BAILED UP

An Australian Historical Fiction Novel

The Australian Sandstone Series 4

MICHAEL BEASHEL

Title: Bailed Up
Series: The Australian Sandstone Series Book 4
Author: Michael Beashel

Publishing and Marketing Consultant: Lama Jabr
Website: https://xanapublishingandmarketing.com
Sydney, Australia

ISBN 978-0-6480569-6-6

Cover by Giovanni Banfi
Image: Great North Road ½ Mile North of Wiseman's Ferry
Sketches in NSW 1881 to 1886 /James A.C. Willis
Dixson Library, State Library of New South Wales

Contents

Characters

Tradesmen/Labourers
Gerry Riordan, stonemason
James Donovan, master stonemason
Lawrence Toole, metal forger
Dougal Simpson, quarry worker

Businessmen
Patrick Hughes, foundry owner
Sean Hughes, Patrick's son
Jacob Greenberg, gold merchant

Donovan Family
James Donovan
Anne Donovan, his daughter
Colleen Donovan, his wife

Police
District Inspector Dermott O'Flynn
Superintendent Hands

Military
Lieutenant William Dodds, overseer
Sergeant Daniel Morgan, scourger
Lieutenant Derrick Bates

Convicts
Fergus Dooley
Francis Murphy

Wiseman's Ferry
Brian Walsh, innkeeper
Jess Walsh, his wife
Deirdre Walsh, their daughter

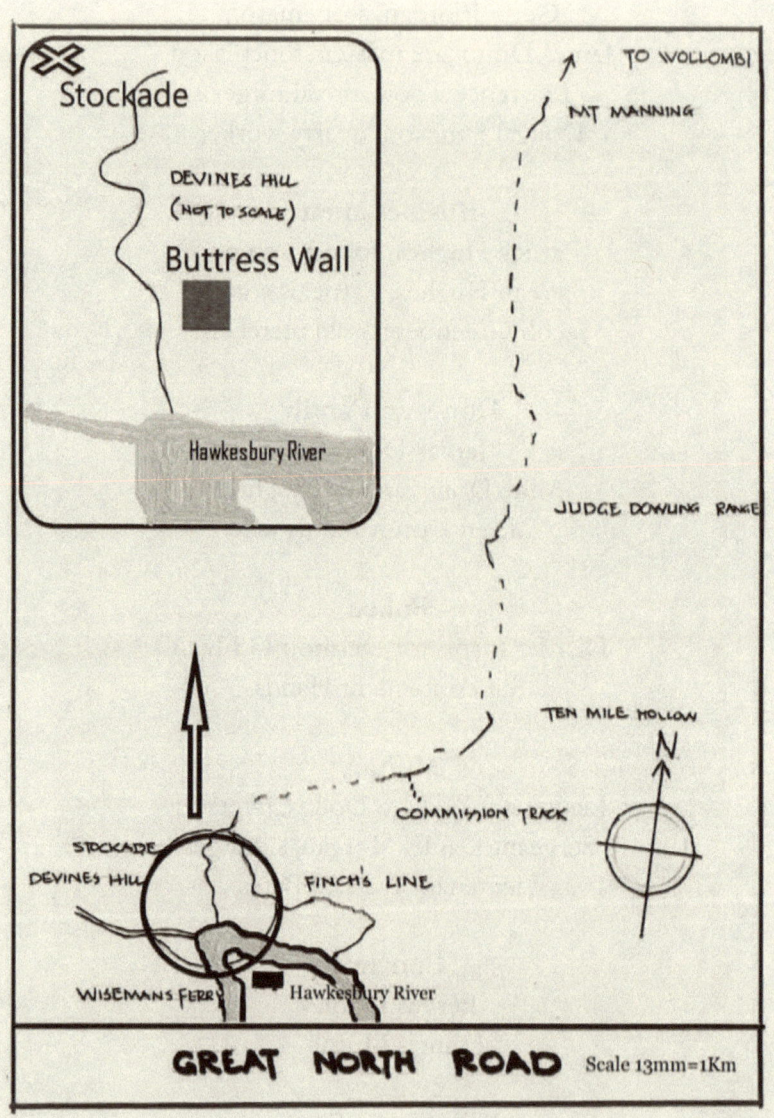

Stockade

DEVINES HILL
(NOT TO SCALE)

Buttress Wall

Hawkesbury River

TO WOLLOMBI

MT MANNING

JUDGE DOWLING RANGE

TEN MILE HOLLOW

COMMISSION TRACK

N

STOCKADE
DEVINES HILL

FINCH'S LINE

WISEMANS FERRY Hawkesbury River

GREAT NORTH ROAD Scale 13mm=1Km

Chapter One

The midwinter night was cold but Gerry Riordan was warm, because he was seated in the bar room of the Drawbridge Hotel with his best friend and drinking companion, Lawrence Toole. The Drawbridge stood on St Patrick's Street in the centre of Cork and it was a favourite of many a tradesman and labourer on a Saturday night when work was over. Tobacco smoke settled above the tables, swirled around the four singers near the fireplace, and mingled with the welcome scent of hops.

Gerry leaned away from the smoke and glanced at the window, which showed that the January night outside was as black as Satan's cloak. Inside, though, there was the heat of the room, beer was filling him and he was happy. His work had meant shovelling, splitting, sweating and stooping over the last seven years, and by it Gerry Riordan had achieved one worthy thing: he was now a certified stonemason.

Gerry looked at Lawrence Toole. His friend, three years his senior, was a metal forger: blond-headed, of average height and wearing a jacket that was a tight fit over his muscled arms and shoulders. Gerry said, 'You know, I can get my hands on a jacket that'd fit you.'

Toole was sceptical. 'Oh, aye, and what's wrong with it?'

'Nothing, It's near new.'

'And what else?'

Gerry laughed. 'I'm offering you a gift, my friend. Take it. My brother's about your size, bar height and all—'

'Now, don't get cheeky on me just because it's been a big day.'

Gerry smiled. 'It has been a big day.' He could feel the edges of his stonemason's certificate pressing on the lining of his jacket pocket, but he dared not put the document on the table, which was wet with beer. 'My brother doesn't want the jacket. Ma bought it for him but he already had one the same. So,' Gerry slapped Toole on the forearm. 'It's yours, anytime. Just say so.'

Toole nodded. 'Thank you. Thank you. Now,' he said, raising his voice over the din from the adjoining table, 'I have something for you.' He placed a package on the table, the size of a playing card. 'It's a small gift I made for you. You now being a tradesman. One of us.'

Gerry shook his head in surprise and opened the gift. 'Grand! Thank you.' He brought out a silver medallion. Looking at the well-crafted image in the shining metal, he smiled. 'St Stephen, the patron saint of stonemasons. He'll look after me.' He went to pocket the medallion.

'Wait,' Toole said. 'Look on the back.' Gerry flipped it to find a different figure on the other side. Toole went on, 'That's the sign of St Eligius, the patron saint of metal forgers.'

'And the word "Ex"?'

'It's Latin for "from". From one saint to another.'

'Ah, a nice thought, my friend. Thank you.'

'Now it's your shout, and make it Jamesons this time.'

'Something to celebrate?' Gerry stood up and smiled. 'We have! Of course. Keep behaving yourself while I'm gone.'

Gerry navigated through the standing crowd as he approached the bar. Men sensed his six-foot-three-inch frame before he got to them and made way. Two of the labourers who worked on St Mary's Cathedral smirked at him in a way that he did not like and he felt anger rising. As a rule he was quick to act if anyone provoked him but he remembered that he was now a tradesman, a rung above this pair on life's ladder. He scowled at them instead and concentrated on the barmaid. 'A bottle of Jamesons, if you will, and two glasses.'

'Got the money, Gerry?' she said with a cheeky smile. Gerry put a note on the bar and she nodded. 'Coming up.'

Gerry took the bottle and glasses back, sat down and poured for himself and Toole.

Toole took his glass. 'Now you've got your ticket to lay stone, you'll want to think about where you'll ply your trowel.'

Gerry nodded. 'Aye. I am thinking.'

'And I'll bet Miss Donovan has got to be part of that.'

The whiskey was welcome. 'She will be, I hope. Have to finish the cathedral work for her father first. Then decide what I'll be doing after that.'

'Right.' Toole pointed at him. 'She likes you, you tell me.'

'She does. That's a blessing and a problem.'

The fact was that Anne did like Gerry—but her father did not. James Donovan, master stonemason, had taken Gerry on as an apprentice seven years before, and housed him in one of the work sheds at the rear of grand Donovan House, where the master lived with his wife and only daughter, Anne. Gerry had served his boss well but there had come a time in the fifth year of his apprenticeship when Donovan noticed something almost like a friendship developing between Gerry and Anne. Donovan's workers were always respectful if they came into contact with his beautiful, good-natured daughter, and she was pleasant in return, but such encounters were rare and the idea of her meeting any of them by design was unthinkable.

Two years ago, Donovan had ceased to house Gerry and had told him to find a roof elsewhere. No words passed between them about Anne but Gerry knew why he was not lodged on the master's premises any more—it was to separate him from the young woman he had come to love. From then on he was only supposed to go anywhere near her if he had to work in Donovan's sheds or pick up tools there during the day.

In his youth, James Donovan had made his money from his trowel, but by middle age he had achieved wealth and standing in Cork and he would expect his one and only daughter to be courted by the city's finest young gentlemen, not a fresh-minted stonemason who still had traces of the bog—albeit bog on a twenty-acre family farm. For the last two years of Gerry's apprenticeship, he and Anne had had to meet in secret.

'You could work anywhere in Cork now you're out of your time, Gerry,' Toole said. 'But I suppose Mr Donovan will want his pound of flesh first.'

Gerry gave a wry nod. 'He's had a big piece of me already. These last two years I've just about starved with the way he's treated me.'

'Go on, you haven't got any thinner. You still take up a big piece of this city.'

'You know what I mean—under my indentures he's supposed to give me shelter and one feed a day. That's what I had until Anne started to like me. Then that man punted me out of the Donovan shed and into a room in Philput Lane. Donovan says the rent is dearer there than what he allowed in the indentures, so I have to use some of my meagre wage to top up. My lodgings are not far from the cathedral, sure, but it isn't right. Not right.'

Toole poured more whiskey into his glass and Gerry's. His blue eyes twinkled. 'And you've tried to get him to compensate you. Yeah?'

'Four bleeding times I've asked him, but no go.' Gerry shook his head.

'Now you're certified, you'll want to pay your parents back the money for your indentures.'

'Been thinking about that. I'll work in Cork for, say, half the year—then the rest out and about. That should please Donovan; he'll be getting value out of me for six months at a stretch. The other half of the year—well, I'll have to make more money if I'm going to have the hand of Miss Donovan, and a journeyman's work pays better.'

'How old is she now?'

'Seventeen,' Gerry said, twirling the whiskey in his glass.

'So, you've got three years on her, but she's not of age.'

'I can do the sums, my friend. She's not free of her father yet.' Gerry poured for them both. He'd better order a meal for them if they kept up this happy drinking. 'Anne likes me a lot and I just have to hope that she'll wait for me.'

'You can see yourself marrying her?' Toole said. 'When she's of age, of course.'

'Indeed.'

'If it was up to her, it sounds like she'd take you on, although I'd give her fair warning about you.'

Gerry laughed. 'Nothing like support from my best mate. I'm dreaming that she will and it's made me doubly happy tonight.'

'Well, I've enjoyed this, Gerry,' Toole said. 'It's been grand, but I have to go.'

'No, really? Stay for just one more?' Gerry eyed the bottle.

'Parents are in town and want to see me, and that's good. Good night, my friend. See you at work on Monday. And again, welcome at last to being a certified stonemason.'

Gerry stood up and clasped his friend close to him. It was good to have that bond. 'Give me regards to your Da and Ma.'

Toole went off and Gerry sat back. Life was good. He knew a girl who liked him a lot and there was a future with her. The certificate in his jacket with today's date, 5 January 1828, would get him a tradesman's wage, and he had work for his trowel. He smiled: life wasn't good, it was bleeding grand.

* * *

It was the heart of the business, money was literally made from it, and it required sophisticated management—yet it seemed medieval, this foundry's furnace, one of Cork's biggest. The fire was illuminating the surrounds like a cave and James Donovan half expected devils to pounce on him. He edged closer, the heat burning like hell, the brightness almost forcing his eyes to close as he stood transfixed. On the other side of the flame was a leather-aproned man, a puddler, who was moving a crucible with confidence, not spilling a drop, his elbow-length gloves a protection from the heat. The liquid brass that he poured into the mould would cool and become a coat of arms to replace the one at the Cork police station.

The floor was lumpy, formed from the cooled detritus of many previous fires, and Donovan was careful not to stumble as he took another pace forward and brought his hand up, feeling the heat of the molten metal radiate towards it.

'Careful,' a voice said behind him.

Donovan turned to the man. 'Tidy result by the looks of it, Mr Hughes.'

Patrick Hughes smiled at him. 'Our men have been on it all day, Mr Donovan, and I'm glad you think so. I love to watch, myself. Never tire of it.'

Hughes was beyond middle age, solid and well dressed, too dressed for in here, Donovan thought. Hughes struck him as socially ambitious.

The molten metal bubbled and Donovan stepped back.

'It's nearly done,' Hughes said. 'You can see the levelling in the pattern is what we wanted. You agree it's quality work?'

'I believe I've seen enough to be convinced.'

'Good. Then you've a mind to place an order?'

'If your quote is reasonable, Mr Hughes.'

Hughes glanced at the puddler then back to him. 'We can talk about this on Monday.' He smiled. 'Perhaps at your club?'

Donovan said without enthusiasm, 'Twelve o'clock for a meal?'

'Thank you. I can't attend but my son will.'

'Mr Hughes,' the apron-clad man said. 'That's it for me. Shall I leave this to cool?'

Hughes nodded to the puddler then pointed to the mould. 'Here, Mr Donovan. Take a closer look.'

Donovan scanned the cooling brass. 'It looks grand to me, but I've little knowledge of your trade.'

Hughes smiled. 'It's good, then, that we have. Thank you, Kieran.' He took out a padlock key.

The puddler removed his gloves and took the key. 'I'll tidy up and lock up?'

'Please do, then get yourself home to your family.'

'Thank you, sir, and goodnight.'

'If you don't mind, Mr Donovan,' Hughes said, 'I have a function to attend. It's Saturday evening, after all. I'll see you out.' At the foundry entrance, Hughes turned to him. 'Good night.'

Donovan watched the foundry owner amble down the street to his gig, then started walking in the opposite direction along St Patrick's Quay towards the bridge. The River Lee's ice patches showed grey and dirty, and the wind sliced through him like a sharp-edged trowel.

James Donovan put on a good show but in fact he was down and desperate. His Cork stonemasonry business was all but out of cash, and payment for his valuable commission for the restoration at St Mary's Cathedral would not save him. He felt the problem was bigger than he was, and when he looked for an economic scapegoat he cursed the English. Thirteen years it had been, an unlucky thirteen years since 1815 and Napoleon's capitulation. The Irish economy had slowed after the war and now it had stopped. The famine of 1826 hadn't helped and he had made a recent speculation in bonds that had become a disaster.

He turned into Ship Street and headed home. The bright metal he had just seen in the foundry glowed in his mind. He could see a solution to financial ruin. He need only wait until the end of the following week to put it in place.

* * *

Gerry stepped up his pace along Glenmire Road, having spent a pleasant hour on Sunday afternoon strolling along Cork's Grand Parade. In the fading sunlight a chill accompanied him, which was not helping the effects of his drinking with Toole the night before. The breeze brought his russet-coloured hair across his eyes and he brushed it back.

Soon he was close to Donovan House, one of many mansions on the waterfront: a two-storey stone residence with arrogant gables and boastful wrought iron. Treading behind the back wall of Donovan's sheds, Gerry unlatched a gate and entered the rear yard, overlooked by the windows of the first floor of the house. He scanned the windows, satisfied himself he was unseen, and opened a door of the nearest shed, where he had arranged to meet Anne.

She was there, in a fine dress and a bonnet that set off her dark hair. Her full-lipped smile widened when his eyes met hers. 'Grand,' Anne said. 'I was starting to worry.' She was pretty, clear-skinned and tall—very tall for a woman, which embarrassed her but pleased him, with his unusual height.

He took her hands in his. 'Here I am, Anne. I said I'd come.' For a moment he felt how precious this was, being able to meet, even in a shed that had the stamp and smell of stonemasonry. He looked around at the dusty old place.

She noticed this without being able to read his thoughts. 'Do you miss this?'

How humble and practical it all was. A rack of punch-hammers stood next to three rows of wall-fixed chisels, all wrapped in oil-soaked cloths. Stacks of hod boards, some smeared white with old plaster and some—like himself—new, and yet to feel the years of work. The shed next to this was similar in size and under its small window was a rope-wired bed with a thin mattress. Gerry's home for five years.

Perhaps she could read his thoughts, because she let go of his hands and went to touch a pair of stone emery wheels. 'I used to watch Da work here when I was young. I didn't mind the dust and the dirt.' She looked up at him. 'But I've missed you.'

He laughed. 'It's only been seven days.'

'And it seems like a month,' she said, her green eyes sparkling. She moved closer. 'When I'm not with you, the hours and days drag by. Do you feel the same?'

He nodded. 'Aye.'

'Yet,' she said, 'when you're with me, time has no value. It's just the two of us.' She smiled at him. He wanted to kiss her, but he hesitated too long and she moved away. 'You're determined to have a go on your own, then?'

They'd talked about naught else the last time they'd been together, and she had not accepted that he should exercise his freedom as a journeyman. The word 'jour' was French and meant 'day': with his new certificate he could work by the day or week or month, depending on the job, wherever he chose. He rested his hand on one of three barrows stacked side by side. 'I am.'

'I can't convince you to stay here in Cork the whole year?'

'I'm twenty years old and off your father's books. As a journeyman I can accept work all over the county. A new-minted stonemason.'

'You'd still be one if you worked for Da all the time.'

'It's not the same, Anne. It's not. Not to me.'

She kept silent for a while. 'Then I concede.'

That was unusual for her. The idea occurred to him that she'd wanted him to be independent all along: she'd waited for him to argue his case, be strong in that, and come to the decision himself. She was clever. He said, 'I've got a lot to learn.'

'My father thinks so, too.'

There was the rub. Gerry had no illusions about himself when it came to dealing with people. He was gangly and said little, and he knew it. Stumbled and stuttered over words like a drunk on a cobbled path. With anyone except family, or his friend Toole, he had trouble expressing himself. Then he'd fallen in love with Anne Donovan, a strong-willed and passionate girl who could have her choice amongst the blades who circled Donovan House like gamblers sensing a game. But it was Gerry she wanted. And by a miracle, with her he spoke more freely and didn't fall over his words.

She said, 'When are you going to tell Da that you'll be a journeyman when the cathedral's done?'

'Soon,' he said. 'I have to finish all the work on the altar.' He brought her closer. There was a lemon scent on her and her glossy lips were parted.

Her breath quickened. 'We're safe. Father's not due back yet.' Her voice was husky.

Gerry frowned. 'I'm not scared of him.'

'Nor am I.' But she just brushed his lips with hers before breaking away. She gave a tantalising smile over her shoulder. 'You might find work in the country when you've finished with Da. How are your parents?'

'Good, from their last letter. Da is extending the barn and wants my help. It's hard being wanted.'

Anne stepped close again and poked him in his middle. 'There you go with your big head.'

'It's the same size as when you first met me.'

'And it's a handsome one. Is that what you want me to say?'

Gerry smiled. 'At least I only have to look at my face once a day while shaving.' He pulled out his medallion. 'Look what Toole gave me.'

Anne took the object, her eyes brightening. 'It's beautiful. He must have spent hours on this. Saints front and back?'

'Aye. I'll treasure it. From one saint to another, through the workers they stand for.'

'That's well said, even poetic.' Anne returned the medallion to him. 'Will you wear it all the time?'

'Aye.' He paused. 'It could get dirty on site, though. We'll see.'

She stood back. 'In return, do you like my new bonnet?'

To Gerry, Anne could have worn anything and still be beautiful, but he looked her over. Her dress was simple yet well-tailored, her bonnet the same. 'It's grand. Grand.'

'I'm glad you like it.' She smiled again. 'Here we are in the only place where we can be together. I feel I can talk to you about anything, and I'm glad for just your company. But it's going to get harder and harder to see you, Gerry.'

'Why?'

'Because of what I feel for you. I want to see you more often and I'm frightened that I can't keep that a secret. Some day I'll make a slip-up, I know. It's just a matter of time. I don't think Da has stopped being suspicious about us.'

He brought her close. 'I want to keep seeing you. I'll wait until you come of age, I'll do anything you want. Until then, will you keep meeting me like this? Will you let me hold you like this and say how I feel about you?' He would have said, 'And kiss you?' but he still could not read her signals—he knew she was attracted to him but couldn't tell how much.

She put her hands against his chest. 'I shouldn't, Gerry. I'm doing this behind my father's back and I don't like that. I love him and will not hurt him. In one way I don't like feeling so strongly about you.' Before he could protest, she stepped away. 'It's not that I don't like being with you. Of course I do; that's just the problem. But I feel so torn, because I hate deceiving my father and my mother. It's not right.'

Gerry chose his words. 'But I don't want to lose what we have. For now, can't we go on as we are?'

'And you'd be happy with that?'

Gerry was determined to kiss her before he left. 'Forget about the future for a while. Let's just enjoy each other's company when we can.'

Anne nodded. 'All right, Gerry.'

Gerry eased her closer again. 'I must let you go back to the house. See you next Sunday?' He pressed his lips to her smooth cheek.

She ran a hand down his chest and he shivered. She whispered. 'Yes.'

Anne sighed as she stepped out of his arms and he wondered whether he should have been bolder and captured her lips. She went to a wall rack and removed a chisel, came back and handed it to him with a cheeky smile. 'If you're asked why you were here today, this chisel is your excuse.'

'Smart girl.'

'I am. Till next week, then. Sunday after Mass.' She gave him a radiant smile, slipped out through the door and closed it behind her.

James Donovan came home early that evening, greeted his wife and then went to sit in his study. At his desk by the window, he heard a door click across the rear yard and looked out. Anne was walking across the paving to the back door of the house. Where had she been, that she wasn't coming in the front door?

Then he saw a tall, well-built man come out of the shed at the corner of the yard and go through the gate to the street. Gerry Riordan. Donovan went cold, got up and made his way downstairs. He waited in the hallway by the closed kitchen door.

Anne pushed open the door and looked at him, startled. 'You're home.'

'Yes,' he said. 'I just saw Gerry Riordan leave the yard. What was he doing here? And what were you doing?'

Anne took off her bonnet and hung it with her scarf in the hall cupboard. 'Father, Mr Riordan was here to collect some tools. I happened to see him and speak with him. It was innocent and I—'

'I forbid you seeing him on your own! And I've told you why.' Anne looked at him, her lips pressed together. Donovan sighed. 'My dear, I'm only looking after your interests.'

'And I can't do that?'

'There are other young men you should be meeting,' he said. 'Ones with more promise.'

'Mr Riordan is not poor, Father. He does not come from a poor family and he's now a certified stonemason. His brother runs a prosperous farm in Kildare owned by his parents. He—'

'Anne! He's not for you. Dear Lord, he's got a limited future. He's not from here. He's arrogant and strong-willed.'

'He's not a monster, Father.'

'I didn't say he was.' Donovan relented a little. It was no good trying to make Anne a prisoner in her own home, yet. 'You're young and you don't see the full picture of the man. I do and what I see, I don't like.'

She came towards him. 'I need to go to my room.'

He allowed her to pass. 'Mr Sean Hughes,' he said. 'Now, there's a bright young man, a businessman, a gentleman.'

She turned to face him and her shoulders slumped. 'Mr Hughes seems a nice person, Father. He does. But he's old.'

James became irritated. 'I wouldn't call thirty old.'

'I would.' She turned away and walked up the stairs.

He spoke after her. 'Just keep away from Riordan. Anne. Look at me.' She turned and faced him. 'You are not to see Riordan on your own. Do you understand?'

Her look was more sad than angry and a part of James Donovan felt for her.

'I understand, Father.'

* * *

The next day, James Donovan crossed the centre of Cork's Grand Parade and glanced at the clock tower. Its chimes started clanging out the noonday time. He approached the building and nodded to the uniformed attendant who held the door open for him.

'Chilly Monday, Mr Donovan, even for January.'

'It is that.'

The door closed after him, shutting off the sounds of the street.

Donovan walked over the plush pile and inhaled the club's affluence. It always made him proud to be a member of the Cork Corporation, a guild whose membership was limited to wealthy and influential Cork residents. No business door was shut to him, and money was the key to all of them. Yet it hadn't always been like this. Thirty years ago, Catholics like the Hugheses and the Donovans had been excluded.

Ascending the stairs to the first-floor drawing rooms, his pride took a hit. Looking around at the seated gentlemen and receiving a nod from one or two, he felt that the members must already know about his cash-flow predicament. Nothing was secret for long in the city.

The young man he was to meet stood up and smiled. Sean Hughes was three inches taller than his father, slim while his father was stocky, and had handsome features. Donovan could see he had a lithe strength not unsuited to foundry work.

Donovan put out his hand. 'Mr Hughes. Have you been waiting long?'

'I was early, as a matter of fact.'

Keen. That's good. 'Sit back down, then. Care for a drink?'

'Bushmills, thank you,' Hughes said. 'They've got some vintage stock, I hear.'

Nothing but the best. Donovan ordered drinks and sat opposite his guest. Doing business in the club was frowned on by members but not forbidden provided it was done with tact. Loosening his jacket, he removed a sheaf of papers and, glancing around so as not to be seen, he placed them on the table between them.

Hughes glanced at them. 'What's that?'

'We'll talk about that soon.' He smiled. 'You keep well?'

'In good health, thank you.' Hughes looked around. 'A beautiful place. I'd like to come here more often.'

A not very subtle hint that he and his father sought to be members of the Cork Corporation. Their drinks arrived and Donovan tipped his Waterford crystal against Hughes's. 'I think we might arrange that, if we can do the right business together.'

Hughes's brown eyes twinkled in excitement.

'Now, Mr Hughes, we are both members of the congregation of St Mary's and I have the honour, as you know, to be one of the cathedral's trustees and chairman of its building committee. From that committee I have full power to award contracts with my business.' He smiled. 'We are about to award a commission for doors that are to be fitted to a new tabernacle. I can't share the approved sketches with you here but I could provide you with a set at your foundry this afternoon, including detailed drawings of the bas-relief motifs. As a Catholic I know you'll be familiar with the old tabernacle on the altar of St Mary's, consecrated to hold the leftover Host after Mass. We're replacing it with a marble tabernacle that will have two doors in the front, faced in gold bas-relief.'

Hughes looked impressed. 'The effect should be beautiful. How big are the doors?'

'They're each fifteen inches high by twelve inches wide. There will be a solid polished brass perimeter frame, two inches wide.' Donovan sipped more of his drink.

'And the cathedral has approved this?' Hughes asked.

'Of course.'

'Good, Mr Donovan. Please go on.'

'On the front of each door will be two sheets of solid gold. The top sheet will have the letters IHS in bas-relief.' He looked at Hughes. 'Clear?'

'The timber backing and the first gold sheet are straightforward. Skill will be needed for making a mould for the top sheet in bas relief. Concealed hinges on the doors … anything else?'

'That's it.'

'Mr Donovan, if our foundry received your commission, we could manufacture just what you have described.'

'I see. How long would it take you to make the doors?'

Hughes sat back. 'We'd have to source the gold. That's a large outlay.'

'Which bank do you deal with?'

'The Agricultural and Commercial.'

'We'd be happy for you to source it from them, and have it certified by Mr Jacob Greenberg.'

Hughes smiled. 'Then that shortens the time period. In two days we could make a mock-up on base metals for your approval. Then we'd make the final product. If we were awarded the commission today, we would drop all orders and just do yours. From receipt of the gold and your detailed motif drawings, the doors can be made in a week.'

'Good,' Donovan said. The club's members were not numerous around them and were well out of earshot. 'Now, all we have to talk about is the price for the work.' He slipped Hughes a piece of paper and his guest looked at it.

Hughes sipped his whiskey. 'We'd need to charge a little more than that, I'm afraid. Skilled labour is expensive, and we've just refurbished two kilns.'

'All businesses face rising costs,' Donovan said. 'The men around you here would agree with you.' He leaned closer. 'The thing about our corporation is that we help each other. It's required as part of the corporation's ethics.' He hoped the younger Hughes would get the hint. No price reduction, no membership for Hughes and his father.

'I don't think we can quote very low,' Hughes said.

'There is another foundry that's keen to quote,' Donovan said.

'Taylors?'

'Yes,' Donovan said.

'They won't give you the quality.'

'I think they will,' Donovan said. 'If you can't bring down your quotation, I'll have to consider them, I'm afraid. It matters little to me, personally.' Donovan was glad to see a frown cloud his guest's face.

'We'll struggle to make money,' Hughes said. 'But, very well, we'll meet your figure for the work. I'll let you know how much brass and gold we'll be using when I've assessed the plans.'

That would have satisfied Donovan but he wanted to press on the manufacture. 'What about five per cent less?'

Hughes paused. 'Would you agree to two and a half?'

Donovan waited the appropriate time then put out his hand. 'Done. But I want no drop in quality.'

'Of course not. I'll get onto them this afternoon,' Hughes said. 'I believe we can make beautiful pieces. They'll be finished for inspection next Monday afternoon, the fourteenth.'

'Another?' Donovan tapped his guest's empty glass.

'I shouldn't really, unless a meal partners it.'

'One more and we'll eat,' James Donovan said and ordered another round.

'The other work at St Mary's,' Hughes asked. 'How is that getting along?'

'The trustees have changed the design of the candelabras yet again but we've got the new ones in hand. The altar's built now. It just needs the marble top and the tabernacle, both of which are nearing completion. The tabernacle itself is a simple box made of marble. I'll send you the plan of it, along with the plans for its doors.'

Hughes nodded. 'You have many trades to manage, Mr Donovan. Being a trustee comes with a heavy responsibility. You are well organised. On this tabernacle, we'll see you right.' Hughes gulped down his drink. 'Do you need anything more from us to … you know … to recommend us to the corporation?'

Coarse as river sand, this man. 'Rest easy, Mr Hughes. My recommendation will be entered here tomorrow. Within a week, you should get some good news.'

* * *

Patrick Hughes sat in his study with Sean that night, sharing a whiskey. Patrick looked at his son and said, 'He meant it?'

Sean poured another glass of Jamesons. He glanced at his father, who nodded, and he filled his glass as well. The study fire belched a shower of sparks up the chimney.

'Said it was good as done.'

'I don't believe it,' Patrick said. 'You just come in and say it, like announcing dinner.'

'We're now recommended members of the Cork Corporation. Mr Donovan will lodge it tomorrow but acceptance is a formality.'

Patrick stared at his son. A Dublin man to his core, he had never got close to joining the club—not even after twenty years in Cork as one of its main businesses, a leading foundry. The Cork Corporation was a closed club, where only Cork's select gained entry. Sean had managed a stunning outcome.

Patrick picked up his drink. 'Have you arranged with Donovan for them to collect the doors?'

'The Tuesday after completion, Father, Donovan will send a wagon to our foundry for them.'

Ice cracked in his glass. 'Escort?'

'Just the two men picking them up.'

'Armed?' Patrick said.

'No, they're trusted tradesmen, a stone mason and metal forger who are both working on St Mary's Cathedral. They'll inspect the doors and then deliver them to the cathedral.'

Patrick smiled and slapped his knee. 'So, how did you get the commission?'

'I reduced our quote for the manufacture,' Sean said.

'Five per cent lower than what they wanted, I'd guess.'

Sean smiled. 'Not quite, father. Two and a half, and it's in the contract. Supply of the metals is in the contract too, of course. We're sourcing the gold from the Agricultural and Commercial, with Donovan's approval.'

'Well done! You read it all? The whole document?'

Sean looked at him. 'Have no worries, Father. It's done its work for us already. Mr Donovan needed a high-value deal like this to convince the senior members to get us into the club.'

Patrick stood up. His knees cracked and he steadied himself. 'That sounds like a reason, I suppose. It's all in your hands now.' He leaned over and patted his son's shoulder. 'I'm off to bed.'

Sean topped up his glass and felt for the contract in his jacket. In fact he hadn't read it all through—he had been too full of the idea of how impressed his father would be that he could do business transactions on his own. Still, better to set his mind at rest. He pulled the document from his pocket and spread it on his father's desk.

'Sean?' His mother came into the study. 'Are you retiring soon? The maid needs to tidy up in here.'

Sean smiled. 'I am.'

He stood up and looked at the contract. It was signed and done and the price was right. He folded it and slid it into one of his father's pigeonholes. It was all right. What could go wrong?

* * *

In a small parlour on the ground floor of his boarding house, in Philput Lane, Gerry waited for Anne. The clock on the mantel struck eleven. This Sunday Anne had promised to come to his lodgings for the first time. She should be heading here now, after Mass.

He moved the parlour curtain and looked out. There she was, crossing the street. His excitement rose. She stopped outside his front door and looked around. The nuns were always about, hunting in pairs for their wayward students, with watchful eyes. Anne came in and he greeted her in the hallway.

'I'm glad you came,' he said.

She looked worried. 'It wasn't easy, Gerry. My parents are out visiting but they'll be back home by one.'

Gerry frowned. He felt as though her father was circling them. It was a risk for both of them, to invite Anne to his rooms. But she was worth it.

'Come on,' he said. 'The landlady has gone to see her sister and the other lodgers are away. We have the place to ourselves.'

They walked up the stairs and he unlocked his bedroom door. It was a simple but large room and in good condition, with a window, double bed, chest of drawers with jug and bowl on top, wardrobe and chair. Gerry left the door open an inch; he did not want Anne to feel trapped.

Anne pulled off her scarf and bonnet. Her hair fell free: long, thick and shining. She sat on his chair and asked polite questions, as though this were an ordinary conversation. 'How are your parents? And your sister Maeve?'

Maeve lived in Cork. 'Maeve is well, thank you. And everything's grand on the farm. What about you? Your classes?' Anne attended the forty-student school attached to the convent of the Presentation Sisters.

'French and German will be hard this year, but it's my last so I'll put up with it.' She grinned. 'Sister Evangelina is a tyrant and has it in for me.'

Gerry moved to stand in front of her and hold her hands. Her green eyes were enticing, her lips inviting. 'What are we going to do?'

'Do? About what?'

'Us.' He drew her up and lowered his face to hers. Her eyes widened and she smiled, her lips open. He kissed her mouth, gentle at first. Her lips were warm and just as he had imagined they would be. She pressed back and he held her more tightly, experiencing the pleasure and other new sensations.

Anne broke away, her face flushed. 'That was … nice.'

He brought her closer again but she turned and sat back down.

She smoothed her hair, and as soon as she lowered her arms he took one of her hands again. 'I love you, Anne Donovan.'

She smiled up at him. 'I know you do.'

'And?'

Her face softened. 'What I feel and what we can do about it are two different things, Gerry. We're not free agents to do as we please. Oh, Gerry. You see that?'

It seemed like a setback, but at least she hadn't said that she didn't love him. She was being practical. As always. Her body was enticing and he had to be strong.

'You're hurting my hand,' she said.

'I'm sorry. You must know I want you.'

She looked down and he thought he'd said too much. But when she looked up, her face was calm. 'I do.'

Now was the time. Ever since Christmas he'd thought about it: he had to make her see that she was the one for him. And he needed to know if she would make the same commitment. 'I want to marry you.'

Anne was shocked at first, then blinked and stood up. 'Marry me!'

'Yes.' He grinned. 'I want to marry you.'

She kept staring, then touched his face, her fingers running down his cheek. Her gaze moved away from his own and he found it hard to guess what she was thinking. A tremor of doubt ran though him. Then she spoke.

'We can't marry. Not yet.'

'I know that. But when you're of age—'

She said in a wistful tone, 'The sisters in class say all problems can be solved.'

Gerry smiled at her. 'So, how will we solve this?'

Anne squeezed his hand. 'I'll wait. That's what I'll do. You work so hard, I know you'll be able to save money. The more you save for us—'

'The more I'll prove to my parents and yours—'

'Exactly. I'll be eighteen in June. Then we'll have three years to make my father change his view of you and stop forbidding me to see you. And when I'm twenty-one I'll be free to choose you for myself.'

He brought her closer again, rapt. 'So you would marry me?'

'Yes.' But she searched his eyes, without smiling. 'Will you still love me when I'm twenty-one? What if you had to leave Cork? What if you fell in love with another girl?'

'You're my girl.'

'And I like you … very much. Even more than I can say.' She touched his cheek. 'I must go; I must get home. But please see me again. I take risks when we do that.'

'I know.'

'I very much want to keep seeing you. Now, doesn't that tell you something?'

'It does.' He kissed her again but managed not to make it too lingering.

She did up her bonnet. 'Let's meet soon. I'll send a note via Chrissie, my maid.'

'Grand.'

* * *

Next day, Gerry was at work on the altar at St Mary's Cathedral and he couldn't get doubt out of his mind: how would he ever earn enough to satisfy Anne's father and recompense his parents for his indentures?

He flung the excess mud from his trowel and stood up. Something else wasn't making him happy either. 'Ronan! Get yourself down here.' A pock-marked giant of a man, about Gerry's height but wide as a gate, came up to him. Gerry pointed his trowel to the mortar near his feet. 'This is shite. I want more cement in it.'

The giant folded his arms. 'Nothing wrong with my mud.' He smirked. 'Maybe the mason's got it wrong.'

'There's nothing right with it,' Gerry said in a quiet but anger-filled voice. 'I've told you t-twice already. Mix it like I said or I'll look for another labourer.'

Ronan moved closer, his stale breath wafting in Gerry's face. 'Mr High-and-mighty, aren't you, now you're out of your time?'

'Don't matter whether I'm green or a master,' Gerry said. 'That mud won't work.'

'Fight is it?'

Gerry turned to the sound and there was his mate, Lawrence Toole. 'No, Mr Toole. Not unless Tiny here wants one?' Gerry put his hands on his hips, eyeballing his labourer. 'Do ya?'

Ronan glanced at the newcomer, then down at Gerry's feet, and took up the board and its load. 'More cement?'

'More cement,' Gerry said with a hard grin, 'and mix it right.'

The labourer left and Gerry took a swig from his water bottle. The early afternoon chill bit at his face but his sweat stuck to his clothes.

'Mr Donovan wants us,' Toole said.

'And why is that?'

'Dunno, Gerry. Come on.'

They weaved and eased their way through the scaffolding surrounding the altar. Gerry glanced back at his work. Nearly finished, with half a day to set the marble for the tabernacle.

'It'll still be there when you get back,' Toole said following his friend's gaze.

Gerry smiled. 'All right for you. Your bit's done.'

'Mine's easy.'

They cleared the nave and went out into the weak sunshine. Lawrence Toole was more than a competent metal forger. 'Forging b-brass isn't easy,' Gerry said. 'Don't come at that.'

'Keeping it clean is the go. Only thing to do is wrap it in oiled rags.'

Gerry slapped his friend's back as they walked towards the site huts. 'Keeps your mess off the altar rails, you mean.'

They trooped into the site office, where a coal fire clipped the chill from the air.

Donovan was seated at his desk. Gerry noticed that the master mason's spotted face showed the influence of drink even more than usual. The skin was pink and the ruptured capillaries on his nose looked like threads of black cotton. Donovan said, 'Close the door.'

Toole complied and stood beside Gerry. Donovan glanced from one to the other. He cleared his throat. 'Can I trust you two?'

Gerry glanced at his companion, who smiled.

'Don't get cheeky on me, Toole.' Donovan banged the desk with his closed fist. 'I can make your head ring if you cross me. Told that to your boss just the other day. Now, as I said. Can I trust you?'

'To do what?' Gerry asked.

'Ah, there you have it. I've got a job for both of you. I want you to collect a box tomorrow morning from the Hughes Foundry. The box will be strapped but not locked and will contain the new tabernacle doors, which should have been made to these specs.' Donovan lifted a rolled-up plan and gave it to Gerry. 'Here. You'll inspect the construction of the doors and Toole will check the precious metalwork. I'm not expecting faults, but you never know. Once you're satisfied, get them here quick and in one piece, and don't dawdle.'

'Are they at the foundry itself?' Toole said. 'I have a mate who works there.'

'They are,' Donovan said, 'and they're in a box ready for pick-up.'

'So, they're made of gold?' Toole said.

Gerry's ears pricked up. 'Gold?' That would be almost a sacred task, bringing gold doors for the tabernacle on the new altar.

'Gold, my lad.' Donovan smiled. 'You're a quick one, Toole. Said that to ya boss too. Yeah,' he pointed to the plan now in Gerry's hand, 'the gold plates are in bas-relief within a brass frame in each door. Now, don't go spraying it around that you're collecting them. You go, pick up the box and get back here. Just that.'

Gerry said, 'We'll need a cart.'

'You'll get one of my wagons from the yard. That's all, and tell no one about this.'

They turned to walk out but Donovan said, 'Riordan. You stay.'

Toole smirked at Gerry without Donovan seeing, then left. Gerry faced his boss, wondering what questions the man was going to ask him now.

Donovan was brusque. 'You're out of your time. What are you going to do now? Who are you going to work for?'

'I'd like to stay in Cork.'

Donovan sat back and looked at him. 'That's big of you. Now that I've seen you into a trade, I expect you to keep working for me.'

'Part of the time.'

Donovan's face became red. 'All of the time, my lad.'

Determined not to rile him, Gerry said, 'I'm not obliged to, but I will work for you. Let's say six months a year, for three years.'

Donovan opened his mouth to speak then paused. 'I'll think about that and after the altar's finished we'll talk some more. I've spent a lot of my time training you up and it's cost me money as well, Riordan. That means you'll work for me until I'm satisfied.'

Gerry held himself in. Donovan's tone made him angry but he couldn't afford to make a total enemy out of Anne's father.

Donovan glared at him. 'And another thing: while you're finishing that altar, think about this. Stay away from Anne.' Donavan pointed a finger at Gerry. 'You hear me. She's not for you.'

Gerry's jaw tensed. 'Is that all?'

'Get back to work. I've warned you more times than I've counted bags of cement. If I see you with her again there'll be hell to pay for you. I want that last tabernacle slab done today, Riordan.'

Gerry turned and left. In the early years with Donovan, Gerry had copped the man's bullying abuse, thinking it would ease off with time, but it had got worse when Anne began showing interest in him. Gerry knew there was nothing wrong with his work; in fact he got praise from his peers for his stone masonry. They'd told him his choice of stone and its deft laying was instinctive and talented. Perhaps that was another reason why his boss hated him—maybe he was jealous of his craftsmanship.

Back at his work he found a fresh batch of mortar and got cracking.

Squaring off and tapping the stone into place, he knew he had to choose. Stay with Donovan for the sake of being close to Anne or go it alone and use his skills to earn more money, more quickly. He wanted to marry her—which was the surest way?

* * *

Next morning James Donovan closed the window of his site hut, shutting out the dew and the chill. He went back to his desk, confident that this crucial conversation would not be overheard.

On the other side of the desk sat a man in his early thirties, of average height and with a weather-beaten face that was distinctive because of a two-inch scar on the left cheek. This was Dougal Simpson, odd-jobs man and petty criminal, who worked as a labourer in Baker's Quarry, on the outskirts of the city. Donovan looked at him with distaste.

'The job I want you for. It's on today. Are you ready?'

Dougal Simpson scratched his upper lip. 'Been ready for a good while.'

'Have you got enough money on you?'

'I have, Mr Donovan, and I'll add that to the fee you'll owe me.'

Donovan nodded. 'Just do the job and we'll square everything when you've finished.'

'That I will, Mr Donovan.' The man smiled, puckering the scar on his left cheek, just under the eye.

'You've obtained a wagon and horses?'

'I'll have to pay a fellow Ribbon Man for them and any damage that's caused. He's got a livery stable that can hide the horses and wagon till the hue and cry settles down. He won't charge me to keep them there. He owes me a favour.'

Donovan pointed at the green ribbon in Simpson's jacket lapel. 'Then I suggest you remove that ribbon.' Ribbon Men were an illegal activist group that targeted the landed gentry, and they knew each other by a green ribbon worn in the buttonhole. Here in Cork, in the south, they did not often tangle with the law, but they had an influence. Simpson did as he was asked.

'The livery man can be trusted to keep quiet?' Donovan said.

'He can. Don't fuss yourself.'

'Give me his address.'

Simpson picked up a pencil, wrote the details and handed them to Donovan.

'And that scar? Easy to identify.'

Simpson laughed. 'Knife fight. I tell all the ladies I got this at Waterloo. It impresses some of them.'

'And it might impress the police, too. Hide it, mask it somehow.'

Simpson nodded.

'Make it clean and quick. No mistakes.'

'Piece of cake.'

In St Mary's cathedral, fifty yards away from where Simpson and Donovan were talking in the site office, Gerry gripped the marble slab for the top of the tabernacle and laid it in position. He stood back and with string line, plumb bob and level he checked his work. After mixing up the grout, he filled the joints at the reveals of the opening. It wasn't a mandatory step, as the door frames would cover the joints, but the constant opening and closing of the heavy gold-plated doors would otherwise weaken the joints near their fixings and the joints might crack over time. Not for him. He used a sponge to wipe off the excess mortar and continued with his task.

One hour later, a horse's whinny alerted him and he left his work area and walked to the cathedral entrance. Donovan's empty wagon came to a stop, with Toole at the reins.

'Get a move on,' Toole said and grinned. He kept his voice low as he said, 'It's Tuesday and it's time to pick up those lovely gold doors. Your boss says that if he doesn't see you leave in five minutes, you'll cop it.'

Gerry got on and sat beside his mate. Toole clicked the horses and they were off.

They headed down Cathedral Street with the January sun just winning over the chill, but Gerry pulled his jacket tighter nonetheless. 'You still haven't said yes to my brother's jacket.'

'Jacket? Oh, I'd forgotten about that.'

'Well, my friend, if you don't want it, the church would welcome it.'

'No, no. I'll have it, thanks.'

Gerry said, 'Good. It's hanging on the outside of my wardrobe, so the next time you're at my lodgings, grab it.'

'That I will.' The wagon went on and they kept quiet for some time. 'Hard to think,' Toole said, 'that in the bottom half of the world, it's summer.'

Gerry looked at his friend. 'Where have you been reading about that? In the newspapers or some book?'

'I like reading and I like to keep up,' Toole replied. 'Don't want to work with me hands all my life.'

They stopped at Roman Street to let the traffic pass and one of their two horses dropped a pat.

'What?' Gerry was surprised. 'You're a natural, the best I know in your work. Why, there's a future for you. Those altar rails you've made with that fancy pattern—I've seen nothing else like it. Get the guild to look at it. Maybe submit that and get your master's ticket.'

Toole laughed. 'That's years away, my friend, and it takes money to pay the guild fee.'

'Then what will you do to get it? Marry a rich l-lady?'

'Maybe,' Toole said, 'and maybe I'll emigrate.'

Gerry was shocked and his foot slipped off the front carriage board. 'Emigrate!' Toole had a full life ahead of him in Ireland. 'You're daft, you are! No one does that. This is your home.'

'It is,' Toole said with pride. 'But there's money aplenty for ironmongers in New South Wales.'

'New South Wales! You are bloody daft. You've never spoken about it.'

'Doesn't mean I haven't thought about it,' Toole said.

'And leave your best mate, yeah?' The breeze freshened as they turned into Camden Quay, the coolness dampened from mist that still lay on the River Lee.

Toole shivered. 'In Sydney now, it's hotter than a Cork August.'

'Give up your mad ideas,' Gerry said, 'and tell me how they'd have made them doors. With pure gold!'

'Gold bas-relief, my friend,' Toole said, 'and they must be beautiful to see. Gold's a wondrous metal and I'd give two months' wages to have made them. It's soft and needs support if it's to be put on the face of a door. But it's a treat to work. Gold's the thing for our altar and Our Lord.'

The wagon entered the foundry yard and Sean Hughes left his office and came out to meet it. On the way he spoke to two of his workers. 'Stay at the gates and don't allow any deliveries until this wagon leaves here.'

They went to do his bidding and Sean walked up to the wagon. He recognised the men from Donovan's description. It would be Riordan who was getting down first—he was nimble, for a big man whose muscles filled his jacket.

Smiling, Riordan put his hand out. 'Mr Hughes?'

Sean simply nodded. 'Good morning.' As the shorter man stepped down from the wagon, he said, 'You're Toole?'

'I am and we've come for the doors. '

'This way,' Sean said.

Riordan and Toole followed as Hughes opened a locked door and gestured for them to enter an office. Hughes locked the door after them and pointed to a table with a box on it. 'The tabernacle doors are in there.'

Gerry went to the box and placed his hand on it. 'Mr Donovan has ordered us to inspect the work before we take them.'

'Of course.'

Gerry undid the strap, lifted the lid and looked at two leather-covered bundles that filled the box. As he unwrapped one of them,

Sean could see that the gold inside made a strong impression on him. Riordan placed the gleaming piece on the table, almost with reverence.

'Like it?' Hughes said.

Riordan looked overcome, just staring at it. 'Indeed. A beauty.'

Toole joined him and unrolled the set of plans that he'd brought with him. 'Let's have a look.'

The men unwrapped the second door and spent ten minutes on the inspection, Riordan checking the construction and Toole checking the goldsmithing. When they had finished, Toole said, 'Your men have done a great job, Mr Hughes.'

'I think so too. Here's the receipt of delivery.'

'Thank you,' Toole said as Gerry repacked the precious doors and applied the strap. 'I'll get Mr Donovan to sign this and we'll return it to you this afternoon.' Toole slipped the delivery receipt under the strap on the box.

'Thank you. Tell Mr Donovan he'll get the invoice tomorrow.'

Sean unlocked the office and they walked out into the yard. Riordan and Toole placed the box on the bed of the wagon between two sacks of sand. Sean's two men opened the yard doors and Donovan's men drove away.

Gerry and Toole progressed at a sedate pace past St Patrick's Quay, mindful of their precious cargo.

'So, tell me,' Toole said, 'what are you going to do about Miss Donovan?'

'I'll keep seeing her.'

'Her Da won't like that, he won't. He's heavying you now.'

'He is,' Gerry agreed.

They headed up Roman Street and Gerry glanced back at the box. All fine there. There were more people on the footpaths as noon approached and more traffic in the streets. Toole watched the horses, keeping them clear of other vehicles.

'So, what are you going to do?' Toole asked.

'Thinking. Thinking.'

'Well, don't take long. There must be plenty more young bucks wanting Miss Anne Donovan.'

'Who?' Gerry said. 'And how would you know?'

Toole grinned. 'Worked you up, have I?' He punched his mate's shoulder, but with little force. 'For example, there's Mr Sean Hughes. I've seen him talking to Miss Donovan a few times after Mass. You've got to act, my friend. She's young, sure, but not too young to make up her mind. If you want her to be yours, make the move.'

Gerry pondered his friend's advice. All very well for him—how was Gerry going to impress the mighty James Donovan when the man hated him? Feeling hot, as though he had too many layers of clothing, he took off his jacket and flung it behind him into the wagon.

They arrived at the intersection with John Street and Toole urged the horses to cross.

Gerry was paying no mind to what went on in the street. 'I can't marry her until she's of age. And—'

Above the din of the traffic, Gerry heard a man start roaring at the top of his voice, somewhere in John Street. He turned to look and saw a wagon come careering towards the intersection, its driver in a panic, yelling at his horses and yanking on the reins without any effect. The horses and wagon were headed towards Gerry and Toole so fast that their own horses reared in fright and then scrambled to get away.

Toole fought to move them on, but it was too late. 'Idiot!' Toole yelled at the other driver, bracing for collision.

Unable to control the runaways, the other driver could do nothing but jam on the brake. This slewed his wagon, which swung sideways to crash against Donovan's. Just before the impact, Gerry and Toole managed to jump free. The runaway wagon stayed upright but Donovan's tipped sideways, shunting the two horses into a tangle of broken and twisted traces.

All four horses were whinnying in fright as Gerry and Toole picked themselves up and gazed in horror at the scene. Donovan's wagon was tilted at a crazy angle. By a miracle all the horses were on their legs and seemed uninjured. To Gerry's fury, so did the other driver, who now leaped down from his seat and ran up to them.

The traffic started up again and vehicles were driven around them, avoiding the chaos in the centre of the intersection. People on the sidewalks remained to stare, shocked by the catastrophe.

Gerry strode forward to face the other driver, a rough-looking man in his thirties with a hat pulled down over his hair and a patch over one eye. 'What in the name of God were you doing?'

'Sorry, fellas,' he said in a high-pitched voice, perhaps made higher by panic.

Gerry shoved him in the chest. 'You nearly killed us!'

'One of me horses had a scare. There's building work back apiece. Some bricks fell near him. Skitted him.'

Gerry grabbed the man and slammed him against his own wagon. 'You mongrel. You poor excuse for a man.' Gerry raised a fist to strike him but Toole grabbed it.

'He's not worth it, mate. Not yet.'

Gerry flung the man aside.

Bystanders stepped forward to help with the horses and Gerry and Toole unhitched them from the traces and tried to quieten them down. One of the helpers offered to inform the police about the accident and Gerry agreed. They ignored the other driver while doing all this, and he took the chance to walk around his own vehicle and assess the damage. But once the horses were taken care of, Gerry turned to him and said curtly, 'Help us get our wagon righted.'

'Least I can do.'

Gerry was now filled with dread about the box with the golden doors inside—had it been smashed with the impact, or flung into the street and damaged? He ran to Donovan's wagon and with a sinking heart saw that it was not in the tray, which was tilted at a sharp angle towards the ground.

Toole meanwhile was looking underneath the front of the wagon. 'Pin's snapped on the shaft. We won't be able to drive this thing back. We'll strap the box onto one of the horses.'

'We can use part of the harness for that,' Gerry said. But where was the box? Had someone picked it up and walked off with it? He was starting to panic when he suddenly spied it on the ground near the rear wheel. *Thank God!*

With the help of two onlookers the group managed to right Donovan's wagon. Toole confronted the other driver. 'What are you going to do about this? Who's going to pay for the damage to this vehicle?'

The other squirmed under Toole's furious look, and the eye that they could see flickered with nervousness. 'I will.' The man pulled out some notes and peeled off two. 'This should be enough.'

Toole's temper settled somewhat. 'If it isn't, Master James Donovan will be claiming the rest from you. Now you'll give us your name and address.'

'Look, I've said I'm sorry. Sorry to hold you up, too. Have you far to go? I could give you a ride there but now I'm late for my—'

'Forget that,' Toole said. 'Your name?'

'Mulveen. Jack Mulveen.'

Gerry said, 'Address?'

'Ellis's quarry.'

At that moment a police constable arrived and the bystanders began to melt away. The constable swept the scene with a grim look, then took out a notebook.

'All right, let's get this cleared away.' He pointed to Gerry's wagon. 'Who's the driver of that?'

'I am,' Toole said. 'And this eejit here should never have had the driving of his!'

'Look, Constable,' Jack Mulveen said, 'it weren't the lads' fault or mine. Sheer accident. I was just coming down John Street—'

'I'll get to you next. Now, your names are …'

The constable had recorded the details and gone, the three men had pulled the damaged wagon out of the thoroughfare, to be collected later, and Riordan and Toole had left, Riordan leading the horse with their cargo strapped on its back, and Toole leading the other. Neither of them was in a good mood, but at least, he, Dougal Simpson had escaped a drubbing.

He pulled his hat further down over his forehead and checked that all the onlookers had dispersed. There was no one in the intersection now who'd been an observer of the accident. After the impact, while Riordan and Toole were dealing with their horses, Simpson's movements had been swift, simple and unseen. All eyes had been on the panicking horses when he picked up Donovan's box from the other wagon. It had taken only seconds to heave it up and slip it onto the tray of his own wagon, then throw his jacket over it. Then he had put an identical box next to the rear wheel of Donovan's wagon and distanced himself from both.

With no haste, Dougal Simpson mounted his wagon and began making his way back up John Street towards a livery stables owned by the fellow Ribbon Man who had a good hiding place and owed him a favour.

When Gerry and Toole arrived back at the cathedral, they tethered both horses and freed the box from its straps.

They were nervous that Donovan would be mad at them for keeping him waiting, and sure enough he strode up to them at once. 'What the hell happened?'

Gerry lowered the box to the ground. 'I'm sorry, Mr Donovan, we couldn't carry this back in the wagon. There was an accident on John Street—everything else is all right but the wagon's busted.'

Donovan's face went red. 'What on earth?'

Toole wiped his brow. 'The police were called and we told them certain sure that it was the other driver's fault. He was an eejit, lost control of his horses and nearly—'

'I don't want to hear about him! I want to know that you've done the job I told you to do! What have you got to say about that?'

Gerry kept his temper and did not back off. His voice was calm. 'All complete, Mr Donovan. We opened this box in front of Mr Hughes and checked the contents. We inspected the doors and approved them. And we got a delivery receipt for you to sign on arrival. Mr Hughes will be sending his invoice tomorrow.' Gerry paused and looked at the box. The receipt wasn't there.

'So where is it?' Donovan said.

Gerry's mind was racing. He was almost sure he'd tucked the paper under the strap when they fixed the box to the horse's back. Had it fallen on their way back? Or wait—had he even seen it when he found the box? It might have blown away in the collision.

'You've lost it,' Donovan said in disgust. 'Haven't you?'

Gerry said nothing, struggling with his recollections.

Donovan sighed. 'Go on.'

Toole was determined that Donovan should not blame them for the collision. 'The police took all the details, Mr Donovan, and we were not at fault. We've got the name of the driver who hit us: Jack Mulveen.'

Donovan turned to him. 'Describe him.'

'My height, probably ten years older. Not sure about the colour of his hair because he wore a hat. Wears an eye patch. From his clothes and his skin I'd say he works outdoors. Has a squeaky voice.'

'Address?' Donovan said.

'He said he works at Ellis's quarry but I'm thinking if anyone went to see him there, they'd find he doesn't.'

Donovan shrugged. 'With that description, he wouldn't be hard to find. How much damage did he cause to my property?'

Toole pulled out the money they'd been given and handed it to Donovan. 'Mulveen said this would fix it. I told him you'll be after him if it doesn't. And the police would like to meet with you, if you want to make a complaint.'

The master stonemason pocketed the money and scratched his head. 'Bloody hell! I can hardly believe this! Can't I get you men to do anything right?'

'It wasn't our fault,' Toole said.

'Didn't stop for a pint, did you?'

'No,' they both replied.

Donovan sniffed. 'Very well, bring the doors into my shed. After all this, I want to have a good look at them.' They followed him into his site office and laid the box on his desk. 'Open it.'

Gerry undid the strap, lifted the lid and stepped back. Donovan leaned over to look inside and his mouth opened. He jutted his chin at them both. 'All right, you pair of mongrels, what's the joke? This isn't funny.'

Gerry stepped closer and leaned in. The leather-covered packages were not in the box. Instead there was a hessian sack. He reached in and pulled it out. The mouth was not closed, and its contents dropped onto the floor—two loaf-sized rocks that just missed landing on his boots.

Toole said, 'What?'

Donovan stood with hands on hips. 'Where are my gold doors?!'

Gerry, overcome by disbelief, looked at his friend, then back to his boss. 'They were in this very box at the Hughes Foundry, Mr Donovan, wrapped in leather. I unwrapped them, we inspected them, and we put them both back. We did.'

'And then we loaded them into the wagon to bring to you,' Toole said.

'You've stolen my gold doors,' Donovan said. 'You've hidden them somewhere.'

Gerry's shock was now replaced by anger. 'We didn't bloody take them!'

'I'm going to the police right now and you boys are coming with me.'

Gerry was at a complete loss. His brain could not cope with the fact that they had left the Hughes Foundry with the doors but arrived at Donovan's without them. How in hell could this have happened?

Toole looked worried too but Gerry sensed a calmness in his friend. Toole gathered himself and got the boss's attention. 'We'll come with you to the station, Mr Donovan. I swear to God we did not steal your doors. That means that someone else must have taken them. The police need to know. Come on, Riordan.'

When Donovan walked out of the office with his two tradesmen, he locked the door behind him. Gerry was so overwrought that he almost laughed at this precaution. The precious gold doors were gone—there was nothing left in that office to protect.

Chapter Two

In the Cork Police Station, which was lit by bright lamps, Gerry's eyes were burning. He and Toole were still here after an hour of questioning, while Donovan had left after giving a statement. The police had requested the box and its contents and Donovan had since sent them to the station as evidence.

'But I t-told you,' Gerry said to the uniformed man sitting opposite them. 'Toole and myself inspected those doors at the Hughes Foundry, put them in the box and went to the cathedral. We never stopped on the way except for the accident, which was no fault of ours. The box was with us the whole time.'

Dermott O'Flynn, District Inspector First Class, shook his head. 'And that's your story too?' he said to Toole.

'It's as he says, Inspector,' Toole said. 'We had a receipt that Mr Donovan was to sign when we delivered the doors at the cathedral.'

'And where is the receipt now?' O'Flynn said.

'We don't know,' Gerry said. 'It must have slipped off, probably when the other wagon hit us.'

The inspector stood up and went to a table beside his desk. He opened the timber box and lifted the hessian sack. 'So, this wasn't in the box when you left the foundry?'

Both men shook their heads.

There was a knock at the door and a constable went to open it.

Another constable entered and stood to attention in front of the desk. Gerry recognised him from the accident.

The inspector pointed to Gerry and Toole. 'Are these the men?'

The constable looked at them. 'They are, sir. Around noon, I was called to a collision near John Street Upper and Roman Street. A wagon had careered into these boys' wagon and I took the particulars.'

'Did you see a wooden box on their wagon?' asked the inspector, not taking his eyes off Gerry.

'No, sir.'

'And the driver of the other wagon?'

'A man by the name of Jack Mulveen, sir.' The policeman looked at his notebook. 'Mid-thirties, about five feet six with an eye patch. Not sure about the colour of his hair—he wore a hat. He lives on site at Ellis's quarry.'

'Were there any witnesses to the accident?'

'Yes, sir, a lot. I have some of their names.'

The inspector glanced from Gerry to Toole. 'Very well, Constable. Take another man with you and I want Jack Mulveen interviewed. You'll find any other witnesses as well, and I want his horses and wagon found. Have you a description of them?'

'Yes, sir.'

'Then get to it. That will be all.' As the constable left, O'Flynn put on spectacles and pulled out a quill pen. He dipped it into the inkwell and started to write. He looked up at both men. 'You say that you had the box all the time?'

Gerry glanced at Toole. 'Aye.'

'So, you received it at the Hughes foundry,' the inspector said, 'and took it to the cathedral, and all the while it was in your care.'

'As we've told you, sir,' Gerry said.

'We have sent a constable to the foundry. Mr Sean Hughes—'

'What did Mr Hughes say?' Toole asked.

'Mr Hughes wasn't available. He's at Whitechurch and will be back tonight. I've asked him to come here and corroborate your story. Or not, as the case may be.'

'It's fact,' Gerry said.

'So you say,' O'Flynn said again and returned the quill to its well. 'Gerry Riordan and Lawrence Toole, you are both under suspicion of theft. Until I can get further evidence from Mr Hughes or eyewitnesses to all your actions during your transport of the missing valuables, you're detained here.'

Gerry leapt up. 'But that's not right!'

'Constable!'

The policeman near the door snapped to attention.

'Take these men to the cells. Give them a meal and blankets. After that, go and tell Mr Donovan that his employee is detained and he's to inform the cathedral board that Toole is as well.'

'Sir!' Gerry pleaded. This was madness but Gerry had no option. What would Anne think of him?

'Right,' the constable said behind them, 'you two, stand up and follow me.

* * *

It felt cool, like the late afternoon air in this Wellington Road storeroom, which was dusty and horse scented. But the gold surface that James Donovan touched was smooth and wondrous, more beautiful because of what it meant to him. He withdrew his fingers and looked at Simpson beside him. 'You were not spotted coming here?'

'No. And the horses and the wagon are hidden next door.'

'The man who owns this place. Did he see the box when you got here?'

'Mr Donovan, he wasn't here and he hasn't seen me for three days. He knows nothing except that I hired his rig and he's to keep quiet about it.'

'Here's the key to Riordan's lodging,' Donovan said. 'He left his jacket on the wagon and I found it in a pocket after my men hauled the wagon away from John Street. Get a copy of it tonight and I'll put it back in the jacket tomorrow morning while Riordan's working in the cathedral. You need to be quick: I don't know how long the police will hold him.'

'What if they let him go now?'

Donovan smiled. 'Then Riordan will be angry that he's lost his key.'

Simpson laughed.

Donovan looked down at the new tabernacle doors, lying in all their splendour on the leather wrapping. 'Get the gold off these as fast as you can. But careful, mind.'

Simpson got to work with a shifter and screwdriver and after ten minutes the double sheets of gold were free of their backings and frames.

'Leave the brass frames in the box; you'll be planting that in his digs later. Have you checked them out?'

Simpson said, 'He's got a nosy landlady with three other lodgers: two sailors both at sea, and a deaf old bastard who keeps to his rooms.'

'All right,' Donovan said. 'Put the gold in here.' Donovan brought up a battered but sturdy port.

Simpson picked up the shining gold plates and slid them in. 'Champion.'

Donovan picked up the port. 'We melt these down on Saturday. You'll be at the furnace at the right hour and I'll give you your fee when the job's done. You'll do your next bit of work in the meantime.' Donovan moved to the door. He pulled on a jacket and gloves, preparing for the bitter wind outside. 'Douse that light.' He waited for the darkness and opened the door. He looked back at Simpson. 'Don't hang around here. You know what to do. No mistakes, mind.'

At six o'clock that night, James Donovan entered his house and looked at his mail. He opened one unfranked note and read it. The police were holding Riordan and Toole in the cells overnight and had requested Sean Hughes to come to the station. Good.

Donovan climbed the stairs, then went to knock on Anne's bedroom door. 'Come into the study, dear,' he called.

He went to the study, where a lively fire was burning, and sat down to warm his hands.

Anne came in with a smile and sat down. 'Da?'

'Gerry Riordan is in custody.'

Her eyes rounded and she gripped the arms of the chair. 'He's what?'

Anne's pained expression cut him like a knife, no matter that he'd handed Riordan to the police for her sake. He drew his chair close and took her hand. 'He's under suspicion for theft and it looks like he's guilty.'

'What theft?' she said.

'It'll all come out, Anne, and it's bad. It's all over for him.'

Her face was drawn. 'He'd never! What's he supposed to have done? Who's accusing him of this?'

'It's no good, love.'

Anne withdrew her hand. 'Tell me. I'll find out anyway.'

'He's at Cork police station, in the cells. I took him there myself, with that metal forger, Lawrence Toole. Look, I should know! They were supposed to deliver the gold doors to me today—'

'For the new tabernacle?'

'Yes, dear. And all they brought me was an empty box. The gold disappeared between Hughes Foundry and the cathedral, and they had it with them all the way. So how can it be missing unless they took it?'

Her face changed colour and she closed her eyes for a second. 'It's a mistake, Father. Gerry would never steal anything!'

Hearing the man's Christian name on his daughter's lips enraged him. He spluttered, 'Riordan's guilty! There's ample evidence against him. Sean Hughes will confirm that tomorrow.'

'Sean Hughes?'

'His foundry made the doors. We know that Riordan collected them and I know he didn't have them when he got to my office. They were stolen on the way: who else could have done that but Riordan and his mate?'

'So you're convinced already, Father? Before hearing what the police decide? What about Gerry's side of the story?'

Donovan sat back. 'From what the police said to me this afternoon, I'd have trouble believing he's innocent.'

Anne stood up, clasping her hands. 'I'm going to see him.'

'You're not!'

She paused then sat down again, her lips set firm.

He tried to control his tone. 'My dear, for your own sake, promise me you won't see him.'

Anne looked hard at him. 'I promise I won't go and see him alone.'

Her innocence and courage shone through, and he softened. 'Love, if that's what you really want, you may go and visit him tomorrow morning on your way to school. But I'm warning you, it'll be painful. You'll be finding him out at last. You'll see him for the thief he is.'

Anne got up. 'And if he's not guilty?'

He'd thought about this. He was so sure Riordan would be convicted that he could promise Anne anything—he'd never have to make good on that promise. 'If he's innocent, then we'll consider the situation of you seeing him.'

Surprised, Anne walked up to him and kissed his cheek. 'Thank you.'

He touched his face as she left and closed the door. He was doing his daughter a favour, if she did but know it.

In her bedroom, Anne wrote with care. She folded the paper and sighed. 'Chrissie,' she called out. Her maid came into her bedroom. 'I missed saying this to you this morning: Happy Birthday. It's the fifteenth, today?'

Her maid smiled. 'Yes, miss, it is and thank you.'

'Well, you can have the night off. But first I want you to deliver something for me.'

'Thank you, miss. Of course, I'll do that.'

* * *

On that same Tuesday night, a worn-out Sean Hughes arrived back at the foundry from Whitechurch. A customer there had haggled for an hour over the price of waterwheel gears that he wanted the foundry to make. At least Sean had come back with an order. It was eight o'clock and the staff had gone for the day. The evening clouds had closed in and he smelled snow in the air. Going into his lighted office, he put his bag down next to his desk. One letter had been separated from the pile of correspondence on it. It bore the seal of the Cork police.

Ripping it open, he read it. The police were making a polite request to see him, when convenient, so he could help them with an inquiry. About what? He riffled through the rest of the papers. Where was his delivery receipt from Donovan for the gold doors? Another thing he had to chase. On impulse, he decided to get the police business over and done with tonight.

He was heading for the front gate of the foundry when the bell rang outside. Opening the gate, he saw a young woman wrapped up against the cold.

'Good evening,' the girl said. 'Are you Mr Sean Hughes?'

'I am.'

'I have a note from Miss Anne Donovan, sir. She asked me to deliver it. I don't need a reply. Good evening, sir.'

Sean watched her go and shut the gate behind him. By the light of a street lamp he read the letter. He had never had a note from Anne Donovan in his life, let alone one so urgent. She was evidently worried about something but she didn't say what. She simply said she wanted to see him, as soon as possible. But it was quite unheard of for him to call at Donovan House this late at night. He shivered; he was so tired. The visit to Anne Donovan would have to wait until the morning. And why not let the police wait, as well?

As it happened, when Sean approached the police station first thing next morning, he saw Anne outside. She came straight up to him and without any other greeting said, 'You got my note?'

'I did, Miss Donovan. I was going to call on you today after speaking to the police. They've asked to see me but I've no idea what it's about. And what, may I ask, are you doing here?'

'You don't know?' she cried. 'Gerry Riordan is suspected of stealing the gold doors for the tabernacle. They've got him in the cells, but he's innocent. I have to see him.'

'God in heaven! The doors have been stolen? No wonder the police want to speak to me. This is incredible.'

'Please come in with me, Mr Hughes, and set them right. I don't know if I can go in there alone.'

Sean was nonplussed. He was horrified that the doors had gone missing, angry with Donovan for letting his daughter walk here to visit a man suspected of theft, dreading what was to come over the loss of the doors. But Anne was so determined to see Riordan. She must like him a lot. For the sake of her reputation, he tried to put her off. 'Shouldn't you be on the way to school? Won't you be late?'

'It's Wednesday,' she said. 'We start late anyway. Please.'

Her plea was too hard to resist. 'All right. Let me escort you.'

They walked into the police station, where a coal fire warmed the space. 'Let me do the talking,' he said to her as they fronted the counter. 'Inspector O'Flynn, please. I'm Sean Hughes.'

The Constable looked up. 'Yes, Mr Hughes. Please wait here.'

The constable went down a corridor and Hughes turned to Anne. 'Will you let me talk to the inspector first? When we've finished I'll give him your request to see Riordan. Do you mind waiting? I'll try not to be long.'

Anne nodded and went to a chair to wait.

The constable returned. 'Mr Hughes, please come this way.'

Anne watched Sean Hughes go and realised she felt grateful to the foundry owner for his consideration, especially since they did not know each other well. In the past year they'd chatted at Mass in their families' company and also at other social occasions. She had found him pleasant to talk to, and good-looking as well, with nice brown eyes. He wasn't tall like Gerry but tall enough, with a strong upper body. He seemed to understand that she was worried about Gerry. How long would that last? The gold doors that had been stolen were the work of Hughes Foundry.

Inspector O'Flynn stood up as Sean Hughes entered his office. 'Thank you for coming, Mr Hughes.' He gestured to a bench facing his desk. 'Please sit down.'

'What is this, Inspector? You believe I can help you with the inquiry?'

'I hope so, sir. Could you tell me about two gold tabernacle doors that were collected from your foundry yesterday?'

'Of course.' Sean paused, then decided to give the inspector all the details before hearing more about the theft. He explained Donovan's order for the doors, their dimensions and manufacture, and the collection by Riordan and Toole.

'You are certain that the doors were in the box and they were taken away by Donovan's men?'

'Yes, Inspector.'

'There was a delivery receipt—where did they put that?'

'One of them slipped it under the strap on the box.'

'And you are certain that the box those two men placed in the back of their wagon contained the gold doors?'

'I had that box under my eye every minute until they drove away.'

O'Flynn paused. 'Then look at this, sir, if you will.' O'Flynn went to a table and lifted back a cloth to expose a large wooden box. 'Is this familiar?'

The box looked just like the box in which the gold doors had been packed, right down to the HUGHES FOUNDRY stamp on the side. 'Yes, it's one of ours.'

O'Flynn opened the box and extracted a hessian sack. 'Then please explain how this and the two rocks it held were the only contents delivered to Mr Donovan.'

Sean gripped the sides of his chair, overwhelmed by the catastrophe even though he'd been forewarned by Anne. 'It's just incredible that those doors should go missing. They're precious beyond belief and they left my foundry intact and well packaged. What on earth is going on?'

'Just as I said, sir, there were no gold doors in that box when it was opened by Mr James Donovan on the cathedral grounds.'

'Inspector, the doors were in that box when they left our foundry. What happened to them afterwards is out of my hands. They've obviously been stolen, but by whom? How the hell would I know? I presume you've interviewed James Donovan and his workers about this?'

The inspector looked at him for some time, then nodded. 'Thank you for verifying that the doors left your premises intact, sir. I'll detain you no longer.'

'But—but then, where are they?'

'That, sir, we are in the process of finding out. Meanwhile we are holding Riordan and Toole on suspicion.'

Sean shook his head. 'You think they took them? Surely not, that's too brazen for words. If you think so, have you searched their lodgings?'

'Indeed we have, sir.'

'And what did you find?'

The inspector said, 'At present we do not yet have enough evidence with which to charge them. They are still persons of interest, however.'

Sean pressed. 'So you found nothing. How can you lay charges?'

O'Flynn paused, then said, 'It may come to that, depending on the evidence.'

Hughes thought of Anne, waiting to hear Riordan's fate. 'But not now. Would it be possible to release the men while you continue your investigation?'

The inspector gave him a speculative look. 'I'd have thought you'd be glad for us to have them by the heels, Mr Hughes, since it's your foundry work that's gone missing! But yes, since we don't have enough to bring a charge against them they can be released for now. However, if we have fresh reason to believe them guilty, we'll arrest them and they'll come up for trial. Do you know of anyone who can give surety for their good behaviour meanwhile? Yourself, for instance?'

Sean glared at him. 'For two men I hardly know? Certainly not!' Then he thought of Anne, waiting and wanting his help. He was sorry for her, but he also felt a little jealous of her obsession with Riordan. What if the man was guilty—why should he walk free on Sean's recommendation? Still, if he helped the man out of this present fix he would go up in Anne's eyes. And if Riordan was guilty and got his just deserts later on, Sean could be by her side to comfort her. He took a breath. 'All I can say is that Riordan and Toole seemed honest men, and they did their duty correctly when they picked up that box at our foundry.'

The anteroom was warm and stuffy and the hard-backed bench on which Anne sat was uncomfortable. She hated seeing the posters of wanted men glaring down at her. Gerry was nothing like them. He was upright, innocent. She knew that.

She loved him. He wanted to marry her. He'd said that he wanted her, too; she had a sense that wanting meant more than kissing. The sounds within the station, clanging keys and moving chairs, reminded her of what she would lose if he were locked away. She would lose all of him, just when she loved him the most.

Footsteps came towards her and she raised her eyes. Sean Hughes was before her—and Gerry. She shot to her feet and grabbed his arm. She was so excited she couldn't speak; she could only smile into his eyes. One step behind Gerry, Lawrence Toole was smiling too.

Gerry put his hand over hers. 'We're free.'

Inspector O'Flynn interjected, 'For now.' He gave the group a severe look and without acknowledging Anne, he spoke to Gerry and Toole. 'You will now retrieve your personal items at the counter. The constable will give you forms to sign. You are not permitted to leave town and you must make sure your presence is known to the police until further notice. Good day, Mr Hughes.' The inspector walked off down the hall and disappeared.

'Mr Riordan, Mr Toole?' The constable beckoned with clipboard and quill. 'Please sign here.'

Sean Hughes stepped to Anne's side and said, 'Would you like to join me, Miss Donovan, while the formalities are done?'

She let Gerry go and went to sit down again, and the two men stood at the counter to check and collect their belongings. She noticed that Gerry did not receive a jacket but he signed anyway—his jacket must be elsewhere. He would be cold when he left the station in just a jersey, as snow was in the air. Tears came into her eyes but she wiped them away.

Unlike Gerry, Toole did have an objection to signing. He said to the constable, 'Hey, that's not my name on this list of yours, and these things on the counter are not mine.'

The constable frowned as he looked at the paper. 'Sorry, this all belongs to another man. Wait here and I'll get your belongings. Then I'll need to itemise them and prepare a document that you can sign.'

'I can't wait for all that! Just get my things. I'll write a list for you myself and sign when you've brought them. Is that all right?'

'It is.'

Toole walked over to shake Sean Hughes's hand. 'Thank you, sir. Very much.'

Hughes nodded and Toole turned back to the counter and started writing.

Gerry approached Sean Hughes and shook his hand also, too moved to speak. Mr Hughes looked from one to the other and Anne realised that at any moment he was likely to drive off in his gig. He might have persuaded the police to release Gerry—but might he still believe that Gerry was guilty? What she really wanted was to talk with both men.

'Mr Hughes, I wonder if you'd care to wait for a while, so we can get to the bottom of this?'

'For a few minutes, Miss Donovan, if I can be of assistance.'

All three turned towards the door and Toole looked up from the counter, where he was still writing his list. He called, 'See you at work, Gerry.'

In the street outside, Anne Donovan did not set off for school at once; she turned to Gerry Riordan instead. Sean couldn't help admiring her poise: for a very young woman to stand about with two single men in the street might have seemed compromising, but somehow she rose above it.

'You're free!' Anne said to Riordan, her face alight. 'And I know you're not guilty.'

Riordan actually blushed. He looked at his boots as he said, 'Miss Donovan, that's t-true and I thank you and Mr Hughes for b-believing in me, but this trouble's not over yet.'

Hughes said to her, 'What Riordan is saying is that there's not enough evidence to hold him and his friend, let alone charge them, but the gold doors have not been found. As far as the police are concerned, Riordan and Toole might have hidden them away somewhere along the route from the foundry to the cathedral. When the box got to your father, all it contained was a hessian bag with rocks in it.'

'I don't care,' Anne said. 'They're not guilty. Someone else took the doors. But how?'

Well, let's think,' Hughes said. 'As you may imagine, I want those gold doors found.' He examined Gerry's face as he said, 'You had the box with you all the time, yes?'

'Didn't take my eyes off it. Well, on the streets I was facing forward. But no way could anyone have snatched it off the back of the wagon—the tail board was up.'

Sean sighed. His gut feeling was that this tall, strong, unassuming fellow was a decent man. But how could anyone else have uplifted the box? An idea occurred to him. 'What about the accident? The collision shook everything up. Your eye can't have been on that box all the time, you'd have had to deal with the horses and get the wagon upright.'

'I'm telling you, the box was there.'

'You're sure?' Hughes said. 'It was in sight all the time?'

'Aye.' Gerry paused. 'Well … when the crash happened, Toole and I had to jump. We picked ourselves up and tended to the horses first.'

'How long did that take?'

'A few minutes. Then we had a go at the other driver. Then I checked on the box and found it next to the wheel of our wagon.'

'Just sitting on the pavement?' Hughes said. 'But when the wagon tipped, you'd think it must have been flung out and damaged, maybe even split open.'

'Yes, I suppose so,' Gerry said. 'But it weren't. It weren't damaged at all.'

Anne put in, 'Maybe the box stayed on the wagon, and someone reached in and opened it. Took out the gold doors and replaced them with rocks. Would anyone have had time to do that, Mr Riordan, without you seeing?'

Gerry's eyes rounded in amazement. 'It's an idea. But I don't think there would have been time to do all that without us n-noticing. And opening the box—we had a thick strap on it, not easy to undo.'

Sean was shaken by Anne's idea. 'All right, what if the thief took the box with the doors and swapped it with another that looks just like one of ours?'

Gerry exclaimed, 'There wouldn't have been time for that either!'

Sean said, 'No? Think. People all around. All eyes on the frightened horses. You and Toole busy, distracted. A quick, neat exchange when no one's looking at the wagon.'

'Wait,' Anne said, 'that makes the crime planned. The thief would have had to prepare a box of the right weight and size, put the rocks inside it and wait for an opportunity ... but the collision was the opportunity. What you're saying is that the accident was set up!'

'It's a possibility, no more,' Sean said. He looked sidelong at Riordan, the big man she was so determined to protect. He said to him, 'It's something you might suggest to the police when they question you again. But I don't know how convincing it would be.'

They were all silent for a minute. Then Anne said, 'Just a second. If it was planned beforehand, that means that the thief knew all about the gold doors and the delivery well in advance.'

'Agreed. In that case the thief could be anyone associated with the work,' Hughes said. He smiled ironically. 'Even me.'

Riordan burst out, 'Not you, Mr Hughes!'

'Or one of the workers at my foundry,' Hughes replied.

Riordan said, 'Or someone connected with the cathedral.'

'Including the board of trustees and my father,' Anne said in despair. 'So many people.'

Hughes looked at his watch. He wanted to end this conversation but he was not going to leave Anne Donovan alone with a common stonemason who was under suspicion of theft.

However, Riordan solved the problem for him. He bowed to them both and said without a stammer, 'Mr Hughes, thank you for the trouble you've gone to today. Miss Donovan, I won't take up your time. You're on your way to school. I wish you a very good day.' And the man walked off.

Sean Hughes took in Anne Donovan with a sideways glance. Her cheeks were pink, her eyes wet. 'Miss Donovan, allow me to drive you to school in my gig.'

She accepted, but they spoke little on the way; her spirits seemed low now that Riordan was not there and needing her encouragement.

Sean's voice was very gentle as he handed her down and bade her goodbye at the school gates, but inside he was cursing the whole business of the gold doors, and just about everyone associated with them.

* * *

James Donovan saw Riordan as he came past his site office. He got up and followed him.

'Riordan.'

Gerry turned and faced him. 'Yes, sir.'

'How come they let you out?'

'They didn't have enough to hold me, Mr Donovan.'

The master mason shook his head. 'You're bloody guilty, I'm convinced of that. You should be damned glad I'm not standing you down. But I'll keep you on.' He smirked. 'Until your trial.'

'The tabernacle's finished.'

'I know that. You can spend the day cleaning and polishing that marble. I want the altar slab and tabernacle shining like those gold doors you stole.' Donovan delighted in seeing Riordan's eyes expand. 'And after that you can repave the front of the sacristy doorway.'

'That's two men's work.'

'You'll do it Riordan. Get on with it. I don't want to see you leave this site until five o'clock.'

Riordan turned without saying anything and Donovan went back to his office.

Dougal Simpson was sitting there. He looked as usual, without the disguise he'd described to James, except his face looked even more weather-beaten because the stubble on his cheeks was denser. Maybe he was going to let it grow to make his face even less recognisable. 'You'll do it this afternoon,' Donovan said. 'It has to be then.'

Simpson nodded. 'Riordan's back at work?'

'He is and I've got him to work late. Plant the box with the brass frames at his lodgings and get out. I'll be here all day, so tell me as soon as you've dropped the stuff, then I'll send a message to the police and tell them to search his room again.'

'Yeah, Mr Donovan.'

'I've got work to do.' Donovan reached for a pile of paperwork. 'Go.'

In the cathedral, Lawrence Toole shivered and pulled his jacket tighter, eager to get away from work and seek the warm fire in the Drawbridge Hotel. He had two more brass scrolls to complete on the altar rails and that would finish him for the day. He'd take an early mark. He looked across at Gerry. Since coming back from the police station, Gerry had said little for most of this cold Wednesday and had his head down working on the marble.

'Gerry,' Toole said. 'I'm leaving early. I thought I'd pick up that jacket from your room.'

Gerry raised his head and mopped sweat from his brow. 'Right. Sure, you can do that. The front door of my lodgings it unlocked during the day. Take my key to let yourself into my room. It's in my jacket over there. See you at the Drawbridge tonight?'

'I'll be there.'

* * *

Simpson collected the box from the livery stable in Wellington Road, loaded it onto a rented cart and headed to Philput Lane. Most people were indoors around fires and stoves, the January daylight was fading and light snow was falling. He left the cart in a lane near Riordan's digs, waited till the coast was clear then walked up the steps. The front door opened with no trouble and there was no sign of the landlady within or on the stairs. With an effort, he carried the box upstairs. He took out the key for Riordan's door, unlocked it and took the box in. He left the door ajar so he could listen for any noises within the house, but all he heard was his carthorse whinnying in the street outside.

He scanned Riordan's room and roamed about, messing up its tidiness but finding nothing to steal. He opened the timber box. Suddenly he heard a noise from the landing outside and flattened himself against the wall behind the door.

* * *

At the cathedral, Lawrence Toole finished his work and got Gerry's attention. 'See you at five.'

Gerry waved acknowledgement and Toole set off.

'Wait,' Gerry said as he came up to him. Gerry brought his hands to his neck and took off his silver medallion. 'Take this,' he said, 'it gets too dirty when I'm working, and I won't have that. Put it on my chest of drawers when you get the jacket.'

'Will do, mate. See you tonight.'

Toole set off for Philput Lane. Walking to Gerry's lodgings, Toole thought about his future. He was going to emigrate. It was a big step but he'd decided. He would miss Gerry and all his loved ones in Cork but he couldn't let go of his thoughts and plans for a land far away. A horse whinnied in the lane nearby, then he turned a corner and looked up at the place where Gerry lived. The façade looked blank but for a second he thought he saw movement behind the window of Gerry's room. Might be the landlady doing some cleaning. Then a man's head flashed by. It wasn't Gerry's.

Toole went on the alert. He couldn't imagine anyone having a good reason to be in Gerry's digs. Had they broken in?

The front door was unlocked as usual and he went in, closed the door behind him and went up the stairs, not making a sound.

He came up to the landing and hesitated. He could rush in and take the intruder by surprise, but he didn't want to frighten the life out of the landlady, if it was just a new lodger being shown around. He listened hard but could hear no conversation. He softly pushed open the door.

He had a good view into the room, which looked empty after all, if less tidy than usual. At once he spotted the jacket Gerry had promised him, hanging on the wardrobe. He walked in, began to look around him, then nearly stumbled across something else—a timber box exactly like the one that had held the gold bas-relief doors. The top lay open and inside he could see the glow of a dull yellow metal. He caught his breath. Not the gold, but maybe brass?

The floor creaked behind him and an arm wrapped itself around his throat. He grabbed it with both hands. A second later, agony seared through him as something cold and solid slipped between his ribs. Everything became faint, then there was blackness and nothing.

Toole slipped to the floor and Simpson pulled the knife out of the body. The quarry worker panted and looked at the blade and the corpse. 'Good end for a metal forger,' Simpson said in a quiet voice. 'The bastard was full of himself.' Seconds passed. He pushed the door shut and locked it. Jesus, he hadn't meant that to happen. He should have locked that bloody door instead of leaving it ajar.

Squatting, he wiped the blade on Toole's cuff and went through his clothes, pocketing wallet, watch and Riordan's room key. The last of his finds was a silver disk. He pocketed that and left behind just Toole's tobacco and handkerchief.

He heard someone walk up the front steps to the house door and listened with an ear pressed against Riordan's door. The front door closed, then what sounded like a woman's footsteps faded from the hall below and there was silence. Sweat filmed Simpson's face as he looked at what lay on the floor at his feet. He calculated his next moves. Then he let himself out of Riordan's room and went downstairs.

The landlady was making a racket with pans and crockery in the kitchen and under its cover Simpson let himself out, quietly closed the front door and paused on the doorstep. There was no one else on the street. He rang the doorbell. Seconds passed, the door opened, and a middle-aged woman looked at him through thick spectacles. 'Evening ma'am,' he said. 'I'm sorry to disturb you on such a mean night but I have an important letter for one of your lodgers, Mr Riordan.'

She put out her hand. 'I'll give it him later. I don't think he's in yet.'

Simpson smiled. 'I saw him come here about twenty minutes ago. I've been waiting because I thought he'd come back out, but he's taking too long. I've got this letter and I need him to give me a receipt for it.'

'Come in, come in then. It'll freeze us both out here.'

'Thank you, Mrs …'

'Hammerton.'

Simpson followed her upstairs, where she paused and got her breath.

She knocked at the door. There was no answer. 'He's not there.'

'Maybe he's sleeping,' Simpson said innocently.

'You'll have to come back, then, mister.'

'Mrs Hammerton, I got to get a receipt. Actually, I have to serve him notice.'

The landlady's eyes widened and she slapped her side. 'I knew it. Yesterday, Stella, my friend whose husband works at the foundry, said that he'd been locked up last night. Always thought he was a bad 'un. I'll open up for you.' She unlocked the door, went inside and next second Simpson heard an almighty scream.

Simpson stepped in. 'Dear God. That man's dead for sure. Don't touch a thing. We should go downstairs. And I'll go and get the police.'

'But I—'

'Ma'am,' Simpson said, touching her arm, 'you don't want to stay here with a sight like that before you. Here, I'll help you down.'

Simpson settled the shaken landlady in the front parlour, shot out of the house and retrieved his cart. He had precious time to get right away, through the falling snow.

* * *

James Donovan was warming his hands in front of the fire in the site hut. He felt good. The sheets of gold were in a safe place, the timber backing of the tabernacle doors was burning in the grate before him, and the brass frames in the original box would now be sitting in Riordan's rooms for the police to find. And he wasn't going to ruin his daughter's happiness by framing Riordan—he was saving her future.

Simpson entered the hut, his face tense and pale under the stubble. 'It's done.'

'The police.' Donovan grabbed his greatcoat and opened the door of the hut. 'I need to tell them to search Riordan's digs again. I'll tell them he just said something suspicious.'

Simpson held him back. 'A moment, Mr Donovan. You don't need to go to the police— they'll be there at Riordan's by now, because the landlady will have called them. I struck a problem today: Lawrence Toole. He walked in when I was in Riordan's room. I slipped behind the door and he didn't see me, but he saw the box and the frames, large as life. There was only one thing to do.'

Donovan's unease rose. 'What?'

'I had to kill him.'

Donovan closed the door, staggered to his desk and sat down. 'Dear God! What ... what was he doing there?'

'I don't know. Think about it: this is even worse for Riordan. He'll get the blame, not just for theft but murder. I fixed it so, and you should be thanking me.'

Nausea filled Donovan and he started to tremble. This was something else. Theft was bad enough but he could have lived with having committed it. But murder! 'This is bad, real bad.'

Simpson shrugged, his expression ruthless. 'It ain't pretty but we're safe as long as you hold it together. Right?'

Donovan's fear was pulsing cold shivers through him and he fought to get on top of it. 'Dear God! It's made this all horrible.'

'I'll not deny that. But no one saw me come or go tonight except the landlady, and she's short-sighted and never got a good look at me. So we're in the clear, believe me. Donovan? You told me to deal with things and I've done so, on your orders.'

Donovan found the strength to respond. 'So what do I tell the police now?'

'It'll go like this. You saw Toole leave here early this afternoon, and five minutes later Riordan followed him.'

'But Riordan's been here all afternoon!'

'I know that, but he could have got away for a bit. Yes? Could have followed Toole and they went to Riordan's and got into an argument about the gold, yes? And Riordan killed Toole.'

Donovan tried to think. 'Yes, I suppose.' His gut heaved. 'Please go. I feel ill.'

Simpson leaned closer to him and said in a low voice, 'Don't go soft on me, hear? Riordan killed Toole over the split of the gold. He wasn't here on site for a while, then he returned. Got it?'

'I hear you. Now, go, go!'

Simpson left and Donovan tried to force down the nausea that filled him. Getting up and steadying himself, he opened the office door, took some icy snow from the windowsill and brushed his face with it. Its sting shocked him and his brain cleared for a moment, but then he imagined the police on the way to see him, to talk to him about the murder, to question him.

Fear swept in with the stomach-churning nausea. One thought dominated his mind. If Inspector O'Flynn were to tap him on the shoulder now and look into his eyes, James Donovan would confess—everything.

* * *

District Inspector O'Flynn entered Riordan's room and looked around, taking everything in. He turned to the pallid-faced constable who was staring at the body and a congealing puddle of blood. 'Mark the time in your notes,' O'Flynn said. 'Five o'clock. Then go outside and keep everyone away. Has anyone been in here?'

'Just the landlady who alerted us and another man. She found the body.'

'Another man?' O'Flynn said. 'Did you get his name?'

'No, sir. The landlady didn't ask him.'

'Hmm. Send up Sergeant Hooper.'

'Sir.' The constable looked relieved at being dismissed.

O'Flynn stepped over the body and looked into the box. Riordan must have brought this here from some hiding place. It wasn't in this room when the constables searched it on the afternoon of the doors' disappearance. HUGHES FOUNDRY was stencilled on its sides in faint letters, and it was lined with leather and what looked like two brass frames.

Beside him, Sergeant Hooper said, 'Sir?'

'Sergeant, take notes.'

The sergeant brought out his notebook. 'What's that he's got in his hand, sir?'

There was a piece of paper clutched in Toole's dead hand. O'Flynn forced open the fingers and withdrew it. He took it closer to the light, read it and rapped the paper against his open palm. 'Go and tell Constable Derry to get a wagon and remove this body to the morgue. I am about to issue a warrant for the arrest of Gerry Riordan for suspected murder.' The sergeant blinked and glanced down at the body. 'Move, man!'

The sergeant left the room and clattered down the stairs.

* * *

James Donovan glanced at the hall clock as he opened the front door of his house. It was six pm. A police officer nodded to him and took off his cap. 'District Inspector O'Flynn, sir, if you remember.'

Keep calm, Donovan told himself. 'Come in Inspector, will you. It's a raw night. He led him into the parlour where a fire was burning well. 'Please sit down. Would you like something hot to drink?'

'I'm on a murder hunt, sir, and time is of the essence.'

'Murder?'

O'Flynn kept standing. 'Yes sir, at Philput Lane this afternoon.'

'Dear me.' Donovan tried to keep his voice under control, then realised that anyone told of a murder would be shocked. He had no need to look relaxed during this awful conversation. 'Who was killed?'

'We're trying to verify the circumstances of the death. There was evidence on the man's body to identify him but until we're certain, and next of kin are notified, we can't release what we know.' O'Flynn paused. 'Do you know where Mr Riordan is, or where he may be?'

'Is he involved?' Donovan said, trying to keep his voice calm.

'Just answer my question, please. Do you know where he is?'

'Is my stonemason a suspect?'

'It's early days, but we're pretty sure our suspicions are correct. Now, sir, where is Riordan?'

'He's most likely to be in the bar at the Drawbridge, drinking with Lawrence Toole.'

O'Flynn's expression changed. 'Are you sure he's with Mr Toole?'

'I can't be sure, no. But they're best friends and that's their favourite pub.'

'That's very valuable information. Thank you. Now I must go. Good night, sir.'

Donovan closed the front door after the policeman, then walked to the parlour and drank a full measure of whiskey. He sat down and looked at the flames.

Colleen Donovan came into the room followed by Anne. Donovan looked up, thinking how serene and comfortable his attractive wife always seemed. How could he have taken the risks that now threatened their perfect family life? She said with a slight nervousness in her blue eyes, 'Was that the police, dear?'

'It was.'

'What did they want, Father?' Anne said.

'There's been a murder in Philput Lane. A metal worker was killed.' He was looking at his daughter and he saw her eyes flash at the name of the place where Riordan lived.

'That's terrible,' Anne exclaimed. 'Why did the police come to talk to you?'

'Just a question about two of my workers, Anne. But nothing we need to discuss tonight. Donovan's is not affected.' He put his glass down and for the first time since he'd been with Simpson, he felt a little better. It was all inevitable now: Riordan would be charged and convicted of the murder of Toole. Time enough tomorrow for his daughter to hear the news—he was not going to make her suffer tonight. 'Come, let's have dinner.'

As they went to the dining room, Anne gave him a pleading look, but he pretended not to see it.

* * *

Gerry had finished his first beer and asked the barmaid for another at the Drawbridge bar. It was just past six and there was no sign of his mate. Probably having a feed somewhere, which was all right, but it was unusual that Toole hadn't told him. Gerry took the beer, retired to a quiet corner and sat down.

It had been a torrid two weeks, with mixed fortunes. Getting his certificate, proposing to Anne and completing the altar slab and tabernacle. Then the whole catastrophe with the doors. Gerry felt that he'd failed his Lord in not protecting them. Some knight, he chastised himself.

It was worth getting drunk tonight but it was still only Wednesday. Where was Toole? The chatter in the pub started to quieten and there were raised voices at the entrance to the bar room. Then people near him stepped aside, as a police sergeant came up to him with two constables.

'Gerald Riordan,' the sergeant said, 'You are under arrest for the murder of Lawrence Toole.'

Gerry heard the voice but the words had no meaning. It wasn't until the manacles were clapped on him that he realised. 'Murder? My mate, Lawrence Toole? He's dead?'

'Come on,' the sergeant said, 'and don't give us trouble.'

Gerry walked out of the bar room, but only because he was pushed from behind. His mate had been murdered? It was impossible to believe.

Chapter Three

On the day of the verdict, the cell walls seemed to squeeze Gerry out of the basement and up into the Assizes court. He entered the dock, aware of murmuring voices, body odour and the staleness of the packed court room. The jury sat on his left. Their faces were impassive, giving no sign either way of their morning's deliberation, but Gerry sensed what their decision was and his stomach tightened as he looked around. His parents and sister were there and some seats away from them were the parents of Lawrence Toole—the father's face fixed with hate, the mother looking down.

Then Gerry saw Anne. Her lips trembled and she forced a smile. He stumbled as his gaoler pushed him into a hard seat. The benches in front of him loomed dark and foreboding. The clock showed two minutes to two and the sign below it glared out the date, Monday, 11 February 1828.

One month ago, all he had had to worry about was how he was going to marry his love. Now, he had to fight for his life.

His lawyer, a young nervous man, had done his best as far as Gerry knew, but the evidence against him for murder was telling. The police had a sworn statement from James Donovan that Gerry could well have left the cathedral site on the Wednesday afternoon when Toole was killed in Gerry's room. He thought of his own death. For a second the rope would burn his throat, then the shock of the fall, then pain, then nothing. He could sense that Anne was looking at him but he kept his head bowed.

The prosecution insisted that around midafternoon on Wednesday, January 16, Gerry Riordan had murdered Lawrence Toole at his lodgings in Philput Lane. Motive: he did not want to share the spoils of the gold they had removed from the tabernacle doors after stealing them. Part of the evidence consisted of the box stamped with the Hughes insignia and containing the brass frames for the same doors, which was found in his room. Gerry couldn't convince his lawyer that he hadn't been near his digs since dawn on the Tuesday morning.

The Crown also had the most damning item—a handwritten note that had been found in the dead man's hand. This note described the theft of the doors, then went on to say that Toole feared for his life because he suspected Riordan would try to do him out of the proceeds from the gold. Toole had written the note to point to his murderer if he was killed. The prosecution did not speculate how he came to have the note in his hand when he died, or how the murderer had missed this fact—the note itself was fatal.

Poor Toole. Gerry again felt the loss of his best friend, made worse for him by the Crown's allegations. They argued that following the theft, Riordan had hidden the gold sheets somewhere without informing his accomplice and gone to his digs to meet Toole on the Wednesday afternoon. They had fought and Riordan had killed Toole.

During the trial the prosecution had cross-questioned Gerry about where he had secreted the gold. He continued to deny the theft and the murder, and any knowledge of where the gold might be. But the truth from his lips was not enough to save him.

The clock struck twice and Gerry's empty stomach tightened.

The judge appeared in the courtroom and all rose. Some words were said as Gerry sat, unable to make sense of them.

'The accused shall rise.' Gerry forced himself up, his legs weak and sweat running in a line down his back. The jury foreman stood as well. Murmuring rose from the crowd and the judge banged his gavel to order silence.

'Foreman,' the judge said, 'have you reached a verdict?'

'We have, Your Honour.'

'And how do you find?'

Gerry flashed a look at Anne, who stared at him, cleared-eyed and calm, as though to give him strength.

'We find the defendant guilty.'

Gerry's knees gave way and he grabbed at the rail in front of him.

* * *

It wasn't equipped like the Hughes Foundry but the vacant warehouse near the River Lee would do the job. The fire source was uneven, the puddler inexperienced, and the plate-sized crucible misshapen. James Donovan had wanted to wait until the trial was over for a few weeks, but they had to be here on the day after Riordan's conviction because this warehouse was the only one available. And Jacob Greenberg, the man who'd give them cash in exchange for the gold, was leaving for New South Wales on the following Monday.

Greenberg, a Jewish gold assayer and merchant, was a lean man with a beard and respectable clothes. He and Donovan watched as Dougal Simpson pumped bellows to make the fire roar with an intensity that brought out the sweat on Simpson's face and caused the others to stand back. Donovan looked out through the windows. There was no one outside to see what they were doing. Inside, the windowpanes reflected the flames of the fire.

'Why are you leaving Ireland, Mr Greenberg?' Donovan asked. 'For safety, since you'll be taking this gold with you?'

'No,' Greenberg said, 'I've been planning to emigrate for some time. There are excellent opportunities for trade in New South Wales. The financial potential in the colonies is far greater than in Ireland, and my voyage has been arranged for some time. I leave for Australia from London.'

The gold melted, puddled and spat. Simpson now with gloves, apron and mask, took the handles of the bowl and carried it to a tray of moulds placed on a nearby bench.

Donovan pointed to the molten gold. 'And this will be your capital.'

Greenberg shrugged and said in a self-deprecating tone, 'It will help.'

It would do more than that, Donovan thought.

Simpson poured the gold from the doors of the tabernacle into the moulds, each four inches by one inch by a half an inch deep. A golden drop caught on the lip of a mould, then rolled down to the gleaming surface of the new ingot.

'Steady,' Greenberg said. 'Don't waste any.'

Transfixed by the glowing metal, they waited until all the moulds were filled. Simpson put down the crucible, took off his mask and squatted by the fire. He pulled off the gloves and with one of them wiped his face.

'How long for them to cool?' Donovan asked.

Simpson looked up and grinned. 'I ain't an expert but I reckon an hour. I'll put them near the window. That'll cool them more.' Simpson stood up then pulled out a clean rag from his pocket. A silver disk that had been caught in the cloth fell onto the floor.

Greenberg picked it up and looked at it. Donovan could see that it was a medallion of fine metal, with tradesmen's icons on both sides. Greenberg remarked, 'This has class. Saints front and back.'

Simpson smiled. 'Nice piece of work, to be sure. Found it near the site office.' He laughed and took it back.

More likely he stole it from Riordan or Toole, Donovan thought. Or even from Riordan's room?

Greenberg, watching him, stepped forward. 'Mr Donovan, as agreed, I'm ready to give you the equivalent in cash for this gold. Minus the percentage discount, of course, for my discretion and the inconvenience.' Greenberg gave a knowing smile. 'But we must wait until the ingots are cool before I can take them away. You'll be staying here with them, Mr Donovan, while I go and fetch your payment?'

Greenberg flashed a wary look at Simpson as he said this, and James Donovan could hardly blame him. Greenberg knew the gold was from the stolen doors but he had not been told how it had come to the warehouse. He could guess, however, that Simpson was involved in the theft. In addition, everything about the Riordan trial for murder was known about town, so Greenberg could well suspect that Simpson was connected to that crime as well. He would not want Simpson left alone with the ingots for a second.

'I'm not going anywhere,' Donovan said. 'I'll expect you back here within the hour, Mr Greenberg, with the amount we agreed on, and not a penny less.'

'In an hour then.' Greenberg pressed his felt hat onto his black curls and left, keen to be away.

Donovan eyed his sinister accomplice, not liking his company any more than he suspected Greenberg did. Donovan had made sure Simpson came without a knife or other weapons today, and there was no threat to the gold—Simpson might fancy making off with it but a man like him would not have the slightest means of disposing of it. He was getting a large fee instead, from the cash that Greenberg would bring for the gold. Donovan felt the danger of the situation, nonetheless—he had linked himself with a murderer.

Simpson handed Donovan another pair of gloves. 'Give me a hand.'

Together they lifted the tray of ingots closer to the window. Even through the gloves, the heat of it was strong.

Simpson opened the sash and the breeze rushed in. The man closed his eyes. 'That's better.'

'You cocked the whole thing up, you idiot.'

Simpson frowned. 'What?'

'Killing Toole.' Donovan shook his head. 'I never wanted that.'

'Are you still on about it? I had to, no choice.'

Donovan leaned against the factory wall, its coolness seeping through his coat. Since the murder, he'd been a changed man, moody and sleepless. Any fleeting moments of the peace he felt with his family had been outnumbered by dark thoughts. Nightmares often woke him, and he would sit up in bed, sweat sticking to him. Colleen had suggested he see a doctor and he had had to brush away her concern, puzzling her. He growled at Simpson, 'I never had murder in mind, you bastard.'

'I didn't either. But it was that or let Toole rush out and call the police. You should thank me—I had the nous to write that note and put it where anyone could see it. You have what you wanted. Riordan's fat is in the fire and you'll get your money.'

Donovan watched the gold turn less lustrous as it cooled. Yes, he'd get his money. But the price was high—a human life. He shivered and felt a desperate impulse go through him. 'I don't want the money! It's tainted.'

Simpson moved closer to him. 'Say that again?'

Donovan met his stare. 'You heard me.'

Simpson grabbed Donovan's lapels, pulled him from the wall then slammed him back against it. 'Now, you listen to me. Not long ago you wanted this gold for the cash you'd get for it. Money that would save your bacon. You wanted it more ... more than the air you breathe. You had to have it.' He pressed his hand against Donovan's chest and pointed a finger at him. 'Just because the getting of it had a hiccup, don't go all weak on me. Don't think you can sidle your way out of it! Don't think you can betray me and leave me in the lurch. You're in this up to your eyebrows and you'll take your money, even if I have to ram each note down your throat. Then you'll give me my due and I'll keep quiet about you. Otherwise I'll see you ruined anyway, Donovan, gold or no gold.'

Donovan grabbed Simpson's hand and flung it away, but all the fight went out of him and Simpson could see it. This was a burden Donovan had made for himself, and he'd have to bear it for the rest of his life. Maybe in time his remorse would fade and his conscience quieten—maybe. He shuddered at the thought of what his family would think if they even had an inkling of what he'd done. His shoulders slumped. 'The deal stands.'

Simpson slapped him on the back. "Course it does! Now you can be happy.' He turned to the tray and tapped the sides with a hammer to loosen the precious metal.

Donovan watched him. Happy? He'd be alive and debt free but an accessory to murder. Happy? That wasn't a word he'd use.

Simpson stopped tapping. 'And what about that payment? Greenberg is handing you twelve hundred quid. Is that the best you can get?'

'The bank valued the gold at eighteen hundred pounds sterling. Greenberg gets an agreed twenty-five per cent discount to take it off my hands. The rest is mine.'

Simpson sneered, 'Minus my cut because I did all your dirty work and supplied the transport. You agreed to two hundred and you'd better see me right.'

Donovan was amazed that Simpson in this mood was not trying to screw more out of him at the last minute. But maybe the man was as terrified as he was, underneath. After all, he was the one who'd committed murder.

Donovan was curt. 'You'll take it and be damned.'

Simpson pondered, then said, 'Done. When Greenberg comes back with the cash, I'll take my share and disappear.' He pointed with the hammer. 'And you, you'll pay your debts, Mr Donovan, and forget about me.' He smirked. 'I said forget, and if you feel you're about to go soft in your pants—don't. I can kill, and I will again.'

* * *

Gerry stretched out on his bed and gazed at the walls in his cell. The bricks were laid with skill and he concentrated on the quality work. He had to stop his mind from straying onto his fate. The last fourteen days locked up had nearly killed him.

He'd been sentenced, but not to death. He wouldn't hang. The gold sections of the doors hadn't been found and there were no witnesses to the death of Toole, and no proof that Gerry had been in his lodgings at the time. The jury's verdict was 'guilty', but the judge considered that Gerry was not guilty 'beyond a reasonable doubt' and therefore he received not the death sentence but gaol for life.

In a state of shock, he hadn't slept for the first three nights. He breathed. He ate. He shat. That was all.

By the end of the first week, his tormented brain took over. Shock went and anger filled the gap. He struggled to work out how the two crimes had been committed. Had Mr Hughes been right about the gold doors? Maybe they had been snatched after the collision in John Street, or the whole box had been switched for another. No trace had been found of Jack Mulveen or his wagon and horses—was he the thief? This puzzle gnawed at him, but it was nothing in comparison with his grief over Lawrence Toole. Why had his friend been killed? Sadness filled him yet again.

To stay sane, he had to focus on something else. Think about the brick walls that hemmed him in, and the stone foundations. The Cork prison was only four years old. Donovan had laid stone in it and Gerry had spent time here as an apprentice. His boss had been less of a bully during that job, tough but fair. Anne came to mind and Gerry shook his head: he could not bear to think of her or imagine what she might be thinking of him. She was lost to him forever. He had to banish her from his mind, or he would go mad.

His muscles tensed. His breathing became short and shallow. Pain radiated behind his closed eyelids. To distract himself, he ticked off a familiar list: square, plumb-bob, string line, straight edge … square, plumb-bob … his breathing started to return to normal and he opened his eyes. Forcing his torment to one side, he stared at the walls again.

Now the prison. Picture building it again from the ground up, course by course. He closed his eyes and drifted off.

* * *

Sean Hughes was facing Patrick Hughes across his father's desk. The catastrophe of the missing gold doors had just reached another level and his father's questions were urgent.

'You're telling me those doors weren't insured for loss or damage before they left the foundry?'

Sean said, 'No, we didn't need to insure them because I thought they were Donovan's responsibility all the way to the cathedral.'

'Right, and that's what you told me, son,' Patrick Hughes said, 'in this very study, the day you put the contract on my desk. But now, you're telling me you were wrong?'

Sean couldn't hold his father's gaze; he dropped his eyes. Embarrassment filled him. He'd let his father down, a sin as great as any son knows. 'I'm sorry Father. Yes, I was wrong.'

'I don't know how you could have got so muddled. It says right here in the contract that the goods were our responsibility until the doors were installed into the tabernacle, on the altar, in the cathedral.' Patrick Hughes paused. 'What have you got to say to that?'

'I didn't read the contract, Father.'

Patrick Hughes's shoulders sagged—shoulders that not long ago had packed hard muscle. 'The nub of this is what it's going to cost us. You agree: the doors weren't insured because you wrongly assumed they were Donovan's property once he'd collected them from us?'

'Yes.'

'So we're liable for them, whether they were lost, stolen or went up in smoke. And we can't claim any insurance for that loss. What, in your opinion, are we now obliged to do?'

Those words said it all. Fair enough. He'd got himself into this mess because he had signed a contract without reading it— a commercial blunder of the highest order. It was hard to say the next sentence. 'We'll have to make another pair of doors. With new materials, including more gold.'

Patrick closed his eyes. 'The replacement cost?'

Sean hesitated. His father hadn't remonstrated with him yet. It somehow made the next statement harder to pronounce. 'Over two thousand for the materials, plus the labour.'

The blood drained from his father's face, as if he'd just learned he had the typhus. 'We can't meet expenses like that at the moment. You know how bad trading conditions are. The foundry is mortgaged to the hilt. We'll have to mortgage this house to tide us over. We have no choice.'

The ultimate shame. All his life, his father had impressed on Sean that the family home must be held inviolate from the banker's grubby hand. Now here they were having to raise money on it to keep the business afloat. He shook his head. 'Surely, with some belt-tightening, selling something …'

His father leaned over and patted his knee. Sean didn't notice at first that Patrick's devastation and wounded pride had evaporated, replaced with something else. His father's eyes were twinkling. 'If I counted the number of mistakes I made at your age, we'd have had this house mortgaged a dozen times.'

Sean's throat started to thicken with emotion. His father had forgiven him.

'Come on,' Patrick said, 'start writing up the things we need to do.'

Sean got up and addressed the inkwell and paper on his father's desk.

'You haven't been the first to be tripped up by a sharp contractor and you won't be the last. Donovan's won this round but the game is still on. Get those doors replaced—now! As each day passes, our reputation suffers if we don't deliver.' He pushed himself up and grabbed his cane. Standing to his full height, he placed his hand on Sean's shoulder. 'And next time, when the contractor picks up those doors from our foundry, they're his when he touches them.'

His father departed and Sean took a deep breath and started on his list. An ink blob dropped from his nib as he paused. He wasn't as equanimous as his father. Donovan had swindled him. Sure, he and his father were now members of the Cork Corporation because of this deal, but that was a very steep a price to pay.

The two gold sheets from the doors were in someone else's hands at this moment, and it burned him up to think he had to replace them. Where was that gold? Probably melted down. It certainly hadn't turned up anywhere. Who else had known about the doors, apart from the parties involved? Jacob Greenberg, gold merchant, for one. Since the trial, Sean had heard that Greenberg was emigrating to New South Wales and had left town. A coincidence? Greenberg had certified the value of the gold at their foundry and now he was gone.

* * *

In Cork's Fin Barre's chapel, the air whistled along the pew that pressed against Anne, seeming to want to pass through her. Her prayer ended with a plea. 'Dear Lord,' she whispered, 'protect my Gerry. Let him not suffer.'

Her fingers on her beads, she started the Rosary. The third Hail Mary finished and her mind drifted back to the third of March, two and a half long weeks since she'd last seen Gerry. As a minor she had no permission to visit a prison alone and her parents would have forbidden her to go, but she had realised who could help her. Sean Hughes.

She remembered sitting in a crowded visitors' room at the prison. A table in front of her with a chair opposite, Mr Hughes seated on her left. Only one thing soothed the rawness of her mood. The prison wasn't ancient and didn't feel like a dungeon. And Gerry, she was told, had his own cell.

The door to the visitors' room had opened. To her, the noise of nearby conversation had seemed to die down as Gerry entered, in manacles, with his gaoler. Her heart pounded in shock. His face was pale, making the dark red of his hair even more striking. His mouth was turned down as he looked at her and his eyes were haunted.

She stood up, as did Sean Hughes, then they all greeted one another in low tones. Gerry sat down and just stared at a space between Anne and Sean. The silence started to press on her like a great weight. Then they spoke, about small things, meaningless things like the winter weather outside, the prison food and such. She'd been nonplussed, lost, wanting to ask him about the state of his mind, whether he could sleep, what his cell was like, whether he was warm enough—but after five minutes he'd stood up and had gone away.

Anne pressed her beads and the tears came back. Her cheeks felt wet and cold. She rose, made the sign of the Cross and left.

* * *

Dougal Simpson was enjoying himself in a private room at the Drawbridge. His new coat and breeches felt odd on him, yet he was getting the looks. He'd had to be sharp-witted in order to explain his newfound wealth. A distant relative had left him a big inheritance; that was his story.

Life was grand. Riordan had been locked up for over five weeks and would stay there until the end of his days. Greenberg was on the high seas and Donovan's mouth was shut.

'More bubbly?' a voice beside him said.

A young woman snuggled against him, her cleavage on display, and she giggled when he squeezed her waist. With them were just a few friends and some female company.

'Why not?' he said. 'We're here to celebrate.' He poured out the rest of the bottle. 'More champagne, my lad,' he said to one of his new-found drinking friends. 'Off you go.'

The lad stood up and blushed as a woman's hand brushed his thigh. He pushed it away and she pouted.

Simpson grinned at her. 'He'll be right back, love, and you can carry on where you left off.' Laughter erupted and he felt fingers touching his mouth, stroking his moustache.

The girl sitting next to him was flushed and her mouth was parted. She leaned closer and spoke in his ear, her hand on him, squeezing him. 'There's a room just for us, upstairs. I want you—now.'

He looked at her. Two months ago, he would've been lucky to get a shilling whore, and now he had the choice of Cork's finest night ladies. 'Why not?'

Meanwhile, in the evening coolness, Sergeant Hooper rubbed his forehead and considered the lady who was sitting inside the carriage opposite him, twenty yards or so down the street from the Drawbridge Hotel. Mrs Dunleavy was a respectable woman, middle-aged and of sharp mind. She had come to the police about a crime and now Sergeant Hooper was with her because she was convinced she could identify a criminal.

Mrs Dunleavy's story had begun just before Christmas last, when she had been standing inside the Cork branch of the Bank of Ireland, near a front window, attempting to find a name in her address book. She noticed a man was standing on the street just outside that window and found it odd that all the time she'd been in the bank, he had neither come in nor walked away; he just hung around on the footpath.

He remained where he was until she was about to leave, and then to her horror armed men burst into the bank and she was forced to the floor like all the other customers while it was robbed. The robbers' faces were disguised, and they escaped with all the money from behind the counters. As Mrs Dunleavy struggled to her feet, terrified, she could see out the open doorway. She saw the man who had been loitering in the street run with the robbers and disappear down the street. He must have been their lookout.

Despite strenuous police efforts, the robbers had not been caught. Mrs Dunleavy had given them her description of the man she thought was their lookout: of average height, a weather-beaten face with a scar under the left eye, a thick moustache—but he had never been found either. However, Mrs Dunleavy was being driven down Patrick Street today when she spotted the very man entering the Drawbridge Hotel. She had at once stopped the carriage, remained in it to observe, and sent her driver to the police station to demand that they act. Hooper was now in the carriage with her and a constable waited further down the street, keeping an eye on the entrance to the Drawbridge.

'Ma'am, are you quite certain it's the same man?'

'Sergeant, how many times do I have to explain? My dear friend was also in the bank when it was robbed—she nearly had apoplexy from the shock. It was awful. I'll never forget that day. I remember every second of it and I remember that man. He's one of those villains who robbed the Bank of Ireland. He's guilty as Pilate!'

'If you're prepared to identify him, we'll bring him into custody. Anything further you can tell me about him, ma'am? Colour of hair?'

'I don't know, he wears a hat. But I can tell you about his clothes. On the day of the robbery he looked like a labourer—he was out of place in the street outside my bank. But today, oh, today he's dressed like a gentleman—nice coat, though it's a bit loud for my taste, and good trousers and shoes. So now he'll be out of place in the

Drawbridge bar; I can just imagine what that's like. Ten to one you'll find him in a private room, splashing his money about—all that's left of the bank's money, no doubt.'

'Thank you, Mrs Dunleavy. If he's still in the Drawbridge, we'll have no trouble spotting him.'

'Then arrest him!' she cried.

'Not only must we ask you to identify him—when he comes to trial you will be witness for the prosecution. Are you prepared to face him?'

'Face him!' she said. 'I'd gladly slice him up, I would.'

'Now, now. There's no need for that.'

Mrs Dunleavy threw the rug from her knees and got down into the street. When Sergeant Hooper descended also, she straightened her dress, fixed her hat and turned to him. 'I'm prepared to go in there and confront him. Are you coming?'

Hooper sighed. It was going to be quite a night. 'Stay here, if you please, ma'am. We'll get him.'

* * *

In the prison chapel, the priest blessed the Host. Love and forgiveness. It was Easter Sunday, the sixth of April, but the day and date meant nothing to Gerry. The virtues of the Holy Season were like a vapour, no better than the River Lee's mist. He wanted out of this place.

Seated in three rows with him were men like him. He'd got to know some of them. A motley lot who hadn't talked about their crimes. Some were readying to leave, forced into transportation for life to New South Wales. Poor Lawrence Toole. He had wanted to go to New South Wales as a free man to earn his fortune, but Lawrence Toole was dead.

It was five weeks ago that Anne had come to visit him. After he had seen her, he'd broken down the moment he got back to his cell. There should have been words between them, words of love and encouragement, yes, even with Mr Hughes there. Yet there were none. All that night he hadn't slept, just thinking about her. Now he tried not to. He knew that his old life was gone. Desperation pressed on him like a stone slab and each night it became a little heavier, reminding him that he'd be in prison for life.

Thank God for his size. Some of the lightweights here got nothing but beatings and rape. During his second week he'd been attacked and he hadn't held back, taking some bruises and torn skin but able, in the scrap, to chew off part of the ear of one opponent. The third week they'd left him alone.

It was an insult to make convicts attend chapel. There was nothing here to thank God for. One of the new prisoners, a wiry man, stared at him. Gerry stared back, willing the man on. Chapel or not, he'd have him! The man looked away.

The service ended and the prisoners filed out. There were rumours that a government man would be coming after Easter to move some prisoners to other gaols. Gerry didn't care. He was angry, alone and looking for a head to kick. That was all there was to it. Nothing else.

* * *

The spring air warmed the garden at Donovan House and made it fragrant. If Anne's love had been beside her amongst the flowers, it would have been a wonderful Sunday afternoon, but she was at a table in the drawing room, writing a letter to Gerry. She was in despair. She knew she had lost weight and her parents worried about her—it was as though she were fading away. Gerry was drifting away, too—she could sense it. But she must concentrate on her words. This was the sixth letter she'd written since she'd seen him that one time, and her previous letters had gone unanswered. Just a note from him in response to this one would bring her back some hope.

Looking through the window, she scanned the sky, seeking inspiration and help. Had prison changed Gerry? Sean Hughes had used friendships with government officials to get reports on his well-being. What Sean told her was alarming—Gerry had been in fights, showed insubordination and bad attitude. That wasn't her man. Yet she understood his anger. Like Gerry, she was angry too, at the guilty party that had ripped her man away from her.

Her father came in. James Donovan had a spring in his step these days. A big debtor had paid a handsome settlement and they were in the money. He frowned, looking at her writing tablet. 'It's a waste, darling,' he said. 'The rogue's not answered any of your letters.' Her eyes expanded in surprise and he nodded. 'Your mother told me you've been writing to Riordan. And what's it been? Six weeks since you've seen him and no reply. Come on, we're going to town. There's an orchestra playing and we've been invited.'

'Very well,' she answered without enthusiasm.

He sat beside her. 'Your mother would be happier if you'd eat more. You're looking wan. Anne nodded. 'I'll try. Father, Gerry's innocent. I know. He's—

'He's guilty, Anne. The courts proved it.'

'I'll never believe it. No matter what.'

Donovan sighed. 'Your life will be a misery if you can't accept the plain facts about that man.'

'I've been thinking who else could have stolen those doors.'

'What?' he spluttered.

'It was common knowledge on the day, Father, that gold doors were being delivered to you at the cathedral. So, all the workmen at the cathedral, everyone at Mr Hughes's foundry, the draughtsman who drew up the plans, anybody could be the guilty party.'

'But not everyone had the opportunity or the motive to carry out the theft. Now listen, my dear. You must stop thinking over and over about Riordan's crimes.' He held her hands. 'It'll only get you worse. He's guilty and he's serving time.'

'For life,' she said. 'It's life, Father. No reprieve.' She started to cry. He put his arm around her and she leaned on him. 'It's not fair. He's innocent. He is.'

* * *

Gerry's shackles clanged and the man in the prison visitors' room glanced down at them. Gerry was used to the sound and was curious that others even noticed he was in chains; they were part of him, like his eyebrows. His visitor turned his attention to the papers on the table in front of him. A government man, Gerry sniffed; ill-fitting jacket, big gut and bad teeth.

'Sit down,' Gerry's gaoler said to him, but he remained standing, looking at the open window high above the government man's head.

The man put on his spectacles. 'Convict Riordan. Your sentence for life is under review.' On the windowsill, a bird pecked at an insect in the spring sunshine. 'The colonial office and the justice department are considering the situation in New South Wales—it seems there's a shortage of qualified tradesmen.'

Only three words reached Gerry. New South Wales? That's where Lawrence Toole had wanted to go, all that way away.

'Your sentence can be commuted,' the man said.

His sentence? He leaned forward.

The man looked up at him. 'Convict Riordan? Did you understand me?'

A searing pain exploded in Gerry's lower back, jerking him upright. He lunged at the gaoler, who stepped out of reach, baton aloft to strike again.

'Answer the man, Convict. And sit down!'

Panting with rage, Gerry sat down and rubbed his kidneys. He spoke between his teeth to the man on the other side of the table. 'Say again.'

The reply was dispassionate. 'They need stonemasons in Sydney and you can serve out your life there instead of here. That's it.'

Gerry slumped back and the pain worsened. Sweat filmed on his forehead. 'Me, go to New South Wales?'

'Yes.'

'When?'

'If you agree,' the man said, 'as early as next week.'

'Riordan?' his gaoler said and pushed him upright, his baton pressing against the ache in his lower back. 'What do you say?'

It was still a life sentence but it was out of here. 'I'll g-go.'

The government man leaned over his paperwork. 'Sign here.' He handed Gerry a quill.

Gerry signed and noted the date, 14 April 1828. The man closed his file, got up, nodded at the gaoler and left the room.

'Getting off lightly, Riordan,' the guard said. 'A sea trip to the land of sunshine.' He pulled Gerry up. 'Come on. You're mine for six more days.'

Gerry flexed his hands. Just as well for the manacles. He would've killed the sod otherwise.

* * *

The morning chill still clung to the river, but the late April day would be warm soon. He was being deported from Union Quay, Cork. The first word angered Gerry because he resented the English with their damned King and Country. In 1800, the Irish Parliament had voted itself out of existence by agreeing to the Act of Union, which made Ireland part of the United Kingdom. Which meant that the legal system of Ireland was the same as that of Great Britain. He might as well be a bloody Brit.

Gerry hoisted his irons as they grazed against a sore part of his calloused ankles. The line of twenty convicts in front of him were luckier in being shorter than him. Their trousers reached their feet, the material giving them some protection from the shackles' cursed rub.

'Look at me,' said the tense voice beside him.

He turned to face his sister, Maeve. He was aware of dark eyes in a pretty face. She lived in Cork but worked hard in a humble job, like himself, and he had scarcely seen her since she left the farm and moved to town. Now he would never see her again.

Maeve's lips quivered and her chin jutted out, defiant. 'Ma wanted to come. She did, Gerry.'

'And Da?'

His sister looked down. 'You know he's still sick. She couldn't leave him. The trial nearly killed him.'

Dear Jesus! This had harmed his whole family. There was nothing he could do for them but make sure they got the pitiful stuff he owned. 'My goods in my room. Did you get them all?'

'Aye.'

'The medallion. Look after it. It's silver.'

'What, Gerry? The landlady gave me everything and there was no medallion.'

Gone and lost, Gerry thought, just like Toole. 'I handed it to Toole. It got too dirty on site. It must be with the police—they should give it back to you. And the new woollen jacket, the one Ma bought?'

'That was there. Oh, Gerry, why go to New South Wales? You had the choice to stay in Cork. My neighbour said that a lifer can go on parole after ten years and be allowed to work in a trade.'

Ten years. It sounded the same as life to Gerry. 'I'll start work as soon as I get to New South Wales. The colony needs tradesmen. They'll give me a go.'

'You could have stayed!' she said her voice strained. 'But no, not the proud mason. Had to prove himself, didn't he? Well, that's what you get—'

'G-give it a rest, we have only minutes.' Ahead, the line was starting to move.

'And you'll be gone a lifetime.' She closed her eyes and tears ran down her cheeks.

Gerry raised a manacled hand to touch her.

'Back!' A guard's baton stung like a hot rod.

'Leave off, you brute!' Maeve yelled. 'He's not going to harm me.' The guard walked away up the line. 'How will I know you'll be all right? Do they let you send letters? Maybe Ma and Da—'

He shook his head. 'It's goodbye, Maeve.' At the edge of the Quay, the first convict in the line stepped down into one of the longboats that would take them out to the convict ship. The town-hall bell tolled and on the eighth and final strike, Gerry was shunted forward. 'I-I didn't kill Toole. Dear God, he was my mate.' He looked hard at her. 'And as God is my witness, I'm no thief. Tell Ma and Da that. Tell them I'm sorry for all this.' The pull of the chains made him shuffle forward. Maeve walked beside him.

He looked ahead, not wanting to see her face for the last time. 'Leave me,' he said. 'Now.'

* * *

Anne Donovan had one hour in her father's study to do what she had to do, unless he came home early from the cathedral. She was doing devious work and part of her was sorry for that. But she had to find something here to prove Gerry's innocence.

Careful and quick. Not wanting to alert him by misplacing any objects. She rifled through drawers and desk, cabinets and cupboards, examining papers, searching for some link to Gerry's case. There must be something here! Some detail that her father had recorded but the police had missed, because they were so determined to pin the crime on Gerry. Something everyone had ignored—a document or clue to prove her man innocent.

A file with 'St Mary's Tabernacle Doors' written on it caught her eye and she opened it. There was a thick document within it and about a dozen single sheets. She skimmed through the sheets and then scanned the document, drawn up by her father, which was the contract with the Hughes Foundry for the manufacture and supply of the doors.

Some sections were complex but most of it was quite clear to Anne. She read every clause up to Possession of the Doors, then re-read it, amazed. The gold-plated, brass-framed doors were the property of the Supplier, Hughes Foundry, until such time as they were set into the tabernacle on the altar of St Mary's. Until the time they were set into the tabernacle! Odd. If Mr Hughes had responsibility for the doors, why hadn't he made sure they were escorted by his own men? Why hadn't a Hughes man been provided to supervise when

Gerry was meant to attach the doors to the tabernacle? And another thing. Given that the doors were Hughes's responsibility, and considering their value, why hadn't her father insisted in the contract that Hughes provide an armed escort to ensure their security on the way to the cathedral? It was confusing and worrying.

The hall clock chimed the quarter hour and Anne looked at the loose pages again. From a list of names, one leaped out at her—Dougal Simpson. The note beside it said only, 'Possible help'. Help with what? There was a Dougal Simpson lately convicted of bank robbery, along with a number of accomplices, all named in the newspapers. Could this be the same Dougal Simpson? If so, how on earth could her father have listed him as 'possible help' in this folder that was all to do with the tabernacle doors?

She went cold, and picked up the next sheet with dread. It was the affidavit, signed by her father, stating that Gerald Riordan had been employed on work in the cathedral, as an unsupervised tradesman, on the afternoon of Wednesday 16 January, the day Lawrence Toole was murdered in Riordan's room. The altar where he worked was surrounded by scaffolding and no nearby workers were in sight of it. Thus, neither James Donovan nor any of his employees at the cathedral could certify that Riordan had been working on the altar all afternoon. He would have had time during that period to go to his lodgings, meet and kill Toole, and return to the cathedral unseen.

The sound of wheels outside told her that her father's gig was pulling up and he was about to alight. He was home early, damn! Her perspiring finger moistened another paper. Two words leapt out at her: 'gold', and 'Greenberg'. The key turned in the front door and she slipped the folded paper into her dress pocket, hoping that her father wouldn't miss it. By the time the door opened, she was on the stairs, walking down.

A red-faced James Donovan smiled at her. 'Home early? I thought you had late lessons on Thursdays?'

Anne smoothed down her dress and walked towards him. 'Sister Gene was ill. Can I get you some lemonade? It's so hot outside.'

Donovan nodded and handed his coat to Henry, his manservant. 'Let's have it on the back terrace. It's cooler there.'

'I'll see to it, sir,' Henry said.

Seated in the shade, Donovan took a sip of the cool drink and wiped his face. 'How are you faring? I would hope that with Riordan out of the country, you could find some ease.'

Anne fingered her glass. 'It's only been ten days since he left, but it feels like ten months. I see him on the ship, caged like an animal, exhausted and angry.'

'He's angry because his crimes were found out.'

Anne's own temper flared but she kept it in check. 'No. He's innocent, I know.'

'You're in love, Anne. That colours everything for you. For a while. It will pass.'

She pressed her pocket. The edges of the note imprinted themselves on her palm. 'I'll find the real culprit. I will.'

Donovan's hand jerked, knocking the glass over, spilling some liquid. 'You won't! You'll finish your studies. Leave this whole thing alone. You hear?' He grabbed her wrist but she pulled it away, rubbing the red mark he'd left.

'You hurt me!' she said.

'Will I clean up, sir?' Henry asked standing near them.

'Yes, yes,' her father said.

Her father waited till the manservant had left. 'I'm sorry, dear.'

'You should be! Why does it bother you so much? You think I'm just a silly girl with a torch burning for him? Well I'm not, I'm a young woman prepared to defend an innocent man when no one else will.'

She said it with such passion that she expected her father would be angrier than ever, but he sat back, pressed his lips together and then said without emphasis, 'It's far too late for that. From now on I expect you to concentrate on your duty to your parents and to your studies. Are we clear?'

Anne nodded, stood up and walked away. She would continue as the dutiful daughter while she hunted and dug further for Gerry's sake. The document in her pocket was the first clue in her search; she was convinced of that.

* * *

Anne examined herself in the hallway mirror and decided that she passed muster. Chrissie, carrying a loaded cloth bag, opened their front door for Mrs Donovan.

'I'm coming,' Anne said.

Settled in their carriage in the early May sunshine, Anne took stock. They were going to town to look at fabrics for a new dress for her birthday next month, and she had other plans as well. She'd sent a note via Chrissie so she could meet Mr Hughes this morning at the foundry. She had questions for him about the door-supply contract. Maybe there was something he could tell her.

For the first time in weeks, hope was chipping away at her depression. There had to be something, somewhere, to prove Gerry wasn't a thief, much less a murderer.

As they headed into town, her mother said, 'What colour takes your fancy for the dress?'

Anne concentrated. 'I think I'd like something simple in lemon or pale blue.'

Colleen Donovan said, 'Then that's what we'll look at first.'

Anne no longer had the paper that she had snatched up from her father's desk. She had managed to return it the next day without his noticing. It was the certificate of quality for the gold used in the tabernacle doors. A Mr Jacob Greenberg had attested to the gold's purity when Patrick and Sean Hughes obtained it from the Agricultural and Commercial Bank. It gave her just a little more information about the gold.

In the main street, they alighted near three fashion shops which they often visited, all high class in terms of their fabric and the customers they served. Anne put her plan into place.

'Now, I'm going to enjoy taking a good long time to make my choice. But I'm thinking, you may like to step around the corner and see how Mrs Hamilton is, Mother. You told me she's not been well?'

'They say she's up to visitors but I'd like to see for myself. She worries me a little.'

Anne smiled. 'Then why don't you visit her? Chrissie and I can look around and you can meet us back here in, say, half an hour?'

Her mother hesitated. 'I did really want to look for something for myself, as well.'

'Of course! We have plenty of time. You can still do that when you come back.'

'You'll be all right then?'

'Yes, Mother. Now go.'

Colleen Donovan smiled. 'I will.'

After she walked away, Anne turned to Chrissie. 'I'll see you back here at nine thirty.'

'Very good, miss.' Chrissie looked happy to be given the leisure for looking in shop windows.

Anne made her way to the Hughes Foundry, a walk of about ten minutes.

A smiling Sean Hughes greeted her. 'Good morning. You're punctual, Miss Donovan.'

'Good morning to you, Mr Hughes. I have only a few minutes before Mother and I go shopping in earnest.'

'Any time spent with you is always a pleasure.' That was said with charm, and she appreciated it. 'Come into my office.'

Settled in a chair, she came straight to the point. 'I want to ask you about the agreement you had with my father for the tabernacle doors.'

Sean smiled. 'You're interested in the business side of what happened?'

'And why not?' she replied with force.

He shook his head, startled but firm. 'Because what I have to say on that score may pain you, Miss Donovan. What your father did to us was sharp. The contract stated that the doors would not become the responsibility of Donovans until they'd been set into the tabernacle.'

'Was that a problem?'

'It was, for us. I should have insured the doors or put an armed escort on the delivery, which would have prevented the theft. But they were stolen in transit and we had to replace them.'

'Oh, I see. At enormous cost. I can see why you may feel that's unfair.'

'Yes. Nonetheless, a contract is a contract.'

She sat back. Hughes and Donovan had dealt with each other since, never a problem. But this time was different. 'So why did you sign? Why take that risk?'

Sean shook his head. 'I signed without reading the document.'

So Sean Hughes had made a big mistake. He had been caught out by a document drawn up by her father, which he now described as 'sharp'. However, she was not going to be drawn into any criticism of James Donovan. 'Oh dear.'

'Quite,' he said.

She tried her next subject. 'Do you know a Mr Jacob Greenberg?'

'He gave us a certificate of authenticity for the gold in the doors, the first time we made them.'

'He's a man of good character?'

'I haven't met him in person. As to character, you might ask your father about Greenberg; he's dealt with him in the past.'

She stood up. 'Thank you for your time. I must get back to my mother.'

'Any time, Miss Donovan.'

As she made her return she pondered her father's 'sharp' contract. It had left the gold doors unprotected between the Hughes foundry and the cathedral. And her father had not sent an armed guard with Gerry Riordan and Lawrence Toole when he ordered them to pick the doors up. Whatever the consequences, she would have to find out more about his intentions.

Chapter Four

The fly returned. Its fat belly was bluer than the nor'easter-cooled sky and its back legs vibrated on the blotter. Secretary Childs swatted at it again. It buzzed away to find richer pickings and was lost in a second, hopefully through the window whence it had come. Childs looked out. Some four hundred yards away from his desk in Government House, water rippled at the rocky and sandy edges of Port Jackson. His vista through the trees on the headland was dotted with tents, storehouses, forts, windmills, shops, and Sydney's houses of stone and timber.

Standing up, the secretary flexed his shoulders, and stretched his collar with two fingers. Too hot for an Englishman who'd only been here two years, since 1826. Summer was supposed to be over, and it was May, but it was hot. And His Excellency's next appointment was five minutes late.

'Childs!' came a roar from the adjoining room. 'Is Mitchell coming or not?'

'I'll see, sir.' Childs walked out of the double doors and stopped dead. His visitor had arrived.

'Please come this way, sir,' Childs said.

The visitor followed him to the governor's door. Childs knocked on it and announced him, then went back to his desk for a notebook. He was expected to record this meeting.

The Honourable Lieutenant-General Ralph Darling stepped forward from his desk. 'Ah, Major. Please come right in. Would you like a glass of something?'

'Some water, thank you, sir.'

'Yes. A little early for something stronger. Sit down. Sit down.'

Mitchell sat and adjusted his waistcoat to suit his spreading middle, a middle that supported broad shoulders and a solid head. He looked at the Governor with twinkling eyes. 'Your Excellency is good to see me.'

'Needed to, sir.' He glanced at Childs, who had come into the room. 'Pour us all some water, would you, Childs?' As the secretary did so, he went on, 'Major Mitchell, your appointment as Surveyor General is of the greatest importance to me and to New South Wales. I want to talk about roads sir, roads.'

Mitchell sipped and listened as the governor outlined his ideas about the region and his plans to link Sydney with new land holdings in the north, by a major road. Mitchell nodded at all the right points. He was drawn to the project and excited, because what was asked of him was almost certain to make his name in the colony.

Mitchell cleared his throat. 'Let me, if I may, sir, try to bring your ideas into a short summary.'

'Please.'

'This road is a public necessity? It's been requested by parties who are certain to make use of it?'

'Demanded, sir, demanded. A fine group of gentlemen are convinced that the future prosperity of New South Wales cannot be built without it.'

Mitchell smiled to himself as he recognised the political and commercial power behind the project. 'Very good. Now the road is to be constructed north of Sydney Town, to link it with the lower Hawkesbury and the Hunter.'

'We must see it as more than a road, Major. We must see it as a highway. Of course, sections of it have begun already. Progress is straightforward until one reaches the hills. Further north, you may find that the stretch beyond Wiseman's Ferry is your biggest challenge.'

'The terrain is mountainous, with dense scrub.' Mitchell scratched his head. 'A highway you said, sir?'

The governor handed him a parchment. 'This is your official warrant. You will be fulfilling a great need: settlers in the Hunter must have access to Sydney. The Australian Agricultural Company has a charter to cultivate one million acres of land west of Port Stephens. Sea transport of goods and people up and down the coast is inefficient and takes too long. What is required is an artery to Sydney, a proper sealed and drained highway.'

'Your Excellency, what resources can I call upon?'

'A public work on this scale needs workers of all kinds. Major, we have over sixteen thousand male convicts here, out of a population of just over thirty-six thousand. You'll want convicts and you'll get them—we'll assign as many as you need.'

Mitchell glanced at the parchment in his hand and smiled at the title. 'You have come up with a good name for the highway, Your Excellency—The Great North Road.'

Darling nodded. 'Childs! Display the brief.'

The secretary unrolled a document onto a long table.

'Come, Major,' Darling said and both men went to look. It was a map, which Mitchell recognised: Heneage Finch's survey of 1825. 'Firstly, of course this survey will require revision.'

A huge piece of work in itself, Mitchell thought.

Darling continued, 'But much of the work that it shows, between Bedlam Point and the Hawkesbury River, has been done. The hard grind will be north of the river up to Mt Manning.' Darling paused and ran his finger along a route marked in green. 'It's all thick scrub and rock, as you well know. Sandstone. It will need blasting, levelling and filling in. The scale of this work is unlike anything that's been done in this colony.'

'Resources, sir,' Mitchell said again.

'As I said, Major, convicts.' He tapped the thick brief that Childs had also laid on the table. 'They'll need supervising by trained men, and those trained men will be your key to success, so pick them wisely and give them their head. You'll find everything set out in here. Gangs needed, equipment, animals, all that.' He smiled. 'This brief comes from the brains of many men, most of them well-meaning and some of them with vast experience. But don't take it all on board without question, Major. It will be your task to examine it, interrogate it, throw parts of it out if you think they are not practical or workable. To construct this road, you must get the sequence of events right. You must be confident about the materials and resources needed, and you must control the costs. I want a program of work that can be done. Not some clerk's vision of what's possible.' You get me, sir?'

'I do, sir, I do.'

'Good. I'll have all this sent to your office.' The governor took the major's elbow and directed him towards the door, which Secretary Childs darted forward to open. 'You have my full support, Major. This will be the best road yet built. None of your native trails here! See me in a month with your complete plan. Get help wherever you require it. Your warrant gives my authority. This will be the greatest public work this colony has yet seen.'

Mitchell paused in the doorway, saluted, and left.

* * *

A month into the voyage to New South Wales, it was of no comfort to Convict Gerry Riordan that the transport ship was better fitted out than the ships at the beginning of the century. Their gaolers told them that their on-board digs were luxury, compared with what their earlier brethren had had to put up with, but it felt like a taunt.

Through an orange-sized porthole, Gerry stared at the sunshine, which appeared like a night star, adding little to the dim light filtering down from the grated hatch above. There was nothing, nothing to do but think. Pressed close between one of many near full-height bulkheads were twenty fellow convicts, who mumbled to themselves in their misery. There was another deck of convicts above, men he would never see because they only got rare moments on deck at different times.

After the first week it was as if they'd all been doused with the finest that the Cork sewers could discharge. The smell sat on them and in them. Being pounded by five days of storms since they'd left Cork a month past added seasickness to their misery, the vomit mixed with the staleness.

Sighting a rat, Gerry was beaten to it by a fellow sufferer who snatched at it, grinned at him and bashed it on the deck. Gerry closed his eyes to the crunching sound that followed, pressing his stomach for control while the man consumed the rodent.

He forced himself to relive laying the marble slabs on the cathedral's altar top. Only four months ago he'd been a free man. In as many months or so he'd be in a new land, a convict till he died. His teeth ground together and anger, hot and pulsing, spread through him, as it had every hour he'd been awake since the day he left Cork.

His red-rimmed eyes had closed each night after he'd exhausted every reason for the theft and the murder of his best friend. Scene by scene, he'd revisited the journey he and Toole had made with that box, and the collision. Why would anyone kill Toole? Was his death linked in some way to the box that was found by his body? Wetness coated him and he pressed his wrists together. The murder and the theft must be linked, but why and how? And there was Anne. His memory of her smile lightened his existence for a moment, but then the blackness always returned as she was lost to him.

A yell from behind a bulkhead jolted him. There was the sound of a baton crunching down and the scream became a moan.

The overseer, Peter Adams, hooked his baton back on his belt and walked away from the man he'd hit, on the lookout for anyone else who dared stand up to him.

Dougal Simpson leaned over and hissed in the victim's blood-filled ear, 'Deserved that, you did. Shut up and be nice to Mr Adams, then you might just get extra rations.'

'Like you, you mean,' the man said whimpering.

Simpson smiled. 'Yes, like me.' Simpson had known Adams for years, having pulled off a theft with him in the past, from a rich trader's house. Like him, Adams was the son of a Ribbon Man, but unlike him he had taken on the job of prison guard. However, he had been caught dealing contraband in the Cork prison and had been demoted to overseer on the transports.

Adams feared Dougal Simpson. He might bash prisoners now, but in the past he'd seen Simpson inflict things on people that made his hair stand up. As fellow part-time criminals they had both done the odd job that kept the coppers busy and their own pockets lined. In Cork, Simpson had stashed away £200 from his prior crimes, in addition to his share from the theft of the gold doors. When he was arrested and convicted of bank robbery he could not access his gains—so, for a fee, he had paid Adams to collect them and store them in his locker. That fee also included softer treatment from Adams on the journey to New South Wales, at which place, and at the right time, Simpson would get his cash back and start up his money-making ways again. Adams was frightened of him, so Simpson was confident he wouldn't be double-crossed. It was a matter of biding his time and putting up with the pain now. It wouldn't last a lifetime: in New South Wales, after seven years you could get parole for good service.

His bloodied companion slumped against him and Simpson shoved him away, thinking about what Adams had whispered to him in snatches at mealtimes. Over a ladle of mystery soup, the man had given him information—what type of day it was up on deck, the journey left to sail, what convicts to snitch on. Other convicts glared at him but Simpson kept his own counsel, enforcing his will and ramming his fists into anyone who took exception. In his group he was king, dispensing leniency in return for loyalty, mended garments and better grub.

'Come here.' He pulled his companion back towards him. 'Scream like that again and I'll take half your ration off you. Now tell me again about that missus of yours. Give us a picture. She's got big bubbies, you say, bouncy with fat teats.' Simpson laughed. 'Don't be shy, I saw you rubbing that nail you call a prick, moaning in your sleep like a banshee. Go on, tell us all about her.'

* * *

Anne's mother had allowed her to go shopping again, accompanied by her maid. It was fortunate that Anne had a good fashion sense: two of the dresses she'd ordered some six weeks before were to be made from Italian silk, and the tailor had had to wait for an import of the colours Anne had chosen. On Friday 21 June, the dresses were ready for a fitting at the tailor's, so Anne visited the Hughes Foundry on the way, for a brief arranged meeting with Sean. This time she left Chrissie sitting in the carriage a little way down the street from the foundry. She knew Chrissie was loyal and wouldn't say a word about the messages she took to Sean Hughes and the meetings, and it gave more of an air of respectability to Anne's visit if it looked as though her parents had approved of her using the carriage to come here.

Sean Hughes had news to report; he had spent three hours with the trial judge the previous week and discussed the details of the theft and the murder of Lawrence Toole. The judge, a member of the Cork Corporation, had given Sean permission to go over the court records, and had offered to see whether Sean might interview Inspector O'Flynn about the crimes. Meanwhile Sean was planning to follow up on some of the witnesses at the trial—in fact he hoped to speak to the landlady of Gerry Riordan's former lodgings that afternoon.

Sean said, 'She may be able to tell me more about the man who went upstairs with her and discovered the body. He vowed to call the police but he never came back. One of the other lodgers came home and she sent him for them instead. What was behind the man's strange behaviour? I'd like to know, in case it gives us a clue.'

'It's very good of you to take this trouble,' Anne said. 'I know you can't feel the injustice to Gerry the way I do. And you've lost so much from the theft: the gold that was taken belonged to you.'

He smiled kindly, 'Which is why I'm very eager to get it back, however I can, Miss Donovan. Don't despair: our joint investigation may pay off yet.'

She sighed. 'Everything's changed since that day. It's altered so many lives. Yours. Mine, my family's. At home …' She broke off, worried about betraying her parents' privacy.

But he said at once, 'What's wrong there?'

'Well, Father's profits are improving, and he's got more inquiries for work, but he's so depressed these days.' She managed not to say how much James Donovan seemed to be drinking. 'I really don't know why.'

Mr Hughes said, 'When I see him at the club, he's often alone. Not inclined to mix with the rest of us.'

Anne felt sad. 'Isn't he? But with you, I suppose, it's understandable. I'm sure he must feel awkward about the dreadful business of the doors.'

Without replying, Mr Hughes began tidying up the documents on his desk.

'Time for me to go.' Anne stood up, turned and put on her bonnet, using the glazed office door to check herself. Adjusting the bow, she glanced at his reflection in the glass and got a shock. Their eyes did not meet; he was looking lower, at her bust. Just for a moment, then his eyes dropped to the papers on his desk. He was like that? Odd she felt, but not angry. The look wasn't lecherous, just a glance. A tingle rippled through her.

He stood up, came over and opened the door for her. Sunlight spilled around them and they walked across the yard to the gate. He opened it and stepped out after her, into the street. Anne was glad that the carriage stood in view, even if she was only chaperoned by her maid.

Mr Hughes said, 'Farewell, Miss Donovan. When shall we meet again?'

Anne opened her parasol to the sunshine. She didn't want every encounter to be in secret; it would look improper. 'I'm sure we'll see each other at Mass before long. In the meantime, please leave a note addressed to Chrissie at … at the provedores in Roman Street. Especially if you learn anything new today.'

'I shall.'

As she walked down the street towards the carriage, she could feel his eyes on her all the way. The tingle returned and she thought about Sean Hughes's motives. He said he was following up on the theft in an attempt to recover the stolen gold—but might he be doing all this for her? How should she behave, if that were the case?

Sean stopped on the footpath at the end of Philput Lane. He wanted to find out more about the process server who'd been at the Riordan's lodgings on the day of the murder. No one knew the man's name, the landlady had seen him just the once and few details about him had come out at the trial.

Shading his eyes from the afternoon sun, he looked at his notebook again. The server had come to Gerry's lodgings around five o'clock. What notice was being served? Was it for debt? But Anne Donovan was convinced Riordan would never have got into debt— on the contrary, he was determined to save out of his wages.

Riordan might've got himself into some other kind of mischief, but Sean doubted it. There was something suspicious here. Coincidence or not, the process server had been at Riordan's lodgings at a crucial time, very close to when the murder happened. At the least, it was important to find this man, in case he'd seen something vital.

Sean knocked at number ten and waited.

'I'm coming. Hold your horses,' came the reply. The landlady peered at him through thick glasses. 'Good afternoon. What do you want?'

'Mrs Hammerton, my name is Sean Hughes. I've come to ask about the afternoon Lawrence Toole was murdered here.'

At that moment, a pedestrian walked past, and the landlady leaned closer. 'Don't blab it all over the street! Come in, come in.'

Once seated in her parlour, the woman shook her head. 'Horrible business, that. I'm finding it hard to rent the room. The locals fear it.' She paused. 'So, Mr Hughes, you have a question?'

'My company,' Sean said, 'made the gold doors that were stolen.'

'Beautiful, they must've been, God bless our Church. Grand. And what do you want to know?'

'The man who came to serve the notice on Mr Riordan that afternoon, do you remember him?'

'I'm afraid I do, Mr Hughes, too well. Why?'

'You haven't seen him since?'

'No and I wouldn't want to. Except—'

She stopped dead and Sean waited with some impatience for her to go on. Finally, he said, 'But you'd recognise him?'

She said at once, 'Oh, he was ordinary, really, not tall, not short. Rough sort of face. He went up the stairs with me to rouse Riordan and that's how I found the body.' She shuddered. 'I had to come back down, nearly took a turn. He gave me a hand so's I didn't fall over with the shock.' She paused again, frowning.

'What?' Sean said.

'Well, that was the end of him being any help! He rushed off saying he'd get the police but he never came back. In the end I had to send someone else for them.'

Sean said, 'Did you see the paper, the notice that the man was going to serve on Riordan? Or might it have been a made-up story, to get inside your house?'

The landlady gave him an anxious look and rubbed her knuckles. 'Well, I can tell you but I don't want it to go further—he gave me the shivers, he did. Trying to be nice as pie but he scared me and I wouldn't put it past him to be a liar and a thief. And he had a scar on his face just like that man—' She stopped dead again.

'What?' Sean said. "He had a scar? You've never mentioned this before!'

She went on the defence. 'My eyesight's none too good, so I didn't see it until just before he left this house, when he was leaning over me. But yes, a scar under his left eye.'

'You might have said this when you gave witness at the trial, Mrs Hammerton!'

She stiffened. 'I told what I was asked and no more. Anyway, it wasn't until the bank robbery that I got really afeared of him. Thank the Lord he's in prison. I saw his image in the newspaper, when that gang robbed the Agricultural and Commercial. The article says he was called Simpson. David … no, Dougal, that's right. A thief he was, an accessory or something. If it wasn't that man who knocked on my door on the day of the murder, he must have a double.'

Sean sat and stared at her. Was she making up this latest revelation? She would have told the drama of the murder and trial over and over to lodgers and neighbours. Was she exaggerating the fearfulness of it all, months after the fact? He tried to read her eyes but was defeated by the thick glasses. This was damned confusing, but he might get the chance to check whether police evidence made mention of a scar on the man's face. And then he'd have a name to follow up. Dougal Simpson.

At the station, the district inspector gave him some cautious assistance. 'What I've been asked to do for you is irregular, Mr Hughes,' O'Flynn said, opening a file on his desk. 'But I've received instruction to give you access to this. Now, take your time, because I can only make it available to you once, and you are not to make any notes.' He turned the file around to face Sean.

Sean did a preliminary leaf through, but before he got far, a document caught his eye. It was a smallish piece of paper, crumpled and stained. The handwriting was scrawled across it in splotched ink. With a chill, he realised where the stains had come from. 'That's Toole's note isn't it?'

O'Flynn gave a grim nod.

Sean read it and laid it aside. Then he leafed through the rest of the file, looking for anything else that might relate to Toole. At the bottom of the file he found two receipts for personal goods. He had been in the police station himself when they were signed: he and Anne had waited to one side while Riordan and Toole were at the counter after discharge, receiving their personal belongings. One document was the police list of Riordan's possessions, signed by Riordan. Sean examined the other. 'That's odd.' He struggled with the pinned paperwork. 'Can I take this clip off?'

'I'll do it,' O'Flynn said, and laid both lists before Sean. 'What are you looking for, sir?'

Sean now laid the note found on Toole's body next to the receipt for the personal goods, written and signed by Toole at the police station. He glanced from one to the other, then tapped them both with a fingertip. 'I'm no wizard on handwriting, Inspector, but even I can see that these two are in a different hand.'

'What?' O'Flynn took both notes and scanned them.

Sean said, 'I saw Toole write that list and sign it. So did two of your constables, in this station on the fifteenth of January. That means Toole did not write the note that was found in his hand the next day. It's fake. Someone forged it.'

O'Flynn frowned. 'They do seem different, I grant you. If what you say is true—and I mean *if*, Mr Hughes, we have an issue. But let's not get ahead of ourselves. There are procedures to follow. I'll get a handwriting expert to review these.'

'The fake note points to Riordan. It was written by someone else, to frame him. To me, that means Gerry Riordan did not kill Lawrence Toole.'

O'Flynn protested. 'The difference between these notes doesn't make Riordan innocent. James Donovan confirmed that Riordan had every opportunity to leave the cathedral that afternoon, kill Toole and return to work unseen. And he had the motive for murder, if they quarrelled over the theft.'

'I'm glad to hear that *if*, Inspector, because the motive's unproven.' Sean was startled as thunder crashed on the roof. 'There were no witnesses to say that Riordan was in his rooms with Toole that day. No proof that Riordan was there at the time.'

O'Flynn stood up. 'There is other evidence.'

'Circumstantial,' Sean said. 'And now you have new evidence, that the police failed to find the first time around—the difference between these two notes.'

O'Flynn looked irritated. 'Quite the lawyer, aren't you? May I take it I've done everything I can for you today, Mr Hughes?'

Sean shook his head. 'Jack Mulveen. The other driver. Ten to one that collision was no accident and he either planned it himself or was paid to cause it. What did he say when interviewed?'

'We couldn't find him. Oh, we went to Ellis's quarry, but they knew no one of that name.' He smiled. 'We have since been able to identify the horses and wagon involved in the collision, but the livery stables have no record of the man who hired them and cannot tell us where he might be. I agree, anyone might have planned that collision and paid Mulveen to cause it. Gerry Riordan, for instance.'

'That's supposition, Inspector.'

'It's grist, Mr Hughes.'

'Perhaps.' Sean stood up as rain hummed on the roof, increasing in sound. He gestured at the file on the desk. 'I shall be interested to hear what your experts decide when these two notes have been examined. I believe the difference in the handwriting is enough to throw more than reasonable doubt on Riordan's guilt. Good day, Inspector.'

* * *

The mid-July sunlight streaming across St Mary's nave highlighted the new tabernacle doors. At one time the idea of them had delighted Anne, because they were destined to be the finishing touch to Gerry's work. Now she felt they reflected all her woes.

She genuflected and followed her parents into the pew for Sunday Mass. Kneeling, she said her prayers, listening only in part to the priest's cadenced delivery. During the gaps in her thoughts the gold doors kept winking at her.

Sean Hughes sat four pews ahead of her, with his father beside him. Over the last three months he'd helped her cope with Gerry's banishment, making inquiries that she could never have pursued alone. His latest news was both encouraging and curious. In the police file, he had found two notes supposedly written by Lawrence Toole but one was fake—the one that pointed to Gerry as the murderer. And Sean had discovered more about the process server who had found Toole's body. He bore a strong resemblance to a convicted felon by the name of Dougal Simpson.

The priest started his sermon and she listened for a time, then thoughts of Gerry intervened. He wasn't guilty. She had always known that. But what they'd uncovered still didn't seem enough for the police and the courts. Conviction could only be overturned on appeal and the police were not going to allow that. Sean had warned her that the constabulary were more likely to be embarrassed than impressed by the difference between the notes that they'd identified as Toole's. He had told her about O'Flynn's defensive response when he compared them.

Her father's elbow brushed against hers and she glanced at him. He was mumbling his prayers, as her mother gazed at the altar. Colleen Donovan seemed in a trance and Anne could not make up her mind how to help her mother. Either she knew about her husband's deteriorating health, weakened by the increasing grog, and was stoic about it, or she was oblivious. But Anne knew that her father was in a poor state, and she worried about the cause.

Was James Donovan dying from an illness, and hiding the truth from his family? Anne shrank from the thought, almost certain that something else was haunting him. The only times he appeared animated was when Gerry Riordan's name was raised—and the result was intense anger. A fortnight ago, the police had come to Donovan House to speak with him. After they left, he ordered her into his study and flew into a fury. Anne had been terrified as he ranted at her, telling her to stop meddling in affairs that had nothing to do with her—the commissions at the cathedral, the disasters caused by Gerry Riordan. She wondered how he knew that she would never let these things go: had Sean Hughes let fall something about his inquiries, or was her belief in Gerry just shining through in ways she could not hide? But what struck her most about his anger was that it seemed to come from fear. This puzzled her. Of what could her father be afraid? She stood to say the Creed and strove to concentrate on the words, joining her voice to her father's.

Outside in the heat, Patrick Hughes stood in the shade of a tree in the cathedral's foreground, chatting to friends. When he was alone, he waved to the Donovans to join him.

'You go, Anne,' her mother said. 'We have to talk to Father about the fete. Give him our compliments.'

Anne went up to Sean's father and he smiled at her. 'Miss Donovan, how are you?'

She smiled back. 'Very well, thank you, Mr Hughes, and yourself?'

'I can't complain. It's a warm day but it's nice to see someone as fresh as yourself.'

Anne smiled. 'And Mrs Hughes?'

'She's not been well this past week, but on the mend, Miss Donovan, thank our good Lord.'

'I'm glad. Mother and Father are seeing the priest. They bid you good day.'

Hughes waved to his son, who started to bring the gig over to them. 'I'd walk,' he said, 'but my age precludes. Though my joints aren't so sore when I'm talking to an attractive young lady.'

He was always a charming man. 'Thank you.'

'So, what do you think about our new tabernacle doors?' he said. 'Sean says you're impressed.'

She had to be polite. 'I am and they are beautiful.'

'I'd like to say they're doubly beautiful to me, since we had to make two sets. But I can't help regretting the necessity.'

Sean brought the gig alongside them, just as her parents joined them after all.

'Good morning, Mr Hughes,' her mother said to Patrick.

'And to you.'

Patrick's relaxed demeanour changed as he turned to the master stonemason. 'You're not looking the best, Mr Donovan?'

'It's just a blasted cold, Hughes,' her father replied with a red face, 'nothing more.'

'I hope so. Business still prospers, no doubt?'

'It does.'

Anne noted the discomfort between the two men. She said, 'What do you intend to do for the day, Mr Hughes?'

Patrick's smile returned. 'My wife and I might go down to the waterfront this afternoon, if she's up to it.' Anne watched as Sean helped his father on board, then leaped down from the gig. 'There's some entertainment there I believe,' Patrick Hughes said. 'To my ear, music always sounds best with a sea breeze behind it. I'll see you at home, Sean. Mr and Mrs Donovan, good day.'

Sean accompanied the family to their carriage. Her father hesitated beside it and Anne was struck by his colouring. His face was pale now, like worn whitewash; the redness that embarrassed her, because it betrayed the amount of drink he took, had faded away. His eyes were unfocussed, directed beyond her. 'Father?'

He looked at her in confusion. 'What?'

'You're not well.'

Colleen Donovan took his arm, looking up into his face with concern.

James Donovan seemed to rally. 'I need some rest, that's all.' He helped his wife into the carriage, then stepped into it himself.

Sean addressed her parents. 'Would it be all right if I walked Anne home?'

Anne's mother smiled and nodded. 'It's a lovely day, why not?'

James Donovan said to Anne, 'Mr Sean Hughes will look after you, my dear. We shall see you at home.'

When the carriage drove away, Sean Hughes and Anne set off. Anne did not have her parasol but the hot sunshine went with a little breeze to cool it.

'My father has always been very good to me, you know. There's just one thing I can't talk to him about, and that's Gerry Riordan. Otherwise I could tell him how kind you've been, making all these inquires lately.'

'It's strange that he's been so convinced of Riordan's guilt, right from the beginning.'

'You know he had other reasons for wanting Gerry gone, don't you?'

He was tactful. 'I'm guessing that he was worried about … what you might feel for Riordan?'

Anne nodded and blushed. 'You're very understanding. You've been a good friend to me. Without your help we wouldn't have uncovered what we know.'

He seemed pleased. 'Glad to assist. You know I'm fond of you. But I know that you still—'

'And I'm glad of our friendship. Please, let's just have that for now.'

After a moment he said in a low voice, 'All right.'

'Thank you.' She went on, 'I can't help feeling that Dougal Simpson and the process server who came to Gerry's rooms were one and the same man. Have you found out anything more about Simpson?'

'Only that he's been put away for a long time, for the bank robbery. I have yet to discover which prison he's in. But I'm more interested in his past. I'll let you know what I find.'

'I saw his name amongst my father's papers.' She stopped, realised that this did not put her in a good light, much less her father. She hurried on, 'But it was no more than a mention and I haven't any idea why it was there. I don't know whether he's ever worked for my father. But I spoke to one of his labourers at the cathedral, Ronan O'Brien. I asked him if anyone around the site knew Dougal Simpson or had anything to do with him and he said in a horrible, knowing way that I'd be best asking my father about him. Of course I can't do that, so I'm no further ahead.'

'Really?' Sean Hughes looked startled by what she said, but he made no comment on it. They walked on in silence and she wondered what he was thinking of her and her father. Unease began to grow, which she hid by starting another conversation, about the summer entertainments in Cork. He joined in with a will, and they were even laughing just before he farewelled her at the garden gate of Donovan House. As he walked away, she told herself she was lucky to have him as an ally.

In the front garden she inspected her favourite plants, the rose bushes. Selecting the best, she pinched off a bloom and smelled it. It would replace the one in her room.

A cry from inside the house startled her and she ran through the open door. Raised voices and muffled sounds were coming from the kitchen. When she entered, her mother was standing against the wall. Tears stood in her eyes and her face was red on one side.

'Father,' Anne said, horrified, 'what's happened?'

James Donovan just stared at her, his expression vacant.

'Father, please!'

Anne pleaded with her mother. 'What has he done? What were you arguing about?'

James Donovan stepped towards his wife. He reached out a hand. 'I'm sorry, my dearest. I'm truly sorry.'

Staggering out of the kitchen, he went upstairs to the study. Anne heard the door close and then lock.

Chrissie came into the kitchen as though to speak to the cook, who was out because it was Sunday. Anne could tell that Chrissie, too, had heard the commotion and could not stay away. Without a word, Chrissie put the kettle on the stove.

Colleen Donovan sat down and she and Anne waited in silence until the tea was made and poured for both of them.

'Thank you,' her mother said to the Chrissie. 'You may go.'

'Yes, Mrs Donovan.'

When the maid left, Colleen sipped her tea and said quietly to Anne, 'Don't blame your father. He's not himself.'

Henry came into the kitchen with an anxious look. 'Are you all right, Mrs Donovan?'

Her mother managed to smile. 'Henry, that'll be all, thank you. Please leave us.' The servant hesitated. 'Please go,' she said.

Henry left and Anne thought, *The whole house is aware of this, and none of us knows what to do.* The only thing she could think of was to look after her mother first. She sat down beside her and took her hand. 'What happened?'

'It doesn't take much these days to anger him. Yesterday I rearranged some articles in the hall cupboard and that set him off. And now just after we'd got back—for no reason he came in here, yelling at me. I was scared. The first time in our marriage.' Her eyes glistened. 'I thought he was going to hit me.' She took a breath. 'And he did.'

'Mother!'

'There's something really troubling him, dear. He's been this way since the start of the year.' She paused and looked down. 'He's not the man I married.'

Anne glanced down the hall. 'He's locked his study door but I don't think he should be alone in there. I've got to go to him. Will you be all right?'

'You go.'

Anne found Henry outside his master's study. 'Can you hear anything?' she said. She called through the locked door. 'Father?'

Silence came from the other side and she sensed something was wrong. Anne tried the handle. It was locked. 'Father, if you don't answer me, I'm coming in.' There was again no sound from the room. She put her ear against the door and she heard rustling in the study desk, a pause and a click of metal against metal. She turned to Henry. 'Have you a spare key?'

'I have.'

'Please use it.'

The door opened and she entered the room. Her father was in his chair, holding a shotgun with the barrels pointed at his head. Anne stopped four paces away from the desk, appalled and afraid.

'Sir?' Henry whispered.

Anne slowly approached her father, whose eyes were fixed on her, not the gun. He had a firm grip on the stock, however, while the other hand brought his thumb close to the trigger. She tried not to show her panic. 'Father, let me talk to you, please.'

'There's nothing to say.'

Anne continued to move, stepping around the desk until she was a foot away from him. She kept her arms by her sides and made no attempt to touch him or the shotgun. 'I need to talk to you. This isn't you. Please put the gun aside.'

James Donovan looked up at her, but not into her eyes. 'It's the best way.'

A rivulet of perspiration trickled down Anne's neck. What on earth was she to do next? At that moment Henry moved in the open doorway and her father glanced over in his direction. Anne made her move. Grabbing the barrels with both hands, she took hold of the gun, retreated from the desk and passed the gun to Henry.

'Take it away,' she said, 'and close the door.'

'Will you be all right, miss?'

'I'll stay with him, Henry. Go.'

The manservant left and she turned to her father. He brought a hand to his face and a sob escaped him. She was startled at first, then overcome with compassion, never having seen him this distressed. Going to the cabinet, she poured a generous measure of whiskey and brought the glass over to him.

She knelt beside him and put her hand on his knee. 'What is it? What is it that's made you so depressed?'

James Donovan shivered. 'I can't explain.'

'There has to be a reason. We noticed when you began to change.' Anne went straight to the point. 'You haven't been yourself since Gerry Riordan's trial and conviction.'

'Nonsense.'

'Yes, Father.'

'No!'

'Two things happened then,' she said. 'One, you started to look ill, and two, we got a lot of money.' Her father's eyes were threatening but Anne continued. 'They are related.'

He looked out the study window and back at her. He gave an odd, faint smile. 'Why would you say that?'

She stood up and folded her arms. She wasn't afraid of him like this, just full of sorrow. 'Hear me out, please.'

He was silent for some time. 'All right.'

'You only get upset when his name is mentioned. No other time. Second, there are unsolved aspects of this crime. There—'

'Riordan's guilty, Anne.'

'You said you'd let me finish.'

'Go on,' he said with irritation.

'A process server went to Gerry's lodgings on the day Mr Toole was murdered. There's reason to believe the man's name was Dougal Simpson. A man you knew.'

'I don't know what you're talking about.'

'Dougal Simpson's in prison now, a convicted felon,' she said. Her father remained silent. 'What connection did he have with you?'

'None. Never met the man.'

'But you recognise his name?'

His colour changed, the red and white flaring on his cheeks. 'No, I say. What connection could I have with a criminal?'

She saw the reaction and it spelled something that almost made her walk out of the room with shame. The name 'Dougal Simpson' burned in her memory—written in her father's own hand and kept in a folder at the very desk where he sat. He was lying to her. But she couldn't walk off and leave him alone. He needed her. And so did Gerry, if he was ever to be proven innocent.

She said in a low voice, 'Did you employ Simpson, Father? For anything?'

'No.'

She sighed. 'Let's leave that aside for now. I have another question: why didn't you arrange an escort for the gold doors when you had them fetched from Hughes Foundry?'

He seemed to get a better hold on himself as he said, 'They were Hughes's responsibility, don't forget. He should've arranged the escort.' James Donovan stood up, as though his anxiety and weakness had left him. Anne felt a certain relief. She never wanted to see him so bowed down again, so hopeless.

'Will you be all right, Father? Mother and I, we're so worried. We can't stand by and watch you suffer. Please, you need help. Whom can you consult?'

'That's enough of this. I'm seeing a doctor about my … condition. What happened today won't occur again, I swear. I know you're concerned and that's why I've just given you the chance to get things off your chest. We don't need to have any more talk like this; I'll get my strength back and that's an end of it. As for talking about Gerry Riordan and anything to do with him, you'll leave off now! You hear me?'

'Two more things,' she said.

His face reddened again and his fists clenched. She was glad, in a way, to see him angry. Better that than suicidal. She watched him master the anger, his mouth firm. He didn't answer her but he nodded.

'Our new wealth,' she said. 'Where did it come from?'

'A debtor paid up and then some.'

'Who?'

'That's my business, Anne. He wanted it kept quiet.'

'If you told me, I'd keep it a secret too.'

He reached down and poured himself another whiskey. 'I can't tell you. I'm sorry.'

She felt like shouting at him, *It's all lies! Lies.* This was bizarre, a nightmare. The smell of his malt whiskey filled the room. It was as though she could feel the stickiness of it on her hands, her body. She turned from him and opened the study door. She looked back at him and said sadly, 'I love Gerry, Father, I do, and I'm after facts, not lies.'

Her father sounded weary. 'Riordan's convicted and he'll spend life in New South Wales. You want facts, there they are. Now, no more talk of this to me or to anyone. Do you understand?'

She said nothing.

'I said, do you? Because if I hear one word more, I'll lock you in this house until you see sense and understand what really happened.'

'I know what really happened, Father. I think I know who stole those doors.' She weakened and her eyes misted. 'I just don't know who killed poor Mr Toole, and I can't let myself think that you had anything to do with that.'

She left him and went downstairs, Her legs felt weak and she gripped the banister hard on the way down. Her mother was seated in the parlour. Anne went to her and took her hands. 'I think I know what's haunting him, Mother, but he can't solve it and nor can we.

And so, for all our sakes, I'll not stir things up too much by discussing it. But the drinking—he's promised to talk to the doctor. He's not so desperate he won't seek help.'

Her mother took her hands from Anne's and smoothed her hair. All she said was, 'You must have something to eat.'

'I can't.'

Chrissie came into the parlour. 'Mr Hughes is here, miss. Mr Sean Hughes.'

Grand, Anne thought, what next? 'I'll see him.' She turned to her mother. 'You can't want to see anyone after this! I'll tell him I can't invite him in. But I'm willing to talk to him in the garden, under your eye.'

'You do as you wish, dear.'

Anne went to the door to greet Sean Hughes, explained that her parents were not receiving this afternoon, and accompanied him to the garden. The sun was shining down, but in her world it seemed like a dark and dreary day.

Seated on a bench in the shade but in view of the parlour window and her mother, she turned to him. 'I never expected to see you again so soon! You've surely not gone right into town and back again?'

'No, I turned back when I remembered I had something for you.' He removed something white from his pocket. 'You dropped this in my office the other day and I didn't see it until after you'd left. I've been meaning to give it back to you.'

It was her handkerchief, freshly laundered. After her fraught day, the little sign of consideration touched her. This and all the rest made tears spill over. She stemmed them with the handkerchief and used it to wipe her eyes. 'I'm sorry.'

He was concerned at once. 'What's wrong?'

She was too upset to hold back. 'I've had— I've had a quarrel with Father. About the tabernacle doors.'

He was on the alert. 'Go on.'

'I couldn't make him confess but I'm terribly afraid he—he knew of the plan to steal them.'

'What?' he said. He sounded more troubled than surprised. 'Why?'

'He had business problems at the time. There was a big debt owing to him and he needed the money.' She pressed his arm. 'If he had anything to do with it, I'm sorry, I really am. All the loss and trouble this has caused you.'

He kept silent for a while, taking it in. 'Do you really think he was involved?'

'I can't say for sure. I hate saying such things about my own father. But I think you have a right to know the situation he was in, and what it might have driven him to. You're helping me to find out about the crimes—whatever I discover, however awful it seems, I must let you know.'

'And vice versa,' he said. 'Thank you.'

'But I would hate to bear witness against my father, you see that. Or accuse him of anything.'

'I realise that. I honour your frankness.' He paused, then said, 'You've given me a lot to think about. Can you tell me more about your conversation with him today?'

In the next five minutes, she recounted the whole incident in the study. Now and then he would press her hand and she would reciprocate, too overwhelmed by his sympathy to worry whether her mother saw the gesture. She shed more tears, knowing that he sensed her embarrassment, anger and shame, and pitied her for them.

'He's so unlike himself lately, I can't help being terrified that he was involved somehow in the theft. But there's no evidence.' She looked at him, afraid that he might share today's developments with his father. 'There's really nothing that anyone else needs to know about. Please keep it to yourself.'

'I agree there's no hard evidence to implicate your father,' he said. 'Who can prove Jack Mulveen was Dougal Simpson in disguise? Who saw Simpson swap the boxes at the collision? Who saw Toole being killed? No one yet. Nothing we've found deserves public exposure. But I'm sure you realise—if you want to prove Riordan innocent of theft and murder, then the guilt of another man, or other men, must be uncovered.'

'I could believe my father guilty of involvement in a theft. But involvement in murder—no!' Her lips trembled and her eyes filled again. 'Oh, it's so hard! To choose between Gerry and my father.' A moment passed then a desperate idea came to her. 'What if Father could be made to confess in front of witnesses that he played a part in the theft? If Gerry is shown not to have stolen the doors, and the box in his room was a plant, then he was framed, for both theft and murder. He can appeal for a retrial or a pardon.'

'I see,' Sean he slowly. 'Perhaps. But what happens to your father then? If you succeed in getting a confession out of him, and the police come to believe he masterminded the theft, he's certain to go to prison. The consequences for you would be horrendous. He'd be disgraced. Without the family income, you'd be impoverished. Can you and your mother live with that?'

She moaned, 'I don't know. I don't know. I just need Gerry to be free.'

'Of course you want him free, but …'

Moments passed and she turned to him. 'I'd rather be impoverished than have Gerry spend another hour in chains on the other side of the world because of my father's actions. I want Gerry freed and I want to be with him. I'm prepared to wait, and while I'm waiting I'll seek out the truth. Will you help me?'

'You really want me to set up a situation where your father admits his guilt in front of witnesses?'

Anne stared at him. 'That's exactly what I want you to do.'

* * *

A chortle startled Maurice Silverstein, merchant, and he looked out at a magpie perched near his window. A unique creature, it was big with black and white markings. As if the bird knew it was being observed, it flicked its beak in the man's direction and chortled again. A driver of a dray cracked a whip outside, the bird flew off, and Silverstein, formerly Jacob Greenberg, smiled to himself. The bird had character, which went with the unusual settlement in Sydney Cove, his place of residence since he'd landed three weeks before. The merchant cleaned his spectacles, then picked up the quill and continued with a select list of people he'd left behind in Cork, Ireland.

Eager to make his way in New South Wales, he had arrived with a small fortune in gold and a fresh name to go with it. Time and money spent amongst the Jewish community of London's East End had provided him with a new identity. His curly locks were gone and he was now bald as a melon. Jacob Greenberg had disappeared.

Silverstein had not wasted time: he'd leased a warehouse in Kent Street with an attached office, employed two people and paid his courtesies to the Rabbi, a master carpenter in a thriving trade, who'd introduced him to other Jewish merchants. Like him, they were keen to make their future in capital growth, and the commercial prospects in Sydney were encouraging.

The colony itself, meanwhile, was a rough and ready place. Nothing was worth a compliment, except perhaps the weather, which even in mid-July was sunny. The rest of it he disliked at first sight. The previous governor, Lachlan Macquarie, had apparently tried to do something for Sydney's built form in churches, hospitals, and improved city planning, but sadly there was still much to do.

More importantly, Maurice Silverstein had the gold that he'd acquired at such a handy discount from James Donovan, and he was making the most of it. The Bank of New South Wales had welcomed his bullion, and he was using it as security for loans to fund his fledgling business. He hoped that he would find a valuable associate in a Mr Solomon Wiseman, whom he was due to meet next week.

He had not forgotten other associates, left behind in Cork when he went by the name of Jacob Greenberg. It seemed doubtful whether any of them would correspond with people in New South Wales, or gossip about how Greenberg had acquired his gold—but he was a cautious man, hence the list of names he was compiling.

Silverstein had already made himself friendly with a high-ranking official in the Postal Authorities, who for a fee would afford him access to any correspondence that people on his Cork list might send to the colony. Having prior knowledge of any alarming developments in Ireland was critical to his success in Sydney.

His quill had dried out. He dipped it again in the ink well and added the name Dougal Simpson to the list. This took Silverstein back to the day when his gold had been made into ingots. After returning to the warehouse with the cash, he had handed it over to James Donovan, and Donovan had lost no time in paying Simpson his share. Simpson had been so busy stuffing his pockets that he had let the medallion fall for a second time. Silverstein would have liked to pick it up, but Simpson retrieved it. Silverstein remembered it as a handsome piece. The 'head' side of the medallion showed the insignia of the stonemasons, so Simpson must have stolen it from Riordan. Not from his person, because the big stonemason was too formidable. More likely from Riordan's room, where the murder of Lawrence Toole had taken place.

Silverstein put down the quill; his list was complete with every living person involved in any way with the gold doors. James Donovan, Gerry Riordan, Patrick Hughes, Sean Hughes, Dougal Simpson (alias Jack Mulveen).

'Rebecca,' he called out. 'Please bring me yesterday's orders.'

His attractive and diligent clerk arrived and gave him a folder.

Putting his list in a pigeonhole, he opened the folder and perused a contract. It was for the supply of tools and general merchandise for public works that he'd won on a government tender. If he could obtain more orders like this, his future was assured.

* * *

In mid-July, off the coast of Africa, Gerry looked into the distance, squinting against the unaccustomed brightness, though the air was cool. On land he could see a thick green carpet of trees, broken by sections of grassy plains, over which flocks of birds circled in a cloudless sky. A sight as different from Cork as sandstone was to granite.

This southernmost tip of Africa was vast, and the coast had been ever-present on their port side for weeks. He closed his eyes and breathed and tasted the salt-laden air, clean and pure compared to his confines below. It was Sunday and for two hours the convicts were allowed on the deck of the *Lady Jane*. The horizon might change but nothing changed on board: the guards were just as brutal and his fellow convicts still crouched in the hold, day after day, talking less and less to one another.

Over the next hour he held onto the edge of a paint-blistered hatch, with no thoughts passing through his head. He just listened to the slap of a gust-filled sail, the wind through the rigging, and the creak of the ship as it sailed on to a land he knew not, and to a life so different from the one he'd left.

* * *

In the Drawbridge bar, Kieran Tancread, law clerk, was sipping beer on one side of a partition. On the other side of the same partition, Sean Hughes and James Donovan were deep in conversation. Tancread belonged to a law firm of which neither Donovan nor the Hugheses were clients. He was used to taking notes and if Sean decided these were to be delivered to the police at any stage, Tancread would be seen to be without bias. He was as reliable a witness as Sean could obtain.

But Sean was nowhere near extracting anything out of James Donovan. He and the master stonemason had talked around the theft of the doors for more than half an hour, without Donovan throwing any light on the collision or the events that followed, beyond what everyone knew from the trial.

Sean was frustrated, because he had hoped to trip Donovan into admitting that he knew Dougal Simpson. Only the week before, Sean had gone on site at the cathedral and spoken to labourers to see whether Simpson had ever been there. One of them, Ronan O'Brien, told Sean that his boss had twice been in the company of a man who looked like Simpson. O'Brien was familiar with Simpson's face and had learned his name after seeing it in the newspapers during the bank robbery trial. Even better, O'Brien swore that he had seen Simpson entering Donovan's site office on the day of Toole's murder.

Sean also found out from a friend, one of Donovan's creditors, that the master stonemason had indeed been struggling for cash in January, just as Anne had said.

But Donovan continued to claim that he'd never heard of Simpson, let alone spoken to him—except for having a vague memory of images published during the bank robbery trial.

It was time for Sean to try mentioning Anne, to see if that would crack Donovan's reserve. 'I'm disappointed you can't tell me anything about Dougal Simpson, Mr Donovan. Your daughter has confided in me that she thinks Riordan and Toole were deceived by the man who caused the collision in John Street. Whoever this man was, he managed to get away with the doors and plant the empty frames in Riordan's rooms. He was obviously paid to do so, by someone who knew the delivery was taking place. Miss Donovan suggested to me that you might know more about this transaction than anyone else involved.'

James Donovan stiffened. 'Just what has Anne been saying to you?'

'As I recall, she said, "I believe my father could tell a lot more about those stolen doors than he has ever let on."'

James Donovan sat back and eyeballed Sean. 'That's a scandalous statement, Mr Hughes, and your repeating it to me here makes it libellous. Be very careful: are you sure she used those exact words?'

'More or less,' Sean said. Damn, this was getting difficult and he'd gained no advantage by bringing Anne into it.

'I'm shocked,' Donovan said, 'I really am, at your insinuations. Here am I, I've taken you and your company under my wing, introduced you to the right people. Tell me,' he said leaning forward, 'hasn't your foundry done better since the start of the year?'

'It has.' Sean was forced to agree, though the business was still laden with the debt to replace the tabernacle doors.

Donovan seemed to relax a little. 'Anne spends far too much time brooding about the trial. She's obsessed with that convict, Riordan. I'm afraid she has the whole business distorted in her head, Mr Hughes, and you shouldn't allow her to draw you in. The subject is closed, as far as I'm concerned.'

'You're not prepared to discuss it with her further?' Sean said.

'No, we have far better ways of passing our time in the Donovan family. God give me strength! Unless you want to offend me to the last degree, you'd better forget what my daughter has been chewing your ear about. Come on, you're what, thirty? A thinking man, an intelligent man. Surely you're not going to believe an eighteen-year-old's ranting about something she doesn't understand? All coloured by a schoolgirl's fantasy.'

'But the supposed evidence against Riordan that came up at the trial is inaccurate and misleading. Consider the murder of Toole and the note he had in his hand. Well, it turns out that he didn't write it. The handwriting is completely different from that of the list that Toole—'

'Nonsense,' Donovan said, but for the first time he looked rattled. 'The police are adamant that it was identical.'

'I saw both papers, Mr Donovan. The handwriting is different.'

Donovan's eyes widened in anger. 'And now you're a handwriting expert? You're getting back to dangerous ground, my young friend. Look, Riordan stole those doors, that's what this is about. Right?'

Sean felt he was at a dead end. 'I need another drink. Will you have one with me?'

'I will if you're going to talk sense and not sling insults at me like sparks from one of your furnaces.'

Sean went to the bar and waited to be served. He had pushed things too far with Donovan. Continuing the subject would only make an enemy of him, and it wouldn't help Anne. In fact, it would harm the foundry business. In a flash, Donovan could uncouple it from some of its new wealthy clients, clients whom the stonemason had brought them. Hughes Foundry had been permitted to join the Cork

Corporation under Donovan's aegis and as a result of the deal over the gold doors. If Donovan had engineered the theft of those doors and forced their replacement, perhaps Sean and his father should just put up with it and accept that they'd paid double to join the prestigious club. Bringing up Lawrence Toole's murder with Donovan might just as easily get them kicked out of it.

He paid for the beers and brought them back. On the way he gestured to the law clerk to leave. Kieran Tancread had nothing to record.

Donovan took his drink and held it. 'I'm curious to hear what you'll talk about next, young man.'

'I think the first thing I should do is apologise. '

Donovan stared at him for seconds then nodded. 'Now you're talking sense.'

'I always listen to what your daughter has to say, and I'm willing to oblige her, but in this case I should have formed my own view instead of voicing hers. You know I'm fond of her, don't you?'

'It's obvious to a blind beggar, my boy.' Donovan smiled for the first time.

'Should I be asking you about your intentions?'

'I'd like to see more of her. But you might have other thoughts.'

Donovan placed a hand on Sean's forearm and squeezed. 'We all make errors and this incident should teach you something about honesty. I want to help you. That's all I've ever wanted.' At a price, Sean thought. 'Though you won't see a great deal of my daughter in the near future. Her studies are complete here, and within the next couple of weeks I'll be sending her to Europe to complete her education. If she doesn't wish to leave Cork, she may well fight me on that, but she'll do as I say.

'Can I write to her there?'

Donovan smiled. 'I see no reason why you shouldn't correspond as long as they are letters my wife may read. It will cheer Anne to hear from friends at home. I'll be frank with you: I want her to forget Riordan. You can help with that. Next year, if you and Anne grow close, who knows what may transpire?' He clinked his glass against Sean's. 'Let's drink to that.'

Sean responded. If Donovan had criminal dealings in his recent past, there was nothing he himself could do to expose them. So there was no sense in jeopardising his chances of spending time with Anne before she was sent to Europe.

A few days later, Sean was in the garden of Donovan House, after dining with the family. To his delight, he and Anne were now permitted to address each other on first-name terms. Checking the parlour window first to see whether they were observed, Sean covered Anne's hand with his. They were not under scrutiny, but she eased hers away.

She said, 'So you got nothing out of Father at the hotel?'

'No. I'm afraid he isn't going to talk about the theft to me.' Sean said. 'He might not talk even to people who were involved. Do you have any other names for me besides Simpson?'

'Only Jacob Greenberg, but I've already mentioned him to you.'

'Greenberg, yes, the assayer who certified the gold we obtained from the Agricultural and Commercial.'

Anne brightened. 'Maybe we can arrange for Father and him to meet. When they talk, you might get that law clerk to listen in. Can you do it?'

He smiled. Her innocence was captivating and made him feel protective. He knew Greenberg had left Cork but he didn't want to disappoint her by saying so. Maybe he could string this out, for the sake of keeping that hope in her eyes 'I'll make inquiries.'

'The quicker the better. You know Father wants me to go to Europe soon, to finish my education?'

'Really?' he lied.

'He does, Sean, and I'm not going. I can only help Gerry if I stay in Cork.'

'But you can't defy your father. You're under age. You have to do as he says.'

She placed her hand on his. 'Then follow up on Greenberg and talk to Father. Please, Sean. I've got a month at the most. The French schooling starts in September.'

'I'll do what I can. Now, we'd better go inside.'

On the way into the house he had mixed thoughts. Withholding the truth about Greenberg's absence troubled him; not a good start for a trusting romance with the girl he loved. On the other hand, perhaps it was for Anne's own good if their Cork investigations failed and she had to leave for Europe. Maybe her time in France would dampen, even extinguish, the torch she held for the stonemason.

* * *

Only a few days later, in the Donovan House parlour, Anne and her father locked horns.

'You're going, Anne,' James Donovan said, 'and that's that. You'll have a nice trip to Paris with your mother, then she will accompany you to the school and stay in the neighbourhood for one month while you settle in.'

'No, to keep guard over me! This is so unfair. You said you weren't packing me off until September.'

'You need to learn discipline! You just got the marks to get into one of the most exclusive schools in France and I've paid them a hefty donation to secure your place. All your moon-laden affection for Riordan has made you wayward. You will go, and what's more, you'll not leave this house until the coach comes on Monday.'

Her mother came in and stood beside her. She smiled at Anne, took her hand and led her upstairs. Anne trembled all the way to her bedroom. Her mother shepherded her inside.

'Do what he says, child. I'm being selfish, you see. I've agreed to this voyage to force your father to see a doctor, and reduce his drinking, and he's consented. He's promised me that when we return he'll be fit and content and our lives will go back to what they were before all these troubles occurred. That's worth everything to me, my darling, so please support my decision.'

'Mother—'

'Let's prepare for our trip.

So it was that, on the Monday morning, Anne's three ports stood by the bedroom door, all packed. She didn't have much time. The carriage was due any moment.

She read again her first letter to Gerry overseas, frantic that it might not even reach its destination. Then a chill spread through her. The address! Where had she put it? She jumped up. Gerry's sister Maeve had given her the details months ago, the last time she'd seen her; the address in New South Wales to which one could send correspondence to transported convicts. Where had she put it?

Chrissie was sniffling and fussing in the dressing room. She wasn't happy that her mistress was going to a foreign country redolent with garlic and wine, not by a long chalk. She came out and caught Anne's dazed look. 'What's wrong, Miss?'

'Have you seen my writing compendium?'

'I've packed it.'

'Where? I need it!'

Her maid went to the ports. 'Which bag was it in, now?'

'Come on, Chrissie … hurry!'

Anne picked up the letter and read it again.

24 August 1828
Donovans, Glenmire Road, Cork

My Dearest Love,
I can call you that because you are—my love. I don't know what hell will be like after we die but I do know I've lived it in this house for these many months you've been gone.

There is much to tell you but I'm conscious of eyes other than yours perhaps seeing this letter. What I can, and have no great delight, in telling you is that I've found the guilty party who stole the <u>doors</u>. It was, and this shames me to the core, <u>your former master</u>. Yes, himself. He had debts which needed money to solve. He got that money from selling the doors. You may ask about the murder of your dear

121

and close friend Mr Toole to which the doors' theft was related. On that subject I can add little, suffice to say that the letter Toole wrote accusing you of perfidy was not by his hand. You may remember when you both had to sign for your personal goods at the gaol. The receipt Mr Toole wrote at that time has different handwriting from the implicating note found on your poor friend's body.

Now, the next sentences she knew were stretching things, but she was convinced of them.

So there. You're innocent, my love, as I always knew you were! The master stonemason confessed to me that he'd sold the gold from the doors to a Mr Greenberg for cash, whom you may or may not know. So, do not sink to woe. I will make it my goal to link this man to the crime and get you a new trial. If this letter finds you well, and hopefully you are coping as best as possible, I shall be gladdened with all my heart and hope to remain always in yours.

Anne

She didn't want to tell Gerry that she was going to France. He'd only lose hope of her help if she was away from Cork.

Chrissie stood up with the compendium. 'Here it is, miss. What's that noise? The carriage must be out the front.'

'Give it to me and lock the door.'

'Miss?'

'Just do it.' Anne opened the compendium and rifled through its compartments, her hand slippery in panic. 'And light the candle.'

Her mother called from downstairs. 'Dear! We have to go.'

Anne found the sealing wax, folded the letter and held the wick of the sealing wax over the candle. Pressing the corners of the paper down, she dripped wax over the join, let it thicken and pressed a gold seal onto it. Taking the seal away, she looked at the capital 'D' in the wax as it cooled. Then she flipped the letter over, steadied the hand that held the quill, and copied down the address in Sydney that Maeve had given her.

She blew out the candle. 'Now, listen,' she said to Chrissie, and gave her the letter. 'Hide it in your pocket until we reach the Quay. When I've gone, go and post it straight away. You understand?'

'Anne!' Her father's voice boomed from downstairs. 'Come right now.'

The maid's red eyes filled again as she thrust the compendium back into the open port. 'Miss, I just don't think I can stand seeing you go. I'm grateful to work for your aunt while you're at your studies, but how do I know you'll be looked after proper by a load of Frenchies?'

Anne sighed. 'Come on, we must be brave—it's only for nine months.' She handed the letter over. 'Just post this. It's very important.' Anne opened her purse and thrust some notes in her maid's hand.

Chrissie's eyes rounded in surprise. 'That's too much!'

Anne kissed her maid on the cheek. 'You keep the change. I'll not need our currency for a while. Now, unlock the door.'

Chapter Five

The Cork Police station was active night and day, and tonight, 15 September, was no different from any other. Stuck in his office, District Inspector O'Flynn was irritated and cold. The second condition was making the first even worse. A stickler for detail, he needed all loose ends tied up and the Riordan-Toole case had threads that were unravelling. For nearly three months, doubts had troubled his conscience and now they'd inflamed it.

The Police Force had to be protected from any charge of injustice. As an ordered person, he wanted certainty. 'Get me Sergeant Hooper,' he said to his clerk in the next office.

It was true that Riordan could have stolen the tabernacle doors. Yet in hindsight, the man who caused the collision, Jack Mulveen, might just as easily have done so, by swapping the boxes. Mulveen had disappeared. And where had the gold gone? Since then, none of the Cork banks had received bullion deposits to the value of the doors. It had clearly left the city—had it perhaps left the country? At least one person connected with it, Jacob Greenberg, had gone to London with the intention of sailing to New South Wales. Vanished witnesses, emigration and a forged letter—too many threads unravelling.

Sergeant Hooper came into the room and stood at attention. 'Sir.'

'Sit down, Sergeant.'

The sergeant took off his helmet and obeyed. 'Thank you, sir.'

O'Flynn smiled. 'Not long until your retirement. How long have you served?'

'Exactly thirty years, sir, come the end of this month. September ninety-eight I started as a night watchman. Our new force is a pup but I'm proud of it.' He brushed his jacket. 'We've waited six years just for these uniforms.'

'You're to be commended. We will no doubt toast your lifetime of service at some special function soon?'

'The lads have been kind to arrange something, thank you, sir.'

'Now, to business,' O'Flynn said. He looked down at his file. 'There are four aspects of the Toole murder that need re-examination.'

'But that's solved, sir. Man was tried and convicted.'

'Indeed, but I have some questions. The day of the collision, Jack Mulveen was named as the other driver. We can't find hide nor hair of him. Doesn't that strike you as strange?'

'He hit the boy's wagon, sir. Might have wanted to remain scarce in case there were costs for damages. Or he and Riordan were working together.'

'Maybe. The close-fitting hat and the eye patch. Almost like he wanted to be remembered for those and not his face. Besides that, on the night of the arrest at the Drawbridge, you interviewed that hound Dougal Simpson about the bank robbery. I have your notes here.' O'Flynn looked down. 'He was flashily dressed and he'd been on a spending spree for days.'

'I remember, sir.'

'You asked him how he'd been able to splash around ten pounds that night on the grog and the girls, and his pockets were full of money. He said he'd come into an inheritance. Correct?'

'I think that's right, sir.'

'I made some inquiries, Sergeant, after Simpson was transported. He had no known relatives, no legal representation, and there was nothing in writing in his digs or anywhere else about this alleged inheritance.'

The sergeant coughed. 'I see, sir, that is suspicious—but maybe his cash came from the bank robbery?'

'No,' O'Flynn said pointing at him. 'You've forgotten. We ascertained that the robbers divided the loot amongst themselves and Simpson got little or nothing. They'd coerced him into being on lookout that day. Something about a payback that he owed them.'

'You're right, sir.'

'Two other things, Sergeant. Riordan's landlady is convinced Dougal Simpson was the very man who came to her front door that late afternoon of the murder. I've checked with the court and there're only two firms of process servers in Cork. Neither employs a man fitting the landlady's description.'

'That's odd.'

'Very,' O'Flynn said. 'And the last piece of evidence that concerns me is the note that Toole is purported to have written before he died. Its handwriting is different from the receipt Toole completed for his belongings not fifteen feet from this very desk. I've had that corroborated by an expert.'

Perspiration now filmed on the sergeant's forehead, though the room was cool. 'You mean the note might have been planted, along with the stolen box. That means—'

'There's reasonable doubt that Riordan murdered Toole. Which means we must question whether he stole the doors, because the two crimes are linked. He may have been framed for both.'

'He could have been … yes. Sir.'

'I'm opening an inquiry into the two cases against him.'

Sergeant Hooper seemed to be thinking. 'May I speak plainly, sir?'

O Flynn spread his hands. 'As a man with two weeks to serve, you may.'

'Looking at all this again … well, it won't look good for us and the judiciary.'

'A man convicted wrongly is a failure of justice.'

'Of course, sir. I wasn't meaning—'

'Now, hear me out,' O'Flynn said. 'There are more facts to consider. The tabernacle doors were gold-plated and not a trace of that gold has been found. At the time, you interviewed Jacob Greenberg, who certified the gold supplied by the Agricultural and Commercial Bank.'

'Correct, sir.'

'You'll be interested to know that a week after Riordan's conviction, Greenberg sailed for London.'

'And the connection there, sir?'

'The Port Superintendent here is a friend of mine, as you know. He was acquainted with Greenberg and spoke to him on the day he sailed from Cork. Most of his baggage went in the hold—he was emigrating to New South Wales from London, so he had all his possessions with him. But there was one bag he wouldn't let out of his sight. It was a briefcase, a heavy one. Every step he took before they went on board, and up the gangplank, he lugged it with him. My friend twitted him that he had all his fortune in it, but Greenberg wasn't amused.'

'So you suspect it did hold riches? Greenberg acted as a fence for the stolen gold?'

'He might well have, Sergeant.' O'Flynn stood up and the sergeant did the same. 'In the next two weeks, devote yourself to investigating the loose ends that I've noted. At the end of that time, let's say on the thirtieth of September, you'll give me your report. As your parting submission to the service it may not amount to much, I know. But on the other hand, if your report gives me reason to act, you will be remembered as the policeman who cleared an innocent man.'

The sergeant put on his helmet and saluted. 'I'll get right onto it, sir.'

O'Flynn returned the salute and sat back down. Sergeant Hooper would work hard in his final two weeks of service. He might fail to find anything to support Riordan's innocence but this would not reflect on the police force, since he was retiring anyway. But if his report was significant, he would have the satisfaction of a job well done, and O'Flynn could lodge an application for a retrial.

And then, if the gods were kind, an official letter might be on its way to New South Wales before Christmas.

* * *

The convict ship had at last sailed into Port Jackson and Gerry Riordan was on solid ground. The trees around the vast harbour seemed to vibrate in the heat. Squinting against the sharp light of the sun, he found it hard to stand firm on his feet after months of constant movement at sea. He closed his eyes and a salt-laden breeze wafted in his face.

Like a baker's oven, the heat burned the men who had disembarked. It was a heat unlike even the hottest Cork day and Gerry thought of Lawrence Toole again, and the plans his friend had had for coming here and making something different of his life. Poor Toole. That chance had been robbed from him. Thinking of how Toole had died, Gerry trembled again between anger and remorse.

At the mouth of a stream that flowed into a well-protected cove, the last convicts disembarked from the transport's boats and onto Government Wharf, to stand in three ranks as the overseers checked their irons. Over one hundred souls stood with Gerry looking at their new home, a settlement fanning out from where they stood. A fort stood on one promontory, a battery and another fort on the other. Other huts and buildings hugged the cove as if fearful that the massive continent around them would swallow them up. To the north of the harbour was forest. Tufts of spindly, dirty-green trees covered the banks that rose from the water's edge.

'Move off,' the overseer said.

Gerry's three ranks trooped towards the settlement. After departing the dock area, the second section of fifty convicts from the transport peeled away and headed towards the western part of the inlet. Gerry's continued uphill, where the smell of man's communal living triumphed over the breeze. But he didn't flinch from it; he was inured after months of stench in the transport.

It was some relief to be moving in a straight line and upright, on a level patch of high ground. On their left were government buildings, big and important. Further on, soldiers and men could be seen in the streets, and the occasional woman with male escort or perched in wagon or carriage.

It must be summer or spring, Gerry had no idea: he had not kept track since he'd left Cork, and he'd ignored what others might say.

Anger had made him wild and it had taken weeks for him to temper his rage. He had only come to himself after one particular fight. When he'd won it, he had recognised that the bloodied, whimpering mess at his feet was still a human being. This had jolted and shamed him. But his sense of injustice and sadness remained and coloured his existence. Anything beyond his ken did not matter, and that included what month or day it was. He was condemned for life, and time was not his friend.

The convicts weren't allowed to talk but when the overseers were out of sight they whispered to each other. Now that they'd landed in this new place, Gerry felt suddenly curious. 'What month is it?' he asked the man in front of him.

The man grunted. 'Who cares?'

'It's hot enough,' Gerry said.

'It's late October, I think,' came a voice behind him.

He turned twenty-one on 25 October. How near his birthday was it? Who'd care?

'Convicts, halt!' the chief overseer ordered and they came to a rambling stop. 'Look lively. Left turn. At ease.' A high brick building with pilasters peered down its nose at them, its imposing pediment pointing to the heavens. 'This will be your barracks,' the overseer said, 'where you'll stay at the governor's pleasure. You'll be marched in and allocated your bed, kit, eating utensils and a uniform. You'll make up your hammock and an officer will hand out your duties, starting tomorrow.'

Gerry followed the other convicts into the cool building. Each of the three floors was divided into four dormitories reached by a corridor that ran the length of the building. Gerry might be held here in October 1828 in far-flung Sydney, but the tradesman-like bricks and mortar around him reminded him of the Cork prison six months ago. Now he was in this heat-baked, fly-blown colony for the rest of his life.

Tom Bundy, an Englishman already housed in the barracks, pointed Gerry to his hammock, slung between timbers connected to the floor framing overhead. 'This barracks,' Bundy said, 'is in Macquarie Street, which was named after the governor who went back to England in twenty-one. They called him, The Builder.'

'The B-builder?'

Bundy pointed through the end window. 'See that church? Worked on it I did. The architect who done that is one of us.'

It was a fine building, Gerry thought. 'Can't be—he was a convict?'

'Is. Mr Francis Howard Greenway. It's his design and all, like these barracks we're in.' He looked to see how Gerry was faring. 'Careful with that end—here, I'll do it.' He made a neat tuck of the blankets and stood back satisfied. 'They'll beat you if those folds aren't right. Now, about this place. There's a mess room downstairs and a common room where they make these uniforms. We're not supposed to be in here in the day. Let's go.'

Gerry was issued his magpie suit: a coarse jacket, yellow trousers and a leather cap. He objected that he'd be bound to mislay the cap when he worked; Bundy made him sew a hook on his belt so that he could clip it on.

Going downstairs, they stopped at a landing to let other convicts pass.

'What kind of work will I be doing?'

'Public works,' Bundy said, 'We got some little storehouses to build down near the water at Market Street. Me and you'll be working together, that's why we're hammock mates.'

Gerry nodded. Something to do at last. It might get him to think about building again, something he loved, to work in stone, feel its honesty and simplicity.

Unseen by Gerry, a stranger to him, Dougal Simpson, was looking at the same scene. He glanced at a group of convicts making their way uphill from Sydney Cove. Poor sods, they'd have the slog work. His own mates, heading to the other side of the Cove, would be better served. Adams, his overseer, had told him so.

God the heat! His skin prickled and itched. Flies buzzed at his eyes, and he brushed them away. One ignored his swatting hands and hung around on his lip. He smashed it.

'Simpson,' his overseer called to him. 'Walk with me.'

He peeled away from the group, catching one or two glares from other convicts, which he smirked away. He got better treatment for staying on Adams's good side, easy as that.

'You won't be in Sydney long,' Adams said, chewing on his pipe. 'I've fixed a job for you at Parramatta.

'What?'

The guard smiled. 'You'll get used to the daft names. Parramatta, it's a town inland. There's a quarry near it and the settler who runs it needs a good man. You'll work there for seven years. You'll do well, I'm sure. Now, get back in line.'

Simpson rejoined his mates as they passed a barracks and the overseer walked ahead. Lenient treatment be damned: he hated quarry work. He could have slit Adams's throat and thought nothing of it. Like peeling an apple. Overseers were bastards, all of them! But kowtow, that's what he had to do. For now.

'Likes you he does,' panted a convict near him. 'Wants you for himself, special.'

'Shut your mouth,' Simpson growled. 'Shut it or tomorrow you'll wake with it filled with blood.'

The man kept silent and Simpson grinned. Had them under him he did and that suited him.

* * *

During the next weeks, Gerry worked hard with his new companions in a six-man party. Ten hours a day for five days of the week and six hours on Saturday. On Sunday they rested, washed, repaired their kit and went to a church service. He simmered in anger at his life, and the religion just fanned it with its hypocrisy. But the food was better than on the transport and the water ration kept him alive, just.

Gerry's responsibility was to lay stonework for the foundation walls of the storehouses near the shore. He selected the materials, mixed the mortar, laid the stone, finished it and started another section. No enthusiasm came back to him for his trade. If he'd been a carpenter or a metal forger, he would've carried out the work with the same lack of interest. And he didn't think this was odd. He was just existing.

On the morning of the first day of his fourth week, their overseer, Vincent Martin, a soldier, assembled them as the late November sun was burning their skin.

'All right, you lot,' he said. 'You've been slack and my orders are to make you do better. Riordan, I've heard you're some great stonemason. Well, I've knocked around in the trade and I say you're not, with what you've built so far, not by a long chalk.'

Gerry squinted at the overseer who stood in the line of the sun, facing him. 'Y-you know stone, do you?'

'Steady, Gerry,' Tom Bundy whispered beside him, 'he wants to belt you.'

The overseer grinned. 'I know good stone like I know my dear mother's face, you tall piece of shite. Now, the day's a-wasting so let's get cracking. I'll be back in three hours to inspect the work and it had better be good. Bloody good!'

Bundy pulled Gerry aside as the overseer walked away and they got their kit. Sweat filmed on Gerry's face and his teeth were clenched. 'B-bastard,' he said. 'Wouldn't know stone from lye soap.'

'Leave off, Riordan.'

They started work on a retaining wall close to the water's edge and Gerry's hands shook. He'd have that man. By mid-morning they had completed three courses and were sitting in the shade of a large tree.

'Get off your backsides!' Martin said, coming up behind them. 'Who told you to rest?'

Gerry had had enough. 'We're one course ahead and the lads are doing well.' He pointed to the wall. Pain flashed across his back and he doubled over. Before he could stand up, another lash stung him and he lost it and grabbed the whip.

'Riordan!' Tom Bundy yelled, but it was too late. Gerry jerked the overseer to him and was into the man, hitting him. The others soon started cheering him on. Martin screamed as Gerry punched him in the kidneys. Two men in uniform rushed up, grabbed Gerry and pulled him away.

Martin stood up, wiping blood from his mouth. 'Tie him to that tree in the sun,' he panted, 'and let him sweat. We'll see if twenty lashes makes him obey.'

They chained him up with his arms and legs positioned to improve the effectiveness of the whipping. Gerry steadied himself for what was to come. He'd seen men scream under the whip but he swore to himself not to let out a sound, not give the bastards any satisfaction. After the fifteenth lash he thought he would weaken but gritted his teeth to endure the rest. When they'd cut him down, Martin screamed at him, saying that the next time he would hang. Gerry believed him.

At midday, when they had to go back to the barracks to eat, Bundy walked by Gerry and, out of sight of the overseer, gave him a cup of water. 'We'll be back later, Gerry.'

That night in the humid barracks, Gerry lay on his stomach, the marks of the 'cat' still stinging. When the evening breeze died, the mosquitoes hummed, hovered, settled and lanced him. The doctor had given him something but it didn't help much. His pain started nightmares and his sweat, salty and hot, stung his wounds.

'Are you awake?' Bundy said.

Gerry controlled his breathing to respond. 'Aye.'

'The bastard deserved what he got but you didn't. I got to tell you, Riordan, take it easy. If you don't, you'll end up on the iron gangs on the road. That's nothing like this. A sixteen-stone man I knew come back only after three months and the poor bastard was just a stick, a stick I tell you. A piece of kindling.'

Gerry said nothing. Dawn couldn't come fast enough but he filled every moment with ways of not going back to work. Each movement spiked a different pain. If he shifted his shoulder he would feel it in the small of his back. If he lifted his neck a certain way, or his arm, there would be another jab of agony. All he could do was lie still and let the mosquitoes pick at his ears and sting him wherever they liked, which was nothing compared to the throbbing of his wounds. He seemed to sleep for about five minutes, then the bell rang for him to start a new day in hell.

The water lapped beside their work site in the mid-morning heat. In an Irish harbour on the other side of the world, Gerry might've felt some satisfaction in the work of his hands. Here he felt nothing but sunburnt. His work mates were the same, though some were more fortunate than him because their arms, necks and faces tanned to a brownness like the natives they'd seen in town. Gerry's skin just burned to egg-sized blisters, his hair and freckles, like his attitude, refusing to adapt.

Rumours abounded that they would all get a special Christmas dinner. That was the only milestone Gerry had heard about. He still refused to keep track of the date. If he added up his days spent in this carved-out hunk of dry continent, he'd be digging himself into a deeper dell of disgust.

He handed his canteen to Bundy, who took it and slurped. 'Don't drink it all,' Gerry said, trying to get a rise out of his mate, but Bundy passed the canteen on to another man, picked up his mattock and continued digging.

Selecting a cut block, Gerry placed it on a bed of mortar. He positioned the stone, aligning it with the blocks on the course below, close to the string line. He tooled the joints. There was silence from the men around him. He understood the reticence that convicts showed towards each other as they tried to come to terms with their lot. Only last week, Bundy had encouraged Gerry to work with the system, accept his convict life and get on with it. Gerry had listened but said nothing. The first chance he got, he'd go bush.

There'd been no repeat of the whipping but Gerry's reputation, like his back, was now marked down—a troublemaker. Another fight and he'd be transferred to rough labour. His irons did not help his state of mind. He was hobbled like one of his Da's animals. Sunburned, chained, with no escape, he was up to his neck in misery.

Their new overseer exited his site hut and came up to them. He was a man called Donnelly, of average height with a stocky upper body. 'Righto, lads. Got a word from the boss. We have to finish this section by Christmas.'

He said 'Christmas' as though it mattered. Was the man devout? Gerry smiled for the first time since he'd been in Sydney—but to himself. Donnelly was an Ulsterman and proud of it, though he appeared tolerant of Catholics.

'Does that mean we get more Christmas pudding?' Bundy asked with irony.

'It means you'll get none if you don't finish that wall. Now, I want a word with you all. Put your tools down and come into the shade. Riordan, leave that last block and get out of the sun.'

Gerry regarded Donnelly with suspicion but did as he was told. Why would an overseer care if his convict gang got his orders standing in the blazing sun or in the shade? Like a pack of ageing spinsters, he and the other five trooped in under the trees. What did Donnelly want from them? One day last week he had let them finish early, and the day after that he had given them better rations. Why? Gerry knew they'd pay—somehow.

Donnelly took off his hat. 'Right, you men have been working the same way since I took over. Your progress is good but it could be better. You've got one week to finish the job and I want ideas. Smart ideas of how to work better together and get more done.'

So Christmas was that near? Ridiculous images filled Gerry's head. The bustle before Christmas in the city of Cork. His parents' home on the farm, with its warm fires, steaming food and laughter.

Donnelly's voice cut through. 'Riordan. What do you think you could do better?'

Gerry frowned. 'Don't know.'

Donnelly grinned. 'You do! Come on man, I've seen your work. You're good. I want some of that skill here.'

'You're the boss,' Gerry retorted. 'We do whatever you want.'

Donnelly eyed another convict. 'Bundy. What do you think?'

'Sorry, sir. Not used to thinking or being asked.'

'Well I'm asking, and,' he looked at them individually, 'I'll make good on good work.'

'Why?' Gerry said.

It was said with anger and the others dropped their heads in silence. Bundy glared at Gerry in warning.

Donnelly pursed his lips. 'Good question, and one I'd ask if I were in your boots.' Donnelly again inspected each face before him, which riled Gerry further. The man was looking down his nose at them. 'I'm aware of the crimes you men committed to get yourselves in this fix, but—'

'I c-committed no cr-crime,' Gerry blurted out. He clenched his fists. 'I was dumped here.'

'As your overseer, that means naught to me,' Donnelly said. 'What's important is the work you do now. That's what adds up in my book. Now, who has any improvements to offer?'

Gerry leaned against a tree as one of the other men spoke up with an idea. Then the chattering started. They talked amongst themselves rather than Donnelly, and their grim faces became animated. Gerry couldn't believe it.

Fury tore the words from him. 'What's wrong with you? This is forced labour you're talking about! You're stuck here doing hard work with no pay and you're going to let him make it harder? You're living out a sentence most of us don't deserve and you're acting as happy as eejits in a pub with free beer!'

The others shut up and stepped back, while Donnelly came up to him. 'What's your problem, Riordan? Gerry isn't it, boy?'

Gerry's hand formed a fist and he swung.

Donnelly caught the fist in his hand as though he were snatching a ball. 'Now, why do that?' He forced Gerry's hand down and held onto it, surprising Gerry with his strength. 'You come with me.' Donnelly pulled him away. 'Don't move, boys, I won't be long.'

Donnelly hauled Gerry behind the site hut as if he were a lightweight. 'Now listen and listen good. I don't give a beggar's turd for what you're here for. You're in my gang and you'll do as you're told!' He squeezed harder on a nerve in Gerry's wrist, the pain making him wince. 'I tell you to do something, you jump to it, and I'll have no cheek or disobedience. Now, I'm going to let you go, but make a daft move like that again and I'll knock you cold.'

He let go and Gerry rubbed his knuckles. Donnelly was a cool one, no mistake, and Gerry couldn't work him out. Yet.

The overseer tilted his head to one side. 'You've surprised me today, Riordan, by opening your mouth for once. I've seen the way you work and how you lead the men. But you hardly say a word.'

'Nothing to s-say.'

The overseer gestured at their surroundings, baking in the heat. 'This is all you've got now. When, for Our Lord's dear sake, are you going to accept it?'

'Never.'

'How old are you?'

'Twenty-one,' Gerry said.

'And this is hell for you? I've seen worse.'

'I'm not guilty,' Gerry said.

Donnelly sighed. 'We're all guilty of something, lad. Look, you've got skills. Show them, work better and you'll see rewards in time.'

'I'm doing what I need to do.'

Donnelly looked at him for a long time. 'I've been here a while. I've seen men like you, good men but poxed with hatred, and the hatred kills them.'

'I'm not guilty.'

'So you say.' Donnelly paused. 'All right, get back to the others. You'll come to think my way soon.'

Gerry walked away. 'I'll never think any different. Never.'

* * *

Anne Donovan was singing the last of the Christmas carols with her fellow pupils in the common room of the Lycée St-Germain. Her mind, though, was in New South Wales. The last four months had flown by because she'd forced herself to study, trying to push aside the cruel injustice done to Gerry. Ever since Colleen Donovan had got back to Cork, she'd been sending reassuring letters to Anne about her father. And Chrissie, her maid, confirmed that her parents were well. Last week, Anne had received her Christmas present, not Gerry's arms around her, but the next best thing. Chrissie's latest letter had said that Cork police were pursuing an inquiry into Gerry's trial and conviction. It was wonderful news! News that Sean Hughes did not repeat in his three polite, discreet letters.

The fire flashed sparks up the chimney and she was handed a glass of mulled wine.

'It's Christmas,' her friend said. 'We're allowed a little sinfulness. Cheers to you and yours.'

Anne wiped a tear away. 'Thank you, Jeanne, and yours.'

'I've got you a present,' Jeanne said.

'I got you one, too.'

They swapped their gifts and Jeanne smiled. They had both chosen a box of candied chestnuts. 'Give us a kiss,' she said.

* * *

Maurice Silverstein was in his Sydney office, examining a sealed letter that lay on his desk. Over the last six months, business had been good. His expanded warehouse now held sufficient stock to meet part of the growing demand for public works in the settlement, and he'd just put on his fifth worker. His visits to synagogue had brought him introductions to influential Jewish companies who, knowing Mr Solomon Wiseman well, were keen to place orders with a profitable business.

The letter was dirty and creased from a sea voyage of close to five months and there was a small tear in the corner. He could safely tamper with it: no one would notice the damage. Holding the seal close to the candle flame was enough to soften the wax and he was able to lift it off without tearing the paper. He could reseal the thing and have it delivered if he felt like it. But he suspected he wouldn't.

He opened the letter and smoothed it out on the desk, the address uppermost. It was post-marked in Cork on 15 January 1829 and addressed to Convict Gerry Riordan, care of the NSW Judiciary. Silverstein's post-office friend had passed it to him two days after its arrival. Silverstein prepared himself and turned the paper over.

He scratched his bald head, put on his glasses and read it all. What he saw made his hands tremble and he dropped the letter on his desk. Clasping his chest, he rushed to the window and flung it open and breathed, once, twice. It named Jacob Greenberg as a receiver of stolen goods!

Returning to the incriminating document, he read it again, and sweat broke out on his forehead.

So there. You're innocent, my love as I always knew you were! The master stonemason confessed to me that he'd sold the gold from the doors to a Mr Greenberg for cash, whom you may or may not know.

The cursed James Donovan had a daughter who was besotted with Riordan. Had Donovan really confessed to her about the gold? It seemed a dangerous thing to do—was the young woman lying to her lost lover? But the horror of it was that she had named Jacob Greenberg in her letter. Did that mean she would really go to the police with the information and her father's confession? His brow felt damp and cold. He ached with fear.

Five months ago the letter had been sent—and in it she had said she was contacting the police. Anne Donovan had had all this time to spread Greenberg's name around and cast suspicion on his hasty departure from Cork after the doors were stolen. The police had also had five months to follow Greenberg's trail to London and perhaps uncover what he'd done. Created his false identity. Taken his gold to New South Wales and set himself up as a merchant in Sydney. Did they have the power to track down Maurice Silverstein?

Bailed Up

***

Dougal Simpson was sitting on his stool in his Parramatta quarry office and out of the glare of the mid-February sun. What he saw out the window—a wagon with four women in it—frustrated him because he wanted to do something about the best-looking amongst them. When she moved, her good bits pressed against the fabric of her uniform; even under its tucks and pleats her curvy form was unmistakable.

It was not enough for him now to just look at her when the women turned up. Each Tuesday they came from the Female Factory in Parramatta to collect the quarry's laundry and for a small charge return it clean and mended the following week. Three weeks ago, the dark-haired one had started glancing his way. This morning she smiled at him and he sensed that the extra wiggle of her hips was just for him.

He had a plan. Feeling in his pocket for the coins he wanted, his hand closed around the silver medallion. It had survived from Cork, secreted on his person, and every now and then he rubbed it for luck. He felt it had got him this job at the quarry, which he no longer minded. A lucky charm for him. Well, it hadn't brought Toole much luck! Simpson congratulated himself for taking it from the body.

His work was easy: boring, but better than breaking his back building roads. Since October, he'd impressed his quarry overseer with his hard work on supervising the cutting of the rock and general ordering and organising. Then, since Christmas, he'd got the plum job of recording the stone ordered by the buyers. That's where his real talents started to shine.

The sawn rock was sold by the ton. Simpson supervised the recording of the stone on the quarry weighbridge and filled out the docket the waiting buyer would give with his payment at the hut on exiting. Simpson had worked out a way of making extra money out of this arrangement. For cooperative buyers, carefully picked by him, he'd record on the docket ten per cent less than the actual recorded weight of the stone. For this service, such buyers would gladly slip him a few shillings, depending on the overall load. The bigger the load the greater Simpson's 'commission'.

A risk he knew was worth taking. He had a skill in picking the right buyers who would play the game. Some didn't and he had a standard answer for those: he told them that the scale was faulty at times and that he would reduce the weight recorded so the customer wasn't caught short. But most customers picked up on his idea and saved a coin or two on their purchase of the stone.

The quarry was prosperous and the owner could afford it. During January, Simpson had made a tidy sum. Not much, just a little each day. As a convict he received no pay, but his little earner at the quarry made up for that. Meanwhile Peter Adams, his previous overseer, had his former savings stashed away.

A young stone cutter was sitting in the shade having his rest. 'Bob!' Simpson called to him.

'Yeah.'

'Get yourself to town and pick up that new drill. Take the big wagon and take your time.' Simpson would have the quarry to himself for a while, since his boss was in Sydney buying new jigs.

'Right.'

The quarry stretched over twenty-five acres and provided sandstone, shale and some hard rock for the expanding second city of Sydney, Parramatta, and its surrounds. There was talk of extending the roads to the north and Simpson knew his quarry would benefit. If the quarry made money, so would he.

Laughter made him turn to the four girls returning with their laundry on the loaded wagon. It stopped at the quarry hut and the slim, dark-haired girl climbed down, her ankles showing for a fraction. She skipped to the hut and popped inside, peering at him in the darkness.

'You gotta write on this,' she said. 'We've got fourteen bags today.' She smiled, handing him a piece of paper.

Simpson smiled as well. She had nice teeth, a rarity. 'I do, do I?'

'I can't go if you don't make your mark.' She stretched her arms behind her back, her uniform tightening over her full breasts.

Dougal looked at them. 'What's your name?'

'Lillian. Or Lilly, I don't mind.' Her scent was musky from the sun.

'I've got something for you.'

She giggled. 'I bet you have.'

He bent down and picked up a canvas bag from under the desk. 'This is my master's laundry. It needs tending.'

She clasped the bag and Simpson held onto her hand. 'You need to make sure what you'll need to mend. Have a look now. It might take some time.' She frowned. 'How about you leave the girls go, and I'll take you back later.'

She removed his hand. 'I'll look now.'

Simpson moved close to the open window, watched the other girls offload the fourteen bags, and marked the receipt. 'She won't be long,' he called to them. He turned back in the shadows, gave her the receipt and cupped her breast.

She looked down at his hand then back at him, her eyes bold. 'It'll cost you.'

He kept caressing. 'How much?'

'Five shillings.'

'I'll give you two,' he said and grinned.

She turned from him, leaned forward and spoke out the window. 'You take all the clean stuff to the men's quarters. I've got an extra order here.'

'You'll be in trouble if you make us late,' said one girl, but in a friendly way.

Simpson stood behind Lilly, out of sight from the wagon, and pressed her against him.

'That's me. Always in it.' She laughed.

The girls picked up the bags and moved away and Simpson closed the door and lifted the coarse fabric of Lilly's skirt, exposing twin hemispheres of white flesh.

She turned to him. 'Where's the money?'

He brought up his hand between her legs, stopping at their apex, feeling smooth ridges and crisp curls. His fingers stroked her as he undid his flies with the other hand. 'Later,' he panted.

'Show me the coin!'

Shoving his hand in his pocket he dragged out loose change, flung it on the desk then pushed her down. 'Undo your buttons.'

Lilly parted her legs as his hands rummaged at her bosom. 'Whoa!' she cried, her elbows back on the desk. 'That's as hard as my laundry stick.' She giggled. 'But twice as thick.'

* * *

The early morning sun had already saturated Gerry by the time the work gang had marched from the barracks down King Street to Cockle Bay.

Tom Bundy hissed at him, 'Now, don't give Donnelly any lip today!'

'Shut up!' Gerry peeled away from Bundy, went into the site hut and picked up a pinch bar and mattock. Not by a long chalk would he toe the line, and why should he? Donnelly, their overseer, was acting like a fair man, but nothing was going to change. Sure, their team had finished the storehouse work two days before Christmas and they'd got more grub and pudding on the big day. But so what? The relentless routine continued.

With tools loaded in the barrows, their group set off to continue building retaining walls. There was no way to escape his life. At first the bush had looked inviting. It was so close to the settlement and seemed an easy escape. But the killings extinguished his desire to flee. White men had been murdered, some barbarously, by the natives. Instead of promising a haven, the bush looked like a natural fence that would confine him in his misery. The thick growth seemed like a threat to the town. He awoke sweating and trembling one night, haunted by a dream in which he ripped away the branches that were choking him. There was no way out.

Bundy demanded that Gerry stop his rebelliousness and obey their overseer at every turn. Gerry had laughed at the little man but Bundy had been serious.

At the work site, the sun bore down and they kept at it. Donnelly came up to Gerry just as he'd run out of mortar and needed more.

Gerry yelled past Donnelly at one of the labourers working alongside the team. 'More mud!'

Gerry stood aside as the labourer brought up the barrow. Somehow the big-shouldered man lost his balance, tipped the barrow and slopped most of the mortar over Gerry's boots. Gerry grabbed him and shoved him onto the ground.

'I didn't mean to,' the man exclaimed, attempting to get up.

Gerry pushed him down again. 'You d-did. It was no accident.'

'Riordan!' Donnelly said. 'Leave him alone.'

The labourer smirked at this and started to get up. Gerry reacted and his fist sent blood spraying from the man's nose onto the mortar.

'Stop!' Donnelly said.

Gerry landed two more punches but Donnelly grabbed him, pinning both arms. 'Get the manacles, Bundy.'

Bundy clapped the irons on Gerry's wrists and Donnelly grabbed a rope from the pile of tools, tied it onto the manacles and pulled Gerry away. He bound him to a tree and stood back, panting, his florid face streaming moisture. 'I bloody warned you, Riordan. You can stay there all day and stew. Tonight you'll go to the barracks under guard.' He paused for breath. 'Tomorrow, you won't be with us. I don't care where you'll be, just away from here.' He turned around and yelled, 'The rest of you, clean up this mess and get back to work!'

'Sir,' Bundy said. 'Perkins can finish the wall. He's good, like.' Bundy glanced at Gerry who glared at him.

'Right,' Donnelly said, 'get cracking. 'This character,' he pointed at Gerry, 'is about to get another occupation.'

He walked away. Bundy sidled up to Gerry and pulled on his irons. 'Told you, didn't I? Gave you enough warning.'

'You wait until tonight,' Gerry said. 'You just wait.'

'I think I'm safe. You'll be in a dark hole called solitary until you cool down.' Bundy walked away. 'Give my regards to the fellows on the road.'

Two days later, four white lines of light formed a square outlining the gate to his cell, if that was what it was—more like a tomb. But the lines were something to bring the reality of time back from the blackness. The night was the worst because that extinguished the lines of light.

A rat scurried across his thigh, searching for the crumbs he'd dropped from his last meal that was hours ago, or was it? Two days since he'd been marched under guard from his worksite to the barracks and flung into this fetid place. Gerry's arms had ached at first then they'd become numb like his legs. It was the trembling that he couldn't control, and the cramps. Even for a man of medium height the hole would be cruel, designed so the prisoner could neither stand up nor lie down. For a man of Gerry's stature, it was torture and his limbs burned in pain.

He jerked as bolts were thrown and sunshine exploded on him, blinding him. Arms grabbed him and pulled. With aching tendons now yanked to breaking point, he screamed. He was dragged along the ground, then let go, and water soaked him, its coldness a shock. The pressure prodded the pain spots, making him cry out some more.

'Get him up,' an unknown voice yelled. 'Change his gear and get him up to the chief. You've got thirty minutes.'

Thus, eight o'clock on Monday morning he found himself overlooking a three-foot wide table that was offset in relation to the three windows in the wall behind it. Gerry would have liked to shift the table just a little to one side. Just inches, that's all it needed, so that the centre could be in line with the middle window. Symmetry was everything. He wanted all things in order like the stone he'd laid as a craftsman—true, square and level. On this sunny morning he wasn't true, square and level.

Three officers sat on one side of the table and Gerry stood to attention in front of it. He'd been made to wait in the anteroom while five others before him had been reassigned. It was his turn now and his legs trembled, unused to standing.

'Convict Riordan,' said the officer in the middle, 'Number 23420. Your period as an assigned convict to work at the governor's pleasure has come under review. Two recent incidents demonstrate to this tribunal that you are not of the character for doing such privileged work. From today the sixteenth of February 1829, you will be reassigned to'—the officer looked down at his book—'Iron Gang Number Four. You'll report to the officers at six tomorrow morning.'

'That isn't fair!' Gerry said spitting out his anger.

'Silence, Convict,' the officer on the left said. 'Dismissed.'

He was marched away, not to solitary confinement but to the barracks. With all the convicts out working, he ate his meal there in silence.

Gerry left the barracks at dawn the next day on an unusually cool summer morning. Decked out in a replacement uniform and with his limbs still sore from his nights in solitary, he hoisted himself into a wagon where he joined fifteen other convicts.

Ignoring his companions, he looked at the streets and buildings he was leaving behind. Nothing had been said the previous night to the convicts he'd worked with these last three months, and Bundy had not been in sight. Maybe Donnelly had done the right thing and kept Bundy out of Gerry's sight. It was better that way.

The wagon rumbled along down Market Street, heading west. There were no springs in the vehicle and every bump jarred his aching ligaments. He had no idea where he was going but if what Bundy said was true, it wouldn't be cheery. With the prospect of worse conditions confronting him, the simple work he had of building retaining walls along the harbour edge now seemed enticing. This was an extra blow against him. Under the first he'd just existed, with moods like anger, sadness and frustration moving over him. How was he now going to live where whip, stick and scrub were commonplace?

His homeland, his family on the farm, his mates in Cork, were now like scenes from a dream. It was as if he'd visited Ireland as a child many decades ago: the greenery, freshness and softness in wet fields were all starting to fade. The wagon rolled on and soon turned the corner into Parramatta Road. They were heading south. Gerry settled against his fellow inmate and drifted off to sleep.

A toot from a ferry woke him and the pain in his knee throbbed, as it had lain at an odd angle for the past hour and a half. It was cooler now, the breeze coming off a river and the wagon headed towards the punt at Bedlam Point. There was no madhouse there; the point had been called Bethlem but common use soon changed the name. There, they were joined by a supply wagon loaded with provisions and another two wagons packed with convicts. Under the eyes and by the orders from six guards they alighted and assembled into their road gangs. Gerry found his No 4 Iron Gang and they got onto a different wagon. It boarded the punt with the supply wagon. The two remaining wagons heading off in a westerly direction.

The vegetation on the north side of the river was denser than the side he'd left, and the road was smooth.

'Where are we going?' he asked the man sitting alongside him.

The slim man frowned. He was in his thirties with copper-coloured hair and fine features. 'What's left of Finch's Line. Up from Wisemans Ferry.'

'Where's that?'

'You're a new one, aren't you?'

'Aye,' Gerry said. 'What's it like?'

The man laughed. 'Hey, Murphy. Tiny here's new to the road. What do we tell him?'

The convict sitting opposite them leaned forward. He was about thirty, small and wiry with lively blue eyes and a mop of fair hair. 'Wiseman's Ferry is where you cross the river going north. There's a big flat punt there, that takes men and horses and what you will. Finch's Line is beyond that, part of the Road, my young friend, and it's a bastard, a true bastard.' He gave a grim smile. 'If the mosquitoes, snakes and the shitty water don't kill you, you'll die by the scourger's whip or a broken back. True, Dooley?'

'Broken back's the more likely, Murphy,' Gerry's companion replied. 'They've got a new scourger up there. His name is Morgan. A mean prick.'

'What's a scourger?' Gerry asked.

Dooley laughed again. 'A scourger, my friend, is something that fell from a poxed sailor's arse and before it hit the ground was pissed on by a mangy dog.'

'Don't frighten the little one, Dooley,' Murphy said. 'What's your name?'

'Gerry Riordan.'

'Well, Riordan, a scourger is a man who has the authority to inflict punishment with a whip.'

'Like the soldier did to Jesus,' Dooley interrupted, rolling his sleeves further up his smooth, tanned forearms. 'Whipped Him. Scourged Him.'

'I can look after myself.' Gerry mumbled.

'Listen to the tall young man, will you, Mr Murphy! A right fighter we might have here.'

Both of them glanced at him with a mixture of mockery and curiosity and Gerry sat back, not letting them get to him. They'd soon see whether he could look after himself. Three months ago, he'd had two fights at the barracks. In the first one he'd used his fists and come off badly. For the second he was ready and he went for it with anything, knees, nails, teeth and he'd won. How he'd go against the scourger with a whip he didn't know, but he wouldn't buckle. 'What sort of work?'

'What work do you do?' Dooley asked.

'I'm a stonemason,' Gerry replied.

'Culverts on Finch's are finished so you won't be shearing stone where we're going. We will be clearing, grubbing out, burning off and splitting timber. That's what we'll be doing.'

The wagon ambled along behind the supply wagon. For the hours that followed both Dooley and Murphy said little to Gerry, other than revealing that Murphy's first name was Francis and Fergus was

Dooley's. Both had worked on the road before, a section south of Wiseman's Station. Now were back on the iron gangs because they had misbehaved on a farm at Windsor.

As they left the Parramatta River far behind them, Gerry studied the forest. Spindly trees that looked as though they were dying stood neighbours to hardwood that soared to over one hundred feet and more. Nothing like the low, moist ferns and bracken at the boundary of his father's farm. No, this was impassable undergrowth, with eye-plucking branches and arm-cutting edges, and snakes scurrying across the track, frightening the horses. What a country.

By mid-afternoon, the two wagons approached a point where a river much wider than the Parramatta flowed by a small plain. It struck Gerry as a pretty spot at first, but his interest almost vanished, like the smoke from one of the guard's pipes. The wagons continued downstream about half a mile, stopped, and the convicts were allowed to get down.

Gerry collapsed when his feet hit the ground.

'Done solitary?' Murphy extended a hand.

'H-How did you know?' Gerry said as he took the hand and got up.

'It shows. Knees are buggered—'

'Quiet you two,' one of the guards said.

They formed up in two ranks, Gerry at the front with Murphy and Dooley, and waited in silence near the punt that would take them across the river. He said to Dooley, 'What's this spot called?'

'Wisemans Station, named after Mr Solomon Wiseman. He was a convict himself but now he's a free man, and a rich one. Owns all the land around here and—'

A crack made Gerry jump. Dooley collapsed, under a lash made of rawhide.

A uniformed man stood in front of them. 'Scum were told to keep quiet!' He rolled up his bullwhip. 'Scum only speak when a guard asks. I see two have returned. Francis Murphy and Fergus Dooley, welcome back.'

This must be the scourger the others had warned him about. The man was Gerry's height plus two inches, as high as an English door and as wide as its frame. A scar crossed his pocked-marked, weathered forehead and his brown eyes glinted in the light of the dying sun. 'Scum hears what I say? Nod, scum, if you do.'

Dooley struggled to his feet. 'I'm sorry, Sergeant Morgan.' He pulled Gerry's trouser leg and Gerry nodded as well.

The scourger stood in front of Gerry, his navy jacket fitting like skin and the centre row of brass buttons polished to brilliance. 'Now who's this?' he said. 'A new lad, eh? Big enough, but let's see how tough.'

A baton appeared from nowhere and Morgan thrust it into Gerry's stomach. As Gerry doubled over, Morgan remarked, 'Not so tough, Dooley, eh?'

'No, Sergeant,' Fergus Dooley replied as Gerry stood up.

Morgan tapped Gerry's chest with the baton. 'Well, my son, you'll be in my team for as long as my lieutenant needs you.' Gerry stood there trembling and pinched the sides of his trousers, anything to keep his fists from adding another scar to the man's face. Morgan stepped back and addressed them all. 'Your job here is to work, to work and work some more. We're building a road, my boyos and you'll be my beavers, my yellow-skinned beavers.' He laughed and slapped his baton against his open palm. 'Morgan's Beavers. We've got more beavers up at the track; some are old, but they'll teach you some tricks.'

At that point a horse and rider trotted up to them and Morgan turned and came to attention. 'Sir!'

'Thank you, Sergeant. Move the men off.'

The mounted officer was slight of build, with fair skin. To Gerry, the eyes showed an active intelligence, but his big, hooked nose, with wide nostrils, dominated the face.

Morgan yelled, 'All right, you heard Lieutenant Dodds. Dooley, you rodent, you've been here and done this before—lead on, you're first aboard the punt. And the rest of you, just because you're my beavers and it's smooth water, don't try jumping into it. Last time that happened, the stupid bastard sank like a rock.' Morgan laughed. 'Fitting end for a felon and a cheap funeral for His Majesty.'

Chapter Six

Gerry studied the vastness of the scrub in front of him. Dooley had told him that the Hawkesbury River that they'd just crossed started inland, well south of Sydney town, meandered roughly north, then formed a big curve before Wiseman's Station. The punt there had been brought up the river on the orders of Mr Solomon Wiseman, after he'd received a big grant of land. To take further advantage of this vital crossing, further along the bank Mr Wiseman had had an inn built for travellers, called 'The Sign of the Packet', though the lads all called it Wiseman's Inn. Opposite the inn, on the other side of the Road, was a grand house built for himself, and the gardens on his land supplied the inn. Plus Wiseman had a government contract to supply food to the convict gangs on the Road.

Beyond Wiseman's Station, Iron Gang No 4 was confronted with virgin country, fearsome, deadly and challenging. They were ascending a newer section of road, punctuated by zigzag turns and some straight sections that crossed over culverts. The new road then petered out and the wagons stopped at a forty-foot-long ragged framework of poles covered and tied together with bark sheets. This was Gerry's new home, as different from the Macquarie Street barracks as sunshine to night.

'Move in,' Morgan said, 'and find yourself a spare sack of straw and a blanket. You'll be fed soon, my beavers, so don't fall asleep or you'll get a taste of my python.'

They went inside. It was murky and stale: despite half inch gaps between the bark-strip walls, there was a funk of sweat mixed with the smoke from half a dozen pipes. Gerry and his two companions found three spare palliasses.

On either side of him, other men lay back and took a break in silence. Gerry felt anger flash through him and his skin prickled. The confines of the hut were nothing like Cork's gaol but they rankled and he felt just as he had after his conviction.

'Grub,' came a grunt next to him. The man stood up and headed for the doorway. Gerry followed him, with Murphy and Dooley.

The meal was good, better than the barracks; mutton stew with damper.

'Have to keep the beasts of burden strong,' Murphy said biting off a crusty piece of damper. 'That's what we are.'

Dooley grinned. 'This meat tastes fresh-killed.'

Gerry ate the lot and was allowed more, which surprised him. It was a new experience, eating outside, with air cooling his back while the cooking fire warmed his front. Night sounds pierced the blackness but when he went to relieve himself on the edge of the clearing, they died away. The cacophony started again as he returned to the fire. Nature—mating, fighting, scavenging and dying. There was a battle going on in the undergrowth not twenty feet from him.

Later that night, trying to ignore the snores and grunts that rose in the humid air, he prayed, something he hadn't done for months. At times his thoughts strayed from prayer and Anne would appear in his mind. For those moments he allowed himself to think about when they had been together, but it got too hard to bear, so he resumed his prayers. Though he was innocent of murder and of theft, he still knew he had sins enough to confess to his Maker—but he sought no forgiveness. His prayers were a plea, to keep himself from something darker, something that every hour was drawing him to finish everything. He felt that only his Faith could stop him from ending his life. He must fight to stay alive—not so he could lead a true Christian life, which included helping others, but to keep from killing himself. Because if he did that, he would go to hell.

Next morning, Gerry's joints were stiff when he woke and his face felt the coolness of the morning. The doorway of the hut framed an eerie light and he got up, stretched and went outside. Most of the men were eating and he grabbed a bowl. It was porridge, sweet and hot.

The lieutenant from yesterday stood near a tree reading a book. Gerry had forgotten his name.

'Muster's in ten minutes,' the lieutenant said, and resumed reading. Gerry had to pass by him to wash his bowl in the boiling water of the camp's cauldron. The officer looked at him and smiled. 'New lad?'

Gerry nodded to him and looked away, noticing three convicts entered his hut carrying piles of clothes.

The officer raised his voice to include the whole gang. 'Kit for the new men! Get yours and get ready.'

Gerry and Dooley went inside together. On each palliasse was a change of uniform: a frock of Parramatta cloth, a striped cotton shirt, a pair of trousers, a cloth cap, long socks and a pair of shoes.

'Hurry, Riordan,' Murphy said donning his gear. 'Miss muster and you'll be on report.'

Nothing fitted Gerry, but he made do and joined the others, who were lined up outside in three ranks.

Standing in front of them was the lieutenant, with a rollcall instead of a book. 'Number Four Iron Gang, I'm Lieutenant Dodds, your overseer. We are building a road known as the Great North Road. Some of you have worked on part of it, from Castle Hill to Wiseman's Station. The section of the road from Wiseman's that you came up on yesterday is nearly complete, and the next section is called Finch's Ascent.' He paused, glancing over them all. 'I have two rules. One, if you work hard, you'll be treated fairly. Two, if you show a history of working hard, you'll be rewarded.' He stroked the side of his prominent nose. 'I'm happy to say that three men who used to work with you are now applying for their tickets of leave, which I believe they will be successful in obtaining.'

'Ticket of leave. What's that?' Gerry whispered to Murphy.

'I'll tell you later.'

'Do exactly what you're ordered to do each day and do it well. The only other thing you need to remember is that I live by rule Number One.' His gaze rested for a second on Gerry and Dooley as he said, 'You met Sergeant Morgan yesterday. He's a man who lives by rule Number Three.' There were a few curious murmurs, which Dodds ignored. 'Sergeant Morgan will supervise you day to day when I'm absent and administer punishment when authorised by me. Formal punishment is performed on Saturdays, which is wash day. Informal punishment can be expected by those who break my rule Number One more than once. Sergeant Morgan is … a necessity amongst you, as am I. We are all here at the order of the governor.' Dodds gave an enigmatic smile. 'Sergeant Morgan and I compete. I pit my total issue of tickets-of-leave versus his total of corporal punishments. Very good. I'll call the roll. You will answer with "Sir".'

Dodds called out about fifty names. When all had been accounted for, the men were marched from the camp into a large area of cleared land. The sun flashed at them from a low angle and its brightness forced Gerry to look down, handy since the surface was pocked with hazards.

After one hundred yards they were stopped at a tree with a blaze on it. Behind it lay forest so thick that Gerry was convinced no one could pass through it.

'Right,' Dodds said pointing to three stacks of tools, 'break out and start work.'

'Come on,' Murphy said to Gerry, 'I know the drill. As we're new men, we're on clearing. They've cut down the big trees in front of us and left us this lot.' Murphy picked up a scythe and Dooley took a machete and bow saw. 'Stand behind me, Riordan,' Dooley said, 'and clean out what I cut.'

The three of them went forward to meet the challenging forest wall. The big trees might be gone but what was left seemed to attack them instead of the other way around. The bush was motionless until scythes, small axes and saws bit into it and then it became angry, fighting back with whipping branches and stinging thorns. Gerry, picking up the cut undergrowth, was saturated with sweat in minutes. On either side of them, along a thirty-yard front, other men were doing a similar job. Beyond the undergrowth, axes and crosscut saws could be heard. A loud crack startled Gerry and he thought it was Morgan at work, but it was a tall gum tree crashing onto the undergrowth.

As the morning wore on, smoke rose when tree stumps were burnt. A whistle shrieked.

'Grub,' Murphy said and smiled. His face was running with sweat and his brown hair was wet. He spoke to a new man named Western, whose hands were red and blistered. 'I'll get you some grease for those tonight. You say you were a labourer? Christ, you've got the hands of a bishop!'

Gerry sat down with Murphy and Dooley, having got used to their company. A fellow convict brought water cans and they drank.

'We'll be grubbing up stumps after our meal.' Dooley spat out some of his water. 'Better, but hard. Hey, here's the tucker.'

The food was good again and Gerry got stuck in. 'What's a t-ticket?'

'A ticket-of-leave, my friend, is a trip to heaven,' Dooley said. He had a pleasant smile; his eyes were bright and his teeth even.

'Don't fool him, Dooley,' Murphy said. 'It's a way out of the irons, Riordan. For good behaviour, after a certain time you might get parole. Know what that is?'

'I think so.'

'Tiny thinks, Murphy. We have a scholar on our hands!' Gerry grinned despite himself. 'And the giant likes a joke … A ticket-of-leave is a certificate that our dear Majesty's government deigns to give to us after a number of years of valued service.'

'Stop your blarney, Dooley. You're no Dublin advocate.'

Dooley looked shocked and pointed a slim yet work-hardened finger at his friend. 'But I would have made a good one.'

Murphy shook his head. 'Get on with you.' He chewed at a tough piece of meat, then brushed away a wet strand of his fair hair. 'It's like this, Riordan. Dooley and me got a seven-year sentence. But after four years of good service we should get a ticket-of-leave. That is, the right to work where we can, and earn a wage.'

Dooley stood up. 'Those lads that got a fourteen-year sentence, they could get a ticket-of-leave after six years.' He stretched out his arms. 'What's your time?'

'Life,' Gerry said.

Both Dooley and Murphy looked at each other. Dooley lowered his arms and Murphy placed a firm hand on Gerry's forearm. 'Then you'll need to wait eight years.'

Gerry's shoulders slumped. He remembered something like this being told to them on the transport coming out, but his mind had cringed from the details.

Murphy sensed his concern. 'So, my short young friend. Work hard and work better.' Murphy glanced at Dodds. 'That man over there might well help you. I've heard he's got lifers a ticket after four years.' Murphy brightened. 'Anyways, that's down the track. From your brogue, you'd be Leinster?'

'Aye,' Gerry said, glad of the distraction. 'Kildare.'

'I'm from Wicklow,' Murphy said, 'and Mr Fergus Dooley here, who's eaten more than he should, is from Meath.'

'So,' Dooley said, 'we're neighbours so to speak.' They all smiled.

Scattered groups like them sat in the sunshine that bore down on them as if trying to roast them alive. Murphy stood and stretched and Gerry copied him, his limbs sore.

For the rest of the afternoon they laboured with shoulders, backs and legs stressed to pain as they ripped out the burnt-off stumps.

* * *

It was a Saturday, and Gerry inhaled the freshness of his kit, liking its smell and feel after the weekly wash in a creek near their camp. Over the next few days, however, the lice would return inside his clothes. He kept a better mental record of the days and dates now. It was April, and Easter would soon be upon them.

When it came, they assembled without leg irons beside three wagons; two for the men and one to collect stores at Wiseman's. Every Sunday, a Church of England minister brought his vestments to their work place on site and the holy words were said. Today the service would be held in a hall positioned between the Hawkesbury River and Mr Wiseman's house.

Boarding the wagon with his mates, Gerry said little. Three months of routine—no stonework, just labouring—had conditioned him not to think, but to do, like the bullocks that hauled away the fallen tree trunks to the sawmills further south. Like them, too, he worked under the whip. His hands were hardened now like mattock shafts and his muscles were as thick as the ropes that bound the great logs. Only his skin showed damage, pockmarked by sun blisters.

Being the last convict to sit down in the wagon, Gerry had a space to himself at the end of the bench, but Lieutenant Dodds climbed up and went to sit beside him, so he pressed against his neighbour to make room. The wagon headed off downhill.

'What a lovely day,' Dodds said. Gerry froze and the men stared and then looked away. Nothing was said for a while. Dodds brushed away a fly. 'You're a stonemason are you not?'

'I am, sir.'

'We will have stone for you to lay shortly.'

Gerry was startled. 'What?' He forgot the honorific in his surprise, but Dodds didn't seemed to notice.

'Culverts and retaining walls, that's what, on a new section of road.'

Gerry fell silent and the wagon continued on. Stone at last, but, then doing that might make him have to think and not just act. But stone again! His skill being used for something he liked to do. Mr Dodds said nothing else for the rest of the journey.

They crossed the river by punt, reversing the way they came three months earlier. A little further on, there was a group of buildings, which they had not been close enough to examine on the journey north. One was a fine-looking two-storey house. Across the road and down a pace was a two-storey, older building. It was 'The Sign of the Packet', known to most as Wiseman's Inn.

'Mr Wiseman owns both those places,' Dodds said to Gerry. 'He calls the house Cobham Hall. He doesn't live there yet; they're still doing the insides.'

The convicts were all looking at Gerry again and Murphy and Dooley were smirking. Was it because Dodds was seated beside him?

He wished the man hadn't spoken to him. Since Gerry had been working on the Road, he hadn't shared more than ten words with the officer, and he wasn't interested in talking to him now.

A girl came out of Wiseman's Inn and walked past the wagons, carrying a basket. She was in her teens, not tall. She walked well with a sway in her step, and the features beneath her bonnet were kind on the eye. Her brown hair was in a ponytail and her well-proportioned figure was clothed in a blue dress with an embroidered white blouse underneath.

A growl of appreciation came from both wagons.

'Steady, lads,' Dodds said. 'That is Miss Walsh, the licensee's daughter. Miss Walsh is in no need of your plaudits. You'll show her respect.'

Dodds sounded firm but there was a smile under the big nose. He would stand no nonsense from the men, but he seemed to understand their reaction. The growl dropped to a few low whistles.

A crack made Gerry jump and Morgan rode up between the girl and the wagon. 'Apologies, Miss Walsh, for that sound.' He turned his horse and glared at the wagon. 'Scum here know no better.'

Dodds stood up as their wagon stopped near the stockade. 'Thank you, Sergeant Morgan. Please bring the men into the hall.'

The big man paused just for a fraction, then barked at the men, 'Right, out of the wagons.'

Miss Walsh had vanished. Gerry sensed that Dodds's call for respect might have saved them all a night without blankets; a penalty they'd endured twice already. They alighted, formed into two ranks and were marched into the hall.

The service droned on and Gerry's mind wandered to the girl. Her brown hair was not as dark as Anne's, her skin was tanned and she was shorter and fuller. Anne. It had been so long, yet he had not forgotten her. This girl here reminded him of what a future he and Anne could have had.

After the service, the convicts were assembled and the roll called.

'Sergeant,' Dodds said. 'Convict Riordan will stay with me. I'll bring him back with the stores.'

'Sir!' Gerry was startled.

The others moved off, some glancing at him with curiosity.

'Come with me,' Dodds said.

Gerry followed the lieutenant around the back of the hall, where Dodds stopped. 'I've studied your specification.' Gerry had no idea what the officer was talking about. Dodds pulled out a piece of paper. 'Your specification says you're convicted of murder. I'd like to hear your story.'

Gerry remained at attention. The absence of his convict mates made him feel self-conscious and he perspired.

'Well?' Dodds said.

'I didn't kill anybody.'

'I didn't kill anybody, sir. Tell me what happened.'

Gerry frowned and a thought struck him. Was this officer a dolly? Murphy Dooley and the other men had not said he was but they were wary just the same. Gerry had seen things on the transport and in the gangs that disturbed him. Was Dodds like that? Why else would he single Gerry out? 'Sergeant Morgan will get me for this,' Gerry said. 'D-doesn't like when an officer talks to us.'

Dodds paused. 'Very well. Perhaps another time you'll tell me. Now, I want you in the party for the work up to Devine's Hill. That's where we're getting into stone.'

He'd heard about the place. There was a new, straighter route north for the Road, starting upstream from Wiseman's Station then ascending to join the end of Finch's Ascent. Land had been cleared in advance and he'd seen the jumper pits where the blasted rock had been split, ready for use on the last filled sections for Finch's Ascent.

'What happens to Finch's, sir?'

'It'll still be used for transporting materials for other sections of the Road but the road from Wiseman's to Devine's Hill, the one you'll work on, will become the new permanent route. It'll be a special duty with better rations and conditions.'

This should have been exciting, but Gerry was worried. Did Dodds want him just for laying stone? Gerry's blood surged with suspicion. 'Why me?'

Dodds laughed. 'You're a stonemason, man! I think maybe a good one, but you'll have to prove it. And call me sir.'

'Yes, sir.'

'Well? Do you want this work or not?'

Clearing and grubbing out was hard but he was used to it. No thought needed, just action. But to work the stone again was tempting. 'I want no favours, sir.'

The overseer frowned for the first time. 'And you'll get none. You remember what I said to you men? Rule Number Two: show a history of working hard and you'll be rewarded. Promotion to the stone party is your reward. Simple.'

A queer English officer with a big nose giving him a leg up. But stone it was and that was something different. Gerry nodded.

'Good. We also need carpenters.'

'F-Francis Murphy and Fergus Dooley, sir.'

'My choices also,' Dodds said. 'From tomorrow you'll all be in that party. I want good work, Convict Riordan. Don't let me down. Now, come and help load the stores.'

When Dodds and the convicts were arriving at the inn, Deirdre Walsh was in the kitchen with her mother.

'Come along,' Jess Walsh said. 'I want those goods checked with your own eyes before they leave here. I trust no man with our goods, king's officer or not.'

Deirdre put her dish towel down, glad of the change of chores. She wanted to see the convicts again. And why not? Two of her friends, both sixteen like herself, were married to ticket-of-leave men. The army lieutenant she was seeing, Derrick Bates, hadn't been here for two months and she missed their time together.

Her father was packing boxes in the store that adjoined the kitchen and opened to a set of double doors to the outside. Nearby, an empty wagon stood harnessed to two horses.

'They'll be here soon,' Brian Walsh said, picking up a clipboard. 'It's the Sabbath but I suppose God won't mind the convicts getting fed.' He grinned at her. 'I've done my bit. You stand by the wagon and make sure the stores are loaded there. Check them off.'

'Yes, Father.'

'Here, lass.' Her father gave her the clipboard and left.

It was quiet outside now, not like this morning. Timing it nicely, she had completed bed making and when the wagons approached she'd hurried downstairs, stopping for a moment to check herself in a wall mirror. She had her mother's looks, which her father said were pure Spanish—olive skin, a sensuous mouth, thick brown hair and eyes that glinted mischief. Undoing the top button of her blouse, she grinned. Her bust was her best asset.

Seeing the wagons slowing to a halt, she had gone outside with her basket and into the smell of the close-packed men. The growl from the wagons pulsed through her as though she'd stepped into a warm bath and she had bitten her lip, trying not to smile. When Morgan had chastised the men, she'd given him no heed. Six months now the brutal sergeant had been up here on duty. She loathed him—what he did and the way he looked. She hated the scar tissue that partly closed one eye but did not conceal a look that seemed able to pierce solid iron. When he was close, he inspected her as though she were on parade and he could see right through her clothing.

As she walked out through the open door of the storeroom, a familiar_figure appeared, Lieutenant Dodds. A tall, well muscled convict with russet-coloured hair and fair skin stood behind him.

'Miss Walsh, good morning.'

She smiled. 'Good morning to you, Lieutenant Dodds.'

'Right, Riordan,' Dodds said, 'step forward and give Miss Walsh your assistance.'

The convict didn't move, just stood and looked at her. His eyes were attentive, his mouth was attractive and his shoulders were as broad as their back door. Lieutenant Dodds took out a key and removed the man's manacles.

'Miss Walsh,' Dodds said, 'please show Riordan what you need him to do. He's somewhat slow on the uptake.'

Riordan's skin reddened and he looked down. He didn't like what Dodds had said. But when his eyes met hers again, she saw a spark in them, maybe of anger, maybe something else. She felt a tingle.

'This way,' she said.

Deirdre was very aware of him behind her as she went into the dimness of the store. On purpose, she stopped and turned, and he bumped into her.

'S-sorry, miss.' His hand brushed her arm. She liked the touch of his fingers. He had a different accent. His was a voice from an eastern county of Ireland, lilting.

'Pick up those boxes over there,' she said to him, 'and put them behind your wagon.'

'Yes, miss.'

'I'll check them off. Then you'll load them up.'

He nodded.

'Right, Riordan,' Dodds called from outside, 'get moving.'

It took a while but Riordan duly took care of the wheaten meal, salt, beef, pork, sugar, pease and soap as the sun crept higher. Deirdre made sure he had to brush against her now and then in the confines of the storeroom—a forearm here, a knee there, like a caress. She was distracted and excited in a way she hadn't known before. This was so unlike being with the civilised Lieutenant Derrick Bates. Riordan was tall and strong, yes, but he was a convict, and hardly spoke. Despite this there was something about him, something which interested her. When the last box was loaded, Deirdre felt disappointed.

'On the wagon, Riordan,' Dodds said and he turned and removed his hat. 'Thank you, Miss Walsh, and good day.'

'I wish you and'—she caught her breath because Riordan was looking right at her—'a good journey back.'

When Dodds and Gerry mounted the wagon for the drive back to camp, Dodds had Gerry sit beside him on the driver's seat, without manacles. The wagon wheels bit into the ground as Dodds shook the reins. The horses took up the load and headed along the bank towards the punt landing. Gerry was tempted to turn back for a last look at Miss Walsh but managed not to. She was something else. He mused about her seductive body and the way she'd stood close sometimes while he was loading up the stores. What was he supposed to make of that? He also wondered how much Dodds had noticed.

'We have just under two hours to get back to camp,' Dodds said. 'We can say nothing on the way, or we can talk. What's it to be?

'Talk about what?'

'Sir.'

Gerry grimaced. 'T-talk about what … sir.'

'I've been here for a year and see, all types,' Dodds said. He steered the lead horses around a rain-eroded crater. 'At the start I made mistakes. We all do. At one stage I thought that a certain convict had potential.'

For what? Gerry thought.

'And I was right. He might have earned his ticket of leave and made something of himself.' Dodds was quiet for a while, his face set. 'But he couldn't see that, and it ended in tragedy.'

This trip was going to be trying if Dodds was going to chatter all the way.

'Now,' Dodds continued, 'I've seen how expertly you work. And just now, how you deal with civilians—cooperative, and no cheek.'

Gerry kept silent, hoping Dodds would follow suit. At the landing, the lieutenant eased the horses onto the punt and they watched as the driver turned the cable wheel, pulling the punt twelve hundred feet across the Hawkesbury.

The clear waters rushed by and both men stayed silent. When the punt touched the other bank, Gerry shifted away from his companion and waited while the wagon moved out of sight of the riverbank. There were no other vehicles on the road. He gazed at the vast, dense bush on each side. Was this the place to deal with Dodds? No one would witness the attack if he decided to go for him and then flee.

He thought of the three men from their gang who had tried escaping last month. The military had gone in pursuit with native trackers and hauled them back to camp within two days. Sergeant Morgan had smiled when they were brought in. He was grinning even more when he finished the drubbing and blood coated their backs like paint.

It would mean much worse, if he was caught after striking an officer. And if he killed him, he'd hang. But if Dodds touched him, he would do it. Kill him here and make for the scrub.

'At trial, you were convicted on two counts,' Dodds said, and Gerry tensed. 'Theft and murder. But you claim you're innocent.'

'I'm not guilty, sir, of either crime. Or any crime, for that matter.'

'So why were you condemned? And which happened first, the theft or the murder?'

It occurred to Gerry that if he kept on talking, Dodds might be content to listen and leave him alone. 'The theft. It happened while I was working on Saint Mary's Cathedral in Cork.'

'I know Saint Mary's,' Dodds said and closed his eyes for a fraction. 'Detailed columns and flying buttresses.'

Gerry glanced at him in surprise. This officer had travelled. 'I was working in marble for the altar and tabernacle. There were doors being made for the tabernacle, faced in gold bas-relief, that I was to fit in place once they were finished.'

'Gold bas-relief? Beautiful. So, there was restoration going on at the cathedral. Any other craftsmen involved? Tell me about it.'

For at least half an hour, Gerry found himself describing the work that had gone into St Mary's, and about others' achievements as well as his own—like Lawrence Toole's fine work on the altar rails. He was not conscious of Dodds except as a willing listener by his side, so he rarely stammered, and he even felt a sense of satisfaction in this account of good things past. When he got around to the doors again, Dodds prompted him to talk about the theft, and he told the bitter story of how the false case had been made against him as thief, and then how he had been framed for the murder of his best friend.

'You've no idea who *was* guilty of the theft and the killing?'

'Wouldn't matter if I did, sir. The box was found in my room and so was my friend. Stabbed to death.' Toole's face appeared before him, as Gerry had last seen him. He had just given Toole his silver medallion to place in his digs, and Toole had said three simple words: *See you tonight*. Sadness overwhelmed him.

'You were close?' Dodds reached for a water bottle.

'We were sir.'

Dodds offered the bottle to Gerry, who glanced at him sideways. He still couldn't be sure whether Dodds's interest was dubious. He shrugged and slaked his thirst. 'But I got convicted of my best mate's death and here I am paying for two crimes I didn't commit. That's it. Enough about that.' He placed the bottle back below the seat.

Dodds kept quiet for a while. At times he slapped the reins to urge the horses up a steeper incline. 'You're angry,' Dodds said eventually. 'That influences your thinking about things.'

Of course he was angry! Gerry retorted, 'You would be too, sir. Sent to this place with no future.'

'A man can make of life what he wills.'

Gerry turned on him. 'Easy for you! Sir.'

Dodds smiled. 'It might surprise you to know that I was forced to come here myself.'

'You chose to join the army, sir. You're here because you obey orders. That's nothing like being condemned for murder!'

Dodds nodded, his lips pursed. 'You're angry that you've been unjustly convicted.'

'I am.'

'Then you need to control that feeling, or you can't move onward.'

Gerry grunted. Bull dust! The same sentiment the minister had gone on about this morning. The grace of God? A crow squawked from a nearby branch. Lucky bugger, it could fly anywhere.

'I had no choice either,' Dodds said. 'My father had debts. I accepted a transfer here because it was a promotion, and that meant I could send some of my pay back to help him.'

Gerry stared at him. 'It was your choice to come to New South Wales, sir?'

'That's right.'

Dodds was lying. No one would willingly condemn themselves to a hellhole like this.

'I'm a chartered surveyor by profession.' Gerry gripped the wagon's side as it lurched into a pothole. Dodds glanced at him and caught his surprise. 'Aye. I liked building but I liked the mathematics better.'

'What?'

'Sir, Riordan. I won't remind you again.'

'Sorry, sir, but you surprised me. So the army wasn't your first choice?'

'No, but I'm lucky enough to pursue my profession within it. My expertise is valued in this country. My job is on the Road, measuring and costing the works completed, and those works yet to be done.'

The road surface was newer now, and they were getting close to their camp. Gerry thought about what Dodds was doing: talking to him almost as an equal, giving him details about his life. Why? Because Dodds liked men, surely. He was in his mid-thirties, unmarried, trying to get cosy with a convict. Next thing he'd be trying to touch Gerry.

'Where are your irons, Riordan?' Dodds put a hand in his pocket for the keys.

Gerry reached down and clasped the manacles beneath the bench. He could swing them up now, smash Dodds, cut a horse loose and gallop away.

Dodds smiled. 'You're a big man and in a fight you'd win, especially against a smaller man.'

Bugger can read my mind!

Gerry hesitated, then put his arms out with the manacles loose on his wrists. With the reins held between his knees, Dodds leaned over and locked the irons. Then he drove on.

They reached the camp in silence.

* * *

Timothy Johnson, Clerk of the New South Wales Court, grimaced at the amount of correspondence piled in a tray on his desk. No chance for him to go to the pub in the early afternoon. Why hadn't he stayed on as the judge's clerk, with easier duties? No, for an extra two shillings a day he'd taken this job.

Part of his work was interesting. The part where Britain and Ireland asked for additional details on convicted felons who'd been transported. As Clerk of the Court, he was the first to receive such documents brought in by sea. The mail room took possession of all the Court's mail from each ship's captain and with a witness opened it, stamped its contents with the date of receipt and delivered the correspondence to him.

He verified the date stamp. It was 20 May 1829, two days previous. He spread out the documents accompanying the letter, which he expected to be witness statements, affidavits and the like.

Johnson read the letter. It was interesting, rather different from the normal requests that required the courts to assist on some minor interpretation of law or inform the authorities in England of felons' crimes in the colony.

He read the letter again, reached for his quill and made notes. The Cork judiciary had conducted an inquiry into the conviction of a transported felon, Gerald Riordan. It suggested that the New South Wales courts might well decide there was enough evidence in his favour to hold a new trial. Or they might convene a committee to consider a pardon for Riordan. To this end, the Cork judiciary recommended that two other individuals who had come to the colony, one as a free man and the other as a convict, should be questioned in relation to the theft and murder for which Riordan was convicted. Johnson recorded three names in his notebook: Gerald Riordan, Convict Number 23420; Dougal Simpson, Convict Number 23631; and free settler Jacob Greenberg, Esq.

Reaching for a blank piece of paper, he requested to be given the whereabouts of these men. There would be no difficulty about locating the convicts, and in a place like this the free settler should also be easy to find. Whether the Cork authorities could expect to secure a pardon for Riordan at this huge distance from home was another matter. Johnson was sceptical at the worst, prudent at best. Sanding the request, he placed it in his 'out' tray and sighed.

* * *

James Donovan stood alongside the Cork Quay, revelling in the warm June sunshine. His good cheer heightened as Anne walked down the gangway from her ship. In the ten months she'd been away, she had grown prettier than ever. She had done well during her time in France and as she approached he thought he could see a new maturity in her face and posture. Please God she had used the time to grow away from Riordan. And if not, the letter in his pocket would banish Riordan from her mind once and for all.

'I'm very glad your daughter is safe home,' Sean Hughes said.

James Donovan smiled at the good-looking young man beside him. He had invited Hughes to accompany him because Colleen Donovan was unwell, and he wanted more than one person to welcome Anne home. He was nervous, too, about how she would greet him. Surely she would hesitate to demonstrate before others the resentment she'd shown when she left Cork?

Anne approached them and he went to embrace her but she held her reticule in front of her, her arms across her waist. Her face was cool, without emotion or affection. 'Hello, Father.' Still holding a grudge. He tried to hide the shock of it.

She smiled at Sean, though. 'Sean, you are looking well!'

'Thank you,' Sean said and smiled.

Anne turned to her father again, her eyes now full of concern. 'Where is Mother?'

His anger rose as though she had accused him of something, but he kept control. 'She's had a bout of influenza. It took its toll and she's resting. But she will be all right, dear. She's as fit as I am, really—or fitter.'

'I can't wait to see her.'

They walked to the carriage, where a smiling Chrissie got down and embraced her mistress.

Anne smiled at her maid. 'It's grand to see you.'

'Me too, miss.'

'It's good to be in Cork again,' Anne said as she settled into the carriage. Sean Hughes joined them, as James had intended. 'France was nice but home is home. And Sean, how is business?'

'We're trading satisfactorily, thank you. Orders are plentiful, partly thanks to your father's patronage. My brother Andrew has joined me in the management of the foundry; Father is fully retired now.'

'And is he well, and your mother?'

'As well as they can be, Anne, thank you.'

When they arrived at Donovan House, James wiped his brow. 'Let's get out of this sun and have some cool drinks. You'll stay for one, a quick one, Hughes?'

'If Anne permits me to.'

'Of course,' Anne replied and smiled at him.

Good start, Donovan thought. Give the man some time and Anne would be his.

Much later, after a perfect meal presided over by a happy Colleen, James told Anne he would like to talk to her in the study.

'Not now, James, surely,' said Colleen Donovan, giving him a quick shake of the head. He realised that the letter in his pocket would make Anne miserable and his wife unhappy for Anne's sake. No matter—best to get it over with.

'What about, Father?' Anne said.

'Come with me,' he said.

Anne followed him into the study and sat in front of him, her eyes wide in expectation. Donovan wasn't liking this. Bringing back the past, especially with his daughter, in this very room. But he had to do it.

'I've had word from New South Wales that Gerry Riordan is dead.'

Anne blinked. 'What?'

He stretched out a hand over the desk but she didn't take it. 'It's true.'

Anne's face blanched. 'Dead?' Her eyes glazed over, unseeing.

Donovan pulled out the letter. 'This is from the New South Wales authorities. Riordan contracted an illness on the transport to Sydney and survived only weeks in the colony.'

Her eyes closed just for a moment, then she snatched the letter and read it. She slumped back in her chair and the letter fell to the floor. 'Dead,' she said. 'I can't be-believe it.' She looked stunned, in a daze. 'Why is it addressed to me?'

'I can only imagine he gave your name and address to someone on board ship when he was … failing. They would have been passed on when the vessel reached Port Jackson.'

She stood up. 'It was *to me*,' she cried. 'And you opened it!'

'I could see where it was from. I had to.'

The way she looked unnerved him. A row of creases on her brow showed anger, not grief. Not yet. 'You're happy now, aren't you?' She brought a hand to her mouth. 'You're glad that he's gone.' She burst into sobs and ran out of the room.

James was retrieving the letter from the floor as his wife came in.

Colleen said, 'I asked you not to tell her like this. It might have been better coming from me. I understand a woman's love, at least. I'm not sure that you do.'

James let her walk out of the study without protest. Anne would recover, however painful her reaction and his wife's might be today. In the long run, Riordan's death was good news for them all. He looked out the window at the garden, where summer flowers basked in the heat and the world looked bright and cheerful. He sighed. Inside his grand house, his daughter's heart was breaking.

* * *

Anne walked in the shade of the trees along Cork's riverside, a path where she and Gerry had shared stolen moments. Her body felt numb and she was aware of her own movements only with reference to objects that she passed: a lamp post, a flowering shrub, a clump of manure. During the three weeks since she had known Gerry was dead, she had gone on with each day like an automaton. Sometimes she'd look around, wondering where she was or whom she was with, puzzled, looking at worried faces. On other occasions, she would be in a weird kind of dream and she would be hit by reality, by the letter that had come from the other side of the world to tell her that Gerry had died. An innocent man, punished, banished, dead.

A pebble pressed through her sole and she winced. Gerry was gone and there was no escape from that truth. To prove it once more, she pressed down against the sharp stone and opened her eyes at the July sun. Its blinding brilliance made her shut them again.

She had spent these three weeks in a state of unfeeling. No laughter and no tears. No excitement and no sorrow, just numbness. No appetite and no thirst, just nothing. Sleep when it came in the pre-dawn did not refresh her.

Her mother had wept with her on that day of the letter and so had Chrissie. Since then her mother had striven to comfort her, and both mother and maid had pleaded with her to eat more. Her dresses felt loose on her but Anne didn't care.

The morning after her walk by the waterside, she was eating breakfast when she realised her sense of taste had returned. The sugar on her porridge felt both sharp and sweet. Her spoon hovered over the steaming breakfast bowl and she glanced around at her family.

'Are you all right, dear?' her mother asked.

Anne's eardrum vibrated as though her mother had screamed at her. She hid her reaction and nodded. So her body was capable of sensation again.

She ate the rest of her breakfast in silence. It was painful, but perhaps this was a start, a gossamer link back to her life as she used to know it.

A week after that, Sean was sitting on a shady seat beside her in the garden. He was trying to interest her in an outing.

'I don't know,' Anne said. 'It's too soon.'

'We don't have to stay long,' he said. 'Just speak with some friends at the theatre, then we can leave if you don't want to see the performance.'

'Just for a while, then.' Anne could feel that her links to her life were firming, but she did not really want company. Yes, her taste had returned a week ago and other senses had started to function too. She responded to the feel of her satin bedspread, the fragrance of the roses, sounds from the street. These familiar things were helping her to cope.

But at the same time she knew there had been a massive change in her. She resented her father and resented being in her father's house. No, worse than that—she loathed them. This was the place where she had heard the shattering news that Gerry was gone from her life. This was the place where James Donovan had planned Gerry Riordan's downfall. This house, her father, would forever remind her that a great evil had gone unpunished. A man had been killed, his killer had gone scot free and her beloved had been falsely convicted and died in exile.

This place was overwhelming her. She turned to Sean, hoping to confide at least something of her turmoil. 'I ... I feel haunted here. I have this yearning to get away—from home, maybe even from Ireland.' She looked up into his startled face and tried to explain. 'I feel as if I'm failing Gerry by staying here. It might sound silly to you, but I feel as if I need to leave here and go somewhere else so I can pray for him, like the pilgrims of old. You know how they used to journey to a far-off place to expiate their sins?'

He said, 'I understand. But are you sure you could be happy, separating yourself from ... your mother, the household?' She noticed that he didn't mention her father and was glad of his tact.

She did not reply, just sat beside him, saddened that she could even think of leaving her mother, Chrissie, the peaceful life she had had in Cork. But then the sharp need surfaced again and took hold with a new power. Every brick and beam, every shop and shutter in this town reminded her that her love had died convicted of crimes that in all probability had involved her own father—and she had done nothing to prove her father's guilt.

Sean was looking at her now with anxiety. He was sweet. He cared about her, even though those very crimes had affected him, too. In his lovely dark hair, there were touches of grey, which were unusual in a man of thirty-two. Unusual strains, caused by her father, had come into his life, yet he remained loyal to her. She smiled to reassure him. His closeness was her only comfort now.

* * *

Sean sat beside his father in their parlour, thinking how much he had to be grateful for. After a long career of hard work and endeavour, Patrick Hughes stepped down from his business last year and allowed his two sons to run it. He was dedicated to their welfare and that applied to Sean's choice of a wife—Patrick had been outfoxed by James Donovan over the delivery of the gold doors last year, but he would not stand in the way of Sean's marrying Donovan's daughter. The banns had been read and the wedding set for 25 July, in ten days' time, and Patrick had told Sean more than once how happy it made him that his son's patience had won out.

Anne Donovan saw Sean as her protector and comforter, and Sean was not unwilling to play that role, because he hoped to bring her closer once they were married. But he wondered whether his father would be saddened by what he had also promised to do for and with Anne.

'So, what's the other thing you want to tell me?' Patrick Hughes said as he reached for a glass of lemon cordial. 'Your mother knows, I'm sure, but she insisted I talk to you about it. And how is Anne?'

'She's well. Fussing with the arrangements.'

'They are all the same,' his father said and smiled. 'You won't get much sense out of our womenfolk, or theirs, until the wedding is over. Have you chosen a place to live?'

Sean put a hand on his father's shoulder and hoped that the shock would not hit him too hard. 'We have. We're going to New South Wales.'

Patrick leaned towards him. 'South Wales? Just for a visit, surely. In summer, delightful. Which part?'

'No father, *New* South Wales. You see, we're going to emigrate. The business here—'

'Emigrate?' Patrick's eyes widened. 'Leave Ireland?'

'The foundry is solvent, father, but its debt is heavy. A debt that I caused through negligence.' His father's brow creased but Sean kept on. 'This house is mortgaged. That's not right. You shouldn't be burdened by debt at this stage of your life. That mortgage has to be lifted. But there's no chance we can repay it quickly, the way business is going in Cork.'

'Your mother and I have never said a word of complaint about this. We can live perfectly content with—'

'But Andrew and I have to think about the future.'

'Of course you do. And only last week, Sean, you got that ironwork contract for the new bridge.'

'Which will bring in a profit, yes, but it's modest. Even ten such contracts wouldn't see us right, and we'd risk mistakes in the work from having too many orders. We'd have to employ more people; therefore our costs would rise and our profits would be reduced. We can't get large amounts to pay off the loan's principal and interest. We're paying six per cent on our loan of eighteen hundred. That's two hundred and forty-four pounds a year for ten years. We only just made the first year's payment.' He paused. 'The colonies are the only hope, with me taking advantage of the opportunities abroad and Andrew holding the fort here.'

'But surely you wouldn't think of New South Wales? Why go that far?'

'I've corresponded with merchants in New South Wales, reputable firms. The demand for forged metals is growing at a rate that's not possible here. Wagon axles and tools especially. I can get our debt paid off in two years.'

Patrick sat back, amazed.

'Yes,' Sean said, 'that quickly.'

'You're not just believing that to be true?' Patrick said.

'I've got the figures in my office. I can show you.'

His father looked at him for some time then shook his head in defeat. 'If you say so.'

'The debt can be paid off and your house will be unencumbered.'

There were other reasons for him to leave Cork, that he would not share with his father. There was every probability that James Donovan was linked to the crimes for which Riordan had been convicted. If Sean and his wife stayed in Cork, their lives would be spent in Donovan's shadow and they would each carry a burden of guilt and anger, knowing all along that the master stonemason was escaping justice because they could not bring themselves to speak out against him. They each needed a new life.

But enough of that. 'We have a fine manager here; Andrew is very able.'

Patrick said, 'The business is sound and we'll manage, I suppose. But for you to emigrate, with all your abilities. Goodness gracious, to think of leaving your home!'

'New South Wales offers great things, Father. I hope you'll be no less proud of me while I'm there.'

Patrick's eyes glistened and, self-conscious, he coughed and frowned. 'All that way. How many years will it take to get yourself established? And the length of time to correspond—it's daunting. To send a letter and get a reply can take a year or more.'

'I hope the time will go quickly at both ends.' Sean tried to smile. 'There'll be many a piece of good news to impart.' His father had a look Sean knew only too well. Patrick Hughes was not one to believe false encouragement. 'We'll write often. I mean it.'

His father tried to rally. 'So will we. But tell me, what does Anne Donovan think about you both packing up and leaving us all behind?'

Sean hesitated. How to explain that Anne was desperate for him to help her escape? That the shelter he could give her was one of the reasons that she had agreed to marry him? 'She's accepted it with good will and courage.'

Patrick nodded. 'I have a question that may sound intrusive but I must ask it. Your mother and I have only your happiness in mind, so you'll forgive me. Is she over that convict?'

'I think so, Father. She mourned him for a while, and I can understand that. She was fond of him and she thinks he died because of the injustice that was done him. The short time I knew him, I thought him honest and honourable.'

'From that point of view, it's a tragic story.' His father paused. 'Still, I've seen you two together. There's a peace in your presence and Anne's affectionate to you. And when she gets to Sydney and sees the rabble they call society there—I can only imagine she'll be glad to be married to you and free of the likes of him.'

Sean had no reply to this. He often came close to a guilty relief that he no longer had a rival standing between himself and Anne. He just said, 'I love her, Father.'

'I know you do.'

'And I'll make her a good husband.'

Patrick grinned. 'Wouldn't be a Hughes otherwise!'

Sean pulled out his fob watch. 'I should go. I have to complete the paperwork for our departure.'

Patrick pushed himself up and hugged his son. Sean felt like a boy again, as though his father were a strapping foundry worker once more. Their bond was strong and Sean warmed to its security and love. It might be the last time he held his father so.

* * *

Anne and Sean were in the public area of the Cork Emigration Department. 'A test, yes?' Sean asked.

Anne glanced at him and smiled. Yes, it was, of that wish to leave that had drawn her closer to Sean. On the other hand, signing the documents would dispatch her to another part of the globe—into Gerry's world. But that thought led nowhere, because Gerry was dead. 'Give me the quill.'

They initialled each page. Sean collected them and took them to the counter.

He was a good man and marriage to him would be … acceptable. Gerry's death had changed her. The shock of his loss had pitched her to another place, as if she'd been dropped on the dark side of the moon. But now she could live in that darkness, because it was lit in patches by Sean's friendship and a love that she believed in but could not quite return.

She'd grown up, now she was to marry, and she would receive an extra boon: separation from her father.

'All done,' Sean said, coming back. 'Here's our certificates. We've time to get to the shipping company if we hurry.'

'Will it take long?' She smiled. 'It's such a lovely day. I thought we might spend the rest of the afternoon by the river. Like last week.'

He smiled at her enthusiasm. 'Can we get our tickets first?'

She pressed his hand. 'All right.' They made their way to a cab. Inside, under the canopy and out of sight of people on the street, he kissed her. It was sudden and exciting. As another vehicle passed close by, they separated, then looked at each other and laughed like conspirators.

He squeezed her hand and pulled her to him again.

* * *

On a chilly morning in late August, Gerry Riordan was busy on part of the Devine's Hill line of the Road, well north of the river. This section of road lay between two hills and required stone cut from the defile to be used in retaining walls on each side. Despite the coolness, he had to wipe sweat off his face. 'More stone here!' he called. Standing on the scaffolding, he checked his last course of this section of wall, which was half built. When at full height, it would retain the fill taken from a spur that they'd levelled some hundred yards back.

Road making like this was simple in principle. Ideally the new highway had to go in a straight direction and on an even level, meaning that any hills and valleys in its path had to be surveyed and reformed to plan. The tops and/or sides of the hills were cut by hand and by blasting, to allow the new road to go through. Then the excavated spoil, pulled by bullock teams, was hauled up the road to fill in any hollows. Meanwhile blocks of stone were cut to retain the surface and the sides of the Road, so spoil would not slip away. Drains were created to allow free fall of the valleys' natural watercourses and prevent damage to the walls, which at Devine's Hill would be supported by immense stone buttresses.

Gerry and his party were creating culverts in the newly laid stone, placing keystones and arches through which water would drain. Laying stone at the bottom of each course was a less complicated task, and it was going on at pace. Just about a mile up the trail, where the Devine's Hill line would run, work was nearing completion on a stone-walled stockade for accommodation and storage. It would be a welcome shelter, compared with the tents and huts they'd lived in up until now.

A bullock team brought up a load of tools, and Fergus Dooley jumped from the wagon. 'Hola, Tiny, how goes it?'

Gerry grinned down at him, liking the nickname and getting used to it. 'Come up,' he said. Dooley climbed the ladder and joined him. They watched as four convicts started to empty the wagon. 'We've got a bit to do, to finish this by the end of the month,' Gerry said.

'You'd better get a hurry on, then. Lieutenant Dodds wants you at Ten Mile Hollow. I've been looking for timber for the bridge there.'

Ten Mile Hollow was a new section of the Road being built about six miles northeast of them. 'How's the stockade coming?' Gerry said.

'Just the ticket. I fixed the last door on the last hut this morning.'

'Grand.' They stood in silence, until an explosion about half a mile from them sent a flock of lorikeets shooting into the clear sky. 'They seem to be blasting a lot more,' Gerry said.

'Have to. Dodds says we're behind.'

Gerry's keen eyes returned to the work of his team, some of whom were preparing cut stones, while others built more scaffolding.

Dooley looked down, too. 'I'll help the lads.' He went back down the ladder. Gerry returned to work. His leg irons were gone and he was grateful. This leniency wasn't for good behaviour; it was to keep him alive. A month before, two skilled convicts working in irons had fallen from a height while working on the Road. One had died and the other was injured and not yet back to work. Their loss was felt. So, off had come the shackles.

Selecting a square-sized stone, Gerry started another course, aligning the block and levelling it. He repeated the process with a stone at the other end of the new course, then he ran a string line from it to the first stone. Now to lay the infill blocks. All this work he liked, and it replaced his dark moods and tormented thoughts of Anne. He still had a trade he was at home with, and he was glad of the concentration it required.

The wagon was half unloaded when Dooley waved to him.

'Overseer,' a labourer beside him said in a quiet voice.

Gerry looked away and kept working. He heard Dodds's horse come to a halt below, then the man dismounted and climbed the scaffolding.

'Looking good, Riordan,' he said as he stood beside Gerry. Gerry nodded and kept working. 'I want you to start to think about more than just laying stone. I want you to start thinking as a leader.' He thrust a paper at Gerry. 'Look here. You'll read this list, and tell me if anything else needs to be added to it.'

Gerry read the document while Dodds opened a survey drawing he had in his satchel. He was perplexed. Why see him as a leader? He had an intuition about the general needs of a work party, but that was it. No responsibility, no demands—that was what he aimed for. But he looked at the list, since he was ordered to: two barrels of gun powder, axle grease, one barrel, three by hundred feet ropes, three new frocks and two caps. It all looked right. 'I think that's about it.' He handed the paper back to the lieutenant then had a thought. 'What about four more spades, four shovels and two road picks.'

'Thank you.' Dodds added them to his list. 'Now, I'm off to Ten Mile Hollow.'

'Right, sir.' Gerry paused with his chisel as the lieutenant rode away. A good organiser, that officer, but he was an odd one. Whomever he might be speaking to, convict or civilian, he'd been known to quote daft things from books or plays that he'd read. At first the men thought he might be a dolly, but he was just strange in other ways. It turned out that he might be as fond of women as the next man. Fergus Dooley said he'd once got a glance at a locket that Dodds carried with him, and it contained the picture of a girl. Someone else said they'd heard he'd left a sweetheart behind in Bath, England.

So Gerry couldn't fathom why Dodds took any interest in him at all. If the man liked girls, why was he always trying to talk to Gerry? They were on the same piece of road, but worlds apart. Tapping a stone into place, Gerry thought about the next course to lay.

* * *

Deirdre Walsh moved a branch aside and glanced back at Wiseman's settlement. In the damp shade of a late winter morning, she and her companion were out of sight now. Lieutenant Derrick Bates took her hand, drew her close and kissed her. She responded as the lieutenant pressed himself against her. In her mind, the tall, red-headed convict was holding her, and she gave in to the fantasy. It was the stonemason's eyes and hair, his voice and boyish smile that added another layer of pleasure in her. It was his lips on hers. But Bates began tracing the underside of her breast with his thumb and she disengaged. She frowned at him and ran a hand through her hair.

'Deirdre?'

'I'm not a tavern moll, Derrick. Have some respect.'

He looked red-faced at her. 'Of course you're not! But you gave me signals.'

'I gave you nothing of the sort. Now, what's the news?' She sat on a log, bringing her shawl close about her. 'Here, sit with me.'

'I'll stand if you don't mind.' He paused, awkward, then said in a rush, 'The regiment's being recalled to Sydney soon.'

'Oh?' she said, startled and just a bit regretful.

'It looks as though it will be posted to New Zealand.'

'Oh! For how long?'

'At least a year. We leave on the ninth of September. So this is the last time I can see you. That's why my C.O. gave me permission to come today.' Derrick was watching her, studying her reaction.

She was not sure how she felt—it was all too sudden.

He leaned forward, took her hand and looked deep into her eyes. 'I want you to marry me.'

Deirdre pressed his hand with the thrill of it. Her first proposal, on 26 August 1829. She would always remember it. It gave her a wonderful feeling but it required a quick strategy. 'You're sweet, Derrick and I like you. But I'm not allowed to say yes to anyone, you know. I'm not yet of an age to marry. Father is bound to disapprove.'

Derrick said, 'But if he did approve, would you wait for me?'

She thought quickly and tried to look demure. 'You'll have to ask him.'

Derrick jumped up. 'I'll do it now.'

She held onto his hand to restrain him. 'No, he's away—he won't be back until tomorrow.'

The light died from Derrick's eyes as he told her what she already knew: 'I have to get back to Windsor tonight.'

She smiled. 'There'll be another time.'

'No there won't, not for at least a year! Deirdre, I can't go without an answer. Will you consent to marry me one day, yes or no?'

'Take me on a ride and we'll talk about it.'

'Grand,' he said, 'but … is that all right with your parents?'

'They trust you to act like a gentleman and so do I. Besides, I have the post to hand over to Lieutenant Dodds, up at Devine's. Wait here and I'll get my horse.'

She walked off to the stables. She looked forward to the rest of the day. She could prolong the pleasure of being escorted by an admirer who wanted to marry her, and maybe she could see Riordan, again, who had not minded being near her that day when Dodds had him load up stores at the inn.

* * *

Next morning during the work break, Gerry drank the last of his tea, the tin mug seeping heat through his chilled fingers. It would be spring soon, September. He smiled to himself, realising he'd welcome the sun's heat.

Dodds approached. 'What's got you good humoured this frosty morning?'

'D-didn't think, sir, I'd be wanting the sun as much as I do.'

Dodds smiled. '"But hope of orphans and unfather'd fruit; For summer and his pleasures wait on thee."'

Gerry shook his head at his overseer. Always quoting some poet.

'Have you memorised those words I gave you?' Dodds said.

Dodds had told Gerry to familiarise himself with ten surveying words that he hadn't heard before. He flung his tea dregs onto the fire. 'I have, sir.'

'Good,' Dodds said, and removed a piece of paper from his satchel. 'Here's ten more and their meanings.'

Gerry took it and read out, 'Azimuth, Magnetic, Reduced Level …'

'I'll test you in seven days.' Dodds paused and looked out onto the bush. 'I once helped another man who wanted to learn. His name was Abel Alistair Borthwick.'

That must be the lad whom Dodds had mentioned before. Gerry said. 'What was he like, sir?'

'About five feet four, stocky, with dark hair.' Dodds smiled. 'A bit like you.' Gerry grinned. Dodds became serious and looked up the trail ahead. 'He was innocent too, so he said, and full of anger and bitterness. He was a carpenter and his work was good, damned good. He was humble enough to see he had a way to go, and he should have been planning for his future.' Dodds gave Gerry a bleak look. 'But he was stubborn about that. I failed him.'

There was a pause that Gerry did not know how to fill.

'Enough of this,' Dodds said. 'Now, get Dooley and Murphy down here. I'll be based at Ten Mile Hollow for three days and I want to talk about the work to be done here while I'm gone.'

Gerry set off up the track to where the timber was being milled. At times Dodds was irritating, the way he carried on, like a mosquito at dawn. At others, Dodds impressed him, with his grasp of road and bridge building. Dodds's talk about the convict Borthwick puzzled Gerry a little. How had Dodds failed him? Maybe he'd hear that someday. Maybe.

There was the tearing sound of a two-handed saw that got louder as he approached. He waved to the two carpenters, who downed the big saw and came to him. 'Mr Dodds wants you now!'

Murphy punched him on the arm, but with no force. 'And what does your pal want with the likes of us?'

'He's not my friend,' Gerry said.

'What say, Dooley? Is he a friend to Tiny here or not?'

Fergus Dooley wiped his forehead and glanced at Gerry, who stood with hands clenched and his face menacing. 'Unless you want Tiny's knuckles to remove a few of your remaining teeth,' Dooley said, 'I'd keep quiet.'

Gerry couldn't help smiling. The three walked back down the track to where Dodds awaited them.

* * *

As Deirdre and Lieutenant Bates approached the roadworks, Deirdre spotted three convicts, fifty yards off, walking together towards the spot where scaffolding was built against new work. She recognised Riordan at once and her anticipation heightened. As she and Bates came up to them, the three stepped aside. The others kept their heads down, but Riordan looked up and she caught his eye. She gave him a quick nod, which was all she could do as a civilian riding by, escorted by one lieutenant to meet another.

His gaze flicked over her and Bates, then he lowered his head. There was no smile for her, and she hadn't given him one, but nonetheless she was disappointed. She urged her horse up to the new stonework and Bates followed.

She came to a halt at the foot of the scaffolding and looked up. 'Lieutenant Dodds? I have some mail for you.'

The overseer leaned over a rail above and doffed his hat to her. 'Miss Walsh, a pleasure. But we could've collected that this morning and saved you the trouble.'

'No trouble at all,' she said dismounting. She looked up to see Dodds still looking down at her. 'Lieutenant Dodds, this is Lieutenant Bates.'

'Dodds,' Bates said, touched his hat and dismounted.

'I'll be down in a moment,' Dodds said, and began his descent.

Deirdre undid the flap of her saddlebag and took out the bundle of mail. 'Lieutenant,' she said, 'could you tether the horses, please?'

He led the horses off, heading for a tree about twenty yards away, which had survived the road-clearing cull.

Deirdre stayed where she was, watching Dodds climb down to ground level. The three convicts stood at the foot of the scaffolding, waiting for him. As soon as he got to the ground he gave them orders. This was to get them out of the way so he could talk to Deirdre, but it frustrated her to come so near Gerry and not be able to speak to him. He was only a few paces away, avoiding her eye.

Dodds gave Deirdre an apologetic nod. 'Excuse me for a minute or two, Miss Walsh, while these men do what I've summoned them for.' He turned at once to the convicts. 'Riordan, wait here for now. Dooley and Murphy, there's a pile of timber just been brought up. I need eight ledgers, ten by four and ten feet long, and you'll stack them here as soon as you can. Come, I'll show you where they are.'

To Deirdre's relief, Dodds led the other men away. A glance over her shoulder told her that Bates was still out of earshot. When she glanced back, sure enough Riordan was looking at her, with the beginnings of a smile.

She smiled back. 'How are you?'

The smile disappeared. 'What?'

Affronted, she snapped, 'I said, how are you. Are you deaf?'

He went red. 'N-no I'm not deaf.' Looking nervous, he whispered, 'You can't talk to me here.'

Lieutenant Dodds was coming back to rejoin her, and so was Lieutenant Bates. As they came up, Riordan stepped away to a respectful distance. She felt self-conscious and annoyed.

'Here's your mail,' she said to Dodds, and handed it over.

'Thank you.' Dodds took the post.

Deirdre regathered her composure. Today's exchange with Riordan had begun badly but she had plans to see more of him soon at the inn, and she was not going to give them up.

She said to Dodds, 'I wish there was a stonemason who could work at the inn for my mother. She's dissatisfied with the hearthstone of the big fireplace in the bar area. But there's no one skilled enough to lay her a new one or fix the one we've got.' She pointed to the finished retaining walls further back along the Road. 'While I'm here, I'd like to see your men's work up close, without the scaffolding. Could you show me?'

'That's coursed masonry,' Dodds said, 'on a bigger scale than your hearthstone, Miss Walsh. But you're very welcome to inspect it.'

'Thank you. Unless I'm taking you from your duties?'

'My duty at the moment, Miss Walsh, is to rustle up some tea to offer you and the lieutenant. Convict Riordan here can show you the masonry. Riordan, accompany the young lady to see the stonework you've just finished.' He gave Deirdre a little bow, 'And I'll put the kettle on the campfire, Miss Walsh.'

Riordan came to attention. 'Yes, sir.'

But Bates frowned. Ignoring both herself and Riordan, he said to Dodds, 'Wait up. Is she safe with him?'

Dodds looked amused. 'Riordan is trustworthy, and what's more will be under your eye and mine at all times. Come, Lieutenant, and see how we make our tea on the Road.' Bates looked reluctant, but Dodds gave Deirdre another amused nod and strode away towards the campfire.

Deirdre said to Derrick Bates, 'I'll be with you in a few minutes, Lieutenant,' and he gave a reluctant nod and went off to join Dodds. Was Dodds amused and Bates jealous about her being with Riordan because they had both sensed her interest in him? She shrugged. What did that matter? She had got her way and was alone with him.

They walked down the road without saying anything, both perhaps a bit too aware of the army officers observing them from behind.

He stopped and pointed to the retaining wall that rose above them, the clean golden surfaces of the squared stones streaked with random patterns in dark red, brown, even purple. He turned to her. 'This is sandstone, straight-faced work. It's too soft for a hearthstone. What you'd need is granite.'

'So you're a stonemason, trained?' He nodded and she sensed a confidence in him that she hadn't noticed before. She smiled. 'Are you a good one?'

He folded his arms. 'I think so. Please have a look for yourself.'

She had to pass him to examine the new work and she was aware of his musky, male smell, not unpleasant. 'What were you convicted for?'

He started. 'That's nowt to do with the wall!'

'I want to know.'

'Why?'

Because I'm alone with the convict—shouldn't I know what crimes he's committed? She did not feel fear, however, as she looked up at him. She saw vivid primary colours: reddish hair, sun-flecked face, blue eyes that held questions about her that he wouldn't voice. All she said was, 'I'm curious.'

'I can tell you about this st-stone. It all comes from round here. We sh-shape the blocks—'

'Have you always stuttered?'

'Aye,' he replied but not in anger. Perhaps it made a change for him, having someone betray interest in him. 'What else do you want to know?'

She took a glance at the other men around them. The carpenters were busy and Derrick and Dodds were chatting over their tea. All occupied. 'Show me the joints.' She stood even closer to the wall,

Riordan at her side. 'Oh. There's no mortar here to hold the blocks together.'

'No. All stones are dry laid. The lieutenant says they can't afford the mud.'

She nodded. 'Your name's Gerry, right?'

His eyes widened. Now he knew she'd asked about him. He nodded.

'Well, Gerry, from what I've seen, I think you'd be suitable for the job that needs doing at the inn.'

Lieutenant Bates's strong voice reached them from the campfire. 'Miss Walsh, I'm afraid it's time we were getting back.'

She and Gerry Riordan turned from the wall at the same time and picked their way back up the road. Derrick Bates was on his feet and striding towards her. She said to Gerry, 'When do you come to the inn next?'

'When Lieutenant Dodds says so.'

'I'm going to ask if you can be the stonemason that does the hearthstone.'

'Why me?'

Was he fishing for a compliment about his person or his work? She smiled to herself and told a small lie. 'Mr Dodds said you're the best.'

He nodded.

When Bates got to them he addressed Deirdre at once. 'Are you all right?'

'Surely,' Deirdre said. 'I like what I've seen.' She glanced at Gerry. 'Thank you.'

She took Derrick's arm and Gerry fell back to walk behind them. When they reached Dodds, he said, 'Miss Walsh, you've missed out on a cup of tea. Shall I—?'

Derrick Bates interrupted. 'I'll get the horses,' he said, and strode off.

Deirdre said, 'Thank you, Mr Dodds, but I don't have time to linger. The lieutenant has to ride to Windsor this afternoon.'

'Meanwhile, what can we do about the hearthstone that so worries your mother? We can't have you lacking a stonemason when there are so many in your vicinity! May I suggest Riordan for the job?'

'Oh, that would be perfect,' she replied.

Dodds's smile was polite but she wondered whether there was some innuendo in what he said next. 'Good then, Riordan's your man. Ask your parents to send me a note about exactly what's needed— stone, dimensions and so on—or better still I'll try to check that out myself. Then I'll make Riordan available whenever he's needed.'

Bates came up at that moment and Deirdre gave Dodds her thanks and said farewell before they mounted up. Both men ignored Gerry Riordan, who stood a few paces away, his gaze on his boots. She tried to signal a farewell to him, too, but he did not look up.

Once she and Derrick were out of the others' hearing he said, 'You took a risk there, being alone with a convict. There's no knowing what that sort of man is capable of.'

'Derrick, I'm not some fine and fragile lady like those you'd meet in Sydney. I've grown up at Wiseman's, surrounded by all sorts and with many a convict passing through. I don't want you to worry about me. I have a kind of instinct about who might do me harm and who will not, and I give no quarter to those I don't approve of, I can tell you.' He still looked troubled, so she gave him a big smile. 'Thank you, though, for wanting to protect me. I do appreciate that, I really do.'

'I'd like to protect you for life.' She felt herself colouring and looked away. He took her silence as encouragement. 'You know how much I care for you, Deirdre. With your parents' consent, will you promise to marry me when I return from this tour of duty?'

'What, promise now? You want us to be engaged? But you'll be gone a year!'

'I know that sounds like a long engagement, but I can't bear to leave without being sure of you. I love you, Deirdre.'

She couldn't help feeling a thrill at this declaration but she couldn't say the same words back to him—not yet, at any rate. Her confusion kept her silent. Then she felt she owed him an answer—but how to tell him that she wanted to hold onto her sense of freedom for at least another year or two? 'Derrick, I'm seventeen, an only daughter, and my mother and father have talked about these things with me so I know what they think. They're practical. My mother has always said I'm most likely to marry a soldier or a sailor and I won't say I wouldn't be happy with a soldier.' Derrick gave her a bright glance at this, and she hurried on. 'But one thing my father always says is, no one in the military should make a woman his wife before he goes to war, or on a voyage, or on a campaign. It's too much to ask of them both.'

Derrick leaned towards her, his voice urgent. 'I don't say marry now—you're only seventeen. All I—'

'And nor,' Deirdre said, 'should such a man enter into an engagement. It's not right. My father would never say yes to it. I'm sorry.'

He did not reply and for a while her own words sounded so mean and cruel that she couldn't bear to look at him. Then she did, and she could tell from his grim profile that he was mortified.

He said in a stifled voice, 'You are saying you wouldn't wait for me? There's someone else?'

'No!' It was the truth—Riordan was just a fancy, an unknown, not a rival to this good man who'd just proposed. 'I'm not saying I won't wait. Derrick, in a year's time I'll still be at the inn, and I won't have married anyone else in the meantime, I promise! Come, smile at me and say you understand me.'

He gave her a look of amazement and joy. 'You'll wait? So you're willing to be engaged to me but … unofficially?'

'If you like.' She laughed at his expression and he beamed in return.

There, that was it. She was pledged, but free. She had security, but she could be daring as well. Who knew what excitement the next year would bring?

Now to convince her mother that the big hearth in their bar room needed rebuilding.

* * *

Dodds was telling them what had to be done over the next three days but Gerry wasn't listening, thinking only of what had just happened. Deirdre Walsh had got into his head, the first woman since he'd lost Anne. His Faith and his love for Anne had stopped him from ending his life, but that life had offered no highs or lows. Up until now he'd accepted a blank existence, not wanting to feel or think.

Dodds was droning on, something about props and pressure. Dodds irritated him and that very irritation jolted the dusty and unused parts of him into unaccustomed reaction. Dodds made him *think*, made him want to learn. Whereas he preferred a blank equilibrium, with bright hopes or dark moods kept at each extreme. The kind of equilibrium that showed up on the fancy level he'd had back in Cork, where the bubble in the liquid needed to be in the middle of the glass. Day to day as a labourer he'd worked like the big creatures in the bullock teams, reacting only when prodded, ordered about, fed, unshackled and abandoned to sleep—that was all his life had amounted to. Then Dodds had come along and got him laying stone again.

And now a woman was trying to get close to him.

'Your thoughts, Riordan?' Dodds said, and Dooley and Murphy smirked. 'Forget Miss Walsh. We're talking about timber. Now, what would you do?'

'Sorry, sir. I wasn't li-listening.'

'Then listen now. In three days, this section of wall must be completed and reinforced with the ledgers. Dooley and Murphy will tell you what you've missed while your mind was wandering. Now, back to work. It's winter, in case you've forgotten, and the sun sets early. Get stuck in and keep out of mischief.'

Gerry watched him ride away.

'Come on, Tiny,' Dooley said, 'and we'll show you what we've measured so far.'

He joined them. Deirdre Walsh wanted to see him again. Madness. Kicking a pebble, he concentrated on forcing his 'bubble' back to the middle for the day. Tonight was another matter—he had no control over his dreams. And he couldn't end his life in a dream, so he was safe from the eternal fire.

Chapter Seven

The Devine's Hill section of Road was making progress. All parties on it were challenged by the immensity of the tasks required to build in such novel surroundings. Many new methods had to be introduced. New methods giving rise to doubt, risk and frayed tempers. One man in uniform suffered the same challenges.

Derrick Bates rode hard away from Wiseman's, anxious to get to Windsor before dark. Deirdre would wait until he returned from New Zealand and that pleased him. What didn't was her apparent interest in Convict Riordan. Dodds had been negligent this morning, letting her walk off with the felon alone. Riordan could've secreted a weapon or even a tool and done Deirdre harm. Stupidity, rank stupidity, and he would make his concern felt to the authorities in Sydney. Oh, yes, he would. Let's see how long the big-nosed overseer would last then! Anxious Bates had been, when she'd gone with the stonemason, then angry when she seemed interested in the convict's work. Presumption, for the man to talk to her at all! Bates dug his spurs in, feeling better as the horse responded. He hadn't remonstrated with her for being so casual with convicts; all his hidden anger was for Riordan.

A rider approached and he recognised Sergeant Morgan, the scourger.

Morgan pulled up to him and saluted. 'Sir.'

'How are you, Morgan? Back to work?'

'Scum always need me, sir.' The man grinned, exposing yellow teeth. 'Been visiting the Inn?' The scourger knew of his interest in Deirdre.

'I have and works on the Road.'

'And how are my yellow beavers? Behaving themselves?'

Bates was about to give a simple reply and ride on, then he had a thought. Riordan needed a lesson in manners. 'Mr Dodds seems to give your convicts a lot of grace.'

'How so, sir?'

'By letting Miss Walsh in among them, that's what.'

Morgan's scar widened as if it would split his face. 'Is she harmed?' he growled. 'I'll kill any man who touches her.'

'She is unharmed, Sergeant, but it could've been a tragedy. She was left unattended with a convict called Riordan.'

Morgan's horse jerked and he held it firm. 'Top scum, Riordan, eh.'

'He was talking freely to her, without a man near for protection.' Morgan turned his horse and stared up the road to the inn. Bates sensed he'd sown enough seeds to yield a bumper crop. 'I take my leave, Sergeant,' he said. 'You won't see me for some time. My company sails soon and when I'm in Sydney I'll report to the army about that overseer's lax discipline.'

Morgan saluted and trotted off. Bates smiled. Riordan's back would hurt for a week and justifiably so.

* * *

The morning following Miss Walsh's visit was damp and cold and the convicts were huddled around the campfire.

'Morgan's back,' Dooley said. 'With Dodds away, his whip will get an airing.'

A growl came from the group and Gerry said, 'No overseer, just the scourger?'

'That's it, so keep your head down.'

Gerry nodded. Just stay quiet and lay stone and he'd be all right. He washed his mess kit ready to leave.

They went up to their site and split into groups. Gerry was separated from his carpenters, and the labourers were a hundred yards ahead doing the earth filling. He had enough cut stones ready and worked alone on the completion of the second culvert. It was a specialist job. He finished the keystone and when the weak sun was close to noon he sat down, wiping the sweat from him. No sign of Morgan, so he pulled out the list of surveying terms that Dodds had given him. With a carpenter's pencil he wrote down on the back of the paper the first five that he'd memorised. Checking his list again he started to memorise the next two.

The noise and the sting shocked him: a leather thong cracked, ripped out a piece of flesh on his neck, and he jumped up.

'No time for sitting down, scum. Get down here.'

Gerry's paper glided to the ground. Morgan glanced at it then back to him. Gerry pressed a hand against his neck to stem the bleeding.

'Loafing on your fat Catholic arse at the governor's expense. The reports were right! You're well up yourself, scum.'

Gerry counted to five. Morgan's eyes glittered like the embers of this morning's fire. *Just him and me.* The scourger's horse was tethered fifty yards away. The bastard had skulked up here on foot to spy on him.

'You need a lesson and I need some exercise.' Morgan walked towards him, the paper lying between them. Morgan glanced at it. 'What's this? An escape map?' He kept his eyes on Gerry, felt for it, picked it up and read it. 'Ha, 'tis a surveyor's list, that's what 'tis. Where did you get it, my lanky beaver?'

Gerry pressed his sticky neck, the pain rising with his resentment. 'It's mine.'

'Yours? Well then, there you have it, ambition from a convict no less. You know that's commendable but when you're being fed at the His Majesty's pleasure and provided good work, you must be grateful, not steal time. Words? Words are for free men and gentlemen, my beaver.' He cracked his whip, catching the toe of Gerry's boot, making him jump. 'For learned people, for quality.' He cracked again, this time on Gerry's shoulders, the sting throbbing. 'Not for steaming turds in canary clothes.' Morgan flung the paper away. 'Come with me.'

Gerry had little choice. Help was too far away. And he wouldn't attack the man. That offence would hang him and inviting that would be suicide.

Morgan pushed him to the scaffolding. 'Strip off your shirt and take a grip.'

Gerry held the posts supporting the timberwork and the scourger walked away.

'Another thing,' Morgan said. 'Quite the dandy beaver you are too. Courting the local Miss— Ah, and you've seen the cat before. Fine looking scars, those.'

How did he know about Miss—?

Crack. The force and pain of the cut made Gerry collapse.

'Get up! You poxed excuse for a stone layer.'

Gerry stood and gripped the posts again. Another lash thudded, then another. Think … one of the lads must have talked … crack … Gerry staggered, the blood now in short sharp rivulets down his spine. He counted the next twenty lashes, gore tracking down his back and his legs, agony that was unbearable. Twenty-one and his eyes faded and blackness came.

Cold water shocked him to consciousness. He was face down in the dirt.

'Get him standing.' Gerry heard Morgan say. Firm hands each side gripped him and raised him up. Not more, God please no. The voice went on. 'Clean him up and get him back to work. I'll be back later. I want that wall finished. Otherwise, my learned scholar, you'll get more of my precious python.'

Hoof beats faded and Gerry whispered. 'He's gone?'

'Tiny, it's just me, Francis Murphy. Dooley is going for more water. Lucky we came back, 'cause we finished early. That bastard would've killed you.'

Gerry blacked out again.

* * *

Sergeant Morgan faced an angry Lieutenant Dodds but he wasn't worried. He hadn't exceeded his authority by punishing Riordan, and he'd dealt with angry officers for all of his career.

'He was my best mason,' Dodds said. 'Now, Sergeant Morgan, we're behind two days on Devine's Hill.' Dodds eyeballed him and Morgan was impressed. The lightweight poet was having a go.

'He broke the rules, sir.'

'The rules?' Dodds said.

'Two, sir. The first, no intercourse with locals and the second, no wilful disobedience.'

Dodds snapped, 'Explain how Riordan violated them.'

'Sir! Convict Riordan consorted with Miss Walsh who—'

'Whom I gave permission to.'

'I wasn't there for that, sir, but rules is rules. If all the other scum … convicts, saw the breach there'd be a breakdown in discipline, sir.'

'Damn it man! I was there. It was my responsibility.'

'Like I said, sir, I wasn't present. If you were going to do a thing like that, sir, then you should've told me.'

Dodds moved closer to him. 'I'm in charge of that work gang, Sergeant. I take responsibility for them.' He shook his head. 'Now, the second transgression?'

'Disobedience. Going against your orders. Convict was loafing sir, not working.' He smirked. 'Learnin' himself, sir, he was.'

'What?'

'Yes, sir. Tryin' to learn some words … words you'd use on the survey.'

Dodds didn't look surprised. 'Are you certain? He was reading on the job?'

'Sitting down with the paper in his hand, sir, large as life. Then on top of that he wilfully disobeyed me.'

'How?'

'When I told him to get back and lay stone, he did nothing.'

'Who else was there on the work site, Sergeant?'

'Just the two of us, sir.'

'So, there's no one to corroborate your account of the incident.'

Morgan clenched his fists but controlled himself. Dodds was always keen on Riordan. 'Are you saying, sir, that I'm lying?'

'What I'm saying, *Sergeant* Morgan, is that regulations require you to conduct punishment on Saturdays only. In extreme circumstances you may do so on other days, in the company of an overseer. But this incident happened on a Thursday and I was absent.'

'Yes you were, sir, so I was on me own. Breaking rules leads to breakdown of discipline. Riordan's disobedience was extreme, so I had to act. Make an example of him.'

'Your actions were unjustified, Sergeant, and against regulations. If you repeat this, or anything like it, I'll be reporting you to command in Sydney.'

Morgan relaxed. No problem. This was a reprimand, not a punishment. And if Dodds squealed to the army, Morgan could call on Bates to tell them how slack the man had been over letting Riordan near Deirdre Walsh. He'd cop the lieutenant's blast of anger without further argument. 'Very good, sir.'

'Now, get back and do your job and keep that whip coiled. You hear me?'

'Sir!'

As Gerry lay in the hut after the thrashing, the pain was worse than that caused by the 'cat' in Sydney town, because the scourger's whip was thicker. Besides flaying skin and muscles it had exposed a rib, and the visiting assistant surgeon at first wanted Gerry moved to Windsor. But he was in no condition for the journey, so for the next two days he lay in a quiet, cool hut in the empty stockade, on his stomach, with his head positioned to allow him to breathe. It was just bearable with the laudanum but there was no one to help him keep the flies away. They kept landing on his dressings and on the skin between.

Footsteps padded in on the earthen floor. He swivelled his eyes to see Dodds standing near the palliasse. The lieutenant said, 'I heard what happened from Sergeant Morgan. What's your version?'

'Bastard had no excuse for this, sir.' There was no response and Gerry continued, 'I was having a spell, wr-writing words, sir, that's all. He whipped me for that.'

'Did you do anything else to give him cause?'

'No, sir.'

'So you obeyed him when he ordered you back to work?'

'I did … sir.'

'You're sure?'

'I am,' Gerry said.

A moment's pause. 'That's not what he said but I believe you, and I'll make a note of it. You get well, you hear me?'

There was sympathy in Dodds's voice. Through his pain, Gerry felt a rare emotion. That someone in authority should care what had happened to him! The feeling overwhelmed and would soon embarrass him. He wanted no pity. *Go, please go.* As if he'd heard him, Dodds turned and left the hut.

It took the next four days for Gerry to be up, and then he was assigned to light duties. Morgan was around but kept his distance. By the end of the second week, the scabs on Gerry's back had started to itch, which indicated that the healing process was positive, and the assistant surgeon cleared him to resume work. The retaining wall had been completed by others in his absence and Dodds gave him a new task, supervising a three-week program of drilling and stone cutting further up the track, north of the stockade.

On a dewy morning, Gerry breathed in the redolent scent of the bush on the hilltop above and watched as two convicts prepared the rock face below it for blasting, both glistening with sweat. One held a steel bar called a jumper firm against the rock, positioned so that the other man could hit the top of it with a sledgehammer. Each time the bar was struck, it made a dent in the rock, rebounded and turned slightly, in the action that gave the tool its name. Gerry observed the two men's sure work as in this way they drilled a hole in the stone. Gerry walked away and leaped up to a ledge further above. There, two other men were filling drilled holes with a mixture of gunpowder and saltpetre. When this exploded it would split the stone and widen the defile, its deafening noise carrying all the way to Wiseman's.

Some days later, on the last morning of September, when the spring sun was already burning everyone's skin, Dodds rode up to Gerry's party. 'Riordan,' he called out. 'Got a job for you.' He beckoned Gerry over as he tethered his horse in the shade. When Gerry reached him, he said, 'It's at Wiseman's and you can do it in a day. The materials are all there. We spare you for that time but take longer if need be—I want you to do your best with this job. It's a test.'

'A test, sir?'

Dodds looked at him and ran a hand over his forehead and his long nose. 'Of your skills and your conduct as a tradesman. If you pass the test, I'm going to recommend you as a trusty.' A crow squawked above them and Gerry looked up as the bird flew away. 'Riordan?'

'Sir?'

'I said I'm going to recommend you as a trusty. Meaning you could work amongst civilians on specified tasks, without an overseer.'

'Why would you do that, sir?'

Dodds grinned. 'Suspicious soul, aren't you?'

'It's what the world has made me.'

Dodds paused. 'I'm taking a risk, I know. But I think you're worth it and I don't want you to prove me wrong. I took a risk once on the man I told you about, Borthwick, but it didn't work out. I gave him encouragement to improve his lot, as I've been doing for you. Call it my altruism.'

There he goes again with his words.

Dodds explained: 'My liking to help others. Anyway, Borthwick learned, he improved, and his attitude changed for the better. Then he had a setback. I've never found out what happened, or why he dropped back to his self-pity and depression.' Dodds had a hard look that Gerry had never seen on him before. 'The man hanged himself down at Finch's. Hanged himself. A bloody waste.'

Gerry was unnerved. 'Good God. Then why, sir—why take a risk on me? I'm no better: I might just give it all up, like him.'

'Do you want to?'

Gerry shrugged. 'Well, I'll never be a free man again. No hope of getting justice where I am now.'

'And that makes you give up?'

Gerry got angry. 'I'm not a quitter and I'm not soft.'

'No, you're not. And you've learned when to keep your fists to yourself. Last month when Sergeant Morgan attacked you, you could've taken him. It was you and him alone up there. But you kept your temper and put up with a whipping, and that showed maturity and courage.'

Gerry was irritated. He was no saint! 'I'll fight anyone I choose.'

Dodds smiled. 'What about fighting something that you can't see?'

'Sir?'

'Your mind, Riordan. Your mind. It can think violent thoughts and make you do horrible things. Can you fight that?'

Gerry was surprised but gave an answer on instinct. 'I think so, sir.'

Dodds nodded. 'Then I'll persist with you.'

Gerry smiled at his own words. 'It's on your head, then, sir.'

'It is, so don't let me down.'

Gerry looked at the eccentric Mr Dodds. Was he genuine in what he said about the past? Gerry could find out—or at least he might find out from the other convicts whether Borthwick's sorry story was true. Meanwhile Dodds had been straight with him, helped him learn, given him the kind of work he wanted and was now ready to promote him to trusty. Gerry said, 'Keep me in stone with my head down and busy, and I'll have little time for anything else.'

Dodds seemed pleased with that. 'All right. Will you run away if you're not supervised?'

'No, sir.' And Gerry meant it, but for practical reasons—he would die if he did.

'Right, then. You have a hearth to repair, down at Wiseman's.' He handed Gerry a piece of paper. 'I've made a sketch with the

199

dimensions, and the materials you need are all there. You'll take the tools and a barrow down yourself.'

Gerry studied them. 'What's this?' he pointed to a detail.

'A quoin, you know, like a return corner of stone—'

'Of course. Will Miss Walsh be there?'

'Why?'

Gerry reddened. 'No reason.'

'Whether she's there or not is irrelevant to you and stays that way. You'll take the small wagon tomorrow. Load up tonight and get going by first light.'

'I'll do that, sir.'

Early the following morning, Gerry steered the wagon down the Devine's Hill line of road. A breeze wafted against his cheek. He was alone for the first time since he'd arrived in the country, but it wouldn't last. For one thing, he wouldn't trust Morgan as far as he could spit. Likely enough the scourger would find a reason to turn up at Wiseman's and have another go at him. He wouldn't hold back the next time. He wouldn't cop another hiding without taking Morgan down with him—even if he was hanged for it.

The wagon load was not heavy but he took each depression in the Road with care. He didn't fancy being held up on the way, though Dodds had provided him with a pass and a note saying why he was unsupervised. It would be just Gerry's luck for an official on the Road or at Wiseman's to catch sight of his canary uniform and cause him grief.

He kept wondering why Dodds should trust him. He still couldn't understand what the overseer saw in him. His carpenter friends, Murphy and Dooley, had at first poked fun at him over Dodds's attitude, but they were now used to it. They could see that Dodds never gave Gerry better treatment on the job than any other convicts; he just invited his opinion on stonework along the Road. But other convicts were jealous of the overseer's attention. Last night, across the campfire, there had been snide comments about Gerry's going to the inn at Wiseman's unsupervised, and whispers about favours had started. It wouldn't be long before Dodds's plan to make Gerry a trusty spread up the Road and he'd be resented by all.

At the river, the wagon crossed safely on the punt. Gerry turned it and drove along the bank, and the inn came into view. Not far away and across the Road was the house that Solomon Wiseman had built. Gerry wondered if the work inside was all done. He pulled the horse to a stop, got down and went to stand in the main doorway of the bar room of the inn.

A tall, thick-set man was in the bar room, looking Gerry's way. His face was familiar: the inn keeper himself. Mr Brian Walsh, Deirdre's father. Walsh said, 'You want something?'

'My name's Gerry Riordan.' Gerry pulled out the pass Dodds had given him, walked up to the man and handed it over. 'I'm here to work on the hearth, Mr Walsh.'

The man relaxed and pointed. 'It's over there. I know who you are. Recommended by Lieutenant Dodds.' He took the papers from Gerry and scanned them without comment.

Gerry said, 'I was told you have the stone here. My tools are in the wagon.'

'Get your stuff round the back,' Walsh said, 'and I'll see you there.'

Gerry went outside again and took the wagon around to the paved courtyard behind the inn. Walsh came out, indicated the stable where Gerry could put the horse in a stall, and pointed to a pile of granite slabs on one side of the yard. 'There's your stone. Leave the wagon over there and bring everything you need into the bar room. You've got here early enough. Inn doesn't open till one o'clock, so you have until then to get the job done. Here's your papers.' He gave Gerry a keen look. 'Had a feed? Can't do good work on an empty stomach.'

'Thank you, Mr Walsh, I have.'

Walsh nodded. 'Got better grub here. Finish early and we'll fix you up.'

'Th-thank you,' Gerry said as Walsh walked away.

Gerry went about his business in the yard, got everything together and carried it through to the bar room. Going in an out with his gear and stone he saw no one who belonged to the inn. Walsh must be busy elsewhere, Mrs Walsh was probably in the kitchen, there were no staff in the yard and of course there were no customers; it was too early. He couldn't help wondering about Deirdre Walsh, but she didn't appear.

It was dim and cool in the seemingly deserted inn, but there was enough light to work by. Gerry stood before the hearth. The stone flags were uncoursed and with random joints, and the heat from countless fires had forced vicious cracks, like spider webs, all over the surface. No wonder Mrs Walsh thought it unsightly.

'Can you fix it?'

He turned to find that the question had come from Deirdre Walsh. Her hair was pulled back from her face and she wore a navy woollen skirt and light blue blouse buttoned to the neck. He looked back at the hearth, not able to meet her open gaze. He'd hoped she would be at the inn while he worked but seeing her so soon felt like too much to cope with. 'I th-think so. I need to rebuild it and replace a few bits, but it'll be good in the end.'

'I know you'll do your best,' she said, and took a step came closer. Her eyes seemed bolder than the last time he'd seen her and her lips fuller. Her lavender scent reached out to him. 'Are you starting now?'

Gerry stuck to practicalities. 'Yes. I've got to strip away the old stone, then get the base to key—'

'I'll let you start, then. Can I watch?'

He was taken aback. 'Why?'

'I'm interested, that's why.' She smiled at his discomposure. There was a hint of mischief in her eyes as she went on, 'It may seem ordinary to you, but improving this hearth is a big event. Do you mind having a spectator?'

She might be teasing him but he gave her a serious answer. 'No, it's not up to me to mind, Miss. It's just that all around here will get dusty like, and there'll be a mess.'

'I'll sit out of your way,' she said and she whipped away a chair from a nearby table with a dexterity that impressed him. 'Will I be all right here?'

'As you wish, Miss.'

Very aware of her, and also aware that either of her parents might walk in at any time, he began by spreading a canvas sheet in front of the hearth to protect the floor. Then he picked up his chisels and set to work.

After a moment she said, 'Do you see much of Sergeant Morgan?'

That jolted Gerry but he did not let it show. Had his vicious beating been recounted down the Road? 'Hard not to.' He continued to attack the old stone. A large chunk fell with a thud to the floor.

'They say he's a devil with a whip,' she said. Gerry said nothing. 'An evil man.'

Gerry could hear a door being opened, and he looked towards the bar doorway.

'Deirdre!' a woman called. Then she appeared in the doorway. 'What are you doing?'

'I've finished my chores, Mother, so I'm watching to see how the hearth shapes up.'

Mrs Walsh came up, frowning. 'Don't distract the convict, child. He's here to do a job. I need you upstairs.'

'I want to stay.'

'Come now,' Mrs Walsh said.

Gerry resumed his chipping and scowled to himself. *Mother claims daughter.*

'All right,' Miss Walsh said, 'but can I come back before it's finished?'

'You'll see enough of it when it's done! Now come.'

'He's a convict,' Jess Walsh said as she went up the staircase with her daughter. 'Why show him any attention?'

The excitement of seeing Gerry Riordan again did not make Deirdre less careful about what she said to her mother. 'Oh, it's not him I was watching. You know me, I'm good with my hands and I like skilful work. I'm interested whenever I see good craftsmanship, especially in building.'

Jess Walsh smiled. 'Such odd curiosity, for a girl. You should've been a man—but what beauty wasted, if you were.'

'I don't think admiring good handiwork or building is unfeminine. What would you rather I did while I'm sitting around, embroidery?'

'I don't want you sitting around at all, dear, we've far too much to do. Now open the linen store and let's have the sheets.'

'Or should I be writing poems, like Uncle Tom?' Her mother looked cornered: Uncle Tom was a journalist in Sydney and his hobbies, rarely talked about, were growing flowers and writing poetry. 'Mr Dodds thinks my uncle's a good poet,' Deirdre said. 'He thinks his work should be published.'

'Lieutenant Dodds is a gentle and civilised man, but perhaps too civilised. I've always thought he's too soft to be an overseer. Now, help me with the guest beds and then we'll do the baking.'

They worked for the next three hours and all the while Deirdre was anxious to get back to the bar room and Riordan. Her father came into the kitchen just as they were taking the day's bread from the hot range.

'Mr Wiseman's up from Sydney,' he said to her mother, 'without a word of warning. He's at the house and he wants to see us there now. He'll want to see the kitchen accounts, my dear, and you're the one to explain them to him, so—'

Jess Walsh looked flustered. 'Oh, Lord, the kitchen accounts? I pray Mr Solomon's not going to be wanting me to raise the prices in the bar, it's too early in spring for that!' She flung off her apron and said, 'I'm not going looking like this. Brian, get the accounts and wait for me in our office. I'll be downstairs in five minutes. And you, girl,' she said to Deirdre, 'finish peeling those potatoes, put them in a saucepan and cover them with water. But no cooking, mind, not while I'm not here to supervise. If the midday meal is late today it's the owner's fault, not mine.'

'Yes, Mother.' Good, Deirdre thought, both her parents would be at Cobham Hall for at least the next hour.

When she had finished with the potatoes, Deirdre walked into the bar room. Gerry Riordan looked up from his work, then went back to it without a word and she took the chair as before.

Most of the new stonework was done and it looked a treat. She loved watching the stonemason. He worked without wasting energy, each action deliberate and apparently easy, though she sensed that such ease came only from experience. There were no sudden changes of movement or repeated steps, no scratching of the head. He performed the work like a juggler she'd seen in a travelling show, his eyes and hands working in unison. Deirdre was impressed.

Gerry Riordan did flash one glance at her, his trowel poised over the new stone. Although it was cool in the inn, there were damp patches on his opened shirt and underarms. She could see his pectoral muscles beneath his shirt, and the rolled-up sleeves revealed the taut tendons in his forearms. A pulse throbbed through her and she smiled at him. He nodded and returned to his task.

She said, 'When will you finish?'

'Is it one o'clock yet?'

'It's just past the hour of eleven. I have to set up in here at half past twelve.'

Gerry nodded. 'I'll be done in under an hour.'

'Do you want a drink of water?'

'Yes ... please. My bottle's empty, do you mind filling it?' He held out the leather bottle that had been lying on the floor nearby.

She took it without contriving to touch his fingers and carried it out to the pump. Half an hour left at most, and she'd hardly spoken to him. The clean water from the pump splashed over the spout of the leather bottle and it took a while to fill. Going back over the courtyard, she shook the drops off the vessel but left the stopper out. She could get near him because of his work but that didn't bring her as close as she wanted. Would it ever?

In the bar, she stepped up to the hearth and held out the bottle. 'Here you are.' She could smell him: she was aware of sweat and man and a tincture of something that she couldn't place, but it moved her.

While Gerry drank, she glanced down at the tools by her feet and noticed a piece of paper that held a diagram of the hearth. Deliberately she lowered herself and took her time picking it up. As she stood up, his gaze flashed from her face to her bust, and her pulse pounded.

She did not move away. 'I can see you love your work.'

'Aye.' He stoppered the bottle and laid it down, took the trowel and scooped up a load of mortar.

'Your work's good.'

Gerry was laying the final stone. He was concentrating on it, not her, but a smile crept onto his face. 'And you are an expert in stone?'

He was teasing her. She laughed. 'No … but your results are plain there in front of me. You know what you're doing.'

He set the last stone and tooled the joint, leaning forward on his haunches, the action stretching his trousers taut over his buttocks. 'I got my stonemason's certificate back in Ireland. But I could learn a lot more, if only I had the chance.'

She leaned closer as he put down the trowel. 'You want to be better than the other convicts?'

He stood, taking her by surprise. He moved away and started loading the stone rubble into his barrow. 'I couldn't care less about them. I care about my work. Move back, I've got to clean this up. Have you got a broom?'

He sounded abrupt but she knew having her around disturbed him, and she wasn't unhappy about that. She said, 'I'll get one.' She held out the diagram of the hearth. 'You'll want this back, Mr Riordan.'

By the time she'd come back he'd dumped one barrow load of spoil outside somewhere and was filling the barrow again.

'I'll start sweeping,' she said, catching his eye.

Sure enough, he'd had time while she was out of the bar to remember he was supposed to be polite to her. He looked awkward, embarrassed. 'Thank you.'

Satisfied, she created a pile of dust, dirt and stone fragments, then used a small shovel and brush to lift them onto the sheet he'd used to protect the floor. She pulled it away to clean up underneath and Gerry returned to place his tools in the barrow. Together they took hold of the corners of the sheet, lifted it into the barrow and folded them across the load.

Outside, he emptied the sheet on the refuse pile and went to the pump. She drifted over and watched as he stuck his head under it, then rinsed his arms and hands. She felt as though his work was bringing them together in a natural way. Maybe he felt that too, because all of a sudden he seemed eager to talk.

'I'm glad to have done that hearth. Every job I do, I learn more. It's thanks to the overseer that I get different kinds of work. The more there is, the better for me.'

'I'd love to hear more about stonemasonry and building. My mother thinks I'm mad, taking an interest in these things, but I admire good craftsmanship. It would be grand to have someone to talk to, who knows so much more than I do.'

He looked baffled. 'All I know is what I've done with my hands.'

'Don't you think that's a lot? I bet you could build a stone house, from the ground up, if someone gave you the means.'

'I daresay I could. But that's a dream, isn't it? A castle in the air.' He smiled at her—a broad, warm smile that took the sting out of the retort.

'No, it's a very practical idea. You could show me how to draw a diagram for a house. And then describe how you'd build it. So I could learn how it's done.' She smiled back, glad of finding a way to maybe see him again—perhaps often.

'It's an odd idea,' he said.

'Just because I'm a girl doesn't mean I can't grasp things the way you do.'

Gerry shook his head. 'Fair enough, but look, I'm a convict. I'm only here because Mr Dodds gave me a pass.' He thought for a moment. 'But if Mr Dodds makes me a trusty—'

'A trusty! You might get work in other places.'

'If I get that,' he said, 'then maybe I can see you again.'

Gerry led his horse out of the stall and hitched it to the wagon. 'Tell your father, if you light a fire in here tonight, make sure it's small so as not to crack the new work.'

'I'll tell him, Gerry, and … I'd like to see you again.'

'You want me to teach you about building? But I'm not Mr Dodds.'

She grinned. 'Mr Dodds is a scholar who uses long words and speaks poetry. You're what I need. You'll teach me about real things.'

'I gotta be a trusty yet.'

'Well, go then and be one!' she said.

He nodded. 'Your father said I could get something to eat before I left.'

Grand she thought. 'Well, tie the horse for a minute or two and follow me to the kitchen. I'll fix you something for the road.'

* * *

Ten days after Gerry mended the hearth at Wiseman's, he and his group were seated near the stockade in the shade of a banksia tree, after church service. Meat, potatoes and carrots loaded their plates and jugs of gravy were ready to pour. It was a special Sunday meal because work was ahead of schedule on Devine's Hill—and Sergeant Morgan was not present.

'Even God loves our scourger on this day,' Francis Murphy grinned waving away a fly. 'It's a present to us that he's with his loved ones.'

'Then he'd have the company of himself,' Dooley said with a smile. 'And he deserves it.'

Gerry speared a slice of lamb. 'He's an evil man.'

'Keep away from him, Tiny,' Dooley said, 'and keep your nose clean. That's the best advice I can give you. He's been sniffing around Wiseman's is the rumour, wagging his tail at young Deirdre.'

'She doesn't like him,' Gerry said.

'Got that officer hot for her … Bates,' Murphy said.

Dooley nudged his fellow carpenter. 'Stop teasing the lad, Murphy. You know he's keen on her.'

Dodds came up behind them. 'Well done everyone, fine effort.' A few looked up from other groups and nodded to the officer. Dodds's fairness was respected by most.

'Sit down, sir,' Dooley said, 'and join us. There's plenty here.' He handed the overseer a plate.

'Thank you.' Dodds sat opposite Gerry and silence settled over the group as they tucked into their meal. When they'd finished, Fergus and Murphy stood up.

'Would you like some pudding, sir?' Murphy asked.

'A small portion, thank you.'

The carpenters went to the dixies to wash up and Gerry stood up to go.

'We need to talk,' Dodds said. Gerry sat back down. 'Miss Walsh says that you and she are going to read books on architecture together?'

Another long word. Gerry said, 'On building, sir, yes.'

'How are you going to do that?' Dodds said. 'You're a convict in an iron gang.'

'I damn well know that … sir.'

Dodds frowned. 'You get angry quickly, don't you? That's not good in a convict, gets you into more trouble. What I've got—'

Gerry looked around. 'Sir, I can't talk to you like this.'

Dodds looked annoyed. 'Why not?'

'The other men don't like it. They feel like I'm getting favours and it makes them angry.'

Dodds shook his head. 'I'm disappointed in you, Riordan. That's just stupid envy and resentment—ignore them. I'm here to challenge you, and that's something even your mates can't do. They can't help you get a ticket of leave, but I can. Remember my rule. Show a history of working hard and you'll be rewarded.'

'I'm a lifer. I'll never get a ticket.'

Dodds said, 'Listen, man. Look how far you've come in just a year. In seven more years you're certain to get it.'

'Seven more years in this place, sir?'

'Or maybe less. If you go on improving, make trusty, gain more experience and show leadership on the job, you'll get a reduction on that time. And I'll be here to help:

Devine's Hill has at least another two years to run and I'm not going anywhere.'

All Gerry's early suspicions of Dodds rushed back. 'I don't want your help.'

Dodds shook his head. He leaned forward, his voice low but forceful. 'Listen. Yes, you're a lifer. Yes, you've got years to go before you're ticketed, but one more run-in with Sergeant Morgan and you'll be hanged.' Dodds paused. 'There's one way out of this and it's with *me*. Do you understand?'

'Not sure that I do. Not by a long shot. You're not my friend, you're our overseer. So why the helping hand?'

'*Because* I'm your overseer, you fool. I oversee hundreds of men and I very rarely see any potential in them. But you're different and I want you to make an effort before it's too late and you get obliterated by the likes of Sergeant Morgan.'

'You want nothing else from me?'

'Nothing.'

Gerry smiled grimly. 'Just as well. Because I've got nothing to give to anyone. Doesn't matter what you want, I haven't got it.'

'Riordan, I'm offering you a way to get ahead because you have character. All I *want* in return is your effort.'

The look in Dodds's eyes was earnest. Gerry took a breath. 'That's all?'

'All? You say that too easily. Making a real effort is hard.'

At that moment Murphy and Dooley returned with the bowls of pudding. Dodds gestured with impatience towards Gerry and said to them, 'Talk some sense into this lad, will you? I'm offering to help him, get him out of the doldrums and make him a trusty.'

'I'm not just in the doldrums, I'm stranded,' Gerry said angrily. 'I'm here for crimes I didn't do.' He dug into the pudding, not looking at the others.

Dodds shrugged his shoulders. 'Stay stuck in the past, keep harping on about your innocence, and you'll be here until you die.'

Dooley looked up from his bowl. 'Riordan, wake up. This officer is saying he'll give you a hand, lad. Murphy and me, we'll get out of here in a couple of years, so we won't be around to see you right. Why not accept help where you can?'

Then Francis Murphy poked his spoon at Gerry. 'Tiny, I hate to say it, but you're a cut above us all when it comes to your work. Forget about the others here, we'll sort them out. Use your skills and don't let them go to waste.'

During Murphy's speech, Gerry had been finishing the pudding. But the words got through. He put down the bowl, sat back and folded his arms. There was a glow in his chest, but he still couldn't look his mates in the eye.

Murphy smiled. 'God, now, haven't I made him the proud one?'

Dooley pressed the advantage. 'Getting made a trusty, now, wouldn't that be grand?'

Gerry looked at him. 'It would, if I could get away from here sometimes.'

'Now he wants to leave us,' Murphy said in mock sorrow.

'I know what he wants,' Dodds said. 'Now listen, Riordan. You made a good start at outside work, going to Wiseman's unsupervised and coming back without incident. And Mr Walsh says the job's well done. Sergeant Morgan might want you back in irons, but I'll see that doesn't happen.'

'How are you going to keep that scourger off my back?'

'Sir.'

'Sir,' Gerry corrected himself.

'I'll think of something. There's no point having you back on labouring, and so I'll tell the sergeant. Whereas expertise is needed up at Devine's, on the bridge supports and those buttresses.' Dodds scooped some pudding and held his spoon suspended. 'As for other work, you might drive the stores wagon once a week to Wiseman's. Leave here an hour early, spend that hour on Miss Walsh's studies, load up and be back here with the wagon at the usual time.'

'It could work, sir,' Murphy said.

Dodds nodded and finished his pudding. 'I'm off to Windsor the day after tomorrow. I'll start the process of getting you made a trusty. In the meantime, do what you're told.' He stood up and looked at the carpenters. 'Thank you for the food.'

Francis watched him go. 'He's all right, our overseer.'

'It's that prick Morgan we have to look out for,' Dooley said. 'Now, Tiny, let's get down to the creek for a bathe.' He patted Gerry's shoulder. 'Give you a cool head.'

* * *

Maurice Silverstein unlocked a desk drawer and pulled out a document dated 16 November 1829. It was a large and profitable contract with the New South Wales Roads and Bridges Department, and he was about to have it stamped at the Government Office.

He sipped at a glass of water and smiled. His business had won the tender to supply all tools and equipment for the third section of the Devine's Hill part of the Great North Road project. This included broad axes, saw sets, gunpowder, grubbing axes, bullock collars and gang books … and he would supply them at a tidy profit, even better than the one he'd made from his first agreement with Roads and Bridges. This was partly due to Mr Solomon Wiseman charging a nice low price for transporting the material to the Road.

At a merchants' meeting two months before, he'd met Mr Wiseman again. He remained impressed at what the man had done since he'd come to the colony in 1806. Two hundred acres on the Hawkesbury River had been granted to Wiseman, who had set up a ferry crossing and an inn there, plus a country home: Cobham Hall. He was granted a licence to get cedar from the surrounding forests and send it to Sydney, and he was also paid handsomely by the government to supply food for the convict gangs on the Road.

When Wiseman's transports of timber were offloaded in Sydney, most of the wagons went back empty, with no income to cover the cost. Knowing this, Silverstein had seen a way to transport the materials to fulfil his Great North Road contract, and after only half an hour of haggling, he and Wiseman had agreed on a price low enough to bring a smile to Silverstein's face in private.

Grabbing his hat, he made his way to the Government Office, keen to get the contract stamped. Solomon Wiseman had invited him up to Cobham Hall, and he looked forward to making the trip inland to seal the deal.

* * *

Anne Hughes was on deck, trying to take in the panoramic view of Port Jackson. The harbour was impressive and the buildings of Sydney Town crowded and haphazard. But she forgave their primitive appearance because they were bathed in sunshine, there was natural beauty on the outskirts and hilltops, and a warm breeze blew across the water to the ship. She did wish, however, that she'd taken another passenger's advice and dressed in a lighter outfit; her woollen dress was as constricting as bandages. Sean fared better in cotton tailored trousers and a light-woven jacket. At least their headgear would protect their faces from the sun.

She turned from the vista to her husband. 'It's grand, is it not?'

Sean nodded, glancing down. 'And here's the longboat. Not long now and we'll be on dry land.'

And in a house with proper bedrooms and conveniences, she thought. She really wanted to have it ready for Christmas, just two weeks away.

In the crowded boat, they kept silent on the way to the wharf, anxious not to discuss their domestic matters within earshot of those around them. Her fellow passengers, some of whom had got close to them on the voyage, seemed absorbed now with their own excitements and misgivings; silent like them. Another three boats followed with the remaining passengers and their luggage.

Clearing customs, they drove to see a lawyer with whom Sean had corresponded, signed a lease on a house in town, paid two months' rent in advance and collected the keys. She and Sean wanted a good place in the town, to show they were serious about settling in and building a future. They would soon be seeing potential customers, the names of whom Sean had been given before they'd left Cork. They'd had long conversations on not letting the grass grow before they got their business going.

Sean hailed a double-seated dray advertised for hire. 'Castlereagh Street, thank you, number twenty-three.'

The man loaded their goods on board, Sean assisted her onto the dray's second seat and she sat beside him. There was a board in front of them separating them from the driver. Sean said, 'Here we go. After we settle in, I want to find Mr Greenberg.'

'The colony's population is small,' Anne said as they drew away, 'and Jews would be scarce, I'd think.' She was grateful to Sean for mentioning Greenberg—it showed that he had not forgotten his promise to her, to find out more about what had happened to the stolen gold in Cork. Learning more might eventually prove Gerry's innocence.

They had with them a letter sent to Sean by District Inspector O'Flynn just before they sailed from Cork, giving the findings that had led to a reassessment of the case against Gerry. Anne felt that the need for justice should not die with him; he had to be exonerated in New South Wales. She didn't care how long that would take. O'Flynn had named persons of interests and he considered that the New South Wales authorities were the only ones who could bring the true culprits to justice. Government officials moved slowly, but at least Sean might hurry them up a little.

'And there's Simpson to follow up on,' Sean said. 'I'm sure he's connected somehow. I checked his departure date from Cork.'

The dray pulled up to let a loaded wagon pass, its lead horses straining in the harnesses. Up close, Sydney looked rough and ready. Its buildings were mostly low and built close to the street. The streets themselves were unpaved and the people who walked them wore practical clothes with no hint of fashion. The pervasive smell of animals was heightened by the December heat. But she was here to stay.

For the first time that day, her excitement waned. Along this street where she and Sean rode, Gerry might have walked in the last weeks of his life. All at once it seemed as if he'd just died yesterday. Pain pricked her and she threaded her arm through Sean's.

'All right?' he said.

She nodded and thought of something to distract herself. 'We'll have to buy provisions today, to get us through a week at least.' She brought out a piece of paper from her bag. 'The shops all seem to be open.'

'Not far now,' The driver said over his shoulder that they were turning into Hunter Street.

It must have rained earlier in the day, for the potholes in the unpaved street were full of water. Sean took off his jacket. 'It's muggy, isn't it?' The dray lumbered up the steep hill.

'Like being in a hot house,' she replied. 'We're turning right. This is Castlereagh.'

She looked along the street, where lines of houses alternated with shop fronts. She knew no one here and she didn't care. She and Sean were by themselves; no family, no traditions to keep—bad ones that is— and they could make a life here. She'd be able to help Sean, not in the business per se, but in subtle ways—in the home of course, but also in a social sense, because she wanted to get to know their customers. There was no Cork Corporation here but there would be other associations, formed because of the wealth this colony made from wool. She knew that simple men had grown to squires, running breath-taking acreages of a size not dreamt of in Ireland. Those wealthy settlers, squatters and merchants all had enterprises that required the forging of metals. So they would need Sean's new business.

'This must be it,' Sean said as the dray stopped.

Anne looked at the building. It wasn't much but it would do. A single-storey stone cottage with a verandah. The driver got down and started to unload their goods.

'Open it up,' she said to Sean, 'and let in the air.'

He jumped down, held out his arms to her and smiled. 'Welcome to Sydney, Mrs Anne Hughes.'

* * *

Dougal Simpson was sitting opposite Dempsey, the manager of the Parramatta quarry where he worked. Dempsey was fanning his face in the December heat, a glass of water near his hand. The hut was hot, yes, but Dougal was glad to have it: his own annex, now complete with a desk, chairs and a bed, all of which were attached to the store hut. The only drawback was that he lived alone now: Lilly had been transferred to Sydney, where she worked as a maid. Dougal scowled: he needed a woman.

'You've been a good worker, Simpson,' Dempsey said.

'Thank you, Mr Dempsey. You're very kind.'

'Kindness be damned. You're a natural quarryman, knew that from the start.'

Dougal Simpson smiled. Dempsey was a trader and had other businesses beside this one. He wouldn't know good stone from good food, so it had been easy to trick him. Now, Simpson would test his luck further. 'I have a man coming this afternoon about that Windsor order.'

Dempsey sipped his water, then swatted a fly. 'The one who complained that our price was too high?'

'The same.'

'And you want freedom to negotiate?' Dempsey said.

'Please.'

'No need to ask. And if you want even more freedom, you should apply for your ticket of leave. I remind you again to get it. Oh, I know you have three years before you can apply but—'

'Yes?' Simpson said.

'Blast it man, don't you see? I want a partner and you're it! Get your parole and I'll sell you a share of this place. I want to double this quarry's profits and you're my key.'

Simpson thought of his lucky medallion and smiled again. Another opportunity coming his way since he'd lifted it off Lawrence Toole's body.

'I knew that would make you happy,' Dempsey said. 'I have connections who could help you, shorten the period, so to say.'

Still all legal though, Dougal mused. 'Could some of these connections be persuaded by money?'

Dempsey's face betrayed innocent shock. 'What, a bribe you mean?'

No, this wouldn't work. Simpson scrambled to right the ship. 'No indeed, sir, but we know some charities. Perhaps a donation might swing an attitude the right way?'

'Maybe, but … I don't think so.' Dempsey stood up. 'Got to go to town, so think about what I said. Get your ticket and we'll talk about a partnership.'

Dempsey left the hut, put his hat on and walked away.

Unlocking the second drawer in his desk, Simpson pulled out his cashbox and opened it. Fifty pounds, the proceeds from his skimming at the quarry scales. It was an annual income for a mid-level gentleman and his donation to his freedom. Before he put the box back, he retrieved his lucky medallion and pocketed it.

He got up. One quick inspection of the quarry and he'd be back to talk to his visitor. Peter Adams, who'd been his overseer on the transport ship, was due in an hour and Simpson had something to ask from him. Adams had been looking after Simpson's kit and was now returning it.

An hour later, a trickle of sweat shot down Simpson's back as he clasped the man's hand. 'Mr Adams.'

'Can we get out of this sun?' Adams said, his face red as a rose. 'It's a week to Christmas but I'm like a turkey, baked and basted.'

Simpson unlocked his annex door. 'Come in here. I've an ice box and water.'

'Good man!'

Peter Adams sat down and wiped his face as Simpson poured him a drink. 'This your digs?'

'Not much, I know.'

'For a convict, it's Pall Mall.'

Simpson nodded. He was still that, a convict—but convicted as accomplice in a bank robbery, nothing worse. It was true that in July a constable had been here, asking questions about Riordan and Greenberg and the crimes back in Cork, but Simpson had pleaded ignorance about the whole thing and his inquisitor had been satisfied.

He studied Adams, guzzling his water. He didn't need Adams much longer because he wouldn't be useful in the future. Simpson just had to play him one last time. 'How have you been?'

'Good. Out of the Corps and making money as a gentleman.'

'Excellent!' Simpson said, not believing a word.

'I have your kit. You want it now, I suppose? It's in my saddlebags.'

Dougal did indeed. It might be a little lighter for its stay with the overseer but that was worth it.

'Bring it in.'

Simpson was surprised: his capital was intact, minus the £10 he and Adams had agreed on for the man to look after Dougal's money. He thrust it all into his top drawer. 'How close are you to the courts?'

Adams narrowed his eyes. He could tell this was about money as well. 'As a retired overseer, I know some people. They ask my view about convicts, improved conditions, rations, that sort of thing. But here in Parramatta, I'd need to do some checking.' He smiled. 'I'm not a bigwig here, not like in Sydney.'

The man's a fool.

'I need my ticket of leave,' Simpson said, and held Adams's gaze.

'You've only been here a year.'

'Fourteen months,' Simpson said.

'Whatever. You had a seven-year sentence, so you'll get your ticket after four years.'

'I know that, too.'

Adams grinned. 'You want my help to get it now? It'll cost you.'

Demanding man. Maybe his new job had made him arrogant. Simpson poured for them both. 'I do want your help.'

Adams glanced around. 'You must do all right here.'

'How much I'm paid is my business.'

Adams folded his arms. 'Ticket issue is an important process, involving more than one person. It's long and detailed. It's—'

Simpson controlled his temper. 'Can you help me or not?'

'I might.' Adams smiled again. 'But how much can you afford?'

'Ten pounds.'

Adams slapped his thigh and laughed. 'That, my friend, will get you dinner with a magistrate, no more.' Simpson didn't smile. Adams leaned forward and said, 'My son, you can pay. You have a nice tidy sum in that kit of yours. If you want a ticket, it'll cost you fifty pounds.'

Simpson nodded. He'd already worked out that a government man would take at least £40 for the Ticket and he'd predicted that Adams would pocket the other ten. He took £50 from the drawer and handed it across. It hurt to have it pass through his hands so quickly but what the hell, it was an investment for his partnership with Dempsey.

Adams stood up. 'Done. See me next Monday at the Crown Hotel in Sydney.'

* * *

Maurice Silverstein was sitting opposite Solomon Wiseman, talking business in the shade, on the wide verandah of the latter's grand house overlooking the river. Further down the riverbank, Christians were celebrating their prophet's birthday at the inn, and Silverstein was considering how he would spend Hanukkah in the next few days.

Wiseman was a lean man, with a high brow under hair cut fashionably short. His face was craggy but handsome and he had very straight brows. Crossing his long legs, Wiseman raised his voice over the din of the cicadas in the nearby trees. 'With each trip the wagons make back from Sydney, there will always be five available for your purposes. That's what you're paying for—fill them or not, as your business requires.'

'Thank you.' Silverstein hesitated. Making a regular, fixed payment helped him with his budget, but on the other hand he didn't want to find himself paying for space he couldn't fill. 'I'd like to be sure about the capacity of these wagons.'

Wiseman gave a slight smile. 'It's in the contract, Mr Silverstein—each takes a one-ton load. Perhaps you'd like to see? An empty one stands in the inn yard as we speak. Care for a stroll?'

'I would indeed.'

The two men walked out onto the unpaved road that ran through the tiny settlement. Silverstein looked back at the imposing façade of Cobham House, with its long verandah that ran right across the front, and matching balcony above, both decorated in intricate iron lace. The ironwork would have cost a great deal in itself.

Silverstein squinted at the glare coming from the hard-packed ground under his feet. His lightweight trousers and shirt were ideal on this summer's day, though he could feel the sun beating down through the hat on his bald head. Just as they reached the inn, a young woman carrying a basket walked out a side door. Struck by the sight of her, Silverstein stopped, as did Wiseman. The young woman came towards them.

Wiseman doffed his hat. 'Good day, Miss Walsh.' He turned to Silverstein. 'Mr Silverstein, this is Miss Deirdre Walsh. Her father is my innkeeper.'

That was why Wiseman had introduced her to him, instead of the other way around; he considered her beneath them both. Silverstein, taking off his hat and bowing, couldn't have cared less about her status—he'd not seen a woman more beautiful in his life.

Her voice was cheerful and pleasant. 'How do you do, Mr Silverstein.'

His thoughts were so scrambled, he sounded lame. 'How do you do, Miss Walsh.'

Wiseman said to her, 'Mr Silverstein has a contract to supply part of Devine's, so your father may see him from time to time. Possibly as a guest.'

She said, 'What kind of stores do you supply, Mr Silverstein?'

Her lips were her best asset; they made her smile like sunshine. Her eyes by contrast were like lovely black pearls. He found his voice. 'Tools, in the main.'

'Let's hope you prosper, Mr Silverstein. If you'll excuse me, I've things to do.' She smiled. 'Goodbye, gentlemen.'

The men walked around to the inn courtyard. Wiseman was speaking of other things but Silverstein didn't hear a word. He was in love—with a Gentile innkeeper's daughter! Just like that. It was unbelievable.

There'd been times in his past when an attractive face had turned his head, but *her* face was different. Why? It must be the combination of symmetry, the line of her cheekbones and her eyes. Yes. A face like the biblical Sarah's might have had, and her breasts and hips were ideal for childbearing. It was absurd, the way marriage and children entered his head at the sight of her. His race, religion and culture passed down through the mother, so if he married her, his children would not be Jews—unthinkable.

But he was thinking of her; he couldn't help himself. 'A very nice young woman,' he said as they came to the inn courtyard. 'Is she married?'

'No,' Wiseman said, 'but an army officer is courting her. Why do you ask?'

Of course she was being courted; she was too beautiful to be unattached. 'No reason.'

Wiseman stopped at a wagon parked at one side of the yard, away from the stables. For the form, Silverstein had a glance underneath it; the axles and supports looked well-greased and in good shape. Wiseman said, 'Twelve foot long, as you see, high sides for the safety of the load, one ton capacity.'

'Very good,' Silverstein said, scoping the windows of the inn, wondering whether Deirdre Walsh had gone back inside the building.

'You could back this up to your warehouse doors with no trouble?'

He must change his timetable and come up here more often. What if she got engaged in the meantime?

'Mr Silverstein?'

'I'm sorry, Mr Wiseman. I'm feeling the heat.'

'Let's go back into the shade if you like.'

They retraced their steps to the verandah of Cobham Hall. Deirdre Walsh did not reappear in the road, but Silverstein had to see her again, wanted to see her now. What was wrong with him? Like a youth with a crush. And she wasn't Jewish ... that should have mattered, but in this mad instant it didn't seem to.

'You're happy with our arrangements, then?'

Silverstein looked at him. 'Yes, thank you, Mr Wiseman. Couldn't be more satisfied.'

'Are you all right? This sun would fry a diamond if you're not used to it, even for a moment.'

'Thank you, Mr Wiseman, for your consideration.' Silverstein wiped his brow. 'I may need to lie down.'

Wiseman gave a small smile. He was not going to take this as a hint to invite Silverstein to rest in the house, so he said at once, 'The inn is at your disposal, of course. But the innkeeper and his guests keep a very noisy Christmas. You'd be quieter and more comfortable here in the shade while they finish their meal over there.' He patted Silverstein on the shoulder. 'I'll have Miss Walsh bring you over some refreshments. Don't mind me, I have some paperwork to do, about the timber. I'll be out in half an hour to see how you do.'

Silverstein sat back as Wiseman went indoors, leaving the wide front door ajar, and he shivered with pleasure at the thought of seeing Miss Walsh again. He settled down to wait. The sound of the cicadas waned a little, a quietness spread over him and his eyes grew heavy.

Ten minutes later, Deirdre balanced the tray that Mr Wiseman had ordered through his servant, left the inn and started walking towards the Hall. It was Christmas, which meant she was working harder than usual, but her life was good.

In just over a week she and Gerry would be together, conducting their tenth reading lesson, and she couldn't wait. She was reading big books on buildings and art, while she introduced him to novels. During the early sessions, her mother had been suspicious and wary of her spending time like this with a convict. But after three meetings without any incident her mother had come to accept her daughter's new pastime and trust to Gerry's good behaviour, though she still checked on them at least once every lesson.

Meanwhile Lieutenant Bates had written to Deirdre from New Zealand, saying he missed her already. She would respond to him with politeness and friendliness—the least she could do.

The big house with its wide verandah and the beginnings of a garden in front felt drowsy in the afternoon sun. The insects had stopped their chattering and a lemon-scented silence shrouded her. This was where she was meant to bring the refreshments, but at first she couldn't see anyone on the verandah. Then she heard a distinctive sound and peered through the decoration under the railings. Mr Silverstein was lying back in a chair set by a little table, his mouth open, snoring.

She sized him up again: about mid-thirties she guessed, with a kind face, and when he'd first smiled at her, his eyes had twinkled.

She tried not to make any noise as she mounted the steps, but they were not swept quite clean, and a twig cracked under her shoe.

He woke up, saw her and was bright and alert at once. 'I'm sorry … but the sun and the heat … I must have dozed off.' He jumped up and took the tray. 'Thank you, Miss Walsh. You're very kind.'

'That's quite all right, Mr Silverstein.'

He looked at the tray. 'You have brought two glasses?'

'I have.' She looked at the chair next to his. 'Can I ask a favour?'

'Anything!' He smiled.

Deirdre looked back at the inn. 'It's been so busy in there. It feels like a holiday for everyone else except me! I haven't had a break since I woke up this morning. Could I sit with you a while? That's why there's two glasses.'

Silverstein beamed. 'Is that all? Of course you can.'

'Thank you. If Mr Wiseman comes out, I'll be off. I wouldn't want him to think I'm shirking work.'

'It doesn't sound to me as though you do any shirking, Miss Walsh. Surely you deserve a short break.'

'Oh, good. Let me pour you a drink.' Deirdre relaxed and sat down. She had guessed right; Mr Silverstein was nice. 'Have you been up here before? I don't think you have.'

Silverstein drank half the glass and dabbed his face with a silk handkerchief.

She was talking with a gentleman! From Sydney, what's more.

He said, 'It's the first invitation I've had from outside Sydney since I've been in the colony. I arrived in July twenty-eight.'

'Where did you sail from?'

He paused and she waited. 'England … London, I had a business there. I'm a merchant, Miss Walsh.'

'I'd love to hear about London. What's it like? All I know about is my little patch of river. I read about faraway places all the time. It's even better to hear about them from people who've lived in them.'

Silverstein proved very ready to answer questions and she was able to build picture after picture of London in her mind before she heard the sound of Mr Wiseman approaching through his hallway and had to slip away back to the inn.

* * *

A big tree in the copse between Wiseman's Inn and the Hawkesbury River gave filtered shade from the early January sun. Gerry was sitting there with Deirdre and some new books loaned to him by Lieutenant Dodds. Gerry had *The Abbot* by Sir Walter Scott and Deirdre next to him, but at a discreet distance, held her book, also a novel for once: *Runnemede* by Louisa Stanhope. At Gerry's feet on the rug lay a copy of Johnson's dictionary, which by itself was a book worth studying. For nearly an hour they had been discussing words they'd found, and their meanings.

His 'bubble' was square and centred.

The dejection that had descended on him at the Cork trial hadn't gone away but it was easier to live with, because of three things: this opportunity to study, building difficult masonry and being a trusty. Three things that, without Mr Dodds, he wouldn't have had. He'd be here for life but, if things worked out, he'd get his ticket in time and that would get him back to his trade, from which he would make money.

Deirdre moved closer to him, her eyes animated. 'Christmas Day was busy here. I met a merchant from Sydney, Mr Maurice Silverstein.'

'He was doing business on Christmas Day?'

'He's a Jew, Gerry. He's a gold merchant, and now he's a supplier for the Road.'

'A gold merchant?' he said.

'Yes. Why are you frowning?'

'In Sydney?'

'Yes, but he'll be coming up here as well, now and then. He looks like a bit of a toff but he didn't mind talking to me.'

He heard the tone of approval in her voice. 'You like him, don't you?'

She eased a strand of hair away from her face. 'He was a gold assayer back in England. He told me all sorts of things about London.'

'That's where he's from?'

She nodded. 'He says he is, but his brogue is Irish.'

'What's he look like?' Gerry said.

She poked him. 'You're jealous, aren't you?' Tension started to fill him. He had a sudden image of the gold tabernacle doors; his reason for being here. Without that gold, the theft and murder he was accused of would never have happened. He clenched his fists hard. She looked at him anxiously. 'What's wrong?'

'So, what's he like?'

'Short, slim, bald … glasses, kind eyes and pleasant smile. He seems a nice man.' Her gaze softened. 'But that's all, you big loon.'

He held her gaze for some time and then moved so that his arm was around her waist. Her eyes widened and her bosom rose and fell, the blouse enclosing it as taut as a drum skin.

'I like you,' he said and one breast touched his chest. 'A lot.' A fragrance of starch and lemon filled him. He kissed her. She held his face and their lips moved together. Gerry relished their touch: soft, slippery and smooth. He clasped her more tightly, feeling her against him.

'Deirdre!' her mother called from the edge of the copse.

Gerry broke their kiss and stood up.

Deirdre did the same, then ran a hand through her hair and stepped into the clearing. 'Over here!'

'It's time to come inside.'

Deirdre waved and waited until her mother turned away. She came back to Gerry. 'You like me even more than a lot.'

He smiled. 'So I do.'

'Now, you'd better come back to the inn and pack your stores.' She turned and ran off, her hair flying. He revelled in the movement of her body as she ran. Then when she'd gone he stacked the books to carry them back, and rolled up the rug.

A stolen hour on a riverside. In a moment of sadness, he thought of a similar time with Anne, in a place far away.

Chapter Eight

The town of Windsor was the central hub for the Upper Hawkesbury area. Its surrounding villages, created by Governor Macquarie, relied upon this hub for stores, mail and government services. When Lieutenant Dodds was summoned without explanation to the police station at Windsor, it was in January 1830. It was high summer, and he'd ridden from Devine's. His uniform was dusty and he felt overheated. Entering the building, he welcomed its coolness.

There was another man in the waiting room but Dodds went straight to the desk.

'Lieutenant William Dodds. I'm here to see Superintendent Hands.'

'Come this way, please, sir.'

He followed the clerk down a corridor.

The superintendent was signing some papers at his desk.

Dodds stood to attention. 'Overseer Dodds reporting, sir.'

'Close the door, Dodds,' Hands said, and waited till Dodds had done so. 'Firstly, a report has come from Sydney about an incident with a convict Riordan and a Miss Deirdre Walsh of Wiseman's Inn. It happened during the construction of culverts at Devine's Hill in late August last year.'

Ah. Who had spoken to the army, and why had the army passed this on to the police? No doubt Bates or Morgan had put in a report.

Hands was terse. 'Do you recall the incident, Lieutenant? You were there. On the twenty-sixth of August.'

'There was no incident, sir. Miss Walsh requested to inspect the stonework that I was supervising and I asked a trustworthy man to show it to her.'

'You know it's against the rules for females to mix with convicts?'

'Yes, sir, but at no point was Miss Walsh alone with Riordan. A simple exchange of information cannot be defined as "mixing".'

Hands sat back. 'You have an impressive record as an overseer, Dodds.'

'Thank you, sir.'

'But poor judgment has let you down lately. Riordan was insubordinate to Sergeant Morgan, the scourger, only two days after the incident with Miss Walsh, and he got the lash for it. Yet on the first of October, you gave this same Riordan permission to go unsupervised to Wiseman's, amongst civilians—that is, Miss Walsh and her family. What have you got to say about that?'

Dodds tried to stay clear-headed. 'Riordan behaves impeccably in his work and there are no complaints from Wiseman's, sir. As for the so-called insubordination to Morgan, there was no evidence of that at the time, and in my view the punishment was unjustified.'

'The evidence looks clear enough to me, and you were absent, so how can you assert that punishment wasn't due? Morgan is adamant that it was.'

Dodds wouldn't be put off. 'There were no other witnesses.'

Hands snapped, 'Are you saying that Morgan is lying?'

'I wouldn't go so far as that, sir. As you point out, I wasn't there at the time. I therefore had to weigh a convict's statement against a scourger's, and it was my duty to take Morgan's word. I will say, however, that Convict Riordan shows intelligence and aptitude. It is my opinion that he would not wilfully disobey orders. All my dealings with him bear that out.'

Hands looked at him for some time. 'Both incidents stand noted on your file, Lieutenant, along with my admonishment. No action will be taken against you for either. However, I advise you to be more scrupulous about regulations and less lenient with convicts in the future. Understood?'

'Sir.'

Dodds's spirits sank. Hands was saying that his credit had expired and his next misdemeanour would be treated seriously, with demotion and/or transfer likely. He hoped his instinct about Riordan was correct and he hadn't risked his career on a dud.

Hands went and opened the door. 'Mr Johnson,' Hands said, raising his voice. The man who had been in the waiting room entered the office. 'Please sit down.' Hands resumed his seat. 'This is Mr Johnson from the New South Wales judiciary.'

Dodds nodded to Johnson.

'Sit down, Dodds. This gentleman will now give you new information that has come through from Ireland about Gerald Riordan'— he glanced at a file in front of him—'Convict Number 23420.'

'Thank you, Superintendent,' Johnson said. 'Mr Dodds, the Irish judiciary are requesting a review of the Riordan case, to be conducted in New South Wales if possible.' Dodds sat up, intrigued. 'We are required to interview and investigate two people who came to New South Wales on and near the time that Riordan was transported.'

Dodds said, 'They are?'

'A Mr Jacob Greenberg and a Dougal Simpson, Convict Number 23631. Simpson works at a Parramatta quarry. He was interviewed by the Parramatta police and says that he knows nothing about Riordan and has never been associated with him. We have not located Jacob Greenberg, though he is believed to have sailed to Sydney from London. That was his stated intention when he left Cork after the Riordan trial.'

Dodds said, 'What is the review based on? Is there a chance that Riordan is innocent?'

Hands nodded. 'There are suspicions about Simpson and Greenberg. It appears someone else might have committed both the theft and the murder of which Riordan stood accused. The courts in Ireland are taking this question seriously, Dodds, and they want a careful inquiry here. If it turns out that false evidence was given against Riordan at trial, or supporting evidence was withheld, he may be due for a retrial or a pardon.'

'Correct,' Johnson said. 'As it was, the evidence on which he was convicted was circumstantial. And at least one piece was false. A note supposedly written in the murder victim's hand, incriminating Riordan, turns out to be a forgery.'

Dodds was amazed. 'The judiciary's taking all this trouble for just one convict?'

Johnson said, 'This doesn't affect just one convict, Dodds. The judicial system is under scrutiny here. The way it handles these cases sets precedents, and we have to make sure they're the right precedents for the future of the colony. I doubt whether we can gather enough evidence to prove Riordan innocent, but if there is any, it's our responsibility to find it.'

'Frankly I doubt we will,' Hands said with a sigh. 'We've got nothing out of Simpson, and Greenberg is untraceable.'

'Indeed,' Johnson said. 'There is no record of Jacob Greenberg arriving in the colony.'

'That means having another go at Simpson,' Hands said. 'Dodds. You know your convicts: I wager you can spot a spiv from a saint.'

Dodds smiled. 'Don't know about that, sir.'

'Your record is excellent'—he waved his hand in an impatient gesture—'despite recent history. Most convicts say they're innocent and it's a downright lie, but maybe Riordan is the exception to the rule. With all due respect to the Parramatta police, I want you to sniff out this Simpson. Dig up why he's here, what he got up to in Cork, what he's doing now. If he's had any association with Riordan or the crimes Riordan was transported for, I want you to be able to prove it. Got that?'

'Yes, sir.'

'And Riordan's not to be told about any of this.'

Dodds nodded. 'It would only get his hopes up, sir.'

Hands frowned. 'Be careful, Mr Dodds. I'm warning you.'

'Yes, sir.

'Very good. You have leave to spend time in Sydney and Parramatta that will not jeopardise your duties on the Road. Arrange it, check out Dougal Simpson and keep myself and Mr Johnson informed.'

* * *

Anne made the sign of the cross and she and Sean walked out of a small house into the city streets. Living here was still hard to get used to. It was Sunday, and she'd just been to Mass, not in a cathedral, not even in a church—just a two-bedroom Sydney cottage. True, the faithful were saving up for a church, but it was not yet built, though land had been found for it in the Rocks area.

They shook hands with Father Therry and made their way to their gig. It was St Valentine's Day. She'd bought Sean a small gift and would give it to him this afternoon with the wonderful news that she was expecting. She was in a constant state of excitement, tempered every morning by nausea.

'I'd like to go down to the Governor's Domain this afternoon,' she said. 'We could sit in the shade and get a cool breeze.'

'That would be nice.'

She felt as though everything was beginning to fall into place. The colony's isolation had been the hardest; just getting things had proved a hurdle, because so much was imported. One of the hardest things to cope with was the water rationing. Water in Cork was in abundance, here it was more precious than lamp oil.

'Tomorrow,' Sean said, 'I've got meetings with two suppliers who need forged sections for a new brickworks kiln, and in the afternoon, I'm quoting on bases for two wool presses.'

'Good,' she said.

Sean also had plans for a new warehouse. Their foundry in Sussex Street wasn't even meeting the demand. In just under two months they'd been deluged with orders.

'I've got the police asking about Simpson,' Sean said. 'Where he's located and when we can move on him. But Jacob Greenberg is not in Sydney and there's no record of his coming here.'

Anne sighed. 'Maybe he's still in London.'

'That reminds me,' Sean said. 'The Rabbi who ordered those new menorahs from us mentioned a merchant who may be interested in doing business with us.'

'Very good' she said.

* * *

The Parramatta quarry manager mopped his head in the February heat. 'He's the best quarryman I've had. Now, Mr Dodds, explain to me again why the police are so interested in him.'

'Mr Dempsey, I'm just here to find out what he might know about another man.'

'A convict.'

'Yes, who's serving time for something he's likely not to have done.'

'I don't want Simpson harassed again,' Dempsey said. 'When he comes back—'

'Harassed?' Dodds said surprised. 'Simpson's a convict. Liable to be questioned at any time.'

'He's close to his ticket, Lieutenant … very close.'

Dodds referred to his notes. 'That's early, isn't it? He's got years of his sentence to go.'

'Mr Dodds, Simpson's good at his job … very good. It's weeks away, months at the most that he'll have his ticket.'

'You've given him some responsibility. He must deal with a lot of people from outside?'

''Course he does!' Dempsey said. 'He's my right-hand man. Scores of them, customers, transport people and others.'

'And it's all above board? What did the Parramatta police ask him?'

'Don't know. I wasn't there. But they seemed happy that he knew nothing about this Cork thing you're talking about.' Dempsey pulled out his watch. 'He's due back in half an hour. You can talk with him then. Come on, I'll show you around.'

Dodds was impressed with the quarry's organisation. The Great North Road needed two types of stone; the local sandstone that was quarried in situ, and proper hard stone to support the structural sections. This quarry could supply both.

They stopped at the big quarry scales, which were loaded with stone to be weighed. A customer waited nearby with his six-horse team. One of the quarry's workers read off the weight of the stone and wrote it on a docket, which he handed to the customer.

'What's going on here?' Dodds asked as a crane loaded the stone onto the wagon.

'The customer takes that docket to the front hut. The man there calculates the total—the weight multiplied by our price by the ton—and the customer pays up.'

The waiting customer flicked at his horses and the heavy load moved off, while the man by the scales acknowledged Dempsey.

'How's it going, Jacko?' Dempsey said.

'Fair, boss.'

Dempsey nodded. 'Come on, Mr Dodds, and I'll get you a cool drink.'

They took the path back to Dempsey's hut and Dodds thought about the scales, which were crucial to the quarry's profitability. If they happened to be even slightly inaccurate, the tonnage would not be correct. Beneath the real weight, the quarry would lose money. Above the real weight, the quarry would be charging too much and the customer would be out of pocket. He wondered how often the scales were checked for accuracy.

'Where did Simpson start when he came here?' Dodds said.

'On the drilling and cutting, then I got him on stone selection. After that,' Dempsey said, 'he was on the scales like Jacko there. He liked it, said he enjoyed the numbers like, the measuring. But then I saw his ability and got him to work beside me. But for some reason he would've liked to stay with the scales.'

Something was niggling at Dodds. What was so nice about working at the scales? The customer was right there and could read off the weight that the convict recorded. No hope of cheating the customer. But what if the convict had an arrangement with the customer to put down *less* tonnage on the note ... so he'd get a backhander from the buyer and cheat the quarry? He wondered whether the man he was about to meet was clever enough to run a scam like that.

'Here's Simpson now,' Dempsey said.

Dodds ran an eye over the convict, who'd come to a halt on their approach. He was of average height with a lean frame, a moustache, and a scar on his left cheek. His eyes narrowed unpleasantly when they met Dodds's gaze.

'Simpson,' Dempsey said, 'this is Lieutenant Dodds. He wants to talk to you.'

Simpson came to attention in a mock military fashion and said, 'Do I have to talk to him?'

Dempsey seemed to take no notice of this insolence, but Dodds said curtly, 'You do. Inside, now.'

Dempsey said, 'Take Lieutenant Dodds to your hut, Simpson.'

'Very well, sir, if I have to.'

Dempsey said, 'I'll leave you two to talk. Goodbye, Lieutenant.'

'Goodbye and thank you.' Dodds followed the convict to his hut, sat down at the man's desk and left him standing before it. 'I oversee an iron gang on a section of the Great North Road. A lot of the convict labourers are Irish, and some are from Cork.

There were two crimes committed in Cork before you were tried yourself for robbery and transported—the theft of some gold, and a murder. I'll hear what you've got to say about those crimes.'

Simpson snapped, 'Nothing. Know nothing about them. Told the Parramatta police that, months ago.'

'Then let's start with something you do know about—Saint Mary's Cathedral. You're aware of its existence?'

Simpson sneered. 'Yes.'

'You knew it was undergoing reconstruction at the time? The altar work, the new tabernacle?'

'Never went there but I heard about it. I knew people who worked on it.'

'Who?' Dodds said.

'Plenty.'

'Name a few.'

'The Hughes Foundry,' Simpson said, 'Hampton Plasterers, Donovans.'

'Gerald Riordan, the man convicted of stealing the gold intended for the cathedral, was employed by James Donovan.'

Simpson shrugged. 'He could've been. I never met him.'

'The judiciary in Cork has requested the New South Wales judiciary to review Riordan's conviction and there's a chance he'll be declared innocent.'

There was a definite reaction here from Simpson. Dodds could see alarm in his eyes before he turned his head away to look out the window. After a second, he managed to say, 'Means nothing to me.' But the tone was unconvincing.

Dodds liked the idea of Simpson running scared from now on—he might make some mistakes. He took a punt: 'You were seen around Riordan's digs the day Toole was murdered—got anything to say about that?'

'What? I had work to do that day, other side of Cork. I was nowhere near Philput Lane!'

Dodds shook his head. 'You claim you don't know Riordan, but you do know where he lodged?'

Simpson went on the defensive. 'It was hearsay at the time!'

Dodds changed tack. 'You have an excellent memory after all, Simpson. And Mr Dempsey speaks well of your work here—he says you'll get your ticket soon.'

'Deserve to,' Simpson said with a sullen, wary look.

'And what are your plans after that?'

'No idea, Lieutenant. Is that all?'

Making no move to leave, Dodds said, 'Gerry Riordan is going to be made a trusty in March and I'm predicting he'll have his ticket of leave not long after that.'

'But he's a lifer!'

'I didn't say he was a lifer,' Dodds said in a soft voice. 'I've only said he was convicted of theft. Like you.'

'I guessed.' Simpson tried to rally. 'Well, if he's like me he's got to do four years before he gets his ticket.'

'So how will you contrive to get yours so early?'

Simpson shook his head and did not reply.

Dodds remained sitting. 'When a convict gets his ticket he has more freedom of movement. Riordan's a determined man. He'll be using that freedom to good purpose.'

Again, that flicker of alarm in Simpson. 'But he's not allowed outside the area in which he works.'

'That's so,' Dodds said. He got up, and Simpson stepped back a pace. 'Nonetheless, Riordan wants to prove his innocence. I'm sure he's going to be talking with anyone who can help him with that.' He moved to the doorway. 'That's it, Simpson, back to work.'

Dodds walked out, mounted his horse and rode away. He had got Simpson rattled, which made the man vulnerable and might make him careless. A born liar, Simpson had tried to cover up what he'd done in Cork, but it would be difficult for him to keep that up if Dodds could find out what he was doing in New South Wales—which he was convinced was criminal. Simpson was likely getting a rake-off from the quarry to fund an ill-gotten ticket of leave. Dodds would follow up on his suspicions with people who bought stone from the quarry and get the dirt he was sure was there.

* * *

Dodds glanced up to a point two hundred yards from him where his party had just set up on a cleared section of track. They were about to work on the massive buttresses that supported the walls at each side of the Road, and he was sweating about what his carpenters needed to construct next. He turned to Gerry Riordan instead. 'Have you ever built a crane? A big one?'

'Aye, sir.'

'Where?'

'I worked on one for the Cork gaol.'

'Good,' Dodds said, 'then tell me how you'd do it here. We've got to get stone up to a minimum height of thirty feet.'

Gerry looked up to the work site. 'We build two triangular frames and stand them side by side, a couple of feet apart.'

'How high will they be?' Dodds said.

'Well, if the wall is thirty feet high, then the frames have to be at least half that height. We'll weight the bases using sandstone blocks and connect the frames together with cross members at every four feet. On the top cross member we rest and connect a forty-foot jib made from two ten-by-four timbers. I know it'll work,' Gerry said, 'and we have the men to build it. It's a quick job to fix the pulleys and lay the ropes.'

'Very well. Get Dooley and Murphy onto it. I want the crane ready in three days.'

Dodds turned to his Road drawings and examined once again the work required. The retaining wall would be the highest they'd built so far. The smallest sandstone block measured a fifteen-inch cube, a nearly three-hundred-pound brute. These could be lifted by four men but that way was too slow, so a crane was needed. He sighed. A crane that had to be constructed in the middle of the bush.

Riordan was talking to the carpenters and within a minute they were crouched on the ground, the stonemason drawing figures with a stick in the dew-moist dirt.

'I need sketch paper and a rule please, sir,' Riordan said, looking up at him.

'Here,' Dodds handed over the items from his satchel.

'Thank you, sir.' Riordan took them, looked around, walked to a wagon, pulled down its hinged rear end and started to draw, stopping sometimes to add notes. Dodds knew now he had a leader in the young stonemason and his decision to make him a trusty was justified. This crane, if done well, would make Gerry's ticket of leave more probable.

Ten minutes later, Riordan looked up. 'Sir? I think we have it worked out.'

'Good,' Dodds said and inspected the drawings. What he saw was an impressive start.

'I've got more sketches to do but you can see already that it'll need new timber, sir. Hardwood, and big enough to take the load.'

'Are the carpenters of the same mind?'

'They are, sir.'

'The Surveyor General, Major Mitchell, is coming to inspect the work next week,' Dodds said. 'I want it to be well under way.'

Gerry smiled. 'We'll have your buttress wall started by then, sir.'

Dodds pointed at Gerry's team. 'Timber?'

'I want the lads in the cutting party to pick the best and we'll spend the morning dressing those into shape. I'll need a bullock team, four extra men, and some three-hundred-pound rope.' Gerry pulled out his notebook and pencil and started writing, glancing at his drawings now and then. After two minutes, he had the list.

'Get things organised,' Dodds said, 'and come back and see me.'

Dodds then addressed his own plans. Devine's Hill was an important two-mile section within the Wiseman's Ferry to Mount Manning section of the Great North Road. If they could finish their section up to the new stockade by the end of the year, they would be doing well. Mitchell had given their work the thumbs-up in February and praised the attitude of the convicts. Dodds was satisfied with the work they did but annoyed by having to put up with the sadistic Sergeant Morgan. He longed to get the man transferred.

When Riordan returned, Dodds said to him, 'We're halfway up Devine's now. You've gained an appreciation of just how long it takes to build in this country.'

'And what materials it takes. Four thousand barrow loads for one wall only,' Gerry said, 'and that was just three feet high.'

'Indeed. And now this buttress,' Dodds said. 'It's going to be like building the great pyramids.'

'The pyramids, sir?'

'Three great monuments built in ancient Egypt. They were tombs for kings, the pharaohs.'

'What stone did they use, sir?'

Dodds smiled. 'Limestone. Not like the sandstone here.'

Riordan nodded. 'I know limestone.'

'One of the pyramids was over four hundred feet high.'

'No, sir! No one could build that high.'

'Four hundred and fifty-seven feet to be exact, Riordan, and I can show you books to prove it. They will be of interest to Miss Walsh. Now, I have a billy boiling. Sit down and we'll have some tea.'

Riordan looked up the Road to where ten workers worked with mattocks and shovels in a trench which would hold the first course of stone for the wall. 'Thank you, sir. They'll be all right for a bit.' He sat down and accepted a mug from Dodds.

Dodds said, 'I've never asked about the crimes you were supposed to have committed in Cork, Riordan. But I have read the record.' Riordan gave a start at this and glowered. Dodds went on, 'And if I'm to help you to a ticket of leave I need to hear about them from you. I have some questions for you and I expect you to answer them.'

Riordan's big hand closed around the metal mug he was holding. For a second, Dodds wondered if he were about to throw it into the bushes. A lot of good that would do him! Dodds said, 'Let's start with the worst crime, the murder. Tell me about it.'

Riordan had a hard look on his face, as though he had to nerve himself to speak. 'My best friend was killed in my lodgings ... sir. His name was Lawrence Toole. There was a note clutched in his hand and the court said it proved I killed him.'

'What did it say?'

Gerry looked at him. 'That we stole some gold and Toole worried that I'd kill him to keep his share and mine.'

'This is the gold from the tabernacle doors, isn't it? Go on.'

'He wouldn't have written that, sir. It can't have been by him, it can't. We didn't steal those doors.'

'So, who did you think wrote it?'

Riordan looked haunted, as though the answer to the question was beyond him. Dodds said nothing and finally Riordan said, 'I had problems with my boss. His name's Donovan. He didn't like me, because his daughter and me were friends.' Riordan looked away again and was silent for a moment. He put down his mug and looked back at Dodds. 'It seems so long ago now. Anyhow, Donovan got me and Toole to pick—'

'Toole is the friend who was killed?'

'Yes. Toole and me had to pick up this box from a foundry. The box held tabernacle doors plated with gold.'

'This was the Hughes Foundry?'

'Yes. We picked them up from Sean Hughes.'

'And what sort of man is he?'

'Don't know much about him, sir, but he seemed all right.'

'Had you met him before?'

'No, sir.'

'So you were taking the gold doors from the foundry to Donovan—where was he?' Dodds stirred his tea.

'At the cathedral. But a wagon drove into ours on the way and everything went flying. We had to carry the box with the doors on horseback the rest of the way. And when we handed it to Donovan there was nothing inside it but rocks.'

'Toole was killed the next afternoon, wasn't he? Where were you at the time?'

'Working on the altar at the cathedral, sir.'

'So Donovan had you back at work, even though you lost his precious doors. What did the police have to say about that?'

Riordan frowned again. 'They let us go free because they couldn't prove we stole the doors—and we didn't! It was only when another box was found in my room with the brass frames from the doors in it: that's when everyone had us down as thieves. But I'm no thief and no murderer.'

Dodds decided he had asked enough tormenting questions of this man. 'If you're innocent, Riordan, then all the evidence against you is planted or fabricated. You're not accusing anyone else of being a thief and a murderer, but I want you to think back and give some thought to the people who were around you at the time, and their motives. If you remember anything suspicious, let me know.'

Riordan looked gloomy. 'Why, sir?'

Dodds had his instructions from Windsor: make his own inquiries without informing Riordan. 'Just put it down to my curiosity. You know I like to get my nose stuck into things: it's the biggest part of me.'

Riordan nodded without smiling. 'If I think of something, sir, I'll let you know. I better get back to the boys.'

'Take the billy with you.'

'Thank you, sir.'

There were many characters in this Cork drama and Dodds could bet that one or more of them had framed the stonemason for two crimes. What were their motives? Money, love, ambition, revenge and fear pretty well summed up what might drive someone to serious crime. The main players were Donovan, Hughes, Greenberg, Simpson. Donovan and Hughes could either lose or gain by the disappearance of the tabernacle doors—money? Greenberg knew their value and might have fenced the gold—money again? Simpson was a proven thief, so money was a clear motive for him, and perhaps ambition drove him, too. And fear. If any of these men were guilty, and discovery threatened, wouldn't they be gripped by fear?

He swilled the tea leaves around in the bottom of his mug and tipped them out on the ground. A breeze sprang up and lifted the corner of the plan he had spread across one knee. He grabbed at it and tried to concentrate on today's challenges: masonry, timber, labour and the weather.

* * *

Sean Hughes opened the door from the street and stepped into a familiar anteroom. Taking off his hat, he rang the bell on the bench top. The merchant he wanted to see for future works was one referred to him by the Rabbi.

A young woman came from behind a partition and smiled at him. 'Ah, Mr Hughes.'

'Good morning, Miss Rebecca. I'm here for my eleven o'clock appointment. Is Mr Silverstein in today?'

'Mr Silverstein is attending to urgent business. He says he's sorry but could you make another appointment.'

Sean's manners just won over his irritation. 'This is the second time he's not kept his meeting. Can you give me any explanation for that?'

Rebecca gave an apologetic shrug. 'I'm sorry but, as I said, he's very busy.'

'Oh, very well,' Sean said annoyed. 'Please tell me when he'd be available to see me.'

'In the afternoons is better, mostly late would be the best time, so five of the clock.'

'Here's my card again,' Sean said. 'Please get him to write to me and propose a time to suit.'

'I'm sorry again,' Rebecca said.

Sean left and pulled on his hat then his gloves, the autumn wind numbing his cheeks. What a rude man to keep postponing seeing him! Now he had time to fill before his next meeting, which was up the hill. Across Kent Street there was a pub with its hearth warming the few patrons just before the midday meal. He ordered a pie and an ale and took both to a window that overlooked the street.

Maurice Silverstein was beyond inconsiderate. One cancelled appointment was bad enough but two seemed suspicious. Either Silverstein didn't care about Sean and his business or he was avoiding him for some reason. It was worth sticking around to see whether the gentleman would turn up from wherever he was lurking, so Sean tucked into his meal.

He had just about finished when a movement in the street caught his eye. A man had emerged from Silverstein's premises and was putting on his hat as he hurried away. In all the time that he had been sitting by the window, Sean had not seen him go in.

Placing some silver on the table, Sean grabbed his hat and went out with a determined stride. In no time he had caught up with him. 'Mr Silverstein?'

The man stopped and turned. 'Yes?'

'I'm Sean Hughes.'

Silverstein took his hat off to reveal a bald head and peered through his glasses. 'How do you do.'

'I've been trying to meet you,' Sean said.

Silverstein's face broke into an almost convincing smile. 'Of course, I'm sorry, Mr Hughes, of course. I've been so busy with work and—'

'Where are you going?' Sean said.

'To an appointment in Bridge Street. I have my gig close by.'

'Do you mind if I walk with you?'

Silverstein hesitated. 'If you like.' Then he smiled again. 'Of course, you must. It's the least I can do for postponing our meetings. Your foundry is in Sydney?'

He mounted onto the double seat of the gig and Sean joined him. 'In Sussex Street, Mr Silverstein, but I live in Castlereagh. The synagogue is a customer of mine.'

'So I've heard. Let me drive you home on my way.'

'Thank you. I'd also like to provide you with a list of the ironware and other metalwork that we produce, and a list of my prices.' He took a few sheets of paper out of his satchel and handed them to Silverstein, who stowed them in his.

'Thank you, Mr Hughes.' Silverstein shook the horse's reins as it pulled them uphill. 'I'm a supplier to the Great North Road, amongst other ventures. Public or private, many an endeavour requires the work that you produce, and for the buyer, there's the convenience of not having to wait months for imported goods. The synagogue. Is that where you got my name from?'

'The Rabbi told me about you.' They remained silent for some minutes as they reached the top of the rise and then turned into Castlereagh.

'How far along do you live?' Silverstein asked.

'You may stop just here. This is my house.'

Silverstein pulled the horse to a halt. 'I wish you success with your foundry, Mr Hughes. I'll keep your business in mind.'

Sean alighted and put out his hand. 'Thank you for the ride.'

When Sean went in, he found Anne in the parlour.

'Hello, dear,' she said in pleased surprise. 'What brings you home at this time? You're not ill?'

'No, never better. More important, how are you?'

'Come and sit with me. I find it hard to stand for long.'

'Of course,' Sean said. The swell of her stomach was just showing, and she was not far into her pregnancy, but her health had been delicate of late. 'Did you consult the midwife this morning?'

'Yes, dear, she had a look at me and she says everything's going all right. My only trouble is my back hurts a little. I just need to mend my posture. Anyway, enough of me. How did you fare with Mr Silverstein?'

'I had to ambush him,' Sean said.

'What?'

Sean smiled and sat down on a chair next to her. 'The man cancelled his second appointment, just as he did the first. But I was having an ale in the hotel across the road and spotted him leaving his premises. So he had his talk with me whether he liked it or not. I even got him to drive me home.'

Anne laughed. 'What a funny fellow. Will he give us business?'

'Maybe,' he said. 'He looked startled when I accosted him, but later he was as pleasant as could be. Over pleasant, if you want the truth.'

She smiled. 'Let's hope he stays like that. We need people to be nice to us. We'll have a little one to support soon.'

* * *

On the Devine's Hill retaining wall, thirty men were busy, either close-packed on the scaffolding laying blocks, digging in the footings, carting spoil, or handling stone and operating the fancy new crane, another bloody Riordan design! Dan Morgan watched and calculated his chances of causing some kind of accident to take place, and they looked good. There were tools to injure and maim, a risk of a fall—anything that could bring that mongrel down, he would do. Trusty Riordan stood halfway up the buttressed wall, ordering his men like the Duke of bloody Wellington, his stance arrogant, his face confident. Morgan spat onto the grass.

Dodds never worked them hard enough. There he was poring over plans and working the numbers. That wasn't how to get things done. Morgan caressed his whip at his side. The gangs were soft, one man even singing. This wasn't a social gathering! It was a bloody road that needed building and with an iron man to lead it. The convicts were scum and had to be led like scum! Morgan perspired, although the May Day was cool. He had to put two more punishments in his report before the end of the month, otherwise he'd be transferred. A gang that worked adequately without having to be whipped to do so was considered not to need a scourger. This was his gang, and if they didn't need the end of his whip, he'd be allotted another.

Morgan went over his best plan one more time in his head and stepped over to Dodds. 'Mr Dodds,' he said, 'the extra blocks and rope are at the inn. I'll take the spare wagon and get them.'

Dodds looked up. 'I'm going there myself. I'll get them. Make sure the men continue working at this pace.'

I'll make them work all right. 'Very good, sir.'

Ten minutes after Dodds had left, Morgan acted. At twenty-five feet above the ground, on the highest level of the scaffolding, a cockney named Ernest Smith, a diminutive carpenter's assistant, was busy securing braces for the next set of frames. On the ground beneath Smith, two men were working the crane's windlass, hauling a single stone cube up to the working platform. The men's muscles were prominent, sheened with sweat. The ratchet clanked and the cube rose and settled on the planks, making them sag with its weight. The men on the windlass rested while the stone was unshackled and the hook returned to the ground.

Morgan would now stir some mischief.

He tapped both windlass operators on their shoulders. 'Move away from the crane.' Morgan put his hands to his mouth and yelled. 'Smith, get down here.' When Smith joined him, Morgan grinned and said, 'Grab hold of that windlass. You need work to build up those arms of yours.' Morgan gestured to two labourers. 'Don't suck up more of the governor's air! Shackle up another block.'

Fergus Dooley, near the crane, paused in sawing a scantling. 'It takes two men to pull up a block, Sergeant.'

'Quiet, scum, or you'll feel my lovely leather.' Morgan watched as the new stone was brought over and trussed up ready for lifting. 'Don't just stand there, Smith, you whore's discharge! Get this moving.'

Smith glanced at Dooley as though for help but took hold of the handle.

Morgan said, 'You've been slack, my little man, doing all the easy work up top. It's time you earned your ration. Right, take the strain.'

Smith pulled on the windlass, and nothing happened.

'Get it moving!' the scourger said.

Dooley stepped forward, still holding his saw. 'No one man can do—'

Morgan swung and smashed Dooley on the chin with his whip stock. The carpenter dropped his saw and collapsed, holding his chin, blood leaking through his spread fingers.

Morgan yelled, 'I said, move that load!'

Smith pulled using both hands, his triceps strained and his red face creased in effort. There was a pause, then a ratchet clicked and the stone moved up a foot. Another click and it moved higher. Smith strained to engage another ratchet and then let the handle go, holding his shoulder in agony.

'Lift it to the top, I said.'

'He can't,' Riordan said, 'and he won't.'

Morgan grinned and turned as Riordan came up. His plan had worked a treat.

'I'll move it with him,' Riordan said.

'Smith is the man who'll move that stone, Riordan. Now, get back up that scaffolding.'

Riordan said, 'It needs two men on that windlass.'

'Get back,' Morgan said. 'Smith will lift it! Come on!'

Riordan stood in front of him, his face calm. 'He won't.'

Morgan uncoiled his whip. 'That's wilful disobedience.'

In an instant, Riordan reefed the whip away from the scourger. There were gasps around them. Work stopped. 'I want it known before all of you,' Riordan said, raising his voice. 'What's happening here is torture.'

The scourger's scar widened and his eyes shifted from one man to another. Some of the workers were edging closer to him. He took a step back. 'Mutiny, Riordan, and you started it.'

A labourer near Riordan lunged and punched the scourger, another followed and Morgan went down with two men each side of him, kicking his ribs and groin, raising dust. Blood stained the scourger's uniform and cheering started. Morgan covered his head as best he could and then he was lifted and jerked back from the throng by someone who felt like a giant. Next thing the big hands had released him, and through a blood-filled, half-closed eye, he was looking at Riordan's back.

'Keep off!' Riordan said, fronting the group. 'All of you.'

'Let's be at him, Riordan,' a man said, his face lit with hate. 'He deserves it, by the Christ.'

'Leave him to us!' yelled another. 'He's ours.'

Morgan's blood ran cold. *They'll murder me.*

'No!' Riordan shouted, and raised one arm, hand outspread. 'Get back now.' The men shuffled about. 'Kill this man and we'll all hang. Back to work!'

'Right, fellas,' Dooley yelled. 'Tiny's right. The scourger's not worth it.'

Some men moved back, grumbling, then the rest followed.

'Dooley and Murphy,' Riordan said, 'tie Sergeant Morgan up and stick him under a tree.'

When Dooley and Murphy stepped up to Morgan to tie his hands behind his back, he made himself submit. Feeling the blood run down his chin, he raised it to watch, as Riordan climbed the ladder to resume his work on the buttress.

Dooley said in his ear, 'That man just saved your life. Now walk.'

Morgan grimaced, which forced more blood from his cut lip. 'He'll hang now for sure, and he'll have some mates on the gibbet with him.'

The two men ignored this, marched him into the shade and pushed him down so that he sat with his back against a tree. He watched the men resume work and scowled with satisfaction. Now Dodds would have to admit that Iron Gang 4 was a pack of seditious mongrels. Now he had his quota, and he'd never lose this post.

Chapter Nine

It was a week after the 'riot' and both overseer and scourger were fronting the constabulary in the Windsor Police Station. Morgan's scars and bruises were evident. William Dodds, standing to attention beside him, read the date under the wall clock: 15 May. His mother's birthday.

'I've read your reports,' Superintendent Hands said, 'and I'm disappointed, to say the least. You each give different versions of the incident, which is why you're here—to tell me the truth. When I'm satisfied that I've heard it, I'll make my recommendations to Sydney. Sergeant Morgan, you said that the men attacked you without warning. If proven, that's a serious offence. But Mr Dodds says that the convicts were responding to unprovoked violence by you; you were torturing one of the men.'

'Sir,' Morgan said, 'I can—'

'Sergeant, did you or did you not call Convict Smith down from the task he was performing and command him to work the crane?'

'I did, sir, and he—'

'It is not your job as scourger to hand out tasks, Sergeant Morgan. You do not assign the convicts' work; you ensure their diligent execution of it. Now, did you make Smith do this ill-conceived task under duress, thereby causing him injury and moreover holding up the work?'

'It was him held up the work, the slacker! Hauling up the blocks was no new task; they'd been at it all day. But Smith wouldn't do his bit. And when I kept his nose down to it, that other mongrel, Dooley, stepped up to me with a weapon. So he copped it in the face for mutiny, because that's what it was. As you can see, sir, by what they did to me.'

The superintendent sighed, looked at his notes and said, 'Mr Dodds, you were not there at the time, so your account is based on what the convicts had to say to you after the incident. This weapon that Convict Dooley was carrying; you have it down as a saw. Is that correct?'

'Yes, Superintendent. Dooley is a carpenter. He stepped away from his work to explain the function of the crane to the sergeant, with the saw in his hand, but he did not raise it. In the melee that followed, none of the men on site used tools against the sergeant. They were protecting Smith with their fists only.'

Superintendent Hands gave him a piercing stare. 'So they say. It's a remarkably consistent report, Lieutenant, to have come from so many. Self-defence against torture seems to be the theme. Exactly how many men did you question, to compile this?'

This was it, Dodds thought. Top brass wouldn't believe convicts on anything. 'I interviewed ten men individually on the melee and they all told me the same facts.'

'Scum stick together,' Morgan said.

Hands did not object to the interruption and Dodds sensed that Morgan had scored a point. Dodds also suspected that the scourger had set up the ruckus to get at Riordan.

'What justifies the claim that Smith was tortured, Mr Dodds?'

'Convict Smith is five foot two and very slight. He was asked to operate the crane alone but it normally takes two able-bodied men to do so. Pulling the excessive weight under the sergeant's orders caused injury. He still suffers from torn ligaments in both arms.'

'Sergeant Morgan?' Hands said.

'I've seen such slight-built men do the job. Smith could have as well, but he refused to obey.'

'That so, Mr Dodds?'

'He did not refuse, he put all his strength into the pull and moved the block a few feet, but no one could make the full lift to the top. That's why we always have two men.'

'Sergeant Morgan?'

'Like I said, Smith refused to obey and Riordan backed him up and tore the whip out of my hands. If that's not disobedience and assault, I'd like to know what is.'

'Did Riordan strike you?' Hands asked.

'No, sir. Didn't need to. Rest of them did it for him.'

Hands shook his head. 'So you're saying, Sergeant, that the convicts just spontaneously attacked you for no reason. What were they trying to do, in your view? Injure you, maim you, kill you?'

'That's right, sir.'

Hands raised his eyebrows. 'But they were a large group of tough men going for just one. How is it that you're still alive?'

'Because I fought them off, sir. Fighting for my life, I was.'

'So their intent was murderous? Then how is it you ended up with no serious injury, no bones broken, trussed like a Christmas turkey?'

Dodds bit his lip to hide a smile.

Morgan had no ready answer to this, so Hands consulted his notes again. 'Mr Dodds's account gives another reason for the end of this sorry piece of violence. Apparently Convict Riordan plucked you from the melee, stood up to the others and dissuaded them from returning to the attack. By doing so, he saved you from serious injury. He also had you tied up and led from the scene, to protect you from further harm. At his prompting, they all returned to work. That so, Mr Dodds?'

'Indeed. When I returned from the inn, sir, work was proceeding as normal and on time. I saw nothing unusual about the scene except for Sergeant Morgan, who was tied up.'

Hands sat back silent for a moment. 'There's been a flagrant breach of discipline here. Along with disobedience, insubordination and violence on the section of Road for which both you men are responsible, in your separate capacities. Sergeant Morgan, you're transferred to Ten Mile Hollow. You will change your ways there. If you exceed orders one more time in this fashion, your career as a scourger is over. And I'm changing regulations with regard to your use of the whip. It is to be used for punishment only and in every case, you require permission from your commanding officer. If you—'

'That can't work, sir,' Morgan said in a fury. 'Scum need—'

'Sergeant! Do not interrupt me again.'

'Sir.'

'No punishment without approval,' Hands continued, not taking his eyes off the scourger, 'and that doesn't mean, Sergeant Morgan, that progress of the work up on your new section can falter. You will keep the men up to the mark without mistreatment and without causing the kind of injury you inflicted on Smith at Devine's.'

Morgan was livid. 'What, I'm reprimanded and that riotous pack of mongrels get off scot free?!'

Hands snapped, 'Be thankful you're not cashiered! Yes, every man on Devine's will work as usual. Dooley's still carpenter and Riordan is still a trusty.'

There was silence for a moment.

'I don't think that's good, sir,' Morgan said.

'That's my decision. Sergeant you're dismissed. Make the men on your new watch behave, but by the rules.'

Morgan saluted and left the office. When his footsteps faded, Hands stood up. 'I had to transfer the man rather than punishing him, Dodds. Of course, his new commanding officer will get the full report on him, and so will Sydney. But in our neck of the woods ... if the word gets out that we've supported the word of convicts over that of a scourger, we'd have anarchy amongst every gang on the Road.'

'Leaving him with sole supervision was an error of judgment on my part, sir.'

'Perhaps. Though I suspect Morgan had been spoiling for a fight for some time and it would have happened wherever you were.'

'He's been down on Riordan ever since he saw him, sir.'

'And you suspect Morgan planned the incident in the hope that Riordan would stand up to him?' Hands nodded. 'Well, the way it turned out, it looks as though Riordan saved Morgan's life. That's a rare act for a convict!'

'He deserves to get his ticket of leave, sir.'

'It appears he does, but that'll have to wait, I'm afraid. My report won't make pleasant reading in Sydney, and no one figures well in it—yourself included. You realise a transfer is in order for you, too?'

Dodds went to protest, then held his tongue, resigned.

'Three months in Sydney on some investigations I have in mind.' Hands rapped his fingers on his desk. 'I suspect Morgan's a sadist, and I'd like him drummed out of service. But until he exposes himself as the brute he is, I can only transfer him on. That's a risk, too. I don't want him causing a death on the gangs.' He clasped his hands together. 'Right then. You're going to Sydney for a while. I'll get another officer to replace you pro tem while you check some things for me.' He reached over his desk, pulled up a folder and extracted two sheets of paper. 'The costs for bringing materials up the Road have almost doubled in three months but the loads and routes they travel haven't, so something's not right. Investigate that and the other things on the list. Keep me informed and come back in three months when, I trust, things, will be sorted out here.' He smiled. 'There'll either be a new man in my chair because Morgan has killed someone at Ten Mile or been killed himself or—much to be preferred—he's got the message.'

'Very good, sir.'

Hands nodded. 'Now, on your horse.'

Dodds saluted and left. He was disappointed at being off the Road, but then thoughts of Sydney town drew him and his spirits rose. There would be time and opportunity to dig further into what had happened to Riordan in Cork. And he was leaving behind a road gang that would never feel Sergeant Morgan's whip again.

* * *

Inside the office of the Roads and Bridges Department, five clerks and four ticketed convicts slogged at paperwork with their heads either deep in files, filling in forms or in conversation. Odours from boots, sweat and tobacco mixed with the faint smoke from the wood heater. All were making Dodds perspire more. The clock struck ten and he grabbed his coat and file and headed outside where the June wind was scurrying the leaves on the pavement.

The fresh air hit him and he felt he was back on the Road. That's where he liked to be. Four weeks he'd been here and he had heard nothing about what was happening with the gangs. No news was good news? He was unsure.

In those weeks he had tracked down three of the buyers who had bought stone from the Parramatta quarry. Under his implied threat of a departmental inquiry they all admitted to him that Simpson had run a scam with the Parramatta quarry scales that gave them a discounted price on stone in return for a small backhander to Simpson. None would agree to supply an affidavit to this effect, but Dodds did not ask for one. It was sufficient for the moment to know that Simpson had operated—was possibly still operating—this scam, to the detriment of his employer. It was something to hold over the man if need be.

Today Dodds had another opportunity to escape desk-bound duties, this time on the orders of Superintendent Hands. Clapping on his hat, he headed towards Kent Street.

A Mr Maurice Silverstein had the contract to supply tools and other material for the final section of the Road at Devine's Hill, and the trader had recently put up his costs. That was what brought Dodds to Silverstein's office. Opening a door in a shop front he went inside to find a young lady seated behind a counter.

'Yes, sir,' she said, getting to her feet.

'I'm Lieutenant Dodds. I'm here to see Mr Silverstein.'

'Good morning, Lieutenant. Please come this way.'

He followed her and paused as she held open the office door for him. 'Thank you.'

Maurice Silverstein stood up behind his desk and extended his hand. 'How do you do, sir. Anyone associated with the Great North Road is welcome here.'

Dodds clasped Silverstein's hand. 'How do you do, sir.'

'Very well,' Silverstein said sitting down. 'Can I order you some refreshment? Tea perhaps?' The room was not brightly lit but the man's bald head and spectacles gleamed, giving him a cheerful look.

Dodds seated himself opposite the merchant. 'Thank you, no.'

'I love the area up there, Lieutenant Dodds, especially Wiseman's. And the Road is a masterpiece of engineering. You must be proud of it.'

'For my part of it I am, thank you, but there's much still to do.'

'For what section are you responsible?' Silverstein asked.

'Devine's. Up from Wiseman's to the stockade.'

Silverstein smiled. 'Then you're on my patch.'

'Indeed,' Dodds replied. 'When were you up there last?'

'In April. I normally stay at the inn.'

'Owned by Mr Wiseman,' Dodds said. 'You use his wagons, I understand, to transport your goods up there?'

'I do, Lieutenant; we have a regular agreement.'

'I'll be frank, Mr Silverstein, accounts have itemised the transport costs alongside the price you're charging for the tools and materials, and it would appear that those costs are higher than when we first came to an agreement with you.'

The merchant spread his hands. 'Indeed, Lieutenant, you're perfectly correct. You see the tonnages are greater and so is the distance travelled.' He reached behind him, took a map off a shelf and spread it on the desk. 'Let me show you the route our deliveries take these days. Accessibility up country changes all the time, as you well know.' His eyes twinkled behind the glasses.

Dodds left his seat to lean over the desk and Silverstein explained distances and practicalities that convinced Dodds about the increases. When they looked into the goods supplied, Silverstein could show that the quality of many items, especially tools, had gone up—and hence so had the prices charged to Roads and Bridges. Over recent times, demand for tools in the colony had risen but the rate of imports had not, and as a result prices had increased. Meanwhile local manufacturing went ahead, often producing better quality tools but at similar prices. The department would have to accept the situation—but with the saving grace that the quality of the metalwork was improving.

Dodds sat down again, satisfied that Silverstein was trading above board. Naturally the man had not disclosed what profit he was making from his transactions with Roads and Bridges, but Dodds could see it was within reason.

'Thank you for the frank discussion, Mr Silverstein. I wonder if you can tell me a little about your company, its size and capability?'

'Delighted to, Lieutenant. There's myself and two assistants and Miss Rebecca Gabon, whom you've met. I employ three men in our warehouse. I obtain my supplies in Sydney. Imported goods, of course, but tools and so on are increasingly manufactured here. A number of new foundries have opened up in Sydney.'

'I'd be obliged if you could supply names of the best foundries to me.'

Silverstein studied him. 'May I ask why?'

'Government policy, Mr Silverstein. We have a duty to the government to expend its money as judiciously as possible. It's standard to check on new suppliers.'

'Of course. Excuse me. Miss Rebecca!' A pause then footsteps sounded and the door opened.

'Yes, sir?'

'Please make a list of the top four foundries in town and have them ready for Lieutenant Dodds when he leaves.'

'Yes, sir. Will that be all?'

'It will, thank you,' Silverstein said.

The door closed behind her.

Dodds talked with Maurice Silverstein for a few more minutes, finding the exchange pleasant and the man behind the desk shrewd but conversable. He'd noted the man's brogue and said, 'You've been in the colony a year or two, I understand. Did you come here from Ireland?'

'No, London. At one time …' his voice faded and he waved a vague hand. 'But I have no Irish connections now.'

In the silence that followed, Dodds decided to take his leave.

'It's been a pleasure, Lieutenant,' Silverstein said as they shook hands.

In the anteroom, Miss Gabon stood up behind her counter and held out a paper. 'Sir, here is your list.'

'Thank you.' Dodds left the office, put on his hat and stepped out into Kent Street.

There were four names on the list of foundries, the first one being Hughes. The business was in Sussex Street, so Dodds hadn't far to walk. Hughes? A Patrick and Sean Hughes were connected with Riordan's Cork affair, but that was surely a coincidence; Hughes was a common enough name in Ireland. Dodds set off and soon came to his destination.

The heat hit him ten feet from the open street doorway. A sign above told him he'd come to the right place and he entered. The interior was devoted to furnace and forge, and if there was an office it must be behind the premises. At the furnace, a man was concentrating on ladling molten metal into moulds. Sparks hit his muscled arms above his gloves but the man's hand remained steady. He was a craftsman, spilling hardly a drop into the plate underneath. The blaze and the work drew Dodds forward.

'Can I help you?'

Dodds turned to face another man in his thirties, dressed in a pair of canvas trousers and work boots. A white-collared shirt sat under a well-cut jaw, pleasant face and wavy hair. The man put his hand out. 'I'm Sean Hughes,' he said, 'the owner.'

Dodds blinked. The Christian name was Sean—another coincidence? 'Good day, Mr Hughes, I'm Lieutenant Dodds, an overseer on the Great North Road.'

'How do you do, Lieutenant. How can I help you?'

'I've just come from Silverstein's. He tells me a number of the tools and so on that he supplied to Roads and Bridges are made in city foundries. I'd be grateful if you could spare me some time to talk about what we need on the Road, where your metal comes from and how you make tools and equipment.'

'Gladly. I'm ready for a bite to eat. Would you like to join me?'

'I would, thank you.'

'Right, there's a pub not far from here. It serves a tasty meat pie.'

Dodds accompanied Hughes outside. Was this the Sean Hughes from Cork, who had made the tabernacle doors that Riordan was accused of stealing? And if he was, was he guilty of setting Riordan up or was he a victim who might help bring the truth to light? Dodds would tread with care.

Squashed between beer-swilling workers, Dodds sat with pie and beer and tucked in. The meat was indeed tasty and the pastry crisp. 'Thank you for this.'

'Good, eh?' Hughes wiped his mouth. 'You command gangs on the road?'

'One gang on Devine's Hill. Convicts mostly but they're good workers, all of them.' He chewed on a bit of tougher beef. 'I've just come from Mr Silverstein. He gave me your name as one of Sydney's top four metal manufacturers.'

Hughes let out a breath. 'Big of him. I'd like to sell him my iron. But I've put three bids in, only to find I'm undercut by others.'

'That's business, I suppose,' Dodds said. 'What is your price for the metal?'

'By the hundredweight, raw?'

'Yes. In bars, for construction.'

'Delivered to Silverstein's, about five pounds sterling.'

'And you got beaten on that?'

Hughes slapped the table. 'Handsomely.'

'What if I told you that Silverstein quoted twelve pounds per hundredweight to us for iron bars? And a lot of them, I may say.'

Hughes winced, then calculated for a while in his head. 'He's got to pay for the metal itself, then the handling, transport and overheads. Yes, his price structure is about right for him to make a profit. But he could still make a profit if he purchased our iron.' Hughes gave a philosophical smile. 'I think our problem is quantity—there are other foundries bigger and more established than we are right now, that can fulfil larger orders without delay. I'm not worried, though. We're expanding and I've got lots of other work. I don't need Silverstein's business at the moment.'

Dodds finished his meal and drained his ale, impressed with Hughes's even temperament and his acumen. 'How long has your foundry been going?'

'We started in Christmas last year. My father and I had a similar business in Cork before that. My brother runs it now.'

Dodds brightened. 'You lived there?'

'Until July twenty-nine. The family's been there for a generation. Three before that in Dublin.'

'So, you know Saint Mary's Cathedral?' Dodds said.

'Like my own back garden,' Hughes said and smiled. 'You're English, aren't you?'

'From Bath, Mr Hughes, but lately I've developed an interest in Cork. For complex reasons.'

Hughes touched his empty glass to Dodds's. 'Another beer while we talk? I've got time.' He got to his feet.

'Surely,' Dodds replied. This had to be the man.

Bringing the beers back, Hughes resumed his seat. 'We began with small jobs here, such as our first work for the Synagogue, specialist candelabras called menorahs. That's where we heard Mr Silverstein's name. At present we're doing a big order for wagon axles.'

'About Cork,' Dodds said. 'I'd like to ask—'

'Mr Hughes.' A man came up to them and Hughes turned to him.

'Hello, Jack,' Hughes said. 'What's up?'

'There's a problem with the alloys. Sorry, but we need you back.'

Hughes nodded. 'I'll be right there.' Jack touched his cap to Dodds and left. 'Sorry, Lieutenant,' Hughes said. 'I've got to go.'

'I'd like to talk further, if you don't mind.'

'I'm in Sydney for a couple of days, then I'm heading off to Parramatta. Are you staying near the department?'

'I am,' Dodds replied.

'I'll come by and you can shout me a feed downtown.' He gripped Dodds's hand, the fingers pressing hard. 'Goodbye.'

Hughes left and Dodds sat back, amazed at finding Sean Hughes like this, out of the blue. He couldn't wait for another meeting, to get more out of him.

* * *

In the low mid-June sunlight, Francis Murphy was working on the last of the four storage and maintenance huts built at regular positions along the Devine's Hill section. While nailing the planks to the frame he thought about Lieutenant Curran, Dodd's replacement for three months. Murphy glanced up the line where Curran was talking to Riordan and his labourers. So far he seemed a fair man.

There was a rider coming up the road towards Murphy. Not a uniformed man, a civilian, in good moleskins, jacket and cotton shirt.

'Morning,' the man said pulling his horse to a halt. He looked in his thirties, mousy hair under a broad hat, the face not memorable except for a scar under the left eye.

Francis was used to being passed by, not addressed, so the greeting amused him. 'And you are, sir?'

'My name is Dougal Simpson.'

Murphy put in another nail and took a break. 'What brings you up here, Mr Simpson?'

'I'm a partner in Dempsey's Quarry, Mr ...'

The 'Mr' almost made him laugh. 'Murphy. Francis Murphy.'

Simpson looked into the distance at Curran's group. 'We've quoted on dressed stone, Mr Murphy, for the Banks Crossing Bridge.'

'Just finished the main roadworks there,' Murphy said, following the man's gaze. 'Are you here to check on how the stone's been laid?'

'Maybe,' Simpson said, and something in his eyes showed Murphy he suddenly realised who he was talking to. He went on, though, trying to talk smooth. 'The contract allows payment up front and the government knows that good stone is scarce. So we can call the terms.' Simpson smirked. 'Used to be one of you lot. Got my ticket in April.' He looked Murphy over, condescending. 'We had yellow slops, but you're kitted out different.'

Murphy pinched his woollen trousers. 'They're supposed to be black and white stripes but end up as grey and cream. So, what type of stone do you sell, Mr Simpson?'

'Dressed granite and limestone. It's expensive.'

'It is,' Murphy agreed, 'but we only need small sections done with the better stone, just to give the work a nice finish.'

Simpson glanced up the line again at Curran and the lads. Murphy wondered why.

Simpson said, 'Are there any good tradesmen in with you? Stonemasons?'

'There's one up there. The tall fellow in that group.' Simpson turned to look again. 'Some of them are carpenters, like me.'

'All Irish?' Simpson said.

'Fair number of us. From your accent, I'd say you'd be from the south. Right, Mr Simpson?'

Simpson fell silent and Murphy examined him. If he was a partner in a quarry he'd have made a tidy quid, so why the hell would he be here in fancy clothes, crawling around fly-blown scrub? 'Do you travel to all the sites where your stone ends up?'

'Here and there. I've only had my ticket since April, so it's novel to get out.'

Murphy tried a direct approach. 'You've come to see old mates?'

Simpson frowned. 'I'm here on business, Murphy. Pure and simple.'

Lieutenant Curran was now riding towards them. 'Here's our officer now. He can tell you all about the stonework.'

Simpson glanced at the approaching rider and sniffed. 'Another time, maybe. Good day.'

Simpson trotted back the way he'd come and Murphy continued with his work. Odd: Simpson looked skittish about officials. Why?

'Murphy,' Curran called out. 'I want that hut finished today.'

'Yes, sir.'

Mr Curran glanced at Simpson riding away. 'Who was that?'

'A man from Dempsey's Quarry, sir.'

'You've no time to chat. Get into it.'

'Sir.'

Curran rode off.

* * *

Gerry awoke, rubbed his eyes and put on his clothes. Another day on Devine's, but it was Friday and he was going to Wiseman's with Francis Murphy. He laced up his boots, rubbed his hands at the winter chill and joined the others around the campfire for porridge and tea.

Lieutenant Curran came up to them when he and Murphy were both seated on the wagon.

'Right, lads'—he held a paper out—'this is my list. Make sure everything's on the wagon and bring it back in good shape. You understand?'

'Yes, sir,' they both replied.

Gerry hit the traces and the wagon took off. 'He's all right, that officer. Not as good as Dodds, but he's fair.' Gerry paused. 'Dodds has come round to believing I'm innocent, you know. Though what can anyone do about that?'

'He's looking after you, mate,' Murphy said. 'He is.' He nudged his shoulder against Gerry. 'Where we are now may not be the world we want, but there's blue sky in some of it.'

From the inn, Deirdre heard wagon wheels and quickened her steps through the kitchen. She wondered for a moment how she'd feel if it was Lieutenant Bates arriving. The last time he'd written, he'd seemed in good fettle and cheerful, and said he might be returning to Sydney in October. She hadn't written to him lately. Perhaps she should.

Her father and mother were busy at chores and she'd be able to greet Gerry alone. Going into the storeroom, she opened its double doors to the yard. The wagon was there, backed up ready for loading.

'Morning, Miss Walsh.' Francis Murphy turned to greet her from the driver's seat.

'And good morning to you, Mr Murphy,' she said. Her lips parted in a smile as Gerry jumped down and gave her a grin.

He pulled back on the traces of the horses and directed the rear of the wagon further in between the doors.

'I can do the loading, Miss Walsh' Murphy said. 'Got Mr Curran's list.' He came round the wagon and handed it to her.

'Morning, Miss Walsh,' Gerry said, stopping in front of her. 'There are some things on there that you've got stored in the back huts, I think.'

'Yes,' said Murphy. 'You go get them, Tiny. I'll handle the goods in here.'

She smiled at the carpenter. Had Gerry organised this division of labour? She felt a thrill. 'Come on, Mr Riordan.'

What she was planning to do felt wicked. Yes, her parents had accepted that she'd been meeting with Gerry but they were only supposed to be studying together. While Mr Dodds was away there were no new books, so her parents had vetoed the readings.

They passed one hut and stopped at the second. 'In here,' she said. Removing a key from her belt, she undid the lock of the hut and stepped into the warm, musty darkness. Gerry followed. Closing the door behind him, she bolted it.

'Where are the goods?' he said, teasing her.

'They're here, but first I want to talk to you.' She took his hand in hers and he let her. She had strong feelings for him, even strong enough for love, but she wouldn't tell him that. Not yet. 'I want you to tell me what you think of me.'

He looked down, stroking her fingers. 'You're very sweet.'

'Sugar is sweet, Gerry. What do you feel for me?'

His eyes were bright. 'I like you. A lot.'

'But do you love me?'

He sighed and was silent for a moment. 'Love. It's a wonderful word, Deirdre.' He paused again. 'There's so much going on in my mind and you're a big part of that. But my life here is fixed and I've no freedom.'

'You've got more than most,' she said.

'But not as much as I need,' he said and cupped her chin, 'to do the things I'd like to do. I can't think of love, here … no. But I like you, very much.' She was disappointed but she couldn't get angry at him. They had kissed, after all. She looked deep into his eyes and they never left hers—that made her think he did love her, even if he wouldn't say it.

He bent down and kissed her now and she responded. It took a long time before she could detach herself a little. She smiled up at him, her skin damp with excitement, her breathing quick. She closed her eyes, ready to kiss him again, but there came a knock on the door.

'Miss Walsh,' Francis said urgently on the other side, 'your father's looking for you. I've steered him away from here for now.'

'We're coming,' she called. She took Gerry's arm. 'That box near the door. There's a pinch bar on top. Use it to open it, quick.'

He wrenched open the box. Inside were shovels wrapped in greased paper to keep them from rust. 'Take two at a time outside.' She unlocked the door and looked to see if her father was coming, but he was nowhere in sight. 'Bind them together to make a stack.'

Before he took up the tools she grabbed his hand. 'Just remember that you have friends: there's me, and Murphy and Dooley, and Mr Dodds.'

'He's an officer.'

'He's your friend, Gerry and he told me so.'

'Truly?'

'Yes! Get those shovels out. I'll help you. I know Mr Dodds can do things for you and he'll not give up. He's like a terrier, but with a brain.'

She was trying to make Gerry laugh but he didn't. 'Won't do me no good.'

'There you go: silly you are, saying rubbish like that.'

'It's true,' he said as he left the hut with the tools. 'What can it get me?'

She joined him outside with the twine. 'A ticket that's what, a way to earn your living, to be a free man.'

'That's years away.'

'Have hope, Gerry.'

'You have that?'

'I do,' she said.

He smiled. 'You sound like you do.'

After a few moments they had the rest of the shovels outside and ready for pick-up.

'Mr Dodds will come back,' she said, 'and things will change.' She gave him a push. 'Go and see how Murphy is doing, and if he's finished, get the wagon over here.'

'Yes, boss.'

She smiled. 'You know, you big lump, that if you get your ticket you can do what you want.'

'Around here I can.'

'Around here you've got me.' She pulled a strand of hair back from her face. 'That's if you still want me.'

'Why wouldn't I?'

'Hearing is believing.'

'What do you want me to say? I like you Deirdre, a lot. You're good and kind.'

'And pretty?'

'And that,' he said.

She pulsed with pleasure, which vanished as a tall shape came towards them. 'It's Father,' she whispered. 'Tie those last shovels up, quick.'

'Deirdre,' Brian Walsh said coming towards them, 'your mother needs you. Off to the kitchen now.'

'I'm coming, Father. Just locking the hut.'

She spoke in a low voice, her back to her father. 'Find another way to get to see me, Gerry.'

'I will.'

She ran off and Brian Walsh tramped up to Gerry. 'Don't dawdle there, get those shovels bound proper. I don't want any complaint from the Road about damaged goods.'

'Yes, sir.'

Walsh looked at him with suspicion. 'What were you doing with my daughter?'

Gerry stood straight and looked at the man. 'She showed me where the shovels were, Mr Walsh, just all. I have to get the wagon.'

Walsh nodded. 'Then I won't stop you.'

* * *

Lieutenant Dodds looked up from his desk. At first, he didn't recognise the man in a good coat and cravat standing in front of him, then he smiled. 'Mr Hughes, how do you do?'

'Well, thank you, Mr Dodds. Are you busy?'

'Not now.' Dodds said and glanced at the wall clock in the Roads and Bridges building. 'It's noon. There's a hotel across the road, not as good as the one near you, but the food's acceptable and the beer's malty. Interested?'

'Lead on.'

They crossed busy George Street. Hughes wore his smart clothes well and seemed comfortable in them, as he did in his work gear.

Dodds spotted two spare seats in the crowded hotel and pointed to them. 'If you grab those, I'll order. What'll you have?'

'Pint of porter, and'—Hughes looked at the chalkboard—'some cutlets and gravy, please.'

'Right.' Dodds walked up to the bar. He ordered the meals, paid for two pints and brought them over. 'I want to talk about architecture, art and construction.'

Hughes grinned. 'Cheers.'

Dodds touched his glass with his. 'I'm a chartered surveyor for my sins, and as a separate interest I have an eye and passion for detailed work. I've been to your Saint Mary's cathedral in Cork and I remember gold filigree around the altar. Someone said to me the other day that they've enhanced the altar even further. With what?'

'They have indeed,' Hughes said, 'with more gold. There's a new tabernacle with gold doors.'

'Beautiful they must be.' Dodds's nose tweaked to the smell of the lamb and he turned as a young woman placed two plates of steaming meat in front of them. 'Thank you,' he said to her and smiled. 'Just the thing for this cold snap.'

'Are you interested in gold, Lieutenant?'

'Not gold in itself, the fine work that can be done with it.'

Hughes pierced a cutlet and sawed it with his knife. 'I know those tabernacle doors only too well. The Hughes Foundry made them.'

'You did? Tell me about them, please.'

'They had a chequered life. The first set went missing.'

'The first set?'

'Aye. We had to make another.'

Dodds looked up but said nothing.

Hughes was serious. 'Stolen, Lieutenant, and there's a story in itself.' A wind gust rattled the window next to them and Hughes glanced outside.

'And the design,' Dodds said, 'was it intricate?'

Hughes looked back to him. 'Sorry … yes it was. There were two gold plates, one in bas-relief. The back plate was fixed to a timber panel and that was screwed to a brass frame. I can give you a look at the plans, if you like. I've still got them, but sometimes I feel like throwing them out. The whole story of those doors is a tragedy.'

'Because they were stolen?'

'Yes, they were taken somewhere between our foundry and the cathedral, and the gold was never recovered.'

'Were you compensated for the loss?'

'No, the doors were not insured. We had to replace them at our own expense.'

Dodds whistled softly. 'That would have cost you! No wonder you call that a tragedy.'

'Aye. But there's worse. The police pulled in the two men who'd been transporting the doors and tried to nail them for the theft. They had to release them because there wasn't enough evidence, but then one of them was murdered in the other man's digs. There was a box in the room, with the door frames but no gold. It looked as though they'd quarrelled over the gold and one of them lost his head. So he was convicted of theft and murder.'

Riordan! Dodds nearly blurted out the name. Did Hughes think he was guilty? Or had Hughes framed him? Dodds shook his head: he couldn't see any motive on Hughes's side—the foundry would have been massively out of pocket following the theft. He could see Hughes looking at him curiously, so he decided to stick to the subject of the gold.

'The condemned man never let on where the gold was?'

'No.'

'Then how did he dispose of it? You couldn't fence stolen goods of that kind; they'd be traced in no time. Bas-relief doors, made for the cathedral and intended for consecration—they'd stick out like the proverbial. No one would touch them.'

Hughes said, 'Quite. They might be intact, hidden somewhere in Cork. But my father and I long ago came to the conclusion they were melted down by whoever stole them.'

Dodds said, 'Into something like ingots?'

'Yes, small and transportable. So that gold could be anywhere by now.'

Dodds sat back. 'You say "Whoever stole them". You don't think it was the man who got convicted?'

A look of sadness crossed Hughes's face and he avoided Dodds's eye for a moment, putting down his ale and glancing out the window. Then he gave a slight shrug and said, 'My father believes he was guilty of both crimes. James Donovan—our client at the cathedral—is adamant the man was guilty. But his daughter, Anne … she knew the stonemason, because he worked for her father. She'd known him for years and considered him a decent man. She's always believed he was innocent, and her word is good enough for me because she happens to be my wife.'

Dodds looked at him in amazement. Hughes had been robbed of thousands of pounds worth of gold and he believed the culprit innocent, on his wife's say-so. This story Hughes was telling him—it wasn't only about theft and murder. There was love in it. 'You show a touching loyalty to your wife's good judgment, sir.'

Hughes said quietly, 'I'd met the man myself, of course, though not well enough to give him a character reference. But we— I followed what happened after the trial and new evidence came up that pointed away from the stonemason having murdered the other man.'

Dodds was excited. This was getting close to what he'd been wanting to ask Hughes about—the Cork courts' report to New South Wales and the possible retrial or pardon. Hughes had had dealings with the police—did he know how close Riordan might be to proving his innocence? But if Dodds pressed for detail, he was not sure he could keep Hughes talking. He'd noticed that Hughes was holding back the stonemason's name. Why the discretion? There was one obvious reason: to prevent a convict's name being connected in any way with his wife.

Hughes spoke again, his voice low. 'Not that any of that matters now. The man's dead.'

Dodds started and the movement of his hand spilled his pint of porter. Hughes had to lift a sleeve out of the wetness.

'Sorry,' Dodds said. 'Clumsy of me. Dead? You're sure?'

'Yes. Transported in twenty-eight, a few weeks here, and then he died. We have no details of his death and I didn't seek any. My wife was distressed enough as it was. Considering her faith in his innocence.'

Dodds was struggling to see where this conversation could go next, without his blurting out, *But Riordan's not dead!* He said in a strangled voice, 'But you think there's evidence to prove it?'

Hughes rallied and pointed a finger at him. 'See, I told you you'd be hooked by the story. All right, there were anomalies in the handwriting in two documents that related to the crimes. And there was a remarkable resemblance between two people who were in and about the crime scene at the time. I think it could be shown that they were the same person—that person being both thief and murderer.'

Dodds drank the rest of his beer. Was Hughes talking of Simpson? 'This whole business,' he said with all sincerity, 'has had an extraordinary effect on a number of lives, especially yours. The loss of the gold sounds crippling, for a start.'

Hughes gave a grim nod, accepting Dodd's sympathy for what it was. 'Indeed. In fact Hughes Foundry in Cork is still paying off the debt. That's one of the reasons my wife and I are here in the colony—I want to help my brother and father by sending some of our income home.'

Dodds was surprised. 'I must confess to a fellow feeling with you, sir—I left England to take up my post here, largely to assist my own father.'

Hughes brightened. 'A fine goal and may we both achieve it in this new country. That's what I promised my wife Anne, if she'd consent to come here—a new life. I felt we could only prosper if we left Cork behind and made a home for ourselves in a place that held promise.'

'And she is content with what she's found here? So far, I've found it rough but, as you say, full of promise.'

Hughes's smile was fond. 'I think in a way she was more eager than I to leave all our problems behind in Ireland. She has adapted to Sydney in a marvellous way. She was used to a large household, but she's made our small one into a haven. And I'm happy to say there will be an addition to it, in two months' time.'

'Congratulations!'

'Thank you, Lieutenant.' Hughes pulled out his fob watch. 'I have to go, I'm afraid. Thank you for the meal. It's been pleasant talking to you and I feel we have much in common. I'm sure Anne would appreciate your company. Would it please you to dine with us on Sunday?' He stood up and put out his hand.

Dodds stood up and clasped it. 'I'd like that.'

'Castlereagh Street, number twenty-three, about one in the afternoon?'

'Done.'

Hughes nodded and walked away.

Dodds sat down, floored by everything he had heard. He could not help liking Hughes. A genuine, honest man, clearly in love with his wife and careful of her reputation. And ready to defend the innocence of another man at her prompting—the very man convicted of robbing him!

Dodds was eager to meet the former Anne Donovan. He thought of her growing up in the 'large household' in Cork, knowing Gerry Riordan, stonemason, for years before she met her future husband. Had there been a prior friendship there, an attachment to Riordan? Riordan had never mentioned her, though he'd said he'd worked for James Donovan. Was there love on either side? Dodds pitied Riordan if that were so.

The biggest mystery in all this was the correspondent who had sent a letter to Cork saying that Riordan was dead. The letter must have been a forgery, put together by someone who could copy official documents. The mystery correspondent had to be someone who wanted the investigations into Riordan's trial discontinued. The person with the strongest motive for this piece of forgery and misinformation was the thief and murderer in question. And that person was here, operating in New South Wales. Simpson? Or someone with a bit of education: the elusive Greenberg?

Dodds was in a terrible dilemma over his visit to the Hugheses on Sunday. To mention the name Riordan was unthinkable—Hughes had not pronounced it before Dodds and he would be outraged if it were brought up in front of his wife. The whole business of the trial and its aftermath would not be discussed over the dinner table of a respectable woman, worshipped by her husband and in a delicate condition. But Gerry Riordan was alive!

Chapter Ten

It was a simple, well-constructed dwelling at number twenty-three Castlereagh Street in Sydney town, one of many such houses and quasi-stores lining this major street.

William Dodds approached the dwelling, straightened his uniform, got a tighter grip on the small gift he had brought, and rapped on the knocker.

Sean Hughes opened the door. 'Ah, Lieutenant, welcome. Come in. That southerly is bitter.'

'It is that,' Dodds said and removed his hat. He followed Hughes into a modest, warm and clean parlour.

'Dear,' Hughes said, 'this is Lieutenant Dodds.'

Anne Hughes was an attractive young woman of no more than twenty, with dark hair and a slim body, her pregnancy softened by the loose morning gown that fell from a high waist. She rose a little awkwardly from a chair, smiled at him and presented her hand. 'Good afternoon, Lieutenant. Welcome to our home.'

Dodds bowed over the hand, which was small and smooth. He could see why Hughes felt protective of this refined young woman. 'Good afternoon, Mrs Hughes. This is for you.' He handed over his present.

'Boiled sweets!' she said. 'How lovely. I haven't had these since Ireland.'

'We have contacts with importers,' Dodds said. 'I hope you'll like them.'

'Excellent,' Sean said. 'Come into the dining room. Dinner is ready.'

Hughes pulled out a chair for his wife. 'Are you comfortable?'

'Perfectly, dear. Please, Mr Dodds, sit down.'

'Thank you.'

A cook-maid served the soup and they all tucked in.

'My husband tells me you supervise the gangs on the Great North Road. We read a lot about it in the newspaper.'

'The Road is a massive undertaking. It stretches all the way from Wiseman's to Mount Manning. There are work gangs on all sections of it. I look after one such gang of about fifty men. This soup is delicious. My compliments, Mrs Hughes.'

'Thank you.'

Hughes nodded at Dodds and smiled. The conversation during the first course flowed easily. Mrs Hughes was interested in the Road and Dodds found her questions and comments knowledgeable, particularly about construction. This surprised him until he remembered that she was, after all, the daughter of a master stonemason.

She said at one point, 'It sounds as though your accommodation is makeshift, Lieutenant, so unlike the thoroughness that goes into the Road. Why, you're even under canvas some of the time. Does that get you down at times?'

'Not at all. I only need a roof so I can put my head down. The days are filled with work and I enjoy the challenges of it.' He smiled at her. 'I suppose we all put up with hardship when needs be. You must have a little less luxury here than you had in Cork? But I see you've made a comfortable home here.'

Anne Hughes smiled, her green eyes sparkling.

Dodds sat back as the roast was placed on the table. 'Would you ever return?'

'At some distant time, perhaps. Meanwhile I'm very preoccupied with events in the short term.' She added shyly, 'We'll soon have a family to raise.'

Hughes sliced into the lamb. 'Your plate, Lieutenant.'

She went on, 'Thank you for answering all my questions about the Road. It must seem so mundane to you, but I like to hear about the creation of useful things. Even building materials fascinate me!' She laughed at herself.

'Well, I can understand your interest in stone, of course. On the Road it's the most massive material and the most important.'

Hughes passed the vegetables to his guest. 'It's all quarried in the hills where you work?'

'We have to get it where we find it, which means cutting and blasting. A lot of sandstone, and harder stone for some of the culvert sections.'

'You have to dress that stone?' she asked.

'Indeed,' Dodds smiled again. 'You are informed. I've checked to see whether we might buy the granite from a Parramatta quarry, owned in part by a ticket-of-leave man called Simpson.'

Hughes's eyes grew round. 'Simpson?'

'Yes,' Dodds said.

'What's his first name?'

Dodds hesitated. They seemed about to land on dangerous territory. He still could not decide how much of Riordan's past he should be discussing with them. 'I don't remember.'

'It wouldn't be Dougal, would it?' Hughes said.

'That's it!'

Mrs Hughes looked at her husband, who had placed his fork down. Her expression was calm but her eyes seemed to be signalling him to speak.

Hughes said, 'We knew of a Mr Dougal Simpson in Cork, Lieutenant. Describe this one for us, please.'

Dodds did so. It was Mrs Hughes who replied.

'Thank you. That is a description of the Simpson who worked in a quarry in Cork. He was a petty criminal, found guilty of a bank theft and transported here.'

'You had no business with him in Cork?' Dodds said.

Sean was looking straight ahead, clasping his wine glass with a firm grip. 'No business with him. None.'

'You wouldn't want to have any here, either. I've checked in Sydney and Parramatta about Simpson. I suspected he was underhanded and what I've found here in town verifies that.'

Mrs Hughes looked at her husband, then at Dodds. 'There is more, Lieutenant. We think that he was mixed up with a crime in Cork. Some gold doors were stolen and—'

'Yes, your husband has told me,' Dodds said.

'What he didn't tell you is that Simpson may well have been the thief.'

This meant Hughes had shared their conversation at the pub with his wife. Was it time to tell them both about Riordan?

Hughes put in, 'And there's every reason to believe the thief was the murderer—he killed to put the police off track.'

'I see,' Dodds said. 'I'm of your opinion: Simpson shows all the signs of a potential killer. But I'm not sure that the courts here could prove he was guilty of what happened in Cork. Unless he has your gold, of course.'

Hughes's eyes lit up. 'It's not the gold that haunts me, Lieutenant, or even getting Simpson found guilty. What we want is justice for an innocent man.'

'Even though that man is dead.' Anne Hughes's eyes started to glisten. 'I'm sorry, Lieutenant. This brings back something very painful to me.'

'I'm sorry too for that, Mrs Hughes,' Dodds said. 'But let me tell you this: I'm certain that Simpson has been stealing money from his employer, who is now his partner. I've got three quarry customers who've admitted to me in private they were in on the theft.'

'Get them to swear, then,' Hughes put in, his face animated.

Dodds grimaced. 'They told me about Simpson on the quiet. If I press them, they will deny it. No … but if I can get dirt on Simpson's other crime in Cork …'

'How?' Sean Hughes asked.

Dodds placed his cutlery together on his plate. 'I don't know. Maybe you could help.'

Hughes looked at his wife. 'We'll do anything.'

Mrs Hughes stood and pressed her hands into the small of her back. 'I need to be excused for a moment.' Dodds stood up, as did her husband. 'I shan't be too long.' She forced a smile and left them as the cook-maid cleared their plates.

'Come to the fire in the parlour,' Hughes said, 'and tell me more. A port perhaps?'

'Thank you.' Dodds sat on a lounge chair and welcomed the warmth on his knees. He leaned forward, his hands out to the heat. 'One of the convicts in my gang is a certified stonemason.'

Hughes handed him a filled glass. 'I'd have thought as much. Are there any other tradesmen?'

'Two carpenters; the rest are labourers.'

'No absconders or rebels?'

'We get a few, Mr Hughes. This stonemason was a handful for a good while, but he's now a trusty and heading for his ticket of leave. His tale is as tall as he is, and it includes all the facts we've just talked about. He's from Cork.'

'What's his name?'

Anne came up beside them and Sean helped her sit on the sofa.

Dodds knew what he'd say next would shock both of them and change their lives, but he had no choice. Surely the truth was better coming from him, rather than their hearing it in some official or random way. 'Gerry Riordan.'

Anne gasped.

'That's impossible!' Hughes said and stared at him for some time. 'No, no, no … wait. Why didn't you tell me this the other day when we were talking about the trial?'

'You never mentioned the man's name, sir.' Dodds was aware of Anne Hughes's distress but he couldn't look at her. He went on as dispassionately as he could, 'Very tall, red hair and a temper to match, though he reins it in these days. Intelligent, excellent with figures, fine craftsman.'

Anne Hughes's face was flushed. 'It can't be. He's dead; they wrote and told me he's dead.'

Hughes was angry. 'Dodds? Why didn't you tell me at the pub?'

'Mr Hughes, I haven't mentioned anything about the new investigations to the man himself. Though I suspect I'll need to shortly. So

I'm naming him to you with great reluctance, but I thought you needed to know.'

Hughes cursed under his breath, then looked up at his wife, who
had turned very pale.

Anne Hughes stood up, swaying. 'Where is he?'

'Devine's Hill. I'm sorry if—'

Hughes leapt to his feet. 'Anne!' He made a lunge for her but too
late.

'I have to … get out.' She rushed from the room and after a
second's hesitation Hughes followed her. She made it into the hallway
behind, on her way to the bedchambers. But there was a step there,
and before her husband could catch up to her she fell, striking one hip
sharply as she pitched sideways, then collapsed.

Dodds, on his feet in the parlour, heard the dreadful sound of her
falling, and saw the cook-maid rush past the doorway in a panic.

Hughes's voice was agonised. 'Get the doctor, quickly now!'

Two hours later, the two men were still in the parlour. Sean
Hughes, his face drawn, placed another log on the fire.

'I'd better leave, Mr Hughes,' Dodds said, not for the first time.

After Mrs Hughes had fallen, the doctor had arrived, and then
called in a midwife. There was much traffic, with things being carried
back and forth from the kitchen. There had been little sound from the
back rooms, just a moan now and then, to which Hughes sometimes
responded by pacing up and down in front of the fire.

'No … Dodds, stay just a bit longer. Dear God.' Hughes ran a
hand through his damp hair. 'I need someone's company, even yours,
or I'll go mad.'

Dodds felt like a guilty prisoner. His stomach was churning and
his mouth was tinder dry. 'I'm truly sorry, Mr Hughes. I've been in the
most godawful puzzle about Riordan, believe me. Whether I spoke
about him or not, I knew it would be bad either way. But I swear I
couldn't have foreseen the effect.'

Hughes looked at him in a daze. 'You know whom I curse for
this? Riordan, for ever going near her. And the bastard who should

have hanged for Toole's murder. And most of all the swine who wrote that letter. Dead? By God, I wish he were!'

Dodds said nothing. There was nothing to say—Hughes's pain was too raw.

The midwife stepped into the parlour and stood gazing at the floor as if she was inspecting it for dust. Hughes stood up. 'I'm sorry, sir,' she said. 'A boy. Lasted but a minute, and he's now with God.'

Hughes reached behind him, felt for the chair and sat down. 'You'll send for the priest.' He groaned and brought a hand to his face. 'My wife?'

'The doctor's with her. No ill effects, he says. She's resting, sir.'

'I'd best go,' Dodds said.

Sean peered at Dodds as though a piece of furniture had just spoken. After a moment he returned the hand to cover his face.

As Dodds closed the front door, sobs echoed through the little home. The lieutenant felt the weight of guilt on him as if it were two lengths of hardwood bound into a cross.

* * *

Timothy Johnson, judiciary clerk, pointed to three shelves of leather-bound books on one wall of his office. 'That's the master ledger for the last five years, Lieutenant. With its sub-ledgers it holds the records of correspondence received and sent on the convicts.'

'So,' Dodds said, 'if a letter was sent from here to Cork on the death of a convict, a copy would be recorded here?'

'With date and author, by me or one of the other clerks past or present.' He sat back and looked at Dodds. 'But we would have no record, because Riordan is still alive. Isn't he?' Dodds paused. 'You don't know?' Johnson smiled. 'He's in your gang.'

'My apologies, Mr Johnson. I have an unease about his safety. Sergeant Morgan has a vendetta against him.'

'That brute,' Johnson said, 'only needs one more black mark and he's out. He raped a girl in Ulster but the crime was hard to prove. The army had dishonourably discharged him for a similar incident.'

'Handsome.'

'Indeed, Lieutenant. We were desperate for scourgers then and we turned something of a blind eye. But now we have better trained people with no criminal records, so Morgan's days are numbered.'

'Back to Riordan,' Dodds said. 'He's alive and kicking but a letter was written from New South Wales to Cork, declaring that Riordan died a few weeks after transportation here.'

'You've seen it?'

'No, I haven't.'

'So you don't know to whom it was addressed.'

'I think the letter was addressed to Mrs Hughes personally. I might have asked the other day, but during my visit Mrs Hughes had a ... she lost her baby.'

'I'm sorry,' Johnson said.

'Not as much as I am. You see, I told her Riordan was alive. The shock may have brought the baby on.'

'How very sad. But Lieutenant, I think we need to pursue this. However painful for the recipient, I'd like to see that letter. If it was written under our seal, then that's an offence—or two offences, forgery and fraud. I need to see it before I begin an investigation.'

'Will that amount to anything?' Dodds asked, but he knew the answer already.

'In time, perhaps.'

Dodds sat back and pulled his jacket tighter. All the office doors and windows were closed but he still felt a winter draught from somewhere. 'My first guess at who cooked up the letter is a man called Simpson, who part-owns a quarry in Parramatta. He's bent like a bow and he's been skimming money from the business. I'm about to check his ticket and see how easy it was for him to get it.'

Johnson put out his hand. 'Good luck. It's an evil combination. One we come up against at times.'

Dodds stood up and shook Johnson's hand. 'What's that?'

'An underpaid, unhappy government official and the lure of money.'

'So, you think someone in the judiciary might have taken a bribe to issue the ticket?'

'Perhaps. It happens, Mr Dodds. Good luck.'

Dodds turned and left.

* * *

Anne was knitting in the parlour. Sean sat opposite her reading the *Gazette*. She focussed on the date, 13 August 1830. It was just under four weeks since she'd lost her poor premature baby but it felt like yesterday. She looked the same in the mirror, just paler. Her waist was still enlarged, another reminder. Putting her knitting down, she warmed her hands at the fire and reached for her drink of water.

This grief was different from the one she'd felt in Cork when she learned that Gerry Riordan was dead. This was devastation and guilt. In this room, she had not been able to stifle her reaction when she knew he was alive. If she had not lost control of herself, rushed off, she wouldn't have lost her baby. She was a failure as a mother—she had had a fairly normal pregnancy but she had ended it with an accident she caused herself. The pain of this was unbearable. Which sent her thoughts swinging back to the person she sometimes held most to blame—Gerry. He had done this to her. The things he had done in life had altered hers, for the worse. The news of his death had shaken her to the core and the news that he was alive had been too much to cope with. He had ruined her life. Then she relented. No, that was too long a bow to draw. She was lashing out, she knew.

'Are you all right, dear?'

Sean … loving, dear Sean. 'I am.'

He looked at her but wasn't satisfied, she guessed. At night he fretted in his sleep. He suffered as well. She prayed that he grieved for the lost baby and did not wonder whether thoughts of Gerry Riordan disturbed her.

Alive. Gerry was living, breathing, working. Unbelievable. No, true—it was the letter that had been a lie. Amongst the lies and injustice that surrounded his supposed crimes, why should a piece of paper not be false too? She was reaching for the letter in her pocket when the front doorbell rang.

'That'll be Dodds.' Sean put the newspaper down and went to the door.

In the first days after baby Patrick's death, she had hated even the sound of Lieutenant Dodds's name. But she had glimpsed him at the funeral, standing where he thought she would not notice him. And now, as he stood in front of her, running his hat round in his fingers, worry stencilled on his face, she could forgive him for bringing her the truth.

'Mrs Hughes?'

Feeling tears in her eyes, she gestured to a chair near her and he sat down.

'I can't begin to tell you how sorry I am. If I could retract the news about—'

'It's all right, really. It's God's will.' She looked at Sean, who was hovering. 'With his grace, we'll have more children.'

Dodds dropped his head.

'Now,' she said wiping her eyes. 'Dear me, I'd hate to smudge the letter. Here it is.' She pulled it out and gave it to him.

The lieutenant got up again, took it closer to the fire and read it through. 'The paper it's written on looks genuine. Mr Johnson at the judiciary showed me a blank page with the crown, coat of arms and so on printed on it.'

'Maybe someone stole a blank one,' Sean said, 'and filled out the details.'

'Can I keep this? The authorities will investigate it. It's a forgery, no doubt.'

She nodded. 'I never wish to see it again.' A log dropped onto the fire, forcing sparks up the chimney. 'And I never wish to see Mr Riordan again.'

Hughes laid a hand on her arm. 'You're not well yet, dear.'

She gave him a little smile. 'Even when I'm better, I'll never see him.'

Dodds did up a button of his jacket. 'I won't tell him, then, about your being in Sydney? The efforts that you two have made to clear his name?'

'I don't think so,' Hughes said looking at his wife.

'Mr Dodds?' she said, 'you'll stay for some tea?' She wanted to eat, to taste something and enjoy it, wanted something to distract her.

'If it's not an inconvenience?' Dodds said.

'No. Sean, dear, call the cook?'

'Surely.'

Anne watched him go and turned to the lieutenant. 'He's a good man.'

Dodds nodded. 'I observe that you're very fortunate in your husband, ma'am.'

'Gerry Riordan. Is he happy?'

'I couldn't really say. He's had … well, he had a bad patch when he started.'

She bit her lip. 'Is he healthy, at least?'

'Tea won't be long,' Sean said coming back. 'Dodds, I'd like your opinion on this new pick I've designed.' He went to a satchel by his chair. 'I've got the drawings here.'

As Sean rummaged in his bag, Dodds looked at her and she shook her head. Enough. Gerry was alive. That was all she would know about him, maybe all she'd ever know. Gathering up her knitting, she concentrated on her stitches.

* * *

Sean Hughes and Lieutenant Dodds headed down Macquarie Street on a cold morning. They had agreed to meet again before Dodds returned to the Road.

Hughes skirted a rubbish pile, telling off events in his mind. 'Riordan gets sent here in twenty-eight. It's now the middle of August, eighteen-thirty. That's over twenty-two months as a convict. He doesn't have a good record—flogged you say?'

'Twice,' Dodds said. 'It nearly killed him the second time.'

Hughes winced. 'Don't tell my wife that.'

'I won't.

'So, Lieutenant,' Hughes said moving back to let a dray pass, 'what have we got to prove Riordan innocent?'

'Nothing very concrete but there is that letter your wife received. It's my thought that it was cooked up by Simpson.'

'Or a government man in his pay. We could go to Parramatta and ask the police.'

'We could,' Dodds said, 'but that's a closed shop.'

'What do you mean?'

'They were defensive when I went there. Solidarity among the brothers, I suspect. One or two might be on the take but they protect each other nonetheless.'

Hughes stopped at his gig. 'Think, my friend.'

'I've not been your friend when it comes to Riordan.'

Hughes put a hand on his shoulder. 'My wife and I have been trying to free Riordan for years, and that began long before we met you. Whatever my wife may say, I don't think she'll ever be at rest until Riordan's case is clarified. And I'm prepared to keep on inquiring until it's settled one way or the other, because I love her and I want her to have peace of mind. Simple as that. Whatever you do to help, it will be appreciated.'

'I'm grateful you see it that way. This must be hard for you. Give me a day or two back up country and I'll get some ideas. I'll write to you.'

Hughes reached under his seat, pulled out a satchel and extracted a large package. 'This is the official record so far, and notes from Cork, and what I've added myself. I got my clerk to copy it for you. There might be things in there that'll spark your mind.' He shook Dodds's hand. 'You're doing a great deal for Riordan. I hope he appreciates it. How much will you tell him about your investigation?'

Dodds took the package. 'Thank you. Nothing. Not until the authorities are prepared to act in his favour. Ignorance will keep him sane. Keep well, Mr Hughes.'

Bailed Up

* * *

The evening darkness of mid-August settled on the Fortune of War Hotel in George Street, the Rocks. Inside Dougal Simpson sat waiting in shadow but with a view of the bar. The pub was newly built by one of their own, a rich convict, Samuel Terry.

Dempsey's Quarry was keeping Dougal fed and clothed in a fashion to please him but he wanted more. A ticket was as common now as George Street mud on a wet day. He had to have more. Looking down at his *Gazette* he brought it into the light and turned to the Tenders page, ink staining his fingers. Mr Maurice Silverstein had won another contract for the Road. Perhaps a visit to the up-and-coming Jewish merchant was on the cards, because with any luck he might have at least heard of Jacob Greenberg. Simpson had done some sniffing around in Town and it looked as though Greenberg had never come to Sydney. There was no record of him anywhere. So where the hell did he go with those gold beauties? Dougal gave his lucky medallion a rub and glanced at the wall clock. It was just time to buy another beer.

He brought his drink back and eased away a bar girl who'd come up close to him. Maybe later, not now. Moving his chair further back into the shadows, he waited.

The man entered the pub right on schedule and ordered his usual meal and a beer. Simpson watched him and bided his time. When the man had finished and left, Simpson followed him outside, closing his eyes for a fraction to adjust to the chilly darkness. His man walked down George Street and Simpson pulled his coat together and followed, keeping out of the light of the new oil lamps in the street.

Stench from an opened cesspit made him gag and he looked ahead but his quarry hadn't noticed him. He stopped when the man ducked into an alley and then stalked him in the darkness. Simpson smiled at a trickling sound, pulled out his knife and crept closer. His target had one arm pressed against a weatherboard wall, the other controlling the flow. The man made one final shake and Simpson's blade sank into his ribs. The man groaned and slumped. To check, Simpson walked back to the street, which was clear. Then returned to the body and spat on it. 'That's for everything you've done to me, Mr Adams, and all the backs you've skinned.'

After wiping his blade on the victim's jacket and lifting all his coins, he ambled back to the street, adjusting his trousers over the tumescence caused by the thrill of satisfaction. Peace of mind, that's what life was supposed to give him, and he just about had it. Riordan was his next mark but that would take finesse.

Mr Silverstein, now, there was a fellow whom he'd enjoy meeting and bringing around to do business the Dougal Simpson way. His trousers were still stretched taut and he knew just the place. A lively lass with a sweet bottom lived not far away. Relaxation. Much needed after dumping rubbish in an alley, and that's all Adams was.

* * *

Miss Rebecca Gabon knocked and entered Mr Silverstein's office. 'There's a Mr Simpson to see you, sir.'

Silverstein looked up at his assistant. The name gave him a nasty jolt but it was common enough, and this was not Cork. 'He has no appointment.'

'If you look in your diary, sir,' Rebecca said, 'you'll find you have time before the next one.'

'Oh, very well. Tell him I can spare a few minutes and send him in.'

The merchant tidied his desk and adjusted his cravat. He smoothed a hand over his bald head and pushed his spectacles up his nose. With a sense of foreboding he worried about his voice—he was no actor and he'd never been able to raise or lower it to disguise the tone. He felt as much like Jacob Greenberg as if there were a name plate on his door. It opened, he looked up, and a shiver passed through him.

'Mr Simpson, sir,' Rebecca said.

Silverstein gazed at the man he knew from two meetings in a dark warehouse in Cork. 'That will be all. Thank you, Rebecca, you may go.'

His visitor was dressed in a well-cut coat, silk shirt and cravat. Not like the dirty puddler who had melted Greenberg's gold into ingots. But the sharp eyes, trimmed moustache and scar were reminders of a man he thought he'd never meet again. Silverstein couldn't move. This was a nightmare.

Simpson approached the desk. 'Mr Maurice Silverstein, it's a pleasure to meet you.'

The merchant stood up. Suddenly weak in the legs, he supported himself on his desk. He flung out a hand.

Simpson grabbed it and pumped it. 'You look like someone I used to know.'

'But I'm afraid I don't know you.'

Simpson smirked. 'Jacob Greenberg did.'

'I don't know any Greenberg either. Please sit.'

'Thank you.' Simpson took off his hat and gloves and looked around the office. 'Your business looks healthy. I read in the paper that you've been reeling in contracts by the dozen.'

'I've been fortunate.' Silverstein took a deep breath. He owed nothing to this man. Nothing—yet he feared him. 'Now, how can I help you?'

'Yeah, fortunate you have been, if you came here with nothing. But you didn't, did you? Had a nest egg. A nice one.'

'What do you mean?' Silverstein said.

'You had the capital as security for loans, so you could set up big from the start.' Simpson looked around the office, nodding as though all the features told the same story. Then he said, 'I knew Jacob Greenberg in Cork.'

Silverstein forced out a reply. 'Did you?'

Simpkins stared at him. 'I did. And I know what collateral he had when he left.' Simpkins leaned closer and Silverstein moved back the same distance. 'He brought gold to Sydney.'

Moisture filmed on Silverstein's face and started to run down his neck. But he had to appear calm. 'I'm not interested in this Greenberg.'

Simpson's lips formed one straight line and his face was hard, lit as though by that furnace in a warehouse in Cork. 'You're a fool, Greenberg. You've shaved your head and your skin's darker from this cursed sun, but I'd know you anywhere. I know you brought gold here. We were in it together. Remember?'

Silverstein gave what he hoped was a contemptuous snort. 'The gold is mine and you received a small cut from Donovan. There's no connection between us.'

'So what did you do with the gold?'

'It's deposited as security for my business.'

Simpson looked surprised. 'So you raised loans on it? You're doing well—but well enough to pay them all off? You've probably got a bit of debt sitting around. I've got some advice for you about that.'

'You're impertinent. This meeting is over. Get out.'

Simpkins laughed. 'Oh no you don't, Greenberg!'

'My name is Maurice Silverstein.'

'Maurice it is, then. So this is what I've got planned for you and me …'

* * *

As soon as he'd got back to the Road, Lieutenant Dodds had sent a note to Superintendent Hands that he'd returned and sought leave to report to him. Now, on a cold Monday, twenty-three days into August, Dodds stood at ease in the Windsor courthouse building. 'It's all there, sir.'

The superintendent concentrated on the report as a fly crawled across the corner of the desk. He looked up. 'Sit down, Lieutenant.'

'Thank you, sir.' Dodds had given every detail he'd gleaned from Silverstein, the Hugheses and the unsatisfactory Dougal Simpson, including the letter that Anne Donovan had received.

Hands took off his glasses. 'The Post Office are still investigating the letter to Mrs Hughes.'

'I hope they find the source.'

'Indeed, Lieutenant. We're not much better off in the case of Riordan. But we can at least widen our supply net for the Road. Move a bit of the trade away from Silverstein.'

'Deal with Hughes directly, you mean?'

'Or companies like his. Why not? The department's always on the lookout for good prices. Why not get Hughes up here so he can get to know the Road?'

'He's curious to do so.'

'Arrange it.'

Dodds nodded, then said, 'May I know how Sergeant Morgan's faring, sir?'

'Morgan has another two months to go on Ten Mile Hollow. Then he'll be transferred to town. No incidents at Ten Mile so far. Either that's good luck or there's been an improvement in his attitude.'

'And my replacement at Devine's?'

'Mr Curran has presented himself well. I'm putting him in charge of Commission Track.' That was a big section of Road starting just north of the Devine's Hill stockade and extending east for five miles up to the next section, which was Ten Mile Hollow.

'About Riordan, sir—we'll get him his ticket?'

Hand nodded and picked up a file. 'Here's the authority. You can tell him the good news. And explain that there's a proviso.'

Dodds took the paperwork and read it. 'I see. He's to stay in the gang until the end of October.'

'You need him up there,' Hands said. 'Are you going to tell him about Mr and Mrs Hughes?'

'No.'

'How about their attitude? Would they want to see him?'

Dodds shook his head. 'No, sir.'

Hands nodded. 'No doubt for the best. Off you go.'

* * *

Later that day, Dodds cantered to Wiseman's and tethered his horse outside the inn. The bar room was cosy, with its fire warming a few patrons. Taking off his hat, he sat down as Deirdre Walsh walked in.

'You took your time coming here, Lieutenant.' Deirdre Walsh smiled at him. 'Francis Murphy said you've been back a week.'

'The Road has its needs, Miss Walsh. I've been on a survey north of the stockade.'

'Then welcome back. Tired of the big smoke?'

He returned her grin. 'It has its attractions, but your face is sweeter.'

She blushed. 'Go on with you. Are you going to order?'

'Lamb chops look good, and a pint, thank you.'

'Won't be long.'

Dodds pulled out his pocketbook and made notes while he waited. Deirdre Walsh soon returned with his meat and drink. 'For the king's officer,' she said.

'Thank you.' He looked around. 'Bit quiet, isn't it?'

'Yes, I don't know why.'

'Have you time for a chat? Do join me if so.'

She sat down. 'I have plenty of questions for you. How's Sydney? Any stuff on the case against Gerry Riordan?'

'A bit,' Dodds said as he cut into his chop. 'I found out that your Mr Silverstein is doing very well in his business with the Road.'

'He's not my Mr Silverstein.'

'Fancies you, though,' he teased her.

'He does. The kind man even proposed. Though of course I couldn't say yes.'

'Indeed! Miss Walsh, you have so many suitors.' Dodds paused, holding his fork over his plate. He wondered what he felt about this himself. 'How did Silverstein take it?'

'He was surprised. But he seemed all right after.'

Dodds sipped his beer. 'In Parramatta, I spoke to a man who claims he never knew Gerry Riordan in Cork, but I suspect he did. The name is Dougal Simpson: let me know if he ever comes by here, and don't trust him an inch.'

'Not a kind man?'

'The opposite. I also met Mr and Mrs Hughes, of Hughes Foundry. They're convinced Riordan is innocent and they've given me a new line of inquiry.'

Deirdre Walsh clasped her hand and her eyes shone. 'What, what? May I tell Gerry?'

Dodds shook his head. 'They don't want any communication with Riordan, Miss Walsh. So please don't mention their names to him. I only told you because I know how concerned you are.'

'But they're nice people?'

'They are, Miss Walsh.'

She stood up and leaned on the chair back. He could tell his answers, however discreet, had moved her and she was trying to hide it. 'Staying the night, Lieutenant?'

'Thank you, Miss Walsh.'

'Then I'll get that arranged for you and go back to the kitchen.'

At first light the next day, Dodds set out from the inn while dew still filmed the trees. The river glistened, its sheen only disturbed by the punt's wake and the steady current. The completed part of the Road was impressive now, and he took his time in examining it, all the way to the stockade. His horse seemed to appreciate the smooth pavement, and with just a tickle of Dodds's spurs would up speed to a canter in the straight sections. Edgings, bridges and drains were all finished to quality detail and he held his breath in pride that he'd been a part of all this work.

Francis Murphy had told him about Simpson's brief visit to the Road. Simpson must have been checking up on Riordan, surely, but he had not made himself known. Dodds was well aware that he'd made an enemy of Simpson with his questioning. Had he also made Simpson consider Riordan as an enemy? If so, he might be a threat to the stonemason when his ticket of leave took him back to town. At some point, Dodds would have to warn him.

In the morning, Gerry turned to his labourers and gave orders for the day's work. The mist on the ridge tops rose as the sun gathered warmth. He grinned at the stubbornness of the vapour, wedged in the valleys, challenging the sun to burn it away.

It was country he liked. And most of all he liked Deirdre.

For over ten months now he'd seen her almost every week and they'd spent time together reading, with her parents' consent. After the stolen moments in the hut, whenever they had an opportunity, they kissed again. She said she loved him. And he did love her. Loved her for her generosity, free spirit and humour.

One of Deirdre's confidences had stuck to him like a sap-filled piece of bark—that he was worth something to her. That was a turning point for him, because Deirdre had been repeating what her mother had said. He had no idea what Mr Walsh thought of him but he now felt Deirdre's mother was at least partly on his side. Deirdre said Mrs Walsh was impressed that he wanted to improve himself.

But he couldn't declare himself to Deirdre until he was on the way to being a free man, until he could get out of the gang. He was still a convict. Yet somehow, because she loved him, it was a yoke he could bear. In this moment, Gerry was happy. The breath channelled through his mouth and the sound was pleasant and he continued to whistle.

'It takes a pretty lass to bring that about,' said Fergus Dooley, who was nearby gathering some nails.

'It might be her and it mightn't.'

'If I was a betting man,' Dooley replied, placing the nails in the bag at his waist, 'I'd say that Miss Walsh has you in her pocket.'

Gerry smiled. 'It would have to be a big pocket.'

'Deirdre's a nice name,' Dooley said. 'It was my mother's.' He paused. 'Just be thankful, Tiny, that Morgan's away and you've kept your head down and laid stone. And that's fortunate for us all.'

Gerry counted the blocks again and wrote the total on his notebook. 'And Mr Dodds is back now.'

Dooley prodded him. 'What's even better, Morgan's leaving the Road.'

'No!'

'That's the rumour.'

'Thanks be to God.'

They both turned at the sound of hoof beats and Dodds rode up to them.

'Morning to you, Riordan, Dooley.'

Gerry was pleased at the sight of the overseer. 'Morning, sir!'

Dodds dismounted, tethered his horse and ran his gaze up the buttressed wall. 'Last day's work seems fair.'

'We were busting our guts, sir.'

'Your gut is still substantial, Riordan, so that's a lie.' Gerry smiled and Dodds returned his grin. 'You seem in good spirits. You must be slacking.'

Dooley said, 'Sir, it's the blarney he peels off I can't take. Give me back the moody bastard any day.'

The overseer went to his saddle bag. 'At least when he was moody he was quiet.' Dodds pulled out a paper. 'Clean your hands, Riordan.'

'Why, sir?'

'Just do it.'

Gerry did what he could with a piece of rag and Dodds handed over the paper.

Gerry read it and smiled. 'It's my ticket!'

Fergus Dooley slapped him on the back and Dodds held out his hand.

'Congratulations,' Dodds said. 'You'll be here for a while but then you're on your own.'

'Glad to be rid of him, I will,' Dooley said but there was a glimmer in his eyes.

Gerry held onto Dodds's hand. 'Thank you, sir. I owe this to you.'

'You earned it. Now, don't make me regret it. If you get into a joust while you're still here'—Dodds pointed at the paper—'that can still be withdrawn.'

Gerry pocketed the paper. 'I don't care if Morgan asks me to lick his boots, I'll do it.'

'He's on is way out of here, too,' Dodds said.

Dooley clapped his hands together. 'So, it's true!' He started doing a jig and laughed. 'Can't wait to tell Murphy.'

'You get back to work,' Dodds said. 'The both of you. The weather's good and that can't last, so, backs and limbs. Let's be at it.'

* * *

Seated at his office desk, Maurice Silverstein paused with his hand over a document that Simpson was pressuring him to sign. He looked at the wily, scarred face on the other side of the desk. This man was witness to the crime Silverstein had committed in Cork—receiving stolen goods. But he himself was witness to Simpson's involvement in the same crime. And neither of them could betray the other, because if they reported to the police they would be incriminating themselves in the process. So in a sense, Simpson had no greater hold over Silverstein than he did over Simpson. Except that he was a terrifying man to cross.

Silverstein knew in his bones that Simpson was not only a thief but a murderer and would stop at nothing to get his way. Lured by the gold that Silverstein had in the bank, he was determined to rake off a good income from the merchant's business, just as he did from the partnership he held in the Parramatta quarry. The document on the desk was anathema to Silverstein but he had to give in to the man who'd written it. Because he was scared to death of him.

Silverstein scratched his signature on the bottom of the document and handed it to his new partner.

Simpson smiled, took the quill and signed also. 'There, that wasn't so bad. Partners in law.'

Silverstein exhaled and dabbed his face with his handkerchief. 'Quite.'

'Let's celebrate.'

'I have too much to do, I'm afraid.'

Simpson leaned closer. 'My friend, it's Thursday afternoon, not Friday, so you can open a bottle and enjoy some company. You do like women?'

'I am not averse to female company.'

'Then grab your hat and let's go.'

Silverstein put on his jacket and took his hat. God knew where they were going but wherever it was, he wasn't expecting clean air and quietness. He'd have one drink with the man, then return home and try to work out how to deal with him in the future.

Rebecca looked up as he opened his office door. 'Yes, sir?'

'Mr Simpson and I are leaving for the day.'

'Where, sir, in case someone inquires?'

Dougal leered at the girl. 'We won't be back, my dear,' he said, 'and if we told you where we were going, you'd blush.'

Rebecca gave an alarmed look at Silverstein, got no help there and looked at her desk.

'Come on, Maurice, my boy.'

Silverstein followed his partner out into the warm October dusk. 'You'll refer to my assistant as Miss Gabon and I want no loose talk in front of her.'

Simpson scowled. 'I'm not talking business now, Maurice, but pleasure. However, since you insist—who's your banker?'

Silverstein cursed in his head. 'Mr George Brown.'

Simpson stood back on the narrow footpath to let a barrel-chested man pass him. 'I want to meet him.'

Silverstein stepped aside also, mortified to be seen anywhere near his companion in the street. Yet for someone who didn't know the vile man beneath the clothes, Simpson looked well set up, even respectable. He was going up in the world, trampling people like himself beneath his well-shod feet. 'He's very busy. I find it difficult—'

'Bankers work for us, Maurice. Get an appointment with Brown. I'm coming with you.'

Simpson entered a shop and walked down a long corridor. He stopped at a closed door and knocked three times. A small hatch slid open.

'Yes?' a voice said.

'Penny's,' Simpson replied.

The hatch slid back, the door opened and Silverstein entered a space filled with conversation, laughter and smoke. His glasses fogged at the sight of bosoms more out of their dresses than in, and thighs that flashed white against tight skirts.

'Stop salivating, Maurice. You'll give me a bad name. Here.' Simpson grabbed two glasses of wine from a waiter and pushed one into his hand. 'Sit down, for God's sake.'

Silverstein sat, gulped and rubbed his spectacles. Then he sweated. What if there were clients of his here? In gentlemanly fashion they could pretend not to recognise each other—but he would still feel embarrassed, cheapened. Someone sat down on the cushion beside him and a heavy perfume reached his nose.

'You're new, aren't you?'

Silverstein's eyes dropped to the whiteness of her breasts, their crescent areolas peeping above her bodice. Her touch on his thigh made him start.

'Skittish as a colt, too,' she said. 'Isn't he, Dougal?'

'Call him, Maurie, Flo, and make him happy.'

Her hand continued to stroke his thigh and now his trousers were constricted. He sipped his wine and looked at the woman, concentrating on a mole on her cheek. 'How do you do.'

Flo laughed. 'You're a gent and all, God love you! Come with me, dear, where it isn't so noisy.' She took his hand and he stood up with difficulty, blood infusing his face, but no one looked at him. Down another hall, there were alcoves where couples kissed and hugged each other in full view. Silverstein tripped over one woman's leg but she continued to massage a man's crotch.

'Don't worry about them.' Flo laughed again. 'We'll have our own fun.'

She opened a door, drew him through and closed it behind her. 'There's a good love, place the cash on the bed while I get more comfortable. The more you pay, the more you play.'

Silverstein peeled off some notes.

Bailed Up

*** * ***

One week later in his office, Silverstein rubbed his jaw and looked at his partner seated on the other side of his desk. He was in deep with this man, right up to his bald pate. The brothel episode was still on his mind and what Flo had done with him that afternoon still made his head spin. Simpson was a rogue but he was stuck with him for now. Maybe he could get used to drinking more and putting up with the company of women like Flo. Maybe.

'So, my partner,' Simpson said, 'here's my idea about the gold. We have to do more with those beautiful ingots than leave them in a dusty bank vault. They have to work harder for us, and they will. We'll go into the money-lending business, Maurice. That's where the real dosh is to be made. We'll charge healthy interest and get rich.' He clapped his hands. 'Then you'll be able to hold your head up in the synagogue like the rich Jew you deserve to be.'

'A licence is required before one can set up as a money lender.'

'Piece of cake. I know the right people.'

Silverstein closed his eyes.

'Now,' Simpson said pulling over a thick document, 'this contract for the Great North Road ... Stage One Commission Track. Have you been up there?'

'A few times. I use the services of Mr Solomon Wiseman to take the goods.'

'What are his rates like?' Simpson said, still reading.

'Acceptable.'

'So keep the costs low and put a bit more on the price, get more profit.'

'Not a good move at the moment. There's an overseer on Devine's who's been questioning me on my prices. He's recommending that other companies quote to Roads and Bridges. I don't want to lose any business there so I'll keep my prices competitive.' Simpson gave him a sharp look. 'Our prices.'

But Simpson's alertness was for something else. 'This overseer— name wouldn't be Dodds, would it?'

'It is,' Silverstein said with surprise. 'You know him?'

Simpson rubbed the gold knob on the cane propped against his chair. 'A vexatious bastard who sticks his big nose into things he shouldn't. He's cunning and he's got far too much curiosity for his own good, so he'll have to go.'

'What do you mean?'

'You leave him to me. I'll deal with him. He's been giving me grief over a convict you and me knew in Cork.'

'I knew no convicts in Cork.'

Simpson gave a sneering laugh. 'Ah, but you do here. Can't get away from that, can you? Remember Riordan?'

'Never met him. That's the convicted man, Gerry Riordan?'

'The same. He works on the Road. Devine's.'

Silverstein started to perspire and poured himself a glass of water.

'Riordan's got his ticket,' Simpson said. 'The approval came from the Windsor District and it's valid from the end of this month. Ten to one he'll be down here in Sydney like a flash, looking for work and going on about how he's an innocent man and never made off with that precious gold we both love so much.' Simpson smiled. 'So I've got a plan for our stonemason.'

'Plan?'

'Maurice, my boy. Get Riordan here and I'll take care of him.'

'Take care of him?' Silverstein was now terrified. 'For God's sake, Riordan is the last person I'd want anywhere near me!'

Simpson patted Silverstein's hand. 'Don't worry. Just write to him and tell him you want to hire a stonemason on contract.'

'But I don't need a stonemason. Least of all—'

'All good houses need stonemasons, Maurie my boy. You're about to build houses on spec, on cheap land, and then sell and reap the rewards.' Simpson hesitated took out a card from a coat pocket. 'Here's a lawyer for the conveyancing, and he'll act as your land agent as well. Organise it. Just get Riordan here. I'll do the rest.'

Silverstein tried to rally. 'I cannot condone violence.'

Simpson pointed at him and grinned. 'You sounded just like Mr Greenberg when you said that. Maurice, get moving, my friend.' He stood up. 'I've got other things on, so I won't be seeing you for a while. I'm off. Keep your bald head out of the sun until I see you again. With our stonemason.'

* * *

Anne Hughes stood in the open doorway of their cottage and hugged her husband. 'Take care on the Road and look out for yourself. I don't envy you the journey and I'll miss you.'

Sean smiled at her. 'There'll be some discomforts, I expect, but no dangers, love. I'm just an observer. It will be interesting to see the extent of work that's up there and the real scale of their need for iron. Details in contracts don't tell the full story. I have to get the lie of the land.'

'Of course you do, my dear.'

'Dodds will be my guide; it'll be fine to catch up with him again.' He hesitated. 'And no doubt I'll catch a glimpse of Riordan, too. If I come across him I won't ignore him, Anne. We'll talk. He may ask after you. If he does, what do I tell him?'

'You may say I'm well and I still believe him innocent. No more.'

After they had said their goodbyes and Sean had gone, Anne chastised herself for never being able to talk naturally about Gerry Riordan. Her husband knew she had loved Gerry and was worried that she still might. There seemed to be nothing she could do about that. How could she convince Sean that she had no love left for a man who still occupied her thoughts? Today was 25 October, Gerry's birthday. He was now twenty-three.

Anne closed the front door, leaned against it and sighed. A twinge in her tummy made her think of the dreadful day when she had lost her child. The doctor had said she could have more children, but some of that pain would never leave her. Going into the parlour, she took out a letter she'd received from her father.

All was not well in Donovan House. Her mother's health was not good and her ageing father had suffered a series of illnesses. Her fingers shook and she pressed them onto the letter. The scene in her father's study when she had snatched the shotgun from him appeared in her mind, the dark tones and highlights as bold as in a Rembrandt painting. The father she had loved and once looked up to was a cause of misery in many people's lives. If James Donovan had not arranged to steal the gold, Lawrence Toole would still be alive and Gerry would not have been convicted for theft and murder. If James Donovan had allowed her to marry Gerry Riordan, they might all be living near one another in Cork. Instead, here she was in a colony on the other side of the world, with a husband whom she loved, but wasn't in love with—and the man who had been her first love was struggling as a convict in the Australian wilderness.

Sean hadn't touched her since the baby's death. He had caressed her a few evenings past and she'd permitted his affectionate hugs and kisses. But the other thing … intimacy … was absent. She didn't seem to miss it and that worried her.

Gerry's face appeared in her mind. She saw the picture of them embracing in his room in Cork, which did start a feeling in her. However, it was like trying to shield a lit match in a gale—she knew it wouldn't last. The gale was her anger, her deep anger against the man who had ruined her life and cost that of her baby. She had tried to tell herself that it was unjustified, that Gerry was not responsible for the lying letter she'd received telling about his death, for the shock of Dodd's revelation that caused the accident in this very house, and her grief and Sean's over little Patrick.

But she had not let go of that anger yet. In fact in the heat of it she had written a letter to Gerry telling him she hated him, saying she wished never to see him again. And this was true. If she didn't see him, then she might be able to banish him from her mind. In time, her anger would fade into indifference, and she would learn to be content. How could she be anything less than content with the man she lived with, who loved her so?

Chapter Eleven

In mid-afternoon sunshine, Sean Hughes alighted from a coach at Wiseman's Ferry. Stretching his arms, he breathed in the lemon scent from the surroundings, a delight compared to the smoke and filth of the city. He set out for the inn, which was a mere walk away.

He arrived at the front entrance just as a dark-haired young woman came out. She stopped and said brightly, 'Welcome to Wiseman's, sir.'

'Thank you, Miss …?'

'Deirdre, sir. Deirdre Walsh.'

'How do you do, Miss Walsh?'

She smiled at him. 'Very well, thank you. Mr Hughes, I think? We've been expecting you.'

'Yes.'

'I'll send someone to the coach for your luggage, sir. Mrs Hughes is not with you?'

Sean smiled. 'You're a perceptive young woman. You noticed my wedding ring. And no, not this time.'

'Then another time?'

'I think I can persuade her,' Sean said, looking down the street towards Cobham Hall. 'This is a lovely place. With the river right next door, you wouldn't want to be anywhere else.'

Miss Walsh smiled. 'Yes, I'd hate to live in town. Do come in.'

They went into the inn's cool, dim bar room. Smoke tickled his nostrils and the smell of hops seemed to be impregnated in the timber walls, but it was not unpleasant. 'If you show me to my room, Miss Walsh, that would be grand.'

Leading him upstairs she indicated the first door at the start of the corridor. 'This is it, sir. We serve breakfast at seven o'clock, a meal at twelve and tea at six. Is there any place you'd like to visit while you're here?'

'I've come to see the construction work on Devine's Hill. Is it far? I'd like to hire one of your horses after breakfast tomorrow.'

'You're in luck. Supplies go up to the stockade in the morning and I'm riding up to deliver their post. You're welcome to join me.'

Sean grinned. 'That would be grand. Thank you, Miss Walsh.'

The next day was clear and promised to be hot. Sean and Deirdre Walsh rode their horses onto the punt, ahead of the wagon taking supplies up to Devine's.

'Is that a typical load?' Sean asked.

'It is that,' she said. 'There's more convicts on the Road now and that means more stores. Flour, meal, grain and corn all must be replenished because they don't keep well on site, so each week every gang has to send down a wagon to make the round trip. This one's headed for Ten Mile Hollow.'

The river surged under them as the punt moved off. 'We used to cross further down river,' she said holding onto her hair against the breeze. 'That's where the first bit of the Road north of the river was laid, onto Finch's land. It was poorly built, zig-zagged, and a bit was too steep, so we now cross here and go up beside Molly Devine's land.'

Sean absorbed the scenery and the sense of isolation that came from the surrounding bush. Again, they rode ahead of the wagon as it left the punt and they made their way up a low incline.

'When this new bit first started,' Miss Walsh said, 'it was tough going up here. A lot of blasting was needed.'

Sean was no engineer, but he could see what effort had gone into the construction of this early section, especially the bridges. He enjoyed the opportunity to view the new work against a background of the trees, birdlife and the hoof beats of their horses. Now and then he would see a branch would flicker and hear the scurry of wildlife.

'How long have you been here, Miss Walsh?'

'I was born here, Mr Hughes; my father was a settler before the crossing was made on the Hawkesbury, and he still has the farm.

I know all this land. It was nothing but scrub until Mr Wiseman was given a grant by the governor. He's become a wealthy man.'

'He's a Jew, isn't he?'

'He is. There's another who comes up here and has business with the Road.' She turned to him. 'You might know him. His name is Maurice Silverstein.'

'I do! He's not a client yet but I hope to get some business from him.'

'And from the Road?' she said with a shrewd smile. 'There's a military overseer up here that I'm sure you'd like to meet. A very nice man from England.'

'Lieutenant William Dodds. We've met.'

She smiled. 'That's him. You know everyone up here, Mr Hughes.'

'I may even know a few more. For instance, I used to know Gerry Riordan in Cork. Stonemason on Devine's.'

Her eyes rounded in surprise. 'Did you? He's a ... good friend of mine.'

The way she said it betrayed a lot to Sean, though she probably didn't realise it. He was only too skilled at detecting what women thought and felt about Riordan. Damn the man for being a kind of third shadow in his marriage. It had been bad enough when they thought the stonemason was dead: now they knew he was alive, Sean could not help feeling jealous and worrying about Anne. If only Riordan could stay working up here and never come to Sydney.

'But as a convict, he has disadvantages.'

She smiled. 'Not any more. He's got his ticket of leave.'

Sean ground his teeth. That meant Riordan would be in Sydney soon, looking for jobs in commercial and domestic construction. They were plentiful. And no doubt trying to get the stain of conviction washed out of his life. 'I don't know if Riordan has told you his story, but he was convicted of crimes that he claims he didn't commit.'

'Most convicts say they're innocent, Mr Hughes, and Gerry Riordan was no exception when I first met him. In fact he was a brooding and angry man. All six foot three of him. But Mr Dodds took him under his wing a bit. He's a reader, sir, and he's lent books to Gerry and me so we can learn together.'

Sean was struck again by this young woman's interest in Riordan. And it sounded as though it was returned. Maybe Riordan was in love with her. His spirits lifted. 'Dodds is a good man. And fair. He believes in the man's innocence as well.'

'He does. He's delving into Gerry's case and he's already got him his ticket of leave. I'll never forget his help.'

The wagon rolled on, the perspiration trickled down Sean's back and it was only October. Imagine what the convicts had to endure in the heat of January with its flies and the dust, as prolific as ants on a sugar cube.

Halfway up Devine's Hill they came to a crossing worthy to grace Sydney town—any great world city, in fact. It was constructed with coursed ashlar sandstone, thirty feet high, strengthened with even-cut dressed timber, all laid to line and level and skirted with dressed hard stone. It was all the more outstanding in these surroundings—a great monument surrounded by grey-green hills.

'It's good, isn't it?' Miss Walsh said.

'It's bloody marvellous.'

She laughed. 'Mr Hughes! Such language for a gentleman.'

'Sorry, but it's beyond praise.'

The supply wagon rolled on and before long it pulled up outside the stockade. The driver applied the brake. A convict came up to the wagon and tied the lead horses to a post.

'Morning, Miss Walsh,' the man said waving to them. He was dressed in a uniform striped in grey and cream.

'And to you, Fergus,' Miss Walsh said. 'Mr Hughes, this is Fergus Dooley.'

Sean jumped down and shook Dooley's hand whose lumps and ridges felt like the rocks and valleys around him. 'How do you do.'

Fergus looked at him in surprise. 'For a man working at the governor's pleasure … I don't often get a handshake, sir.'

The wagon driver joined them. 'Come on, Dooley, we haven't got all day and this flour will go to mould while you're talking.'

'This, Mr Hughes,' Fergus said, 'is Francis Murphy. A bush chippy with a head of hardwood.'

Sean nodded to the men as they began unloading.

'Come on, Mr Hughes,' Miss Walsh said, 'we'll leave these boys to unload. I'm not sure where Mr Dodds may be but if we ride on up there, we'll find the work gang.'

Sure enough, they soon came across a gang who were completing drainage to a culvert opening. Fifty yards ahead of them, a man stood on the face of the cutting, his height and his russet-coloured hair clear in the sunshine. Sean recognised him at once. The stonemason brought a hand to his face and held it there to shield his eyes as they approached.

'Gerry,' Miss Walsh said, riding to the edge of the road, 'I've brought someone I think you know.'

Sean took off his hat and Riordan dropped his hand and jerked his head back. Then he left the wall and walked down to the edge of the road.

To Sean, Riordan looked fitter, stronger than he had in Cork. The muscles in his shoulders and arms had bulked up. 'Hello, Riordan. You'll remember me for a number of reasons, few of them good. Sean Hughes.'

Riordan just stared. 'Mr Hughes. It looked like you from afar but ... I thought I was seeing things. A ghost from my past.'

'Let's go in the shade,' Miss Walsh said, eager for Riordan's attention.

'Miss Walsh.' Riordan stepped over to hold the horse as she looked ready to dismount.

Sean was having none of that. 'I'm looking for Lieutenant Dodds. Will I find him hereabouts?'

Riordan said, 'He's up with the surveyors on the Commission Track today, Mr Hughes. If you've the time, you'd have more luck seeing him here tomorrow.'

'Mr Hughes is staying at Wiseman's, Gerry. So he could do that— come back tomorrow.' She smiled, as though she would be ready for the ride, too.

The big man smiled back but turned at once to Sean and his face became earnest.

'What brings you to the colony, Mr Hughes? I never would have thought to see you here!'

'Business. I've established a foundry in town. Here for the duration, Riordan—an immigrant.'

Riordan shook his head in disbelief. 'The last time I saw you, sir, I well remember. It was in Cork and you'd been talking with me and Miss Donovan outside the police station, about the gold for the tabernacle doors.'

'Two years or more ago, Riordan, and a lot of water under the bridge since then. No need to talk about it.'

'But there is, sir, because I owed you thanks then, and I do now. I'll never forget. There was a mighty set of reasons for you to hold me guilty, Mr Hughes, but instead you wanted me proved innocent.'

'And still do, Riordan. Look, that's enough.'

'If I could just say one more thing besides thank you. If I could just ask you, the last time you saw Miss Donovan, was she well?'

'She was.' Sean took a breath. 'I hear from Mr Dodds and Miss Walsh that you have prospered in your own way, Riordan. Congratulations on receiving your ticket of leave.'

Riordan bowed his head. 'Thank you.'

Miss Walsh smiled at the stonemason again but her eyes were troubled.

Sean pulled his horse's head around. 'Miss Walsh, I'll have to accept I've missed Lieutenant Dodds today. You'll be my guide back to Wiseman's?'

'If you say so, sir.' She leaned down to pat her horse's neck, her head coming close to Riordan's before he let go her horse and stepped away.

With a nod to Riordan, Sean rode away at a smart pace. Miss Walsh came up beside him after a short delay. After a long silence she started asking him questions about Cork. She asked none about Riordan or his past, so out of politeness Sean answered them all.

They reached the bottom of Devine's Hill before she said, 'Gerry mentioned a Miss Donovan that you knew in Cork. What is she like?'

'As fine and beautiful a lady as one could wish to meet, Miss Walsh. She is my wife.'

* * *

In the shadow of a finished culvert one hundred yards north of the stockade, Gerry was sitting with Lieutenant Dodds. It had been two days since Gerry had been reacquainted with Sean Hughes, who had not returned to the Road despite Deirdre's hint.

Dodds handed him a mug of tea. 'The last brew you'll get like this.'

'I'll miss it, sir.' The steaming liquid had an aroma tinged with the flavours of the bush. 'Thank you, sir, for all your help. It'll be hard, getting used to living in a town again, among strangers.'

Dodds sipped his tea. 'You may see a few familiar faces.'

Gerry gave a wry smile. 'From the transports, you mean?'

'Or Irish immigrants of another stamp. Like Sean Hughes. How did you feel when you saw him?'

The smile left Gerry's face. 'Like seeing a ghost.'

'I've got to know him a little and I consider him a good man. There's something else you should hear about him and since he doesn't seem to have told you himself, I will. He's married. Married in Cork and emigrated very shortly after. He and his wife Anne live in Castlereagh Street and the foundry's in Sussex Street.'

Riordan looked up and caught the truth in Dodds's eyes. Something inside him died. 'Her name's Anne?'

'Her maiden name was Anne Donovan.'

Gerry stared into the bush. Anne—his Anne—married. To the very man from whom he was supposed to have stolen the golden doors. 'I can't believe she'd do that.'

'What?'

'Marry him.'

306

'From my observation, Riordan, they're a very happy couple.'

'She wanted me proved innocent. She said she'd wait.'

'Riordan, you're talking about a lady's private life here and I don't intend to intrude upon it. But I will say that in the months after you were transported from Ireland, and before she married, Miss Anne Donovan received a letter from a New South Wales official saying you had died in the colony. No details, just that you were dead.'

Gerry dropped the mug and gasped. 'What? How?'

'The letter was false, of course. A forgery. The authorities have it and are investigating.'

'Oh my God. Poor Anne.'

'Indeed.'

Gerry put his face in his hands. 'Why would someone tell her I'm dead?'

'It could only be because they had some connection to your past, they saw you as a threat, and they wanted everyone back in Ireland to think you dead.'

'Ah, my parents!' he said in pain. 'Would they know? I have to write to them.' Gerry was dumbfounded, shocked. 'How could I be a threat to anyone *here*?' He stretched his arms out. 'I'm a c-convict in a million acres of scrub.' He pressed his hand against the stone culvert, its heat radiating through him. It felt natural and real, unlike what the officer was telling him. 'Anne, married to Sean Hughes.'

Dodds said, 'Don't hold her marriage against her. That's in the past. You've moved on. You have your ticket. You have a certain freedom.'

'I should get back to work.'

'Stay here and figure this out.' Dodds threw his tea dregs on the fire. 'More?'

Gerry held his mug under Dodds's billy. 'That letter. Who wrote it? You said that someone feared me.'

Dodds filled his own mug. 'It would appear so.'

'I can't hurt anyone here, sir. I don't know anyone in the colony.'

'What about a man called Simpson? He's here.'

'I don't know a Simpson.'

'What about in Cork?' Dodds said.

Gerry shook his head. 'No.'

'Think back, man. It's important. Simpson worked in a quarry in Cork. Did you ever meet him?'

'No. Why do you keep asking about him?'

Dodds put his mug down and folded his arms. 'Dougal Simpson was convicted of a bank robbery in Cork and was transported on your ship with you.'

Gerry was becoming irritated. 'What of that?'

'I've read the police report,' Dodds said, 'and Simpson is connected with the stolen gold somehow. Which means he's connected with Toole's murder.'

'And Simpson's here in Sydney?'

'Came looking for you, he did, up here.'

'When? Why?' Gerry said, his irritation growing. 'I've done nothing to him. Why should he be after me?'

'Answer that and we'll have the reason Anne Hughes got a forged letter.'

Gerry got up. 'I can't cope with this. I can't think straight.'

Dodds stood up. 'Wait, there's mail for you.' Dodds went to his saddlebag, sorted through papers and gave two to Gerry. 'I'm off to Windsor. When I get back, let's talk some more about Cork.'

Gerry looked at his mail as Dodds rode away. From the handwriting on the outside, one was written by a stranger. The other was in a hand that he knew well. Anne's.

Gerry,

I don't know how to start and didn't want to even write to you.

My first letter to you was a confession, telling how the tabernacle doors were stolen.

What letter? He'd got no such letter. He continued to read.

Then I received the letter of your death. I didn't want to live and the dark side of life nearly won me over. Sean brought light into that darkness and I lived again, but not like before—never like before, but Sean loved me, he always did, he tells me often.

Gerry looked away and crumpled the letter, wanting to tear it to shreds. He held his breath and clenched his hands. Exhaling, he smoothed out the pages and continued to read.

When Lieutenant Dodds told me you were alive, I got so shocked I lost the baby I was expecting. So, I have now lost two people whom I loved: one who was dead and one who is dead. Now you're alive, I despise you. I hate you for what you did to me—twice. The first time I didn't want to live. Now you've made me lose my child. I can live on and the hate in me will fade in time but it'll always be there. Don't see me, don't even try to see me. Live your life any way you choose. I don't care. The past is just that and belongs there in its place, untouched and final.

Anne

Gerry ripped the letter up, threw the bits away and, ignoring the second letter, jumped up and attacked his work. She had once been in love with him. Now she was married to another and she'd given birth to his child! A block of stone glared at him, seemed to challenge him to do something to it. Grabbing a clean chisel and hammer, he struck the sandstone, making a crack the width of a hair. Another blow and it sheared. Picking the smaller piece, he struck again, sweat filming on his forehead. She hated him. She hated him because she thought he'd died and she hated him more because he lived.

Crack, another blow, another slice of stone. Ringing pulses vibrated through his arm, jolting his tendons. He pounded again and again. Exhausted, he stopped and looked at the result through a film of tears and sweat. He threw down his tools and ran into the scrub.

* * *

Deirdre was on horseback, watching Gerry at work. The sun was just disappearing below the tree line; he would have to finish up soon.

'He's laying stone,' Francis Murphy said, 'and isn't talking.'

Deirdre sighed. 'You said he got a letter yesterday. You know what was in it?'

'He ripped it up and ran off into the bush, Miss. From one of the scraps I'd say it was a woman's hand.'

Deirdre muttered, 'Oh heaven, not that Mrs Hughes.'

'I wouldn't know, Miss Walsh. He's never had a letter from anyone before, let alone a lady.'

'So, he's slipped back?'

Francis shook his head. 'A long way. He's worse than before.'

A fly settled on her horse's ear and got flicked away. 'It's only been a day. He'll right himself.'

'I don't know, lass. Last night he swung at Dooley, clipped him, and Dooley didn't hit back. We had to restrain the big man. The venom out of his mouth was from the devil himself.'

She sighed. Gerry like this on his last day and Dodds not here. 'What can I do?'

Francis looked up. 'He's coming down from the scaffolding. Let's go.'

Deirdre dismounted and they came up to Gerry. He glanced at them both and threw a bucket of water over himself. His torso was patterned in muscles, a tissue of neat rows and compact pouches. He grabbed a towel and dried himself.

'Last day, Gerry,' she said, trying to sound cheerful.

He grunted and put on a clean shirt. She glanced at Francis. 'Come to the inn tonight and we'll celebrate.'

'I'm staying at the stockade,' Gerry said.

'To sulk?' she said.

He snapped his head at her. 'To be alone and plan! I've got things to do and it's money I want.'

'Quite the businessman now,' Murphy said.

Gerry did up the buttons of the shirt. 'I don't want a fight with you but I'll have you if you say too much more.'

'Please yourself,' Deirdre said. 'Life's given you good and bad. Think about that.'

'Leave me alone,' he said and walked away to the wagon that he was driving up to the stockade. Murphy joined him on the front seat.

She couldn't leave like this. She would be late back to the inn, but it would still be light when she got there. 'Wait up,' she said. 'I'll come with you.' Gerry swung around at her ready to say something nasty, but she met his defiant look with one of her own. He turned back around. They started off.

'I'm going to town to work,' he said. 'The second letter Mr Dodds brought me came from a merchant called Silverstein. He wants me to take on a contract for stonemasonry.' Gerry rubbed his head. 'I don't know Silverstein and I don't know how he heard about me.'

She said, 'Dodds knows him because he's a supplier for the Road. And I know him. He's come up here a few times.'

'I wondered how he got my name.' He didn't look at her. He was silent for some time. 'All I want now is to make money.'

'Money's not everything, Riordan,' Francis said.

'It is to me. I've gone over the numbers to stump up a business. Wages for myself I can forego for a while but I'll need to pay for food, lodgings and a labourer. I'll purchase materials, cement and lime. Blocks will be supplied.'

'From convict to businessman in two days,' she said, her tone terse.

'It can be done.'

'What about me?' she said.

'You can look after yourself.'

'Riordan,' Murphy said, 'that wasn't nice.'

Deirdre threw her hands up. 'Grand. Thanks. I thought we were friends?'

'I'm sorry, Miss Walsh.' He didn't even look at her.

Her eyes expanded and she pressed her lips together, holding her sadness and anger in check. Gerry didn't care for her. Maybe he still cared for Mrs Hughes. 'And the other letter you got?'

Gerry glanced at his companion. 'Murphy here has a big mouth.'

'Well?' she said.

'It was from a girl I used to love. And she loved me.'

She shook her head with foreboding. 'Mrs Hughes?'

He sneered. 'You always were a b-bright one. But now she hates me.'

Surprised, she rode close to the wagon and leaned forward, trying to read his face. 'Why?!'

He turned his head towards her. 'Because I didn't die, and I killed her child.'

Deirdre was shocked. 'She said that? What could she mean?'

'She thought I was dead so she married Hughes. She was expecting a baby when she heard I wasn't dead after all, and she had an accident and miscarried.'

'Oh, how frightful. Mr Hughes didn't tell me a thing about that. But she can't blame you!'

'She does.'

'She's upset, Gerry. She's angry at you, that's all.'

'She's angry and married.'

'Does she love her husband?' she asked. 'He seems like a nice man.'

Gerry kept silent for a moment. 'I don't know. I suppose so.'

She'd have preferred that Mrs Hughes had been definite about that.

'So you're going to town without a single kind word for me?'

The stockade came into sight. 'I'm going to make money,' Gerry said. 'I'm going to be something. Buy what I like and see who I want.'

Deirdre tried to keep control. 'You have it all worked out.'

'I do.'

'And do I fit in anywhere?'

'Maybe,' he said in a quiet voice.

The wagon stopped and she reined in, her hands shaking. 'I'll see you again when you're in a better mood.'

'Then you'll have to wait a while. I'm going to town and I'm staying there.'

She cried out, 'But you can't, your parole means—'

He leaped down from the wagon. 'I only need to front once a month and that's at Windsor or in town. So I choose town. You see, my girl, they've got a guilty conscience. They know I got a bad trial and they're trying to make it up to me. So I've got some privileges.'

Francis glared at his friend, then shook his head at Deirdre. 'I'm sorry, lass.'

She faced Gerry. 'Like I said, when you're clear headed, then see me.'

She rode away, a lump in her throat nearly choking her.

* * *

Gerry hitched a ride to town on a Road stores wagon. On the way he tried reading *Gulliver's Travels*, a novel Mr Dodds had lent him. Gerry liked it but the wagon lurched a bit too much for easy reading. In snatches, his mind wandered to Deirdre. She loved him and he knew that, but what he felt for her now he couldn't say. His feelings were in turmoil, ever since the letter from Anne.

Closer to Sydney the odours of the town—manure, smoke and dust—brought back a memory of Cork on a summer's day. But this was Sydney in late spring: the first day of November 1830. The smells were strong enough to counter the horses' sweat in front of him.

Dodds hadn't come back to camp the previous night, and Gerry was glad. A clean break was what he needed. He wanted to be a new man in this town and forget Convict Riordan. The name Riordan belonged to his foul past. He was going to name himself Gleeson, after an uncle of his back in Ireland. Gerry Gleeson. It even sounded wealthy. New life, new name. Where would he live in Sydney? Not to worry. He'd decide after he'd spoken to Silverstein, who owned property in town.

The wagon traffic thickened as they got to the western end of Sydney's George Street in mid-afternoon, and so did the smell. But the town had an excitement about it. It seemed different from the place he arrived in, unsteady and in chains, from a worm-eaten transport ship. A breeze from the harbour wafted against him and for a few seconds the smells vanished. Then the wind died and the odours returned. Industry was all around him, in the tanneries, forges and joinery sheds. The shops on both sides of the street added their own colour and sounds to a scene that was far noisier than the bush in the early morning, when the birdlife was active.

* * *

Silverstein was in Sean Hughes's office on Sussex Street. 'Thank you for seeing me on short notice, Mr Hughes.'

'Please, sit down.'

Silverstein nodded and scratched his bald head. 'This heat. It's the first of November but you'd think it was the middle of January.'

Hughes nodded. 'Would you like some water?'

'That would be nice, thank you.'

'I'll get you some. Please wait a moment.'

Silverstein liked the man's informality and the comfortable way he had furnished his office. He'd created an almost friendly atmosphere. On his desk lay the gold-framed miniature of a woman. Silverstein reached out and turned it towards him. She was young, fine-boned and pretty. This must be Hughes's wife—very sweet.

'Here you are.' Hughes returned and placed a glass on the desk. 'I see you're admiring my wife.'

Silverstein turned the portrait back again. 'Excuse me, but the image is exquisite. You must be very proud of her.'

Hughes sat down and said seriously. 'I am. I'm afraid she's not well at the moment.'

'I'm sorry to hear that.' Silverstein sipped at his drink.

'So, how can Hughes Foundry help you?'

Silverstein bent down and extracted a paper from his satchel. 'This is your first invoice. It's incorrect, so I cannot pay it in its present form.'

Hughes took the paper and put on his spectacles, sliding them beneath tufts of grey hair. *At least he's got hair.* 'No, I can see here the total lengths delivered and the rate we agreed. There's no mistake.'

Silverstein smiled. 'But look at the quantity. You see, you delivered twenty-five sets in good condition and you've only invoiced me for twenty-two.'

Hughes raised his eyebrows. 'Ah, I was three short in my calculation. Of course.'

'You were. I have to be scrupulous with my paperwork, you see.'

Hughes looked amused. 'But that means you have to pay me more for the consignment!'

Silverstein spread his hands. 'Exactly. Now or next month. Up to you.'

Sean sat back with an appreciative look. 'You're very honourable.'

Silverstein forced a smile. 'Thank you.'

'You're a pleasant exception to the rule. There's been a tightening of cash lately and some of my customers are delaying their payments to us.'

Silverstein felt his face grow hot. He felt like the fraud he was. He was dealing fairly with Hughes over this transaction—and meanwhile he had the man's gold sitting in the bank. 'That's how I do business. If you make the change to the invoice now, I'll write you a cheque.'

'Surely, thank you.' Hughes took the invoice, changed the details and signed it. 'There it is.'

Silverstein wrote the cheque and handed it to Sean. 'I'm sorry to hear your wife's ailing.'

'Thank you. I'll write a receipt.' He took his quill. His eyes glistened. 'I've been very worried about her. Sadly, just under four months ago, we lost our first child, before term.'

'That's tragic.'

Hughes handed over the receipt. 'It was a great shock.' Hughes cleared his throat. 'My wife received some startling news. Someone she was very fond of and had thought to be dead was found to be alive. As a result, she fell and miscarried.'

'The person she thought was dead—was this a relative?'

'No, an—an acquaintance. She had received the news of his death in a letter sent to Cork. But the letter was false. The man is still alive, here in the colony.'

Silverstein stood up, a little unsteady.

'Are you all right, Mr Silverstein?'

Silverstein managed to say, 'Very distressing. I'm so sorry. Good day, Mr Hughes.'

'I'll see you out, Mr Silverstein, and thank you for your honesty.'

The foundry doors closed behind Silverstein and the street started to blur. His heart seemed to be bursting out of his chest. He forced his legs forward and focussed on the lamp posts in the street, counting them as he walked past.

When he'd forged that letter about Riordan and sent it to Anne Donovan, she'd been a faceless figure to him, a woman he'd never met, and who mattered only because she was the perfect person to convince the Donovans and the Hugheses and anyone else connected with Riordan that the man was dead. To put off anyone who might try to follow the trail of the gold and come anywhere near Jacob Greenberg. But she wasn't faceless to him now. She was a living, breathing woman who had lost a child because he had written her a letter full of lies.

Dear God, what have I done?

* * *

That evening, as Sean closed his front door after him, he smelled something burning. 'Dear?' he said. 'Are you there?'

Anne came out of the kitchen, her hair in disarray. 'I'm sorry. I was tending the stove. The cook-maid's ill and she's with her mother.' Sean came to her and went to kiss her lips but she turned her cheek to him instead. 'Did you bring the cash?'

Hughes took his jacket off and hung it up. 'No.'

Anne frowned. 'Sean, I need that money in hand! We have bills to pay, the grocer for one; I need oil for lamps and we need to get—'

'I know, I know. Don't keep reminding me, please. We'll have money on Thursday. Silverstein's just paid me extra for an incorrect invoice.'

The burning smell increased. Anne turned. 'Oh dear.' She ran and dragged a smoking lamb roast from the oven.

Sean came to help her. 'How did you get this so wrong? Once the fire in the range is hot enough, it's only a matter of timing.'

She ripped off her apron and flung it on the table. 'You're so good at tending fires; you can rescue the meat. I'm going to my room. Call me when dinner's ready.'

Anne sat on her bed and cried. She was failing Sean, who worked so hard. She felt useless at home, a burden on their new business. But the real burden was the debt laid on it by the replacement of the gold doors. Their profits for their first year had gone into paying back the Cork loan. And it worried them both that their customers weren't paying their bills on time and cash was scarce. For some reason, every task she tried to take on was difficult.

There was a knock on the door and Sean came in. 'Dinner is ready, dear.'

Anne reached out to him and he came and sat on the bed. 'I'm sorry,' she said, 'I really am.'

He smiled. 'It's all right. It's not a disaster, just a bit of knife work needed.'

'I'm no use to you.'

'Don't be daft.' He picked up her hand and kissed it. 'I could say the same to you. But we'll manage. I'll get the cash from the bank on Thursday morning.'

She nodded and slid off the bed. 'Good. But I'll go to the bank and get the money. Just give me the permission slip so they'll know who I am. I'll go every Monday to check our balances and get cash.' She smiled. 'That'll be my job from now on.'

'A proper little businesswoman. We'll see.' She felt fobbed off and he relented at once. 'If I get really busy, I'll see if you can help me. Come on and eat. You need to test the quality of my potatoes.'

Later, in the bedchamber once again, she looked at her reflection in the mirror. She had changed in six months; her face was wan, with more lines on it than a music score. Sean was undressing and she slipped on her night gown and got into bed. 'Tell me about the Road again. Do you really think you'll get a contract there?'

'I think we could.' Sean sat on the edge of the bed. 'There was this girl up there who was very helpful.'

She pricked up her ears. 'How old?'

He smiled. 'Seventeen, maybe eighteen.'

'What did she look like?'

'She was attractive and had a nice ... well, she was nice.'

'Pretty? Like I used to be?'

Sean reached out and stroked her arm. 'She doesn't compare.' He got into bed and cuddled her.

'I'm very tired,' she said. 'I'm sorry, dear.'

He sighed and kissed her. It was gentle. There was a warmth and feeling in it, but she broke away and turned from him.

'Good night,' he said.

After he'd doused the lights, she lay there still and awake. When Sean had returned from the Road, she had asked him about Gerry and he'd told her about the brief encounter. Then he'd reminded her that she hadn't wanted to know about Riordan, that she didn't want to see him. *And I don't.*

Sean fell asleep and she tried to but felt restless. It'd been over six months since Sean had touched her but up to last month she hadn't missed it. Now she did. She should have welcomed Sean just now, pressed him to her breasts and loved him. It would have been good. Tears came to her because she couldn't understand why she couldn't do it. He was a good man, a good provider and faithful to her. And he loved her. More tears came and she bit her finger, trying not to cry aloud, or he would wake.

She said her Hail Marys for the All Souls. After the third, she settled and drifted off.

* * *

Maurice Silverstein was in his office, looking over his desk at Gerry Riordan, whose strong form made the chair he sat in look like one made for a pygmy. It made Silverstein nervous, though there was no logical reason for that—to his knowledge, Riordan had never laid eyes on Jacob Greenberg, so could never dream of his connections with Cork, the trial, the gold.

'Please read through the contract,' he said, pushing it across the desk. 'What you've told me convinces me you have the skills for the work I need done. And as it happens I've seen your work on Devine's Hill. Lieutenant Dodds told me you led the team on the stonework.'

Riordan took the two-page document. 'A lot's due to the lads in the gang.' The chair under Riordan squeaked, giving Silverstein the feeling that its collapse was seconds away. Riordan paused in his reading and the chair became silent. 'I see the contract's for ten weeks.'

The man has no trouble reading. Good. 'Ten weeks is ample, according to my partner. He's an expert in stone. If I want you for another job after that, I'll issue a separate contract.'

'Sounds fair.'

'You'll write your address on that contract when you sign. Have you digs in town?'

'No, Mr Silverstein, not yet. Anywhere you can recommend?'

'Try Henry's Pub in George Street. It's cheap and clean.' There was a knock on the door and Rebecca appeared. 'Sir, Mr Simpson is here.'

There was little space in Silverstein's office and Dougal Simpson had to press himself behind her to get through. Rebecca blushed, extricated herself and closed the door after her.

Simpson looked at the stonemason. 'Gerry Riordan?'

'Aye,' Riordan said, rising from his chair.

Silverstein filled the silence. 'My partner, Mr Simpson.'

Riordan remained standing and Simpson turned to Silverstein. 'Afternoon, partner.' He pulled a chair nearer to the men and eyeballed the mason. 'I was up the Road some months ago.'

'Looking for me,' Riordan said. 'I heard.'

Simpson lowered his eyelids. 'How did you know?'

'Lieutenant Dodds told me.'

'Ah! A good man, that officer! No, I wasn't looking for you but I saw the quality of your work. We want you for stonework to begin with, but later it might be brickwork. You'll lay bricks?'

'Aye.'

He glanced down at the paper in Gerry's hand. 'You can see from that document that we pay good rates, Riordan.'

Riordan said, 'I'm ready to sign this. I'll be putting down my new name. I'm changing it to Gleeson.'

'Not wanted by the law, are you?' Simpson laughed at his own joke.

'New life, new name.'

Simpson stood up. 'I'll leave you to handle the details, Silverstein.' He put out his hand. 'Where's your digs in town?'

'Henry's, I think,' Riordan replied. He took the hand, showing a little surprise that it was offered.

'I know it. Let's have a beer there soon.'

Riordan nodded, still looking surprised. It gave Silverstein a surge of guilt to see Simpson barging into the life of this man, when in secret he was planning to take that life away.

Simpson let himself out and Silverstein got through the business of signing the contract. As Riordan leaned over the desk with a quill in his hand, Silverstein said, 'Town's not the safest place for anyone to live. There's rough fellows here who'll slit your throat for a farthing. Keep a watch out and don't go into any dark alleys.'

Riordan completed both signatures, stood straight and picked up his copy of the contract. 'I've got size on my side and a friend or two here.'

Silverstein stood up and crossed the office to usher the big man out. 'You may have, but scum have no scruples and they often hunt in packs. Who do you know in Sydney? Irishmen, no doubt.'

Riordan said with irony. 'I couple of lads I met up at the Barracks in Macquarie Street might still be about, who knows? And from Cork, there's Mr Hughes. I met him on the Road and he's got a foundry in Sussex Street. You know it?'

Silverstein's head buzzed. His voice sounded thin. 'I know Mr Hughes but we don't do business. Goodbye.'

Silverstein closed the door and leaned against it. His stomach churned and his forehead was damp. As if he were careering down a steep hill, knowing that a fall was going to happen, but with no notion how bad it would be.

Simpson was going to kill Riordan and he himself would be an accomplice. He crossed to the desk and with trembling hands unlocked and opened the middle drawer. The letter that he withdrew was creased and dog-eared. It was Anne Donovan's first letter to Riordan when he was transported. Like him, it had sailed halfway round the globe. But it had never reached the man. Silverstein had intercepted it.

Heartfelt words sprang out at him from the page.

You're innocent, my love as I always knew you were! The master stonemason confessed to me that he'd sold the gold from the doors to a Mr Greenberg for cash, whom you may or may not know. So, do not sink to woe. I will make it my goal to link this man to the crime and get you a new trial.

This letter was incriminating, which was why he could never let it be seen by anyone in Sydney, let alone its rightful recipient. Why had he kept it all this time? He was about to tear it up when Anne Donovan's sweet face came into his mind. He replaced the letter in the drawer and locked it.

* * *

In the early morning sunshine, Deirdre Walsh was checking her list of goods to buy when she got to town. Gerry had been in Sydney for two days, as far away from her and Wiseman's as the moon. But luck was now on her side because there were purchases to be made in town. Her mother was needed at the inn, so she was making the trip herself, with Harry the groom taking turns with the driving.

She put her list away as Lieutenant Dodds rode into the courtyard and doffed his hat. 'You look exceeding well, Miss Walsh. But how is your father? I hear he's injured.'

'Good day to you, sir. He's cranky. Not from the pain but from the embarrassment.'

Dodds grinned. 'They tell me he was kicking a dog. What happened, it bit back?'

She smiled with him. 'No thank goodness—he was injured another way. Our dog King was being set on by a stray. A big brute. Mother tried swatting it with a broom but Father went in with his feet. He missed his target and bashed his ankle on a bollard. It's swelled up like a swag. He let out such a yell the beast ran off and we haven't seen it since.'

Dodds laughed and dismounted. 'Well, he can rest while you go to town. You'll have Harry by your side. And myself as escort, with your father's permission. I have business with the Roads and Bridges Department.'

'Today?'

He tethered his horse. 'Tomorrow, but I'm leaving this morning. Are you taking the wagon?'

'I am,' she said.

Dodds nodded. 'When are you leaving?'

'At nine o'clock.'

'Have I got time for breakfast?'

She smiled again. 'If you're quick, Lieutenant.'

Twenty minutes later, Dodds had wolfed down the rest of his bacon, which had been crisp and tasty. In the courtyard he mounted up, while the groom readied the wagon and horses. Deirdre was already on the wide driver's seat. 'Morning, Harry,' Dodds said.

'Morning, Lieutenant.'

Harry slapped the reins down on the backs of the two horses and the wagon moved off, with Dodds trotting alongside.

They were silent until they'd left the Hawkesbury behind, and then Deirdre smiled over at Dodds with a wistful expression on her face. 'I need some cheering up.'

Dodds could guess why, but he wasn't sure how confidential she might be within hearing of Harry the groom. 'Would this be because a certain gentleman has been less than amenable?'

She gave a little laugh. 'It's just a mess, from start to finish. First he won't stop brooding, next he's mad for money and nothing else. But that's just bluff and talk.' She caught his glance at Harry and said, 'Don't worry about Harry, Lieutenant. He has an earful of my worries now and then, don't you, Harry?'

The man nodded and looked away, a little embarrassed, perhaps, but silent.

Dodds was concerned. 'He was unpleasant to you?'

'That's the least of it, Lieutenant. About as warm to me as a slab of fancy ice sitting in Father's cold store.'

'As bad as that?'

Harry gave the horses a little more leather.

'He makes me so angry sometimes,' she said. 'I could kill him, I really could.'

'The man has that effect on people, Miss Walsh. On the Road I was dealing with a sullen, stubborn convict. What you've had to deal with is yet another side to the man—or maybe he's still a boy.'

'Oh, the black moods are back, I'm sorry to say. That letter he got last week—'

'I know,' Dodds said, to stop her from naming Anne Hughes. 'It was full of anger, from a woman in great sorrow, and it caused him pain. Riordan took it hard. I can't blame him. Well, what we must do is find him in Sydney and knock some sense into him, again. I take it you're still interested in him?'

'Right now, he's the last thing I want to worry about. Father's given me a list of goods to buy, with little money to spend on them.'

'You're a good trader, Miss Walsh. You'll manage.'

'I'm glad someone has faith in me.' She looked around and smiled. 'I love the bush. Its smells, space and sounds. It gives me peace.' She kept quiet for a time. 'Gerry's going to see Mr Silverstein about a contract for laying stone.'

Dodds was surprised. 'Silverstein's a merchant. Deals with tools and such. Why would he be interested in giving Gerry a job as a stonemason? That's odd.'

'Silverstein has property that he wants to develop.'

Ever since they'd left the inn he'd been aware of a familiar, welcoming smell from a large basket behind her. 'Have you got food on board?'

'Of course. Fresh bread, ham and ginger beer.'

'Just what I might have expected from you,' Dodds said.

'We need it on the way,' she said. 'It's an eight-hour trip. But if I have to stop and feed you every hour, we're going to be late in Sydney.'

'Just a little snack, then.'

'Later.'

'You're a hard woman, Miss Walsh.'

'And a sensible one.'

He smiled. 'Did you know Simpson was up at Windsor flaunting his newfound wealth to Superintendent Hands? He was flinging coin around like he'd struck gold.'

'Do you know where Simpson is now?' she asked.

'I was told he was going to Sydney.'

'With him going to Sydney,' she said, 'and Gerry being there too, then all the players in this little plot are gathering together.'

'I'm impressed Miss Walsh. I am. You're a fine student of mystery and intrigue. But Sydney's a big town and it's not certain they'll all meet. I hope they don't before I get to investigate what's going on. Dougal Simpson is the one who worries me. I'm convinced he's behind the theft of those benighted cathedral doors and I suspect he's after Gerry.'

She looked at him in panic. 'Gerry's in danger?'

'It's possible. Do you know where he's lodging?'

'Me?' she said with a bitter tone. 'Of course not. But you could see Mr Silverstein and maybe find out.'

'Good idea.'

'What's your business at the department—or is it all official and beyond the likes of me?'

He smiled at her. Her spirit always impressed him. 'The usual reports. Major Mitchell wants them detailed and complete to the last jot. I admire him as engineer and surveyor—meticulous and demanding, just as he should be. I've also got to bone up on the next section of Road, up through Judge Dowling's Range.'

'What will you do after the Road is finished?'

'That's years away.'

'And then what?'

'Why, Miss Walsh, I'm touched that you brood over my fate so zealously.'

She made a face. 'It's not like that, you goose. It's just that you've become such a part of our lives and I'm going to miss you.'

'Is this an amorous approach, now that Mr Gerry Riordan has rejected you?'

'Not on your life,' she said, but she was smiling just the same. 'Reach me that jacket from behind the seat, would you, there's a good officer? It's getting windy.' He did so, she put the jacket on and then had Harry pass her the reins so she could drive for a few miles. Dodds rode a little further back, leaving her to it.

After an hour or so he drew level again and said, 'We need to get Mr Gerry Riordan to see sense. We also need to find out what this Mr Simpson is all about.'

Just after one o'clock, Harry pulled the wagon off the road and into the shade. The aroma from the food got even stronger and more pleasant. Deirdre broke off some bread, laid a thick slab of ham on it and gave it to him. She did the same for Harry.

'Fit for a king,' Dodds said and opened the ginger beer.

* * *

It was dusk when Harry unhitched the wagon and stabled the horses at Stuart's Hotel in Bridge Street, and went off to stay with his parents, who lived in the Rocks.

With Dodds at her side, Deirdre looked up at the building. 'Mr Wiseman told us this is the newest hotel in town. Father promised me dinner here as a treat for my eighteenth birthday.'

'And when is the big day?'

'The fourth, tomorrow.'

'Well, Miss Walsh, if you haven't prodded sense into our newly minted ticket by then, I'd be honoured to offer you a good dinner here.'

'My Uncle Tom is already invited, and Father is certainly not expecting me to invite Gerry Riordan! But he'd be delighted if you came, Lieutenant. I'll be glad of your company.'

'You're very kind.'

She brushed the worst of the dust from her clothes. 'Thank you for listening to me for hour upon hour. I've never found the trip so pleasant before.'

'All the pleasure was mine, Miss Walsh. Do you want me to escort you inside?'

Deirdre glanced at him. She knew Dodds was staying at his usual accommodation near the department, but he was too polite to walk off and leave her in the street. Nonetheless, she didn't want to enter the foyer of a hotel on the arm of an officer, when both of them were single and unattached.

'Thank you, sir, but my booking's made so I'm sure they'll lose no time admitting me. I look forward to seeing you tomorrow evening. At eight?'

He smiled, kissed her hand and walked away.

* * *

Smoke from a score of pipes and cigars irritated Sergeant Dan Morgan's eyes and his stomach was stretched from an afternoon of Henry's ale. Life in town was easy but the chances of excessive flogging few; too much protocol and too many eyes. Give him the bush any day and the freedom it offered. He burped and finished his beer as the barman lighted the lamps.

If he wasn't to pass out or vomit, he'd better eat something. He hailed the barman for a plate of chops and potatoes. The pub's patrons were a mixed group; whalers, soldiers, merchants, clerks and government people like himself imbibing on this Thursday night. One was a russet-headed man with broad shoulders who towered over his fellows. Riordan.

The plate landed in front of him, its greasy smell mixing with the smoke. He tucked in, keeping a weather eye on the tall man. Riordan must have his ticket, to be drinking free like this with tradesmen and the like. Morgan crunched down harder on a tough piece of mutton. His blood stirred as he remembered that day near the work-site scaffold, the cheeky cockney Smith and humiliation that followed. The jibes and jokes that had lasted for weeks after, all the way up to Ten Mile Hollow.

That Papist stonemason was to blame for the worst moments Morgan had had on the bloody Road. He deserved getting it in the neck tonight. But to start a blue in a pub while in uniform was not a good idea. It would have to be outside and in the dark. No matter. He ordered another ale and kept an eye on his quarry.

Chapter Twelve

In Henry's Hotel, Gerry was enjoying himself. It was his fifth beer and the alcohol was coursing through him, making him feel rosy about his future. He'd been drinking since late afternoon and had met some tradesmen who, like him, had won contracts in town.

'Your shout, Riordan,' his companion said. Gerry had not yet filled in the right forms to have his name changed to Gleeson. It didn't seem so important now that he was in work and getting satisfaction from it. Not to mention an income.

'Right.' Gerry walked the short distance to the bar and leaned on it. 'Three pints, please.'

The barmaid smiled. 'Sure, love. You'll be a big boy when you grow up.' She turned the tap, waited, then placed the beers on the bar. 'There you go.' Gerry paid her.

His drinking buddy took one of the glasses. 'Thanks, matey. Here's to you.'

The ale filled his throat and he settled down to the pleasure of talking to another craftsman.

The pleasure did not last because after a while his casual acquaintance went home and instead of friendly faces across the table he had pictures in his head of the Drawbridge bar room in Cork, and the smiling face of Lawrence Toole. And the tormenting smile of Anne Donovan.

When he was drunk enough, he walked out into the street and headed for Hughes Foundry. It was in Sussex Street and they probably lived there too. He had to see Anne, with her husband or without. It was evening but not too late. He'd make a fool of himself but the beer had given him courage. No letter would keep him away. Face to face, he wanted her to tell him that she hated him. He concentrated on walking in the right direction. The pub's noise faded behind him but he'd only got a short distance before the beer in his bladder became too much. A space between buildings beckoned, but he hesitated. Someone had told him not to go into places like this alone. Then the urgency increased. He ducked into the darkness and relieved himself.

'I'll wait till you finish, Riordan.'

Gerry stared towards a bulky shape silhouetted against the street lamp. The voice was familiar.

'Hate to leave a man with his dick on show.' It was Morgan.

Gerry stepped back but was not quick enough. The scourger's knuckles smashed into his jaw. Pain flashed through his head and he was off balance, one knee dropping to the pavement. A fist found his stomach and he doubled over.

'Stand up, you Southern turd, and fight me.'

Gerry sprang up, feinted and stepped back, the whoosh of another punch missing his nose. 'You need a lesson,' Morgan growled, 'and I'm going to give it to you.'

Morgan swung a boot at Gerry's groin. Gerry grabbed it and flung it upwards, tipping the scourger on his back. Gerry leaped on him, pinning down the man and landing two punches, blood spurting from the scourger's nose and mouth. Gerry's fists stung but he landed another punch. The scourger slipped an arm out from Gerry's grip and jabbed at a rib. Gerry groaned and Morgan hit him on the nose. Blinded, he got up and the scourger landed a kick to his groin, on target this time.

'Now, I'll finish you.' Morgan hit Gerry in the same rib and heard a crack. 'Good, and here's another.'

Gerry lurched to one side, pain stabbing through his ribs. Morgan missed him and Gerry grabbed the scourger's head and smashed his forehead into Morgan's nose.

'Shite!' the sergeant screamed. 'You filthy shite.'

Gerry stood back and slammed a boot down on the scourger's knee and Morgan collapsed. Gerry raised his boot and was aiming at the ugly face when a movement caught his eye.

A tall constable stood at the alley entrance. He leaned into the darkness and raised a lantern. 'What's going on here?'

Gerry slunk back into the blackness and looked behind him. At the other end of the alley, the glow of another street lamp beckoned. He made for it as the circle of the constable's lantern came closer.

As Morgan struggled to get to his feet, the constable was joined by two men, one short and slight, the other heavier set. The three came up to Morgan.

'Are you all right, Sergeant Morgan?' the constable said.

Morgan tried to focus through his swollen eyes. It was comforting that the constabulary knew him. He'd nail Riordan for assault now for sure. 'Help me up.'

The two bigger men assisted him and Morgan took a look at the smaller man standing by. Even in the gloom, there was something familiar about him.

The constable looked both ways down the alley and back at Morgan. 'My brothers followed you from Henry's, Sergeant, and to their surprise you went after Riordan. So we waited till Riordan softened you up for us. We'll finish the job ourselves.'

Morgan was fully alert now. The smaller man spoke up. 'Ernest Smith, Sergeant, remember me?' He touched his shoulder. 'Fair wrecked me, you did, on that damned crane. Now it's your turn to feel what that's like.' He laughed.

The cockney! That damned man on the scaffold that day. Morgan's eyes expanded and he tried to run but was gripped hard.

'Hold him fast,' Smith said.

The others held him while the cockney tied Morgan's arms behind his back. He then took his brother's baton and inserted it under Morgan's right armpit. Grabbing both ends, he began to twist. 'Put a gag on him,' Smith said, panting.

Morgan's muffled cries filled the damp darkness of the alley.

* * *

In Henry's saloon bar, Gerry sat in pain with his back against one side of an open-topped partition. Noise from the public bar behind him was getting louder as noon approached. Pain radiated from his cracked rib, his nose felt busted, his left eye was closed.

'Another drink, love?' the barmaid said, coming up to him. Gerry shook his head. 'I said to the boss you've been lucky to live,' she said. 'Your face is fierce.'

Gerry smiled and the creases stretched his stitches, hurting him. 'At least I don't have to look at it.'

'You should never have gone down that alley, you know. There was a man called Adams who was killed like that a while ago. He came here on a transport ship in twenty-eight—didn't last long, did he? Look after yourself, love.'

She went away and he swore. He remembered Adams, the filthy mongrel of an overseer on the ship. Probably killed in revenge. And revenge would keep Morgan here, still dangerous. Morgan would attack him again. It was just a matter of time.

Then to his utter astonishment, Deirdre Walsh walked into the bar room, with Lieutenant Dodds by her side. They looked around, spied him and walked straight over.

She got to him first, horrified, with Dodds following. He was half standing when she got to the table but collapsed back onto the bench.

She sat down opposite, examining his face in distress. 'What happened to you?'

'A fight, that's all.'

Her eyes expanded in shock. 'That's all! You look like you've been through my mum's mincer.'

Gerry winced. 'The face isn't the problem.'

'Who did it?' Dodds said, sitting down next to Deirdre so that both their backs were to the room. She was the only well-dressed woman in the bar—it was no place for females except those who were in the trade of being on show.

Gerry muttered, 'Couldn't see him. It was my own fault. I went into a dark alley.' He said to Deirdre, 'This is no place for you. You shouldn't be here.'

'I'll enter where I want and I'd like to see them try to throw me out! I'm an innkeeper's daughter, you big loon. Now listen to me because I'm worried about you.'

'You needn't be. I've got a contract for ten weeks on good money and Mr Silverstein wants me to build houses for him.'

Dodds said, 'We know that. I visited Silverstein today to ask him where you might be lodging and he said here at Henry's. Thank God we found you. He also told me something disturbing—he's gone into partnership with a man called Dougal Simpson. Have you met him yet?'

'Aye.' Gerry placed a hand to his side as the pain renewed itself. He was damned if it would stop him working tomorrow, though. The money was too good. 'He's a partner in a quarry as well.'

Deirdre sat back on her chair, patted her face with a handkerchief and glanced at Dodds. 'Gerry, Simpson's a snake. Mr Dodds spoke to the police today and they're as suspicious of him as we are. It looks as though he's cheating his partner at the quarry and if that's the case he's probably cheating Mr Silverstein.'

Dodds put in, 'I can't believe Silverstein would agree to deal with the man unless he was under some heavy obligation to him. And I've heard Silverstein's lifestyle has changed for the worse under his influence. Big spending on'—his gaze flickered towards Deirdre and he finished lamely—'big spending altogether. Strange for a merchant with a head on his shoulders.'

'Well that's nothing to do with me,' Gerry said.

Deirdre leaned over the table and put a hand on his arm. All the dark troubles flew from his mind with this closeness and he was aware of no one in this crowded room but her. She said in a firm, warm tone, 'Gerry, listen to me. You think you've only met Simpson the once, but really he's been part of your life for years without anyone guessing. And listen to Mr Dodds, because he's been digging things out for you and he'll tell you how.'

So Dodds told him the story of what had happened in Cork, from the time when James Donovan ordered the tabernacle doors from

Hughes Foundry, until the day Gerry was marched onto the transport bound for Sydney. It was a story made up of raw facts and hearsay and suppositions and more recent discoveries, but Dodds's dispassionate account added up for Gerry. It all fell into place and he could see the thread of the gold running through it as though it were the light of truth.

He bent his head. 'Donovan hired Simpson to steal the gold. Lawrence Toole surprised Simpson when he was setting me up for the theft. Simpson killed Toole. Greenberg left Cork with the gold.'

'And you got convicted for the crimes,' Deirdre said.

Dodds said, 'So you see, Riordan, Simpson is the key. He's already been convicted as a thief in Ireland. If we can get him into police hands here, and he's proven a killer, then you'll have proven your innocence.'

Gerry closed his eyes. His voice was leaden. 'It's all too late.'

Deirdre touched his arm again, more urgently this time. 'Gerry, you're in danger. Simpson murdered your friend to conceal what he'd done with the gold. And you're working for him! If he suspects that you've seen through him, he won't hesitate to kill you.'

'I don't know how they'd prove he killed Toole.'

'Evidence,' Dodds said. 'If they compared the writing on the paper found in Toole's hand with Simpson's own handwriting I believe they'd be the same. And there's no shortage of papers in Simpson's hand at Silverstein's.'

Gerry shook his head, then regretted it. 'I want a new life. Don't keep dragging up the old one.'

Deirdre cried out, 'You say he was your best friend! He was killed in your room and named a thief. And you just want to forget him?'

Dodds followed her up. 'Riordan. Don't you want to avenge Lawrence Toole? Isn't that worth anything to you?'

Gerry swung round at him and winced, holding his side. 'Yes, Toole was my mate. I'll never forget him.'

'Then do him a service!' Dodds replied. 'Find out who killed him. He deserves that.'

Gerry stared at him. His forehead was filmed in sweat; he felt almost faint from what he'd heard from Deirdre and Dodds. He looked from one to the other, his lips tight. At last he said, 'I owe him that. I do.'

Deirdre sighed. 'Now you're talking sense. We have to get Simpson to say something about his past. At a moment when he's comfortable and thinks he's safe—to Silverstein?'

Dodds said, 'We must find a way to overhear something incriminating, or better still get the police to hear it.' A chair scraped on the other side of the partition. 'We should talk away from here. Riordan, are you up for this?'

'To get Toole's killer? You have my word on it.'

* * *

Dougal Simpson was sitting at a table in the dining room of Stuarts Hotel. He was twirling his lucky medallion because this felt like a lucky day. He thought of the three blocks of land bought at cheap prices in his name and Silverstein's, and ready for the houses that Riordan believed they were going to build. *Nice trap that.*

Maurice Silverstein walked up to his table and sat down.

'Bottle of your best bubbly,' Simpson said to the nearby waiter.

'It's Sunday, sir, and we don't serve alcohol here before sunset.'

Simpson gave the man a vicious look. 'Breakfast then. Maurie? What'll you have?'

'Two boiled eggs, toast and tea, thank you.'

'And I'll have two eggs and bacon, tea and toast.'

'Yes, sir,' the waiter said and left them.

Silverstein looked around at the crowded dining room and Simpson studied him. *What a pushover.* Simpson was the man's partner without having put up a penny of capital. All the capital was in the bank under Silverstein's name. That was going to change today.

'What I want to talk about now is the gold.'

Silverstein rolled his eyes. 'Not that again.'

'Maurie my boy, money should be talked about any time, especially when it's your money. I want the bank account in both our names. Equal partnership, equal access to the capital.'

'I can't grant you that,' Silverstein said. 'When it comes to expenses you've made me lay out more than I ever have in my life. That's all the indulgence you'll get from me.'

'Yes, it's good to see you bent on pleasure.' Simpson leaned forward and squeezed Silverstein's arm. 'Flo likes you, she does.'

Silverstein glanced around. 'Careful, Simpson, please.'

Simpson smiled. 'She likes you so much, she's written to you. Yeah, she's a bright one our Flo … anyway she put it all down on paper, what she likes about you, what you two do together. I have her note here.' Simpson pulled it from a pocket and slipped it across the table. 'Read it. It's sweet.'

Silverstein looked at the document as if it was his death warrant, then pushed it back. 'What, she wants me to set her up? That won't happen.'

Simpson started to eat with relish. 'No, for now it's sweet stuff between you and her.' Simpson wiped his mouth and chuckled. 'But think of the scandal if the papers got hold of this. Think of the loss of respectability, the damage to our business. Just when you're doing so well. Some of the things you and Flo do together make me blush to the crown of my head, Maurie, they do. I'm not sure I can keep on associating with you unless you meet certain conditions. Like making me a signatory to your bank account.'

'This is blackmail and I won't have it.'

'Is that so?' Dougal sat back and pondered his partner for a moment. Silverstein was sweating. 'Then maybe something simpler would convince you.' He slipped his hold-all to one side. Under it was a stiletto and he stroked it, its blade glinting.

Silverstein's eyes were fixed on the weapon in horror. His voice was a whisper. 'All right … all right.'

Simpson covered the blade and sat back. 'See, easy. You meet me at the bank at your convenience and Mr Brown's and we'll sign the papers.'

Bailed Up

* * *

On Monday morning, a week after he'd come to town, Gerry was sitting in the Bank of New South Wales in George Street. He'd put in his papers to open an account and was waiting to be called to the counter. Preoccupied with the turmoil of events since he'd arrived in town, he did not look up for some minutes. When he did, he saw a tall young woman at the counter, with a trim figure and dark hair tied under a bonnet. Anne.

He stared as if to make sure the image was real. She nodded at the teller, who then went away. She looked down at a piece of paper, her profile as fine as he remembered. Yes, it was his Anne.

Standing up, he took three steps towards her. 'Anne, it's me.'

Turning, she faced him and her green eyes widened in surprise. 'You!' She studied him, no doubt seeing the stitches, cuts and bruises on his face and neck.

'Don't judge me by …' His voice failed him.

Her jaw hardened and her lips formed into a straight line; those lips that had once kissed him. 'It's been some time.'

'Here you are, Madam,' the teller said behind her. Anne turned to the teller, who looked past her at Gerry. 'Excuse me, are you with this lady?'

Gerry shook his head.

'Then please stand back, thank you sir.'

Gerry went and sat down while Anne received her money. She put it into her purse, adjusted her bonnet and walked towards the door, not glancing his way. Shocked, he stood up and followed as an attendant opened the big door for them both.

Outside, he caught up with her. 'Anne? Don't you have any time for me?'

She stopped and shook her head. Her lips trembled. 'I'm sorry.' She stood back against the wall of the bank and looked at his chest, not his eyes. 'Sean, my husband, has told me everything about you. It was hard to hear but I trust … you're well and that you'll prosper.'

'I'm working in Sydney now.'

'I'm pleased for you,' she said without emotion.

'I can meet you after work. Please.'

'We've nothing to talk about.'

'That's not true!' Gerry pressed her elbow and she closed her eyes. A shiver passed through her.

'You wrote me a letter and said things that hurt like the devil. Don't I have the right to give you an answer?'

She looked away. 'I must go.'

Gerry kept hold of her. 'I'm staying at Henry's in George Street. They have a lounge there for ladies. A few minutes this afternoon, that's all I ask. I'll be there at four-thirty.'

Anne disengaged her arm. 'I'll never see you.' She paused, her eyes filling with tears. 'I cannot.' She walked away.

Anne had forgotten the cash in her purse as she swung it round and round like a toy. She wanted to smash it against the nearest lamp post. Passersby gave her a wide berth but she hardly noticed. Her pulse raced and her skin prickled, not from the heat that filmed her back with perspiration but from anger, seething anger at him; his eyes, his stance and his mouth. He was injured; that had affected her. But she had hardly spoken a word to him.

Down George Street she went and missed the turnoff to Market Street and backtracked. He hadn't changed much, still the same attractive smile, the same broad shoulders and there was more bulk on him. And his skin was tanned. He was all she could think about and this must stop. She headed down to Sussex Street.

The foundry came into sight and Anne clasped the purse to her, conscious of the cash inside. It was near midday in the blazing sun but pickpockets never ceased work and were never far away.

Her blood still boiled. In a town like Sydney, she should have known she and Gerry might meet by accident, but this had thrown her. She prayed it would never happen again. Going into the foundry, she made her way to the office to give the money to Sean. Nothing would make her tell him about Gerry.

When Anne got home she decided to plan her part in the church fête. She started to list the tasks to do and the people involved. At times she would glance at the clock. There was no need because Sean wouldn't be home till six but there was another reason in the back of her mind. Gerry had asked to meet her at four-thirty.

At three she finished and went into the bedroom to lay out fresh clothes. In her bath she washed herself, conscious of the feel of the sponge on her skin, and she knew why and hated herself for it. She dressed in her best dress, knowing what she was doing and loathing herself even more. At four o'clock she left home and made her way downtown.

The man at the desk looked at her with a formal expression. 'Madam, can I help you?'

Anne felt self-conscious. Here she was about to meet a man alone. Something no married woman with morals would do, but she was forced to answer. 'I'm here to meet a Mr Gerry Riordan in the lounge.'

'If you'd like to go through, Madam, you may find Mr Riordan there. If you don't, I'll send a boy up to his room.' The way the man said 'room' made her think Gerry's must be a modest one.

Anne said, 'I'll try the lounge. Where is it?'

The man pointed to a large entranceway on the other side of the foyer. 'Through there, Madam, next to the dining room.'

With a straight back and no haste, she walked into the lounge room alone. There were three occupants seated in armchairs: a couple talking together in the far corner and a man reading the newspaper. She realised there was no anger in her now, just nervous anticipation. There was pressure in her stomach and her legs felt like jelly. She chose a chair in the opposite corner to the couple and near the closed doors of the dining room.

Gerry entered from the foyer. His red hair was neatly cut and his clothing was nothing to be ashamed of but she hardly noticed that: she could see amazement and happiness in his eyes at the sight of her. She could tell he had not expected her to come, and felt too over-whelmed to speak.

She did not rise and he sat down opposite her at once so as not to draw attention. 'You're here,' he said. 'Thank you.'

Anne clasped her purse as if it held diamonds. She tried to cling to her self-control in the same way. Her voice sounded strangled. 'I didn't want to come and I shouldn't be here.'

'But we have to talk.' He paused, just looking at her. 'In that terrible letter I got on the Road, you said you'd sent me another one. But I never heard from you after I left Ireland, Anne. Did you really write to me here?'

'Yes,'

'When did you send the letter?'

'After you sailed away.'

'Well I didn't get it.'

'What?'

'I didn't. And I want to know what you said in it.'

So, he'd never received it. It must have been lost at sea, or fallen victim to a careless post-office worker—who cared whether convicts got mail? She thought of all the heartfelt words she had poured onto that single page on the morning when she left for France and seized on the one thing that might mean the most to him. At least, the one truth she could tell without betraying her feelings. 'My letter said you were innocent.'

'Innocent? But you already knew I was and you'd told me so. What else was in the letter?'

All at once she had to tell him. At least the truth about the gold. 'My father arranged to have the tabernacle doors stolen. I have no evidence but I'm certain. I suspect the gold was melted down and he sold it to someone to solve problems at Donovans. I hated him for it but I love him too.' She closed her eyes. *And you. And you.*

His shoulders sagged. 'Donovan. He threw me into gaol just to … save himself.' And to keep you away from me.' Gerry's fists clenched and unclenched, and she sensed he was going to punch something. His eyes were forced shut and she felt his pain, then he opened them. He avoided her gaze. 'That must have been hard for you to bear.'

He was thinking of her before himself. There was no accusation for her, though she'd kept James Donovan's guilt from the police and Gerry had been found guilty instead. Tears filled her eyes and she wanted him to hold her. She pressed her purse harder. *Be strong.*

She said in a rush, 'And after I sent that letter I got the official notice from here. To say you were dead. It said when you … were dying you gave my name and address to someone and asked for me to be informed.'

'God!' He put his head in his hands. 'Lieutenant Dodds told me this the other day. I felt for you. I remembered how I loved you then. If you loved me the same way—what would that do to you?'

He was considering her again. Not himself. He was speaking of love in the past. Anne pressed her hands and knees together and trembled. 'It was one of the cruellest things I've ever known.'

'That's when—not long ago, I mean—that's when Dodds told me you married Sean Hughes.' He looked away, then back at her.

The way his blue eyes held hers, she knew he had heard about her keenest grief. 'When Lieutenant Dodds told me you were alive, I had a fall, and my baby didn't survive.' Dropping her head, she let her tears fall on her lap. She was facing the other patrons but she didn't care.

He moved to sit on her armrest and hold her. She sobbed at so many things; her lost love, her lost baby, her marriage to another, all that while dampening his shirt but still he held her, not letting go. After some time, she rummaged in her purse, withdrew a handkerchief and wiped her eyes and looked up. 'I've made you wet, I'm sorry.'

Gerry stood up and sat opposite her again. He leaned forward and took hold of her hands. 'I don't want you to hate me. I couldn't bear that. I've done nothing to you. I was accused of robbery I didn't commit and a murder I didn't do. I was shipped round the world to be a slave and put through torture.'

His closeness reminded her of their secret meetings in Cork and his look made her warm and secure. The smell of him, his strength, old times, mixed and competed with one another to arouse her. His face came closer. His eyes widened.

He drew her up and she followed him into the empty dining room. They kissed. Deeper and longer than at any time in the past.

'Anne, my Anne.' His hands pressed her back and she thrilled within his embrace as he kissed her again.

The door behind her pushed against them and they separated.

Before she even knew who had caught them out, Anne wiped her eyes and settled her hair. Her passion was replaced by acute embarrassment.

The girl who appeared before them was attractive and a little younger than herself. She took in all of Anne with just one expert inspection. 'I came to see that you were all right,' she said, looking at Anne but meaning Gerry. 'They said you were in the lounge.'

Anne went to walk past her.

Gerry said. 'Mrs Hughes, this is Miss Deirdre Walsh.'

Anne went back into the lounge room. The others followed her. Anne faced the woman. 'How do you do.' Her cheeks felt hot.

'Pleased to meet you, Mrs Hughes,' Miss Walsh said. 'This must've been a very important occasion, for you to meet Gerry alone.'

Anne thought, *Direct, even rude, but accurate.* The woman was pretty, with tanned skin and big eyes. 'I should go,' Anne said. 'Excuse me, Miss Walsh.' She turned to Gerry. 'Thank you for clearing up a few things for me. I hope that the future brings you all you want. Goodbye.'

Gerry gave a bow but said nothing. She could tell he was beyond speech. His eyes were full of pain. She walked away.

The moment the woman left, Deirdre faced Gerry.

He stammered, 'What … what are you doing here?'

She glared at him. 'You call that a greeting?'

He flinched. 'W-would you like to sit down? How have you been?'

She went to a chair and sat down. 'So now you're thinking about my welfare?'

He took the chair opposite. 'I am.'

'You've been horrid to me. Is that the first time you've seen her?'

'Yes. Since Cork. That is, there was once outside the bank …'

'How convenient these little meetings can be. She's beautiful, like they say.' Deirdre took off her bonnet. 'How are your ribs?'

'Getting better.'

'I'm glad. Did you invite her here?'

'No … well I said we had to talk about the past and such.'

'You wanted to be alone with her. And you were—in there.' She pointed to the dining room. 'To kiss her. You were kissing! I saw you break away.' She stood up. 'If I hadn't come in when I did, would you have kept on? You were just about to. I could tell.'

Gerry looked around at the other patrons. A man reading a newspaper looked up and frowned. 'You don't understand,' he said, his voice quiet but angry.

'I know when a woman's in love. It was written all over her face.'

'It isn't like that!'

'Oh, you were talking about the weather? I don't think you were.'

'Sit down, please.'

She stood her ground. 'Tell me why she came to see you here, a married woman. Tell me she didn't want you.'

'We were close … once.'

'That was then,' Deirdre said. 'What about now?'

'I won't lie to you; in Cork we talked about getting married. Then everything fell apart and now I'm in Sydney and she's married and that's it.'

Anger made her face flush. 'She still wants you. She took a big risk to her reputation coming here.'

'I won't see her again,' he said.

'Don't say that. Please don't say that; it isn't true. I just came to see how you were. Who you see is up to you—man or woman.' She walked to the entrance of the lounge and turned back to him. 'Goodbye.'

* * *

In her house early that evening, Anne heard a knock on her front door that startled her. Since she'd seen Gerry that afternoon, she had felt a bit like prey being stalked by a hunter. Her blood pulsed and her skin prickled, but not with discomfort; there was a pleasure and an excitement in everything.

She opened the door. 'Oh, you must be Mr Silverstein. I'm so sorry, I'd forgotten—my husband let me know you were coming. Please come in. He's in the back garden.'

'Thank you, Mrs Hughes.' Silverstein bowed.

'Do sit down.' She patted her face with a lavender-scented handkerchief. 'Would you like some refreshment?'

'Thank you, no.' Silverstein sat straight-backed in a chair looking at her. 'The miniature in your husband's office does not do you justice. You are even more beautiful in person.'

He was saying it as a polite compliment but he sounded sincere, almost sad. She was touched. 'You're very kind.'

'Welcome, Mr Silverstein,' Sean said, coming into the room from the hallway. They shook hands. 'May we offer you a drink?'

'Thank you but no,' Silverstein replied, sitting down again. 'Please hear me out. I'm afraid I am about to destroy any esteem you may have for me—and perhaps even destroy my business. I'm in your hands.'

Sean sat down and Anne followed suit, too stunned for speech. Their guest took off his spectacles and she saw that his dark eyes were full of emotion. He looked lost, but there was a kind of desperate resolve in his stance.

'You, Mrs Hughes …' Silverstein said. He bit his lip and tears filled his eyes. He blinked them away. 'Mrs Hughes, seeing you here in your home, seeing you as a woman who has gone through sorrow, makes me certain I'm doing the right thing. I must make a confession to you.'

'Confession? About what?' She sat open-mouthed, baffled.

'My actions caused the loss of your baby.'

There was silence for some seconds. 'Mr Silverstein,' Sean burst out, 'what are you saying?'

'I must go back in time, to Cork. I must tell you about the gold that was stolen during your delivery of the tabernacle doors, Mr Hughes.'

Sean and Anne looked at each other. She sensed a shadow from a damning threat enveloping her, putting her on alert. All pleasure from the afternoon had gone.

'Explain,' she said.

Silverstein sighed. 'The thief melted down the gold plate and I paid cash for the ingots. I knew the quality of the gold—I certified it for your bank, Mr Hughes, though we never met.'

'That was Jacob Greenberg,' Anne said. 'He was the assayer.'

'I am that man.'

Sean sat back, lines on his forehead. 'You are Jacob Greenberg?' Sean looked at him for a long time. 'My God. Do you still have the gold?'

Silverstein nodded. 'Yes. I got it at a discount, of course. Most of the cash payment went to your father, Mrs Hughes, since he had arranged the theft.' He gave a little bow that Anne found grotesque. She felt as though she had been hit. 'There was a small fee to the thief, Dougal Simpson.'

'Now your partner!' Sean said with wonder and contempt.

'The same. He has been trying to take over my business because he believes I'm in his power. I decline to be ruined by him. I would prefer to put myself in your hands and let you know the whole truth. Then it will be up to you whether I'm ruined or not.'

Anne's demon was threatening to crush her but she had to ask. 'Did Simpson also kill Lawrence Toole?'

'I think so.'

She was relieved somewhat. It was terrible to her to think her father might have been involved. 'But you aren't sure.'

'Not absolutely, Mrs Hughes. But at the melting down of the gold doors, Simpson had on him a medallion.'

'A medallion?' Anne said.

'Yes, with saints engraved on it. He still has it. I think he stole it from Toole.'

344

Sean leaned forward. 'Do you know how much pain you've caused over that gold? Do you?!'

'I can tell you I do.'

'I'm calling for the police.' Sean went to the door and Silverstein stood up.

'I'll deny saying any of this.'

'But Anne is a witness.'

Silverstein spread his hands. 'She's your wife. Her testimony is inadmissible. You must let me tell you the rest.'

Sean's shoulders slumped, then tensed again, grabbed the man and shook him, balling a fist to strike.

'No, Sean!' Anne said. 'Don't.'

Sean pushed Silverstein away. 'Tell us everything. Everything!'

Silverstein nodded, sat down and put his spectacles back on, as though to hide behind them. 'When I tell you, you'll consider me the cruellest of men.' He glanced from one to the other. 'But I have already placed it before God, and He will be the judge.'

Sean sneered and sat down. 'Go on.'

'I'll do anything … and I mean anything,' Silverstein said, 'to make up for the pain I've caused you. But nothing will replace your little one.' He brought a hand to his face and then shook his head. 'I intercepted your letter, Mrs Hughes, the one you wrote to Mr Riordan from Cork. In it you accused Jacob Greenberg of receiving the stolen gold. I did not want that accusation to lead to me. I made sure your letter was not delivered to Riordan.'

Anne's face got hot and she pressed her knuckles to her cheeks. 'You read my letter? Oh, how could you?'

Silverstein took a shaky breath. 'I also arranged for a formal … yes, a forged letter … to be sent back to you, saying Riordan was dead.'

Anne's eyes widened in anger and she stood up. 'No!'

Sean leapt up and grabbed the man again, pulling him up and slamming him against the fireplace. 'Mongrel! You bloody mongrel.' He lifted his fist again to smash into the flushed face and paused, his arm trembling in space.

Silverstein's face was calm, his hands at his side. 'Hit me. You have every right, but my shameful story is not over.'

Sean flung the man from him and turned to face the fireplace. 'Go on.'

Silverstein adjusted his jacket and rubbed his shoulder. 'I don't know what you did, Mrs Hughes, when you got my letter ...'

His mouth was moving but the words were muted. Anne was back in the streets of Cork, unable to function other than to breathe, back in the time when she'd heard Gerry was dead. The man in front of her was saying something. She closed her eyes and forced herself to listen.

Silverstein said, 'You were told that Gerry Riordan had died. That was a lie. Therefore, when Lieutenant Dodds told you he was alive, the shock brought on a tragedy.'

Anne rose. 'Yes, I lost my baby.' Blood raced through her. Silverstein was in tears, his bottom lip quivering. 'Get out,' she said. 'Get out of my house—now.' She pointed to the door. 'Get out!'

Sean went and opened the door. He addressed himself to somewhere above Silverstein's head because Anne could tell he would have preferred to kick him down the steps. 'You can go. We need to rid the stench from this place. Be in your office at seven tomorrow morning.'

Silverstein turned and walked unsteadily away.

Chapter Thirteen

In Castlereagh Street, Anne made a cup of tea after breakfast. Her mind was still full of how things had changed for her, the moment Maurice Silverstein walked into her home. For Sean's sake she had wanted him to get his gold back from Silverstein but she had no idea whether that would happen. Sean had confronted Silverstein in his office the next day but he didn't tell her anything about it and he had not gone to the police, as far as she knew. All he would tell her was that he had 'joined forces' with Lieutenant Dodds against Simpson. Aside from that, her husband was not sharing anything with her. Nothing about the crimes in Cork, her father's part in them, and especially not Gerry Riordan. And it was impossible for her to talk about them herself.

The knocker rapped against the front door and she went to open it. On the step stood Deirdre Walsh. 'Good morning, Mrs Hughes. I'm sorry to intrude this early. I got your home address from the foundry.'

Events seemed to be washing over Anne in waves. Helpless, she fell back on good manners. 'Come in, please. Can I get you something? I've just made tea.'

'Thank you, no.' Miss Walsh took off her wide-brimmed hat, which she wore instead of a bonnet. It was unfashionable but did not lessen her attractions.

'Do leave that on the hall table. The parlour is this way.' Anne led the woman into the room and gestured towards a chair. 'Please sit down.' Miss Walsh perched on the edge of it and looked around the room with her big bold eyes. Anne bristled. 'To what do I owe this visit?'

'You may not wish to tell me, but I have come to ask: why did you meet Gerry Riordan yesterday?'

Right to the point! Anne gasped, admired her courage, but did not answer.

'Why would a woman married to a man like Sean Hughes, whom I've met and admire—meet Gerry alone?' When Anne was silent once more, Miss Walsh went on, 'You were desperate to see him.'

'If you already have the answer, Miss Walsh, there is no point in your seeking mine.'

Miss Walsh held her angry look. 'Yes there is. I want to know; do you still have feelings for him?'

Anne glanced out the window at the gardenia that she and Sean planted in the little strip of garden out the front. It was struggling to grow, a bit like her in the colony. She looked back at her visitor. 'There was a friendship between myself and Gerry Riordan—no, more than that. We developed an understanding in Cork. Since then there's been a tangled mess that I cannot work out. You have no idea: stolen mail, forged letters, old news and lies … I needed clarity. That's why I had to see him.'

'You were embracing when I came in.'

Right to the point again. Anne clenched her teeth. 'Gerry and I had planned to be married, Miss Walsh. That's how close we were. You must understand that.' She bent down and straightened a piece of lace on the table.

'But you're married to another man.'

Anne closed her eyes for a second, then opened them. Miss Walsh's lips were set in a firm line, willing her to answer, as though it were some kind of guilty admission.

'Yes.'

'Ah. You hesitated. You're married, but not with your whole heart. You still love Gerry, don't you?'

Anne felt tears spring to her eyes and held her breath. Love? Was that what had riveted her lips to Gerry's as they kissed behind that door in the hotel? It was a question she couldn't even answer for herself. She gathered her thoughts and exhaled. There was one simple truth that she could tell this woman. 'Sean is my husband and I'm devoted to him. He is a fine man; a good man and he loves me.' Anne shook her head. 'Now I think I'm owed some answers from you. Do you love Gerry Riordan?'

'Yes.'

'Has he asked you to marry him?'

'No.'

Anne could not help a stab of satisfaction at this. 'Are you free to do so, if he should ask?'

Miss Walsh looked down. Her air of confidence had gone. Anne assessed her. She was young, eighteen at the most, so parental consent would be required. An innkeeper's daughter ... In this strange society, women of that class did marry ex-convicts. She expected a defiant 'Yes' but Miss Walsh's answer was almost wistful.

'I'd do anything I could to marry him. If he wanted me.'

'Has he said he loves you?'

The girl lifted her chin a little. 'Not as such. But he can be considerate and caring. I think he did love me, at least until you turned up. Now he'll have to get over you.'

Bright girl. 'You think because he's seen me, he wants me again?' *Well, he was full of longing when I saw him, and so was I.*

Walsh glanced at the clock and stood up. 'I must leave. Our groom's waiting with the wagon at the livery stable and we're headed back to Wiseman's.'

Anne stood with her. They were near each other and without thinking she placed her hand on the other's sleeve. 'If you love him, then fight for him.'

'Fight you, you mean?' Miss Walsh shook off the hand and headed for the front door.

'I won't see him again.' Anne found that hard to say but she meant it. 'I won't seek him out or go anywhere near him.'

'He'll most likely stay in town and work,' Deirdre said facing her. 'That's where the money is. So you'll see him somehow, bound to.' The girl took up her hat and tied the ribbon under her chin. 'You never answered my main question. Do you love him?'

Anne opened the door and looked outside. It was quiet, with few people around. 'What I want and what I can have are two different things, Miss Walsh. I can't be close to Gerry, but you can. I won't help or hinder you. Whatever happens is in God's hands.' Anne felt the tears return to her eyes. 'It's difficult to say this but I wish Gerry would return to the Road and marry you. That would make things simpler for me.'

Miss Walsh looked at her for a while then nodded. 'Thank you for your honesty. I'll fight for him.' She put on her hat. 'And I'll fight you for him if I have to.'

Anne closed the door behind her and let herself go, her hanky sodden in seconds. When the tears were over, she went back into the parlour and drank cold tea and went over the words she had said to the other woman. *I can't be close to Gerry.* They struck her anew. Because there was a man with whom she could be close—her husband. Yes, Gerry aroused her, but Sean was a man too and she wanted his closeness more than ever. He loved her, he had given her a child and might again, and she did love him in her own way. Sean deserved a woman who responded to him with all her heart. In time that might be so.

* * *

Dougal Simpson glanced at the wall clock at Henry's. 'It's nearly eight and good old Maurie is waiting to see us.' He half-closed one eye as he looked at Riordan across the table. The big stonemason was relaxed in his company these days, so unaware of his danger that it was all Simpson could do not to laugh in his face. It was enjoyable, watching the man he was about to eliminate drinking his ale in contentment. 'Come on, finish that. Calling us in at night, Silverstein must have something special for you and me both. Something with money in it for me, and more stonework for you.'

Riordan drank up and they left Henry's and made their way to Kent Street. Simpson placed his arm up on Riordan's shoulder. 'It's good that Cork friends stick together and help each other.' He burped. 'Good … yeah. What do you do for fun, Gerry? Like the women?'

'Aye.'

'Good lad, because I know a few that'll make your dick hard as a mattock handle and use it in ways you've never dreamed of. Maurie knows that well. I look after Maurie in that way, and he looks after me. We've got an appointment at the bank tomorrow that will seal our deal for good.'

Simpson knocked on the door of Silverstein's. 'Open up, Maurie my boy, it's your partner with a friend.'

Locks rattled and the door opened. 'Don't shout, Simpson,' Silverstein said. 'Hello, Riordan. Come into my office.' He let the two of them in and went to lock the front door.

'Don't bother, Maurice,' Simpson said. 'There's just us. Got a bottle handy?'

They trooped into the office and sat down.

Silverstein poured whiskeys for Simpson and Gerry, and Gerry took his with appreciation and some surprise. But after an afternoon on the beer, it would be a change. Silverstein then told them about another new site in town that he'd just purchased. He would build houses on it and sell them on for profit.

Simpson grinned. 'At thirty per cent? Now you're talking. But why are you sweating, old man? It's cool in here.'

Maurice Silverstein blinked, then smiled weakly. 'Profit always excites me.'

Simpson slapped his hand on the desk. 'Spoken like a trooper.' He pulled out his chain and twirled his medallion.

Gerry watched the silver disk as it spun. 'Excuse me, sirs, but what's my part in this?'

'You'll be in charge of the stonework,' Silverstein said. 'You deserve to be operating as a tradesman again. You're well trained, and a Cork man, just like Simpson here.'

Simpson nodded. His medallion was resting on his thigh. 'Good old Cork. That was where I got my first break on the way to fortune. Long way from here, but first step to riches.'

Gerry glanced at the medallion. It looked familiar for a moment but the fumes in his head made the image on it indistinct. He took another sip of whiskey.

'Jacob told me all about that,' Silverstein said. 'But it was a big step into misfortune rather than fortune for a while there, Simpson.'

Simpson gave his partner a wary nod.

The conversation kept taking weird turns. 'Who's Jacob?' Gerry said.

'My cousin,' Silverstein said, looking at Simpson. 'Jacob Greenberg. He benefitted from the theft of the gold tabernacle doors from Saint Mary's Cathedral.'

'Just a minute!' Simpson said.

Gerry put down the whiskey glass and his fists clenched. 'Yeah, what are you talking about, Silverstein? You're related to a thief? And you know who was convicted of stealing that gold? I was.'

Simpson sneered at him, 'And the murder of Lawrence Toole. Don't forget that one.'

Gerry leapt to his feet. 'He was my best friend!'

'Don't care and never knew him,' Simpson said.

'Oh yes you did.' Silverstein had perspiration filming his brow. He leaned over his desk and said into Simpson's face, 'You killed Toole. Jacob Greenberg swears that you were the murderer.'

Gerry was so stunned that he took a step away.

Simpson stood up, goggling at the merchant. 'You … damn you … Greenberg is a liar, a thieving dirty liar.'

The medallion dangled in Simpson's hand and the next second it was in Gerry's. He examined it, his brain reeling. 'This is the medallion Toole gave me! The saints on both sides—'

Simpson snatched at it. 'I got this here, my friend. Not in Cork.'

'No one else could have fashioned this!' Gerry cried. 'Saint Stephen on the front, Saint Eligius on the back. You stole this from Toole, right there in my room where he died.' His breath caught and his head felt as though it would explode.

Simpson's face became hard and he stepped close to Gerry. 'I don't put up with men nosing into my doings. Take me on and I'll show you what happens to them.'

But Gerry wasn't going to strike him: not yet. He was convinced Simpson had knifed Toole but there was no weapon on show here in Silverstein's office. To get the man out of his face for a moment, Gerry leaned back over the desk, his long arms supporting his weight, the medallion clattering onto the polished surface. 'I could crush the two of you, one hand for each. But you'll answer my questions first.'

Simpson pulled a knife from his jacket and held it against Gerry's stomach, its point piercing shirt and skin. 'Shut up or I'll use this.'

Gerry was looking into Simpson's eyes, right down to the depths. 'You killed him, you bastard!'

Simpson said, 'Toole had to go. Men who think they can mess me up—they've got to go. Peter Adams—killed him, too. So no loose talk about me, Riordan, or you'll go their way. Nice bit of steel in the gut works every time.'

Behind Gerry, Silverstein screamed, 'For God's sake!'

Simpson's gaze flickered and Gerry took his chance to lift his weight off one hand, twist, and shove the blade away at the same time. But Simpson was quicker. The steel as it went in felt less like that of a knife, more like a chisel piercing stone.

Behind Simpson, who was turning to get away, Gerry saw two men in uniform crowd through the office door. They collared Simpson right in front of him. Gerry brought his other hand around and felt for the knife. There was blood under his fingers and a mist across his eyes, as other men came into view, mouths open, shouting. But there was no sound.

* * *

353

Gerry opened his eyes to see a well-fashioned plaster ceiling. A voice came from beside him.

It was Dodds. 'Welcome back, Riordan. You're in hospital.'

Gerry wanted to turn his head, sit up, but his whole body felt leaden, except for the pain in his chest and stomach. Swivelling his gaze, he made out Dodds and Sean Hughes looking down at him. 'What hospital?'

'The Rum Hospital, Macquarie Street.'

Gerry said, 'Always wanted to see inside that. Am I dreaming?'

Hughes said, 'Riordan? We put you in harm's way without consulting you. Thank God you survived. When you're fit you can belt me one, if you want.'

He was making no sense. The inside of Gerry's mouth seemed coated in lime; he formed his fingers into an open grip and moved it to his mouth.

Dodds said, 'Water. All right.' He reached for a pitcher at the bedside, poured a glass and nodded to Hughes. 'Put a hand behind his head so he can drink.'

Gerry sipped the water and closed his eyes. More pain radiated from his stomach as he swallowed. He cleared his throat. 'So it's your fault I'm stabbed?'

Dodds said, 'We teamed up with a police inspector who's been after Simpson for a time. The inspector only wanted to nail Simpson for crimes done in the colony. He reckoned Simpson killed an overseer called Peter Adams, stabbed to death recently. Well, Simpson admitted that to you and he'll hang for it. We all agreed, the only way to get him to talk about his multitude of crimes was to ambush him, and you were the bait. I'm sorry—we knew he was after you but I never thought he'd go you in Silverstein's office. The inspector wanted a confession before witnesses, hence the policemen who crept into the anteroom.'

Hughes said, 'Don't worry about Simpson: you'll never see him again except in the dock. Silverstein helped set up the trap and you forced the confession out of him. Besides providing crucial evidence. I hope that medallion hangs him for both murders.'

Gerry stared at him. 'Mr Hughes, the gold! The gold that was stolen from you. Silverstein's cousin has it! Jacob Greenberg. You've got to get it back.'

Hughes threw him an odd look. 'The gold has already been restored to me. My wife and I are taking no action against Jacob Greenberg, or Maurice Silverstein for that matter. There are crimes that get paid for in remorse, shame and a yearning for a more honest future. I think both men have learned enough to realise that.'

Gerry closed his eyes. 'So it's all over. I can breathe free. I want to thank you, Mr Hughes, and … and your wife, for believing in me.'

'You may thank her yourself; she's waiting outside until I can tell her you're fit for another visitor. May I?'

Gerry looked up at him. A free man: handsome, fit and well to do. For the first time he wondered whether Sean Hughes might in his way have suffered as much as himself at the hands of fate. 'I'd be grateful, sir.'

Hughes nodded and left.

Gerry turned to Dodds. 'There'll be a trial, and I'll be witness for the prosecution. Does that make me any better in the eyes of the court? Will I get my innocence declared?'

Dodds said, 'Hold your horses, Riordan. You've just been operated on for that knife wound. There's plenty of time to think about what's to come and I'll be around to help you do it. I'm only up at the Road, and always ready for a chat and a char.' He put a hand lightly on Gerry's shoulder. 'Rest. You deserve it.'

When he was gone, Gerry closed his eyes. Only a moment later he felt pressure on his hand and saw that Anne was sitting in the chair beside the bed.

She fingers were light and smooth. 'I thought you were going to die.'

He tried to smile. 'And once you thought I'd hang. This time it would've been real.'

'Don't jest!'

'Sorry.' He slid his hand out from under hers and touched her cheek. 'You're married to a good man.' She went to take his wrist but he laid his arm back on the coverlet. He could feel fever buzzing in his limbs.

She had a blush on her face as though she had fever too. 'Yes, I am.'

'You'll stay with him?'

'I will.'

'Why?'

'As though you have a right to ask that!' But her eyes told him she knew why. 'I owe it to him. He's never reproached me; he's never spoken about the time when you and I ... he's never asked about my feelings for you. And he has such a right to, oh, such a right!' She took a quick breath. 'And I love him.'

He tried not to believe her. 'You love him? But are you *in* love with him?'

'Don't ask me that and don't ask me if I love you.'

He closed his eyes and relived a dream. Of the day when he and Anne held hands and kissed in his room in Philput Lane. 'You know how I felt for you. But you're vowed to him. I'll honour your choice and your marriage.'

Her perfume wafted across him as she bent near him. The coolness of her hand on his forehead dampened his pain. Her breath caressed his ear. 'Keep that with you. Goodbye.'

He lay there in the silence after her footsteps had faded. Alone, but with a lifeline of hope. He was free and proven innocent. A woman he once knew still loved him. And he had a fresh life to build in this country.

There was always a chance at happiness. There was always a way.

Historical Note

Wiseman's Inn is partly fictitious and I've placed it near Cobham Hall, the house built by Solomon Wiseman for his second wife, Sophia.

The civil-engineering project on which the protagonist sweated, loved and lived, was the Great North Road (GNR) project. Part of which is shown in a sketch in the frontispiece. This project was significant: the largest civil-engineering project in New South Wales in the 19th century. I recommend the following wonderfully detailed reference work for those interested in this impressive project: *Blood Sweat and Irons: Building the Great North Road from Wiseman's Ferry to Mt Manning 1827-1832* by Ian Webb.

The effort in human labour that it took to construct this 'highway' cannot be overestimated or overemphasised. The terrain over which it was constructed was arduous. Some of us utilise today machines that seem like dinosaurs in scale and strength, and that have the dexterity to dig, smash, pulverise, lift and load volumes of earth and rock of enormous size. Such machines were absent in the 19th century and it was all down to human labour, metal tools, gunpowder, bullock teams and the dray.

In summary the Great North Road was needed because it took far too long for goods, timber and agricultural products to be brought down by sea from the Hawkesbury/Hunter regions to Sydney Cove. A highway was needed to link the southern part of the greater Newcastle area with Wiseman's Ferry and then on to what is now known as the Hills district of Sydney. What led to the cessation of the Great North Road project was the advent of the steam clipper, which enabled goods and materials to be transferred at greater speeds and frequency.

Remnants of the Great North Road survive, and the Hawkesbury River Heritage Society provides guided tours to see the enormity of the works and in the effort required.

Lieutenant William Dodds is fictitious but Iron Gang No 4 did exist.

More Books by the Author

Unbound Justice (The Australian Sandstone Series Book 1)
Unshackled (The Australian Sandstone Series Book 2)
Succession (The Australian Sandstone Series Book 3)

Unbound Justice

The Australian Sandstone Series Book 1

John Leary boards ship in Ireland in 1850, a young immigrant carpenter ambitious for a new life in Australia. He sails with revenge in his heart--his beloved sister has been raped by her landlord, William Baxterhouse, who escapes on another ship with even grander plans for success in New South Wales. In Sydney, hard workers like Leary and ruthless newcomers like Baxterhouse find a city fired by the Gold Rush and dedicated to creating the finest buildings in the colony.

Leary has a double motive to make his construction company succeed: he has fallen in love with the beautiful Clarissa McGuire, whose family despise him, and Baxterhouse continues to rise in wealth and influence, seemingly untouchable. Meanwhile another woman, Beth O'Hare, is in love with John Leary, and he makes some hard choices--including a climactic showdown with Baxterhouse.

Unbound Justice is now available in ebook and paperback from your favourite online bookstore

Unshackled

The Australian Sandstone Series Book 2

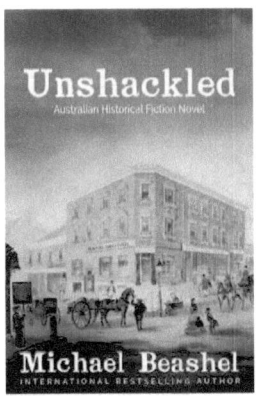

Sydney is booming in 1855 and life looks grand for John Leary: his construction dreams are coming true, his beloved wife Clarissa is expecting their first child and, with his partner Sean Connaire, he has produced some of the city's significant buildings. But success provokes jealousy, and a mysterious rival sabotages a vital Leary site.

John Leary cannot control his own company while his father-in-law holds a majority share, so he arranges a buyout on his own behalf--but this new, silent partner poses a serious risk to the harmony of his marriage. Meanwhile ex-convict Gerry Gleeson makes himself known to John as his uncle and helps him track down the saboteur.

Raw ambition, guilty secrets and undercover deals--will they bring the young builder to ruin or triumph?

Unshackled is now available in ebook and paperback from your favourite online bookstore

Succession

The Australian Sandstone Series Book 3

Leary Contracting has to build it--the tallest hotel Sydney has ever seen. At 55, John Leary employs both his sons in his construction company, but the one he favours is his first-born, Richard. Meanwhile Richard's half-brother, Brendan, gains the respect of the Leary workers because he has 'bricks in his blood'.

John begins the massive hotel project, overcoming city red tape and the jabs of his fiercest competitor. The Imperial dwarfs all around it, with hundreds of workers busting their guts to finish the brutal program. Richard, charming but unreliable, marries well and dazzles the Sydney society of 1885, while Brendan proves himself tougher than he looks whenever real work is required.

John must choose which of his sons will lead Learys into the next century. Only after the Imperial is completed does he make his decision. Succession is the third Australian Historical Fiction novel in The Australian Sandstone Series, a magnificent view of 19c Sydney from the ground up!

Succession is now available in ebook and paperback from your favourite online bookstore

The Author

Born in Sydney, Michael Beashel is an International Bestselling Author. His Irish forebears immigrated to New South Wales in the 1860s and settled in Miller's Point. He spent his youth in Bondi, is married with adult children and lives in Sydney's inner-west.

Beashel was head of Asset Development for a global accommodation services company registered on the NYSE and has made his mark in some of Australia's iconic construction companies. In Sydney, he has restored government buildings such as the Customs House and the Town Hall and completed commercial buildings in the private sector. In SE Asia, he managed a construction division that built apartments and hotels in Bangkok and Ho Chi Minh City.

This industry—its characters, clients, tradespeople, designers and bureaucrats—provides rich material for his writing. He has an eye for the emergence of Sydney's built form, from the early days of the colony to the present, and a love of construction. He says about his writing, 'It's a passion. I revel in using the building industry as a tapestry to weave a great tale seasoned with historic facts and memorable characters. Human shelter is an essential need and I suspect people have a fascination for understanding its context and construction within their societies. Australia still is a young country in terms of large structures but there are many, many outstanding building stories.'

Beashel holds a B. App. Science (Building) from Sydney's UTS and is a member of Writing NSW. *Unbound Justice* is his first novel and Books 2 and 3 *Unshackled* and *Succession* form the first three of The Australian Sandstone Series.

All novels can be enjoyed as standalone stories.

The stone mason Gerry Riordan appears in *Unshackled and Succession* under his chosen name of Gerry Gleeson.

If any interested reader would like to know more about me and my Australian background, please access my following sites:

My website
www.michaelbeashel.com.au

Australian History Videos on YouTube
https://www.youtube.com/channel/UCLETK6K05kne4xhKChBaVAA

Facebook
https://www.facebook.com/MichaelBeashelAuthor

Goodreads
https://www.goodreads.com/author/show/16827192.Michael_Beashel